IF THE TIDE TURNS

RACHEL RUECKERT

KENSINGTON
PUBLISHING CORP.

www.kensingtonbooks.com

KENSINGTON BOOKS are published by
Kensington Publishing Corp.
119 West 40th Street
New York, NY 10018

Copyright © 2024 by Rachel Rueckert

All rights reserved. No part of this book may be reproduced in any form
or by any means without the prior written consent of the Publisher, ex-
cepting brief quotes used in reviews.

All Kensington titles, imprints, and distributed lines are available at special quantity discounts for bulk purchases for sales promotion, premiums,
fund-raising, educational, or institutional use.

This book is a work of fiction. Names, characters, businesses, organiza-
tions, places, events, and incidents either are the product of the author's
imagination or are used fictitiously. Any resemblance to actual persons,
living or dead, events, or locales is entirely coincidental.

To the extent that the image or images on the cover of this book depict
a person or persons, such person or persons are merely models, and are
not intended to portray any character or characters featured in the book.

Special book excerpts or customized printings can also be created to fit
specific needs. For details, write or phone the office of the Kensington
Sales Manager: Kensington Publishing Corp., 119 West 40th Street,
New York, NY 10018. Attn. Sales Department. Phone: 1-800-221-2647.

The K with book logo Reg US Pat. & TM Off.

ISBN: 978-1-4967-4754-9 (ebook)

ISBN: 978-1-4967-4753-2

First Kensington Trade Paperback Printing: April 2024

10 9 8 7 6 5 4 3 2 1

Printed in the United States of America

Because of you,
Brittney, Megan, Mikaela, and Ryan

Cast of Characters

*Indicates a character using the name of a real historical figure
**Indicates a character using the name and known depictions of
a real historical figure

Brown Family

George Brown*
m. Mehitable*
    Constance
    Mehitable (Maria/Goody) Brown**
    Elizabeth*
    Mercy*
Aunt Ruth*

Bellamy Family

Stephen Bellamy*
m. Elizabeth*
    Five older unnamed siblings*
    Samuel (Sam) Bellamy**
Aunt Lamb

Massachusetts Inhabitants

Indigenous
Weetumuw**
Ninigret**
Abiah Sampson, based on Delilah Sampson Gibbs,** a renowned
    healer
Ousamequin**

Colonists

Captain Thomas Hunt**

Cotton Mather**

Sarah White Norman and Mary Vincent Hammon ("Plymouth women prosecuted for 'lewd behavior' ")*

Lydia

John Hallett**

"The poor Reynolds boy"

Dorothy Bradford ("Governor Bradford's wife")**

Israel Cole**

Reverend Samuel Treat**

John Miller ("schoolmaster Miller")*

Pastor Josiah Oakes**

Margaret Hough**

Justice Joseph Doane**

The Abbotts

The Atwoods

The Youngs

Mrs. Walker

Mrs. Smith

Sailors

Lieutenant Evans

Paulsgrave Williams**

John Julian**

Three unnamed divers ("Spain nobles had hired local natives to do the risky diving for them")**

Caleb Dixon

Isaiah Abell

Timothy Webb

Petere (Peter) Cornelius Hoof**

John Brown**

Hendrick Quintor**

John (Little) King**

Thomas Davis**

Dr. [James?] Ferguson**
Alexander*

Privateers and Pirates

Francis Drake**
Henry Avery**
Henry Jennings**
Benjamin (Ben) Hornigold**
Edward Teach,** who later became Blackbeard
Captain William Kidd**
Olivier Levasseur (La Buse/The Buzzard)**

Captains

Captain Young*
Captain L'Escoubett*
John Hamann**
Captain Prince**
Captain Beer**
Robert Ingols**
Montgomery**
Captain Cyprian Southack**

**Individuals named in the *Whydah*'s roster
who are not depicted specifically in this book**

John Fletcher—quartermaster
Richard Noland—quartermaster
William Main—sailing master
John Lambert—sailing master
Richard Caverley—sailing master
Jeremy Burke—boatswain
Jeremiah Higgins—boatswain
Jean Taffier—gunner
William Osbourne—gunner's mate
Thomas South—carpenter

Joseph Rivers
William Lee
Thomas Bernard
John Baker
Robert Danzy
Edward Moon
David Turner
[Edward?] Wood
John Shaun
Simon van Vorst

PROLOGUE

I know this place, how the spindly grass bends against the rolling dunes.

The bite of salt air, the brine of pink Atlantic mornings along the docks.

I know the hideouts for lovers, the townsfolk and the church with its hard pews and shadows.

A barn with a boot print. A whipping post. A cell, real and imagined.

I know every spine of this shore, and the woman whose voice cries and curses whenever storms hammer the bone-white sand where lie the remains of the Whydah *and her treasure, her crew.*

I know something of ghosts, including some who had the audacity to survive.

PART I

SUMMER 1715

CHAPTER I

Maria broke for air as a wave crested. She let out an unrestrained laugh as the ocean tumbled into her shoulders, pushing her through the surf until her knees pressed into the soft shore.

"How did I do this time?" Maria shouted above the roar to her younger sister, Elizabeth, who sat reading on the empty beach.

Elizabeth's eyes flicked up, then back to her novel. "As well as usual."

Which wasn't great, Maria knew. She never waded in deeper than her ribs. But not knowing how to swim hadn't halted her attempts to improve.

Maria scrambled to her feet, shaking out a shiver and scraping away sand. She wrung water from her linen shift, then her braid. Her throat burned with traces of sea. Despite the goose bumps, she glowed with delight. She buried the wet shift inside her basket, then quickly changed into a clean dress.

"I'm missing something in the arm movement," Maria said after drying off. She held out her arms, trying to mimic what she'd seen the fishermen at the docks do when they dove to cut a snagged line. Why were *they* allowed this joy while she was not? She finished dressing and then stared at the bonnet in her hands. She hated the dreadful thing, but over her seventeen years of existence, she'd learned resistance was futile. She sighed, then tied the bonnet on, tucking the damp coil of cornsilk hair away from view.

"There has to be a way to keep water out of my nose."

"Mmm," Elizabeth said.

"Are you even listening to me?"

Elizabeth turned a page. "Imagine what Mama would say if she found out you were at this again."

Maria didn't have to imagine. She knew exactly what Mama would say, having been caught before. A few months back, Maria and Elizabeth had *both* lost privileges of going out, meaning Elizabeth hadn't been able to see her friend, Lydia, for a week.

Maria felt a pang of regret, softened only by knowing that Elizabeth craved these moments away as much as Maria did, a chance to sit with her questionable reading material without prying eyes.

"It would be a shame to spend a life by the sea and never properly venture into it," Maria said. She had always felt so. Such wild vastness, possibility and danger. Adventure and misadventure. Everything she shouldn't feel drawn to as a girl.

But it wasn't "proper" for her to venture into it at all.

"You'll be an eligible lady soon," Elizabeth said without looking up, but Maria heard the sorrow in that familiar reproach. Elizabeth herself might not recognize the base note of sadness, that subtle dissonance, but Maria did. She felt a small, invisible stirring— nothing more. Maria could never explain how she knew these unspoken, unseeable things. She'd tried before, as a child, borrowing language from church. "Whisperings of the spirit," she'd called them, until Mama had warned that God would never send Maria visions. Instead, Maria was instructed to stay clear of Satan's grip, of even the appearance of evil.

Whatever the feeling's name, it was the same tiny pang Maria got whenever she could sense an oncoming storm by the look of a lone cloud or a breeze from the north. Or what she felt after a dream about one of the cows falling ill, only to discover later that the stable lad found traces of red during the daily milking.

Or that unspoken tension Maria noticed between Elizabeth and Lydia whenever Reverend Treat spoke of "unchaste behavior" on Sundays. Maria did not have to look long at her sister to observe her flushed, freckled cheeks when the famous Cotton Mather visited Cape Cod last summer—that cleft-chinned man who'd written about the Salem witch trials two decades ago. The celebrity preacher had delivered a fiery sermon about two Plymouth women prosecuted for "lewd behavior with each other upon a bed."

But perhaps it was all in Maria's overactive imagination. Elizabeth, though a year younger, was better behaved than Maria. More God-fearing and upright.

"We should return," Maria said, retrieving her gathering basket. "I told Mercy we'd meet her by the huckleberries."

Elizabeth glanced at the sun.

"Ready?" Maria said, offering her hand.

Elizabeth sighed, reluctant to part with her story, whatever worlds she escaped into whenever the two of them stole time away from chores—the never-ending mending, washing, animal-tending, cooking, and cleaning. Preparing, always, around the harvest.

Elizabeth snapped her book closed, and Maria hoisted her up.

"There you are!" came a high voice behind the pitch pines.

Maria and Elizabeth swung around in unison, Elizabeth hiding the novel behind her.

"Mercy," Maria said with feigned calm. "I told you to wait for us in the meadow."

Mercy grinned, purple staining the corners of her mouth. "I finished picking early. Did you get the rosemary for the cod?"

Maria and Elizabeth nodded, then stole a glance as little Mercy trotted off, blazing a path for them to follow.

"That was close."

"*Too* close," Elizabeth whispered. She surveyed Maria, making sure her wet hair was properly covered.

Maria gave her a gentle push. "Race you." Then the two of

them picked up their skirts and baskets to sprint after their little sister.

Sea grass whipped at their ankles as Maria walloped with delight, kicking up earth with her boots. A blue heron flew off when they neared, receding into the flawless sky. For a moment, Maria was transported. She could remember Constance chasing her like this, teasing her with taunts as Maria cawed like a bird, always out of reach like the Nauset wind.

One minute Constance was there, carefree, scampering through the golden marsh meadows. The next, severe, grown, then gone. As respectable and cross as Mama. How many years had passed since she'd seen her older sister? Marriage changed people in the worst ways.

I'll never be like that, Maria thought as she ran, then pushed the words away.

When they neared the cedar-shingled house, the three girls came to a stop and caught their breath.

"Who's that with Papa?" Mercy asked with a wrinkled nose.

Papa stood in the doorway, shaking hands with an older gentleman in a velvet waistcoat and a tight cravat.

"Girls," called Papa with a grin when he saw them. "Come. There's someone joining us for supper whom I'd like you to meet."

"More pudding, Mr. Hallett?" Mama offered, passing a pewter bowl. Hallett sat across from Papa, who was seated at the head of the table. Papa hunched over his plate and would not look up from his heap of potatoes until he was through, his normal habit, no matter who was at supper. Tonight might have resembled any other evening, but Maria knew better. They all did. Mama's heightened pitch only confirmed it.

"No, Mrs. Brown, I thank you," Hallett said, holding up a hand. He patted his graying beard with a large cotton napkin. His powdered wig, twice as thick as Papa's, covered his shoulders. "My compliments on the meal."

"My daughters," Mama said, gesturing toward Maria, Elizabeth, and Mercy while Maria pretended not to notice. She had no intention of saying anything. If she opened her mouth, she feared she'd say something wrong—something truthful. Despite her seventeen years, Mama still resorted to the rod.

Was anyone going to mention that, before today, Mr. Hallett was Papa's biggest farming rival?

No. Only she would dare to mention the year Hallett refused to share corn seed, sabotaging Papa's crop season. Or that the two had refused to speak to each other since. Everyone else seemed content to sit here and pretend, as if lying wasn't a sin.

Mama then singled out Maria. "She picked the freshest cod of the catch, a real eye for it by now," Mama added. "An excellent cook."

A stretch. Adequate was how Mama usually described her cooking.

"Delicious indeed," said Hallett without inflection as he picked a bone from his teeth. "Tell me, Mr. Brown," he said, turning to Papa as if the rest of them were not there. "Do you add fish to your fertilizer?"

Just be a body, here in this chair, Maria told herself, already tasting the salt of the sea. *Your mind can go anywhere.* She went over her swim technique from the morning, puzzling out what she might do differently next time.

A swift kick under the table made Maria wince, yanking her back. Elizabeth coughed and shot her a stern look. Maria must have been making the wrong face.

"As I was saying," Mr. Hallett continued, "these funds I donated should secure a much larger meetinghouse. Reverend Treat was most grateful, most eager, when I shared my plan."

"How fortunate for the community," Papa said.

"May I have more?" Mercy asked, legs swinging under her chair.

"Wait to be offered or addressed before speaking, child," Mama said.

"Perhaps the vigor of youth is no great evil," droned Hallett. "I could use a bit more energy these days myself."

Papa grunted in acknowledgment. His gaze caught Maria's disgust, and she detected a sympathetic smile. A mischievous kitten, he'd always called her—"always with the look of a cat stalking a bird."

Then Papa returned to his meal, changing the subject. "It's always a pleasure to host a guest and give thanks for our blessings. As we read in Isaiah, 'If ye consent and obey, ye shall eat the good things of the land.'"

Maria did not join the muttering of agreements, nor in the praise when Hallett mentioned the other great "improvements" he aspired to make to Eastham.

Papa's bay-blue eyes crinkled as he placed his hands on the round of his stomach. The buttons strained along his brown waistcoat. "Is the pie ready, my dear? I'm eager to discuss the grain crop with Mr. Hallett before the night is over. Thievery, this raise in seed price, is it not? With topsoil turning to sand before our eyes?" His gaze narrowed. "And once we dismiss the women, I'd like your opinion on a political matter—property rights and these proposed town 'divisions,' if you understand my meaning."

Hell had to be real, Maria considered as she stabbed at a carrot.

Fallen angels.

Ghastly demons.

Horrid imps disguised as dogs.

All of them, every devil from the Invisible World, sent here to punish her at the kitchen table, forcing her to endure this charade.

CHAPTER 2

Sam clenched his fists as his captain finished reading the list of names.

"Jones. Johnson. Smith. Taylor. Watson."

The mass of sailors on the main deck stared ahead, wringing their caps in their hands, willing for the list to go on longer.

"The rest of you will be dismissed from service once we reach Cape Cod," the captain ended with a cough, pocketing the parchment in his coat and making a retreat to his quarters.

Sam shouldn't have been surprised. They'd been anticipating something like this now that the war over Spain's new king had ended. But somehow that didn't remove the sting. He had no other skills, no other chances to make his way in the world.

A few listeners emitted groans and wails of despair, but nothing louder.

"And what of the rest of us, sir?" Sam said, forcing the captain to stop in his perfectly polished boots.

His reddened, puckered skin contrasted with the false white of his powdered wig. "That's your problem now, Bellamy. I can't control the terms of the British Navy any more than I can control you."

Sam held his tongue until the rat of a man escaped into his hole, hiding from the faces of the men. Rumor had it that he pissed in a silver chamber pot, feeling himself too good to use the "heads" in the bow of the ship like the rest of them.

"Let it go, Bellamy," one sailor whispered with sour breath to Sam as everyone slouched back to their posts. "You'll only make it worse."

"Can it *be* worse?" Sam replied. How long could he watch these emaciated young men haunt the decks, groveling like fearful dogs?

How long could he, himself, be that dog? Kicked time and time again, begging for a scrap of meat and a chance to survive?

But for all his indignation, Sam gritted his teeth and returned to work the lines. His hotheaded speeches did tend to make things worse for himself and others. He could still feel the cuts on his back, the ones from his latest whipping from the lieutenant's cat-o'-nine-tails—all because Sam had taken one good look at the bucket of slop shared between him and six other sailors, felt the weevils crawling through the crumbling hardtack in his hand, and decided to take his concerns up with the captain.

The topsail of the mizzenmast fluttered, and Sam moved to take in the slack. The feel of the rough rope along his callused palms, the sound of the wooden yard knocking against the sail, the texture of the fish-scented planks beneath his bare feet, all felt as natural to him as his own pulse. He'd been doing this long enough—snatched from the docks and made a cabin boy when he was eight years old. None of his superiors, other than Lieutenant Evans, had shown a shred of human decency in the dozen years since.

After tying off a brace line, Sam gazed out at the watery horizon, where he knew they'd encounter land and the reality of mass unemployment the next day. He'd secure lodging with Aunt Lamb in Eastham again, assuming she still ran the Higgins Tavern. He'd find another commission, another way. He always did.

Sam closed his eyes, letting a breeze run along his sun-chapped cheeks and through his black hair. The lungs of nature. The invisible force that governs all souls at sea. That wind began in some faraway corner Sam had never been, going somewhere that no human—regardless of their wealth or status—could predict.

He needed to find another way to live. To truly live. In a way that his father and so many others had never had the chance.

"Back to work, Bellamy," came an order from the quarterdeck. The bark tore Sam from his stupor as he returned to the lines, shame curdling in his gut. That constant gnaw of fear, he knew, was as much second nature to him as any ship. But something deep in him shouted otherwise.

Father, what would you think of me now?

CHAPTER 3

"The sea seems strange today," Maria said, abandoning her potato peelings to stand at the window. Low tide. Swells tinged with yellow-green.

This early in the day?

She ran a thumb down a pane. Too clean. No trace of fog, no salt grit between her fingers—not even a speck of soot from yesterday's cooking fire.

"Four more potatoes should suffice for supper," Elizabeth said, examining the half-filled pot on the floor between them.

Elizabeth was ignoring her again, she suspected, hoping Maria wouldn't bring up the inevitable. But Maria felt determined for a distraction, anything to dispel the dread pooling in her stomach and the "best behavior" cloud that had hung over the house since Mr. Hallett's visit.

It was only business, Maria reasoned when the memory seized her. *Papa minimizing his growing risks.* Mama hadn't mentioned the unexpected guest again.

"What do you say to an outing?" Maria said. She squinted at the large blue blur beyond the dunes across the main road. The sound was just out of earshot. "The vegetables can soak for an hour."

The only response was the scrape of a knife.

"All right," Maria countered, "no swimming this time. Just a trip to the docks. Before we light the wood. Aren't you ready to trade for a new book?"

"You know that answer," Elizabeth said with perfect calmness, tossing an onion wedge into the iron pot.

"Last chance," Maria said, unfastening her apron and hanging it on a nail near the stone chimney with her bonnet. She swatted corn flour from her dress and unpinned the crown of braid wrapped around her head, letting the golden strands fall to her waist in rivulets. She wouldn't be out long, she reasoned. "We *do* need oysters," Maria added with a lilt.

Elizabeth groaned, but scrambled up from the stool, wiping her hands on her long, dark skirt. "Fine. But we have to be back before—"

A creak of the door stopped the sisters in their steps.

"Mama," Maria said, frozen where she stood.

"The Turners' baby came quicker than expected." Mama returned her midwifery bag to the shelf and scanned the modest room, her gaze lingering on the abandoned work, the apron on the nail, then on Maria's loose hair.

"Leaving chores unfinished again," she said. A flinty statement, not a question.

"Yes, Mama," Maria said, staring at the ground.

"To get some oysters," Elizabeth added, and Maria appreciated the gesture. "We could use something beyond the taste of pease porridge, especially with Papa's long hours overseeing the fields."

Mama managed a rare smile, lines edging the features of her regal face beneath her white linen cap. "A wonderful idea," she said.

The sisters exchanged a look.

"It is?" asked Maria.

"Yes, but let's do better. Fresh mackerel." Her emerald eyes mirrored her daughters', but without the youthful humor—a quality Maria could almost remember in her, before the accident.

Mama's gaze settled on Maria. "Mr. Hallett is coming to dine with us again tonight. You would do well to appear respectable, like the well-bred woman that you are, Goody."

Maria set her jaw. She hated it when the family called her by that silly, honorific name. "I'm hardly a woman yet, Mama."

"Maybe it's time you acted like one. You'd benefit from a firmer hand." Mama snatched Maria's bonnet from the wall and handed it to her. "Lord knows we did our best. Your father was too soft to send you away to work like other willful children in the town, but we did try to cure your spirit of pride and disobedience."

Maria's fingers tightened around the cap. "Constance wasn't married until twenty-three."

"She was half as beautiful." Her eyes raked over Maria. "You'll wear your mantua, the navy one your father was kind enough to purchase for you in Boston. Elizabeth, your gray petticoat will do. We aren't struggling farmers or worldly women like some others in these parts."

Elizabeth's eyes widened. "But that dress is only for special occasions."

Again, Maria felt that familiar pang, this time in the form of an undeniable uneasiness. It welled up from the pit of her chest.

No, Maria thought.

No no no no no . . .

As soon as the sisters had passed the town center and were out of sight from the Atwoods' and the Youngs' cottages, Maria let out an animal scream.

"Mr. Hallett is a horse breeder," Elizabeth offered, pushing wisps of copper hair away from her face. "You like horses."

"Not anymore." Never mind how many times she'd drawn out her chores in the barn to talk to Ruby or Snip, spoiling them with apples.

"He might be better than the poor Reynolds boy who tried to court you last summer."

Maria spun around and glared at Elizabeth. No comforts would

erase the fact that Mr. Hallett was a childless, crusty widower—
three times her age—sitting on greedy acres of corn while posing
as a great blessing to the community.

"I am not marrying him," Maria said. "I'm not marrying anyone. I've barely *lived*." Her voice broke, shocked by a truth she'd
never dared to utter aloud, one she didn't totally realize in its full
dimension until the words were out. Maria threw herself on the
hot sand. Her empty basket lay at her side.

Elizabeth looked around, confirmed there were no witnesses to
this public display of emotion, then sat beside her.

"I've never been to Boston," Maria muttered. "I've never seen
a moose. I've never kissed a boy. I don't even know how to properly swim yet."

If Elizabeth felt scandalized, she hid it well. She took Maria's
hand. "It's just another supper. I'm sure you can talk to Mama.
Well, maybe Papa," she reconsidered. "Papa is reasonable. He will
consider your heart's preference, as he did for Constance."

Maria felt the stirring, a feeling laced with bitterness. Her
mother was right: She was no Constance, in more ways than just
looks, so she would enjoy no such privileges. She would not escape this one. Not this time.

"You'd have more freedom, if that's what you want, as a married
woman."

A wind stirred Maria's skirts around her ankles, but she didn't
bother to push down her gray dress. She could imagine what Papa
would say. What everyone always said: "Marriage is ordained of
God, a sacred duty." And maybe it was, a heightened "blessing"
with an extra degree of urgency if it happened to come with a
respected man of means. Maria knew little of the world, but she
knew this much: Money and God governed it all, including her
beloved town of Eastham.

But it was also true that she was old enough now, older than
many women before her. Maria loathed the thought of disappoint-
ing people, despite her proclivity to do just that. Whatever Mama
might say, Maria didn't enjoy being difficult.

She had expected marriage all her life. So why did she feel so unprepared? So repelled?

Was love a preference? A need?

A liability?

Stung by a thought, Maria sat bolt upright. Her eyes narrowed to slits: the pier, the boats.

The water.

She unfastened her boots, removed her fine stockings, and tore off her bonnet.

"Maria?" Elizabeth asked with audible concern.

But Maria was already standing, brushing the sand from her skirts, and running. Running and running toward the horizon. It was all Elizabeth could do to gather both of their baskets and scramble after her, shouting her name.

"Goody Brown!" one fishmonger hollered.

"Is that the Brown girls?"

"Fine clams in stock for your ma."

Maria ignored all the usual calls as she ran along the dock, out of view from the faces—those faces she knew so well, the faces that made Eastham vibrant. Fishers. Sailors. Lobstermen. Traders. Whalers. Maria did not have her sister's patience for books. Instead, she'd come here to sell her lauded weavings while listening to tales of far-flung places filled with quests or unrequited love, stealing any chance she could to learn more about the bigger world around her. Ideas. Politics. Lewd gossip. Snatches of other languages. Ocean-warped newspapers. Anything.

But not today.

She halted at the top of the dock and frowned. Amid the bustle of the day's business, no one took serious notice—not to inquire about her weavings, not even to scold her for her loose hair. But maybe that was for the best. Had she *really* meant for them to see this petty rebellion? Or to endure the less-than-petty consequences?

You're afraid of what they think. You'll always be afraid of what they think.

The soles of her feet burned against the sun-worn wood. A gull circled overhead.

"What . . ." Elizabeth said, breathless and panting as she caught up, "was . . . that?"

"You buy the mackerel for Mr. Hallett. I'm going for a swim."

"But, Goody—"

"Please, I asked you not to call me that anymore."

Sea lapped against the pier. Elizabeth blanched. She looked down at the dark, shifting water, then back at Maria.

"I'll go with you, watch after you. Somewhere shallower, near the shore and out of sight. If you just wait."

"I don't have any more time to wait." Nothing would ever be the same after tonight, Maria reasoned. She had to try.

"But your dress!"

"If anyone notices, say I fell. Throw me a rope if you must."

Before Elizabeth could reach out to stop her, Maria jumped.

A shock of cold. Maria always welcomed that brisk, initial lightning to her system. She closed her eyes, feeling the salt and dark sweep across every inch of skin. The noise, the echoes of waves and rocks and fish and an unseen world. Then, slowly, she pulled her arm up and broke the surface. Took a deep breath.

"Maria!"

She could hear her sister's voice, but the faraway quality remained. She continued moving, arms rotating like a windmill, her legs scissoring away from the pier. Twenty feet away, then thirty. Farther. Skirts dragging heavier than her shift, which she usually wore when practicing her swimming.

I'm doing it, she thought, swinging her pointed toes below to see if she could touch bottom.

But there was no bottom.

She swallowed her nerves, letting the feeling of aliveness fill her, propelling herself as she swam for the beach. Her strong limbs pushing her forward.

Or so she thought.

As her arms fanned around her, her dress grew heavier. Her chest tightened. It took more and more effort to crack the surface for air. She kicked, now frantic.

Maria tried to turn her body, to see where Elizabeth stood somewhere on the dock. To grab the rope. But the sea pulled at her, tugging at her skirts, making her forget which way was up or down, forward or away, dangerous or safe.

She coughed, salt rushing into her mouth, eyes blinded with the sting of ocean.

"Elizabeth!" she tried, unable to see or hear.

Kicking, flailing, swatting at the crush of water.

This is not swimming.

Is it living?

Hope draining, movements slowing. Darkness swirling.

Minutes, maybe seconds later, someone reached around Maria's waist, pulling her up toward the light.

CHAPTER 4

Sam couldn't say precisely what it was about the two girls at the port that caught his attention that June afternoon. His head ached from thirst. He dripped with sweat and felt anxious to bathe, to eat something with flavor, to rest after working since the middle watch—his *last* watch, he reminded himself with bitterness. He still had a dozen crates to unload and favors to ask if he had any chance of securing another commission. His superiors would flog him for slacking off, even in this final hour of their expedition, and he desperately needed to win the good opinion of another captain.

Yet, there was something about the way the redheaded girl juggled two baskets and a pair of boots.

Then the other, the taller of the two, who appeared a few years younger than Sam. The look on her face—a lovely face. Eyes that flashed like some kind of gemstone. Golden hair, wild with wind, like seafarers' tales of Persephone.

He set down his load and removed his tricorn hat.

No, it wasn't that she was beautiful. Beauty wasn't new, however briefly interesting. Rather, it was a sheer determination Sam had seen only in the visage of sailors bent on war or surviving a plague aboard a ship. Sometimes in the glow of a fresh recruit.

Yes, that was the expression. Something visceral. Ambition?

His heart pulsed in recognition. Raw emotion without inhibition.

Courage.

Or, maybe recklessness. Confirmed when the young woman leaped without announcement.

Sam blinked. *Did she just . . .*

A heartbeat later, the girl remaining on the dock shrieked.

He ran to the edge, standing beside the redheaded girl—well-off given the clean white of those lace dress trimmings and the blackened leather boots she cradled. The girl pointed to a disturbed line of water. "She tripped!"

Sam didn't challenge it. Her companion had gotten remarkably far from the pier. Sam looked around. No one else had noticed her plight above the noise of unloading the shipment, especially not with a new brigantine setting sail, too. Then, suddenly, he made out the splashes of a pale arm rising and falling. He watched for a moment with equal parts hope and wonder at her poor but seemingly effective form. Perhaps, if she didn't panic, she could paddle herself to shore.

Then her pace slowed, her motions becoming frenzied as a nest of hair bobbed up and down.

"Find a rope," the smaller girl begged. "Please, can you swim?"

Given the time, Sam might have joked about how, shamefully, so few of King George's Navy could swim. Elites deemed swimming "unseemly," reserved for lowly fishermen. Instead—seeing that the young woman was far beyond the help of a rope—he rushed around in search of something, anything, that could float.

Springing down the platform, he found an overturned barrel. Sam hugged the wide, empty rum cask to his chest, ran, then dove.

When he reached the girl, she was just below the water. Her eyes were closed, her arms clawing for the iridescent surface. She jolted at his touch.

Conscious. Still conscious.

She was heavy as an anchor in her layers of clothes, but Sam kept one arm around her waist and yanked her up toward the barrel, careful not to let her drag him under. Her fingers slipped over the slick surface, the cask rolled, and she fell back under again.

Sam cursed. Ignoring the growing shouts from the dock, and dreading the thought of having to undress the young lady before a crowd, he ducked under and tried again. This time, he grabbed her hand and guided her attention to the top hoop around the staves, locking her fingers around the metal lip. Next, the other hand. Hoisting herself up, she broke for air. The girl gasped, then coughed—violently. Gurgling and weak, but alive. She clutched the barrel with white knuckles.

He reached for the other side of the cask, steadying it with the counterweight of his body. One hand remained on her waist. She coughed again, then spat.

"Are you all right, miss?" Sam asked, treading in place.

Then she faced him, her nose inches away, and nodded. Hair slicked back, but not quite tame. The greenest damn eyes he'd ever seen, bursting with a thousand thoughts in a single glance.

Or was it a scowl?

He ripped his hand off her as if struck, his cheeks burning despite the sweat and water dripping down his temples. She did not flinch in her gaze. And something old and sharp within him broke.

"Maria!" came a cry from the dock.

Maria.

Sam, remembering himself and relieved to break from her stare, waved to signal safety. The white of his sleeve clung against his forearms.

"Do you have enough energy for the return?" Sam asked without looking at the girl.

"Yes, I can swim. At least, I thought I could." She coughed again.

"I saw you jump."

"This isn't what it looks like."

"Oh, then what is it?" The ocean sloshed. Sam pivoted, pointing the barrel toward the voices, and kicked back at the brisk water. She did the same, and they started to move. "Don't worry. I won't tell anyone, though you're lucky there wasn't a stronger current."

"I knew there wasn't a current. I know these waters better than your ilk."

Sam guffawed.

"I do!"

"I believe you. I'm just surprised to hear a good lady like yourself call the king's honorable sailors 'ilk.'"

With only a few strokes left to go, Sam stole another glance. Her cheeks seemed flushed, perhaps from exertion.

"I'm not good," she said, that fire in her extinguished. "Or, at least not well behaved. I'm sorry—what I meant to say is thank you. I've acted very foolishly today." A swell crashed against her back as she gripped the cask. But she didn't flinch from the effort.

Did she mean that? Sam wasn't sure. Her tone mirrored that of people saying what they expected others to hear.

"Don't be sorry," Sam said. "I think you showed remarkable courage. I'd also agree with you that most sailors in the king's 'honorable' navy are a far cry from it."

"I just wanted to swim—to *actually* swim," she said, her voice raw but earnest. "Something for me. Before my life is over."

"Over?"

"I'm to be married."

Sam spotted some of his shipmates gathering a rope to toss. He only had a few moments left alone with her, and he didn't feel the need to challenge or laugh at her statements, however dramatic.

He did not look at her. He did not say it would all work out. He did not ask more questions. It wouldn't be appropriate anyway—for what little he knew about the rules of propriety.

When the rope slapped the water, Sam lunged for it. Then,

swimming behind the girl, he wrapped it tight around her waist. He'd never touched a woman's waist, and her wet clothes clung to her visible curves. He could feel her quick breathing as he finished the tie.

The words tumbled out before he could stop himself: "Do you know where the Bee's River runs off into the bay?"

A nod.

He leaned closer, tugging on the rope to test the knot. "Meet me there at noon tomorrow," he whispered. "I can teach you how to hold your own in the water. For next time."

She whipped her head to assess him. Disdain? Hope? Curiosity? Eyes as large and brave as the question forming on her lips when the crew pulled her up.

CHAPTER 5

After Mr. Hallett's second supper at the house, Maria couldn't sleep. No one at the table had brought up the unspoken alliance forming, and she'd succeeded in not uttering a single word.

Maria might have said something shocking. But she'd had enough consequences for one day. She'd been humbled to a speck of dust. The scrutiny had only compounded the hot anguish of the memory: a salt-burned throat, her public embarrassment, the grueling questions of Justice Joseph Doane—who'd been at the docks to inspect cargo—as to why, given the nature of her accident, Maria still had time to remove her stockings and boots. Elizabeth followed with a quick defense about a blister.

Also, the black-haired boy, that sailor from the docks. His sharp gaze. His strange way of speaking.

His invitation.

"You could have drowned like Governor Bradford's wife!" Mama had shouted when she'd heard about the incident.

After a few hours of tossing, Maria lit a tallow candle, hoping not to disturb her sisters. Elizabeth dozed beside her. Mercy, a head of strawberry curls, snored away in what used to be Constance's bed on the opposite side of the bedroom.

In the flickering light, Maria quietly pulled a Bible from the side table and began reading Genesis. Whether for needed, desperate distraction—or direction—she didn't know.

"Still up?" Elizabeth yawned.

"I'm sorry. I didn't mean to wake you."

"What is it?"

"Nothing."

Elizabeth's eyes narrowed. "We both know you sleep like the dead and have to be persuaded to read scripture."

Maria closed the Bible and slid it back onto the table.

"Is it Mr. Hallett?"

For a moment, Maria wondered what she could tell her sister. Or, if uttering the truth made her all the more dangerous to herself and her family. Maria knew Elizabeth was old enough to suffer for excusing away Maria's behavior. She did not want Elizabeth to be punished for her misplaced loyalty.

"I can read more than books, you know. Something is on your mind."

Maria sighed. "No, not him. Something from the docks."

Elizabeth pulled her knees to her chest, listening.

"The young man who rescued me offered to teach me how to swim."

Her sister drew back.

"He gave me a place to meet him tomorrow at noon, somewhere secluded. And though I know I shouldn't go, I'm not sure I've ever wanted anything so badly in all my life."

Elizabeth said nothing. Maria took her hand.

"I think I will marry Mr. Hallett," Maria said with defeat. "In time, somehow. I just . . . feel it. I know it would be the good thing to do. Mother would be relieved. Father would benefit, forging an alliance. But until then . . ."

Elizabeth pulled her hand away. "You want to ruin yourself. That's how you'll get out of your responsibility—"

"No," Maria said in a sharp whisper. "I want to learn to swim, to be able to carry myself with confidence in the water without any fear—to learn while I still can." To attempt swimming after marriage would be scandalous beyond measure, even by Maria's standards.

She would, alas, have to grow up.

"That sailor clearly knows how," Maria added. "I believe I can trust him." She felt a burn of memory from where his strong arm had gripped her.

Elizabeth raised an eyebrow. The candle flame danced across her freckled cheeks.

"The time will come when you'll never have to make excuses on my account again. I promise," Maria said. "Can you cover my chores for a few hours tomorrow? I'll do the same for you another time."

After a moment of agonizing silence, Elizabeth slipped back under the covers with only her copper hair visible on the pillow. She rolled over, her back toward Maria.

Then, a groan and a muffled answer: "We'll rush through the morning chores. I'm coming with you."

CHAPTER 6

The low tide revealed a long stretch of damp, shell-dotted sand that tapered gradually into the bay. A few terns called overhead. No sign of anyone else. Though Sam knew this beach from his past visits—the calm inner arm of Cape Cod as it flexed against his home of England across the ocean—it had been years since returning to see his relations. And unlike his past visits, today's brought little joy.

I have become the biggest blunderbuss on this side of the Atlantic.

He should have been seeking out a new commission, asking favors and finding out who pulled the purse strings for any new posts. He'd smooth-talked his way into a new crew before, having learned the persuasive talk of a gentleman through studying his superiors' habits and the mottled books in the captain's quarters. Sam could still smell those brown-speckled pages in his child-size hands and hear Lieutenant Evans's raspy, patient voice as he corrected Sam's pronunciation—all those quiet nights beside a lantern, the rhythmic sway of the ship.

But no. Instead, here Sam stood—seeking what, exactly? He nudged a cracked shell with his boot. He hadn't seen it coming: the lack of focus, the daydreams, the way he replayed the memory from the dock over and over until he doubted every detail.

For years he'd studied his fellow sailors with harsh judgment over their silly tales of beloveds at home or encounters with lovers at every port. He shunned their lustful speeches and doubted their boasts and conquests—all predictable, ridiculous, short-lived, and distasteful. Particularly among the higher-ranking crew, who saw themselves as superior, yet leered at women without a thought of their wives at home. The sea is wide enough for many secrets. But his father had taught him better.

Now look at him. Hot-blooded. Desperate to hear her voice again. His insides twisted at the thought of her coming. Then, the thought of her *not* coming. He wasn't sure which was worse. He hoped he wouldn't regret the heavy breakfast Aunt Lamb had foisted upon him at the Higgins.

A hot sun glared. Nothing but the sound of wind and water.

Rather than stand there like the fool he took himself to be, he began assessing a few fallen pines he'd dragged from the brambly forest. With enough wood and rope, he could fasten together a raft. A raft might prove more practical than an empty keg. He'd done as much as a lad, setting "sail" in the River Yeo. Memories of a home that no longer existed.

He reminded himself that his motives were honorable. In a few weeks, he hoped to be back at sea without a single spiced memory to chew. He continued lining up the pine. Anything to keep from glancing up every other minute.

He felt her before he saw her, and his heart hammered. But he did not look up until two figures towered over him and his work.

"You came," he said, standing up and brushing sand from his breeches. He took off his tricorn hat and managed a smile, hiding his surprise that the younger of the two sisters accompanied her.

Her. Eyes greener than the Caribbean Sea. But still no more readable in a glance. It took all his concentration to not look away.

"My name's Samuel Bellamy of Devonshire—sailor in the King's Royal Navy. I'm sorry I didn't get the chance to properly introduce myself yesterday."

The two girls exchanged a glance.

"Maria Brown," she said. "This is Elizabeth."

"Our father is George Brown, one of the most distinguished farmers in Eastham," the younger one offered with a hint of a warning, her chin lifted.

Rich. Of course. Sam suspected as much.

"I'm very pleased to meet you both under much more pleasant circumstances. Elizabeth was my mother's name. Miss Brown, will you be learning, too?"

This disarmed the younger. "Oh no, thank you. I'm here to see after my sister's safety."

"Well, that makes two of us, but I could use your help." He hoisted a smooth beam from the pile of pine. "We'll start by using this as a support." He looked them both over: lighter-weight dresses than the day before, but still difficult for maneuvering. He wouldn't bring it up and had no intention of removing any of his own clothing. At least Maria's hair was braided up this time.

"Until you can sustain your swimming, you must know how to float."

CHAPTER 7

Maria, adrift in excitement and nerves about the prospect of swimming—all while racing to finish the laundry that morning—hadn't properly anticipated what it might feel like to see the young sailor again. She'd seen him as a means to an end. He just happened to be the only man outside of her family to ever come so near to her.

To touch her.

Now, here he stood. A lean but strong build. Tanned skin. A few years older than herself. Eyes dark as night. Cleaner than she'd expect of a sailor, too: a tidy white shirt, black hair pulled back with a ribbon. Given his service in the navy, she wondered why he didn't wear a wig.

She stood up straighter and swallowed her thoughts, her feelings. A lifetime's practice.

"Are you ready?" he asked.

Mr. Bellamy instructed Maria and Elizabeth to remove their shoes. Elizabeth would be getting wet, even if she was only assisting. They all waded out into the bay. Maria welcomed the surprising smack of cold, that tingling of her skin. Mr. Bellamy carried the beam over one shoulder. The salt air enveloped them, setting

Maria at ease. Her ankles sank into the sticky beach as she stared down at the surf, careful to avoid stepping on broken clam shells. When the water hit the sisters at chest-level, they came to a stop.

"Everyone can float," Mr. Bellamy explained. "If you can flip over onto your back and relax your body, you can get far without using as much strength."

Maria nodded. Elizabeth peered behind, scanning the empty shore.

"We'll try here, where you'll be safe. The water is warmer here than in the open sea." He directed Elizabeth to hold the far edge of the beam, and Maria to clutch the middle. He'd hold the other end, suspending Maria between them. "When you are ready, lean back and take a deep breath. Let the air lift you completely."

Maria blushed with embarrassment, her body rigid. Maybe this had been a mistake. But she gripped the wood and did as Mr. Bellamy said.

"Close your eyes. It helps."

Maria did. A warmth glowed behind her eyelids. Then she leaned. Her hair, neck, then back, awakened at the sharp wet, a stinging chill. Her ears filled with that familiar, underwater echo. Her feet lost balance, and her instincts fought to find ground again.

"Take another breath," she could hear Mr. Bellamy say, his voice muffled but discernible. "Yes, like that. Let your legs rise to the surface. Relax all the muscles in your body, and arch your back."

Relax. Breathe.

Despite Maria's skirts, she could sense her body lift. Her limbs, weightless.

"That's it. Now, let go of the support and put your arms out."

Maria's stomach tensed. She felt herself sinking and splashed water up her nose.

"Trust yourself."

Trust myself?

She steadied, then let go. Elizabeth and Mr. Bellamy raised

the beam in response. A grin spread across her face. At last, she opened her eyes and felt the brightness of an unobstructed sky. "Floating feels like flying."

A small wave rippled through the bay, causing Maria to lose her focus and stability. Her feet fumbled along the bottom as she stood again, arms circling.

Elizabeth raised an elbow to block the splashes.

"Well done," Mr. Bellamy said. "This time, I want you to try moving using only your legs. I'll show you how."

Mr. Bellamy handed Elizabeth and Maria the pine support before turning over onto his back and shouting directions, demonstrating how to kick, then fold one's feet in, like a frog, over and over. Elizabeth's eyes widened. Maria tried her best to listen. She really did.

"Your turn," he said. "Once with the support, then without." He took the beam from her, avoiding her fingers. And it was only then that it became clear that he was going to great lengths to avoid touching her again.

After the lesson, the girls hurried back home, toward Papa's gristmill, where they'd stashed two dry dresses to change into before returning to the chores. Judging by the sun, Maria suspected they'd been gone a few hours. Hopefully not longer. Mama might be back from her rounds. But even a beating wouldn't take away the buoyancy in Maria's steps.

"You've burned your face," Maria said, glancing at her sister's freckles, stark against pink cheeks. With Maria's own emotions heightened, the thrill of her adventure, she struggled to read her sister's silence.

Elizabeth huffed. "You're looking like a lobster yourself. Or is that a blush?"

Maria stopped, stunned at her sister's boldness. "Mr. Bellamy was honorable."

"That's what concerns me," Elizabeth said. "Handsome, too. You know how Papa feels about penniless sailors."

"Don't be ridiculous." Her insides lurched. Thinking of Mr. Bellamy as a potential suitor was out of the question. She was, as Mama never forgot to remind her, the daughter of a gentleman.

Besides, she reasoned, she didn't have time to waste on frivolous fantasies.

They walked on, boots kicking dirt onto their damp hems.

"Thank you for coming," Maria finally said. "I know you disapprove, and I'm sorry you didn't get to read today. But I feel I made a lot of progress. Mr. Bellamy, whatever he may be, is a good swim teacher."

"Yes," Elizabeth admitted. "But will you really go again tomorrow? Is it worth the danger to your reputation?"

Maria tried to summon a calmness, clarity. But she felt too heated from the day to think straight. She knew she would go, with or without Elizabeth. "It would mean the world if you came again, just a few times more. But only if you're truly willing. I know this is a risk, my risk, and not your responsibility."

Elizabeth dabbed her burned cheek. "Next time, I'd have the sense to bring a proper hat. A bonnet won't do." She winced. "You owe me."

"I'll make it up to you."

With fresh dresses and Maria's hair hidden from sight, the sisters returned home. They were removing sheets from the line when they heard their mother's voice.

"There you are," Mama said in a tone that made Maria's skin prickle. "Come inside, *now*."

The sisters followed, heads bowed. Maria hadn't prepared an excuse that would cover for Elizabeth's absence, but she had no intention of letting her sister lie or reap the punishment of her own actions.

She was just about to open her mouth when their mother led them into the kitchen. But instead of reaching for the switch, she picked up her midwifery bag.

"Your aunt Ruth needs me," Mama said, fumbling through the

contents and adding a stack of folded, clean cloths. "I've received news that she feels the pains, though her time is not for another few months. I've already told your father. I must leave immediately."

"But that's a two-day journey. Is there not a midwife in Chatham?" Elizabeth said. "Surely—"

"None so good as me." Mama pursed her lips. "Elizabeth, you're coming with me."

"Me?"

"Yes, you," Mama said, browsing through various bottles of herbs. "Since you lack your sister's talent for weaving, maybe it's time you develop an aptitude for another skill. Something more useful than reading."

Elizabeth clenched her jaw. Mama spared no one.

"Goody, you'll manage the home while I'm away. You need the practice. I shouldn't be gone longer than a few weeks. Otherwise, I'll send word."

With Papa overseeing the fields, and Mercy at reading school during the day, Maria felt a swell rise within her. She calmed her facial expressions, giving no signs of trouble, complaint, or excitement—her emotions cold and smooth as a river stone. "I'll see to everything," Maria said. "Take care of Aunt Ruth."

Mama surveyed her. And in her mother's eyes that mirrored her own, she thought she could sense a rare, intoxicating approval. A hope, Maria interpreted, that this unruly daughter of hers might turn out all right, might rise to meet the life she was meant to live.

I will, Mama, Maria thought. *I just need a little more time.*

 CHAPTER 8

The next day, she came alone.

Sam scrambled to his feet. He tented his eyes at the distant sight of her in a gray dress and a wide felt hat, then dropped the hatchet he was using and kicked the rope into a pile. If it was rare for her to be alone with a man, and he very much suspected that would be the case, he didn't want to be standing like a fool holding a potential weapon. He wasn't sure he'd been alone with a young woman either. At least, none like her.

Maria.

"Good afternoon, Miss Brown," he called, waving her over. "Come see what I'm working on today." Not securing a commission. Not working on finding employment, as he should be doing every waking hour, including this one—the reminder a sharp punch.

But to his enormous satisfaction, she smiled back and sped forward to meet him.

"Sit here," he pointed to an upturned log, one from yesterday's unfinished task. "I'm lining up the pine."

"What for?" she asked, a little breathless from the walk.

"You'll see." He sat in the white sand and turned up to meet her face. Circles hung under her eyes, and stray yellow hairs flew away from a tidy bun.

"Is everything all right?"

Her head jerked. "Oh yes. Quite."

His stomach squeezed, thinking about the two of them alone. *Act natural.*

"Your sister?"

"She went away with my mother to Chatham. My aunt is with child and having complications."

"I'm sorry to hear it." Again, Sam found himself unable to read her eyes. Worry? Fear?

Joy?

"Mama left me in charge of the house. I've had to wake earlier to see to the cows and put on the breakfast. It's far more than one person can reasonably do. But . . ." she brightened, "I'll have a week or two to finish my swim lessons."

Only that long?

Fine. *Good*, in fact. He'd be back on a ship before long anyway. Better to be rid of this distraction.

Sam cleared his throat. "That'll be more than enough time. Especially with this." He gestured to the squared-up timber, five feet in length, and picked up the rope. "See what I'm doing, here at the corner with the crossbeam? These knots will cover the whole structure and join the boards. I've flattened them and cut notches for a secure fit. It'll make for a sturdy timber raft for deeper water."

Maria leaned forward. "What kind of knot is this?"

"A clove hitch. A little complicated, but I think I can finish the raft within the week."

"Teach me?"

His eyes widened.

"It'll go faster. I'm proficient at weaving—it's the only chore anyone says I'm good at."

"Very well then." He picked up the end of the rope and wrapped it once around a plank. "You take the short end and cross it to make a slant, then bring it under and tighten." He pulled. "Next, you form an X around the crossbeam, like this." Again, he pulled the rope tight. "To finish, you repeat the first step to secure the X. Then repeat until you cover the length of the plank."

She nodded, then took the rope, adding another X in the procession without error.

"You're a quick study, Miss Brown." He glanced at the sky, noting the time. There was never enough time. "We can return to this later." He grabbed a single beam from the pile. "Let's see how well you remember yesterday's lesson. Then you'll learn to tread water."

Maria set down her felt hat beside his tricorn. A strand of loose hair fell to her chin. He stood and offered her his hand without thinking. She took it, holding it a beat longer than necessary, then brushed out her skirt.

In the ocean again, Sam gave instructions on how to tread water as Maria hooked her arms around the beam. The deep cold surrounded them, the bottom out of reach—something Sam hoped wasn't too soon for Maria. Small waves rippled through the bay along with a briny breeze. Sam noticed the chill sent a shiver through her, but he resisted the ache to pull her closer.

"Excellent work. Keep doing that with your legs. Then, when you're ready, let go of the plank and do this with your hands." He circled his arms inward, showing how he remained in place with his head above the surface.

"Like kneading dough," Maria said.

"Yes, something like that." She was, he imagined, the kind of girl who likely enjoyed fresh bread every day. He wondered what she'd think of hardtack.

She gave the new maneuver a try, her brow furrowed in concentration. A sheen glistened on her forehead. When she felt ready, she let go, fumbling for balance.

Sam saw that she was tired. Maybe too tired for this. The heavy skirts weren't helping. He didn't want to insult her with his concerns, and she'd proved herself determined. But still.

You should have sent her home the moment she showed up alone.

"That's it. Don't stop. Synchronize your movements."

For a moment, she did. Then her chin dipped into the water, and her eyes flared.

"You can—"

But she was already jerking, arms wild as she stretched for the support beam. Sam swam it closer to her. She leaned over the plank, spitting and wiping her mouth. She shuddered, holding the wood in a death grip.

He kept his hands on the pine to steady her. The messy coil of hair at the back of her head dripped. She struggled to catch her breath, and Sam suspected it had more to do with nerves than the amount of sea she'd swallowed. She'd never gone under.

"Why are you doing this, Maria?"

She rolled her head, opening her eyes up at him. "You called me Maria."

Numbskull. "I'm sorry, I didn't notice, I didn't mean—"

"No, no. It's all right." She slid a hand along the beam and rested it beside his. He felt a heat along his fingers that made his pulse pound. "It's not my Christian name anyway."

"Goody is your name then?"

"Ha." She closed her eyes and rested her head on the beam bobbing up and down with the swells. "'The good woman of the house'? Yes, that's me."

A silence fell over them. Another wave lowered and fell. Sam tried to look anywhere but directly at her.

"I share my mother's name, Mehitable," she said. "As in, 'me-hit-able.'" She pulled a face. "No one has ever called me that. And you won't either, *Samuel.* Or should I say Sam?"

Sam stifled a nervous laugh. Nothing but the two of them and the sea. This was dangerous. *You know which direction this tide pulls. Stop it here, now, while you can.*

A smile curved her lips as she opened her eyes again. She pushed onto her elbows and narrowed her gaze.

"To answer your question, I already told you. I want to learn to swim before I settle. Think of it as a farewell to girlhood, something for me."

She'd said her life was "over" that day at the docks. But what had she not said? He wanted her to speak what she meant.

Sam gripped the beam across from her and dared to get closer, close enough to see beads of water clinging to her lashes.

"What do you really want?"

She blinked, taking a moment to answer. "No one has ever asked me that before. I suppose I want to want what everyone else seems to want for me. To fit in, and to feel happy for it."

Sam burned with the urge to reach out and touch her face, aglow with light reflected from the water, to crack that wall blocking off the sea of her soul, restless and bucking, endlessly deep, a strength he sensed, no, *saw*. Even if she did not recognize it yet herself.

"That's not the desire I saw in the young woman who leaped into the open sea."

They'd traveled far enough to stand waist-deep in the water, steps heavy with weight and friction. Sam shouldered the beam, and Maria, tired from the exercise, lost her balance and fell over with a splash. Sam abandoned the plank and scooped her up, heavy skirts soaked. He carried her to the dry beach and set her onto her feet.

She studied him with one eyebrow raised. He shifted, the sand burning his toes. Every part of her dripped with ocean.

"And if you're so clever, then what do *you* want?" she said, crossing her arms over her shaking frame.

You.

Why did he think that? He'd never felt this way around a woman—the few he'd ever been acquainted with. To be fair, it was an unnerving question, what one wants.

"Freedom," he said. Yes, *that*. Freedom from the haunts of his past: the withered crops and the disappointment in his father's eyes when the harvest failed, the untimely deaths, the constant gnaw of hunger, the bite of a navy whip. "I want respect for who I am, not the job I do. I want that for everyone." He could feel his pulse racing, his voice growing louder. "I'm sick of the way superiors act on the ship, the way society cowers to those in power, the intoxication of money. I want to be free of all of it, to live a life for myself without licking the boot of another man." He sighed. "I am bone-tired of the world as it is, how it tramples people in the name of progress."

Maria listened, the lines of her face softening.

"I've passed ships carrying human *beings*, Maria. Men, women, and children in chains, brutally dragged across the sea as slaves." He gestured north. "Do you know where we stand, what happened on that beach in the distance?"

"Yes, the Old Comers first met the natives here."

"Exactly. And then what happened? The Wampanoag shared their food, their land, their farming techniques, their knowledge of survival, and how did they thank them?" Sam scoffed. "The disease the colonists brought devastated them—a disease of illness, yes, but also the disease of greed. Kidnappings. Land theft. Now the colonists who spoke of fleeing persecution perpetuate it."

"You don't believe in fate? In predetermination?" Maria asked.

"No," Sam scoffed. "Predetermination is a weak idea that claims the universe only favors the strong—those who happen to already have power. I believe in change."

They faced each other, their shadows growing with the passing sun.

"Do you believe in God?" she asked, her voice quiet but firm.

Sam considered her. He could feel his familiar zeal bubbling over. Again. "You're sure you want to talk in this way? I might introduce a dose of blasphemy."

"I can handle more than you might imagine."

"Very well. I choose to believe, but not in the superstitious God of the sailors or the ruthless God of the colonists, nor the God of rules taught by the Church of England. I've met many competing ideas about God in my travels. I have hope for a better world. And if there is a God, I hope God is the voice inside that begs us to love better."

They began walking along the empty shore back toward the makings of the raft. Tidal pools mirrored the sky overhead. Sam felt the urge to tell her more about himself, a desire for her to know him. He broke the silence: "A ship took me when I was eight years old. They snatched me from the docks one day and made me a cabin boy—said it would help my family and the parish village. Father was already falling behind on his payments, never able to scrape up enough from tenant farming. My mother passed weeks after I was born. I thought I'd return soon, or be able to send word, and make a difference in our situation." He clenched his jaw. "But I didn't set foot in Devonshire again for three years. My sister led me to the foot of my father's grave. Ashamed and as young as I was, I joined the navy, throwing my anger into battle, into improving my circumstances. My bitterness has only deepened, and I'm broke as ever—and will be until the day I die if I continue this meager trade, my *only* trade. Trapped in poverty."

"Trapped? But you're free to travel, to see the world."

"Few people are truly free, but some more than others. My plight, and yours," he noted, "are nothing compared to those whose lives have been snatched and destroyed against their will. You and I can still walk together like this, talk together like this— improper as it is. No, you and I are trapped by our own doing, for caring too much of what others think and not having the social status or financial means to act otherwise."

She huffed and dropped her skirts, giving up on protecting the hem. "What you're proposing is impossible, especially for women. We live as families, as communities," she shot. "You, a man having seen half the world, preach to *me* about freedom? I've never even been to Boston! I can't own anything or survive without the support of a man."

He blinked. "I didn't mean—"

"Do you know what I risk, coming here to swim? How opposite

our punishments would be, were we caught? Women are scorned for little more than being different. Surely you heard what happened in Salem?"

Sam's eyes narrowed, taking her in. "Forgive my presumptions. I admit there's much I don't understand." He appreciated the way she sparred, speaking to him seriously—that fire he'd sensed in her all along. "But true freedom means living the life you want to live, not the life others have decided for you."

They reached the raft. Maria undid her rope of hair and wrung out the water, her eyes ablaze and unflinching. Everything about that look undid him.

"Don't you think that might be especially important for women?" Sam tried again. "Women erroneously taught that they have weaker souls? You might be guilty of much, but *not* a weakness of soul—not from what I've seen. Would you not want to swim without fear? To travel to Boston? Or better, to live according to your own terms, whatever the particulars?"

"Yes," she said. "Were it possible."

"I want that for you, too."

At this, Maria's expression relaxed. "But it could never be."

Sam bit the inside of his cheek but couldn't stop the tumble of words: "Your life isn't over. It can never be over so long as you make decisions for yourself and not for others. Even choices that impact loved ones must be done from the heart, not out of obligation. Otherwise, that shard of goodwill rots and festers with resentment. You say that your life is over once you marry, but would it feel so if it was the path you wanted and chose for yourself?"

She stiffened. "Maybe not. But consider duty. Hearts are meant to bend to God's design for us. To keep us safe."

"But what if God gave you a heart full of desires you could trust exactly as they are?"

At this, Maria stepped closer, her foot an inch away. Sam could see the flecks of yellow in the emerald of her assessing eyes. His hands shook as his gaze dropped to her mouth. He smoothed his palms against his breeches and inhaled deeply. His body needed to close the gap between them—emotionally, physically. Be damned the consequences.

"Miss Maria Brown, may I kiss you?"

She flashed a smile, then laughed.

Laughed at him.

"This isn't how it goes, Samuel Bellamy," she said, eyes taunting. "I've heard the stories. A man doesn't ask, he acts."

Embarrassment scorched up his neck. Sam stared at the ground, then directly at her. "There are worse things than being respected." He picked up his tools and boots, then threw on his tricorn. "I'll be here again tomorrow, same time." Before he could read into her expression or listen to her rebuttal, he turned on his heel and walked the other direction.

When he peered behind, she stood, fixed in the same spot with her mouth open.

"No one can decide what freedom means for someone else," he shouted over his shoulder. But Sam knew a free soul when he met one.

CHAPTER 9

There are worse things than being respected.

Early in the kitchen the next morning, Maria diced a slab of cow fat to make tallow. She couldn't stop thinking about yesterday, everything Sam had said. What he'd asked.

A lost chance at a kiss—a *real* kiss. And worse, his dangerous, blasphemous ideas that stuck in her mind like sand to wet skin. He talked too much. He certainly didn't understand her life as a woman. Did he even know any outside of a brothel? He'd also dismissed too easily some of the finer points of her faith and community, speaking like a mystic, like one of those men who sometimes came through port with their poets for prophets. A radical. Without the doctrine of predestination, without the belief that God presided over every human triumph and loss, how could anyone make sense of this broken world?

And yet . . .

What of her heart, unruly and resistant? What if her lifelong willfulness wasn't a sin—a sign of being the weaker sex?

What *did* she want? And why had he asked? No one had spoken to her as he had spoken, nor listened to her wayward opinions without shock or censorship.

No one can decide what freedom means for someone else.

And since when was she on the defensive rather than *being* the offensive?

Tossing the fat into the cast-iron pot over the fire, Maria melted the suet—the first step to making the lye soap, Elizabeth's chore now that Maria did all the weaving. The fat sizzled. Her stomach knotted and she felt slightly sick. Her attraction—she couldn't deny it, *attraction*, toward Sam—clashed against his disturbing beliefs and her own uneasiness. She wished she could dismiss him outright and hated the truth to some of his words, but a part of her wanted him to be right, even if it tugged at threads of the tapestry that made up her entire existence. He'd voiced ideas she'd buried deep in the cellar of her mind, so hidden she never had to give them language before.

Maybe she wouldn't go swimming today. Maybe she would. But how to catch up on the chores before Mama came home? Someone had to finish mending Mercy's stockings. Dye the yarn for the indigo-patterned cloth Maria was weaving. Exhaustion clouded her ability to judge the risks. No burning "whisperings" could rise out of such inner conflict.

"Need a hand?" came a voice at the door.

"Come in, Lydia," Maria said, waving away a plume of pungent smoke from the cooking fire as she stirred.

In walked Lydia, Elizabeth's best friend. Her mousy brown hair, parted at the center, was pulled back tight under her white bonnet. Her almond-shaped eyes scanned the room.

"Where's Elizabeth?" she asked, her smile fading.

"Gone with our mother to Chatham, I'm afraid," Maria said, poking at the boiling suet. "Mama got an urgent call from our aunt. I'm on soap duty."

Lydia's chest fell. "Oh. I brought lavender for the scent." She held up a stalk of fresh purple buds.

Maria felt sorry for Lydia. This had been her weekly ritual with Elizabeth, the two of them taking the extra cakes to sell together at the docks. Though Maria sometimes tagged along to sell her weavings, she sensed they preferred keeping their own company as they walked, arm in arm, giggling under their breath.

"Thank you," Maria said as she searched for a cheesecloth. "Here, can you pull this over the top of the leaching barrel while I pour?"

Lydia dropped her things and came to Maria's side. Steam billowed up as Maria slowly poured the melted suet over the cheesecloth. Her forearms ached from the strain, and the girls coughed on the fumes.

"There," Maria said, setting down the heavy pot. "Will you stay until the cakes cool? I'm pressed for time, but you're welcome to sell the extras."

"Actually, I'm needed at home today," Lydia said, clearing her throat and wiping her hands on her apron. Maria felt a wave of relief. She never sensed Lydia approved of her, and she had more than enough on her mind for one afternoon.

Lydia avoided eye contact but held out the lavender. "Do you want this?"

Maria studied the flower, then considered Lydia's face: thin lips, a sharp nose, an understated grace. She was a quiet girl from a respectable family of furniture makers on the other side of Eastham. Her father regularly spoke up during church services. Lydia was a person who wouldn't confuse right from wrong.

Regardless of her feelings.

"May I ask you a question?" Maria asked.

Have you ever questioned your place? Doubted what we've been taught about God?

Lydia tensed. "Anything."

"Does Elizabeth speak to you about me?" Maria said, not sure at all where she was going with this conversation. "I fear I haven't always set a good example. Half of the time, she's the one reminding me to behave. I'm not sure how much longer I'll be living in this house. My parents want me married. But it's difficult to imagine daily life without her."

Has she told you anything about Sam? No. Elizabeth would never betray her like that. Not even to her closest friend. Besides, she wouldn't have had time to before accompanying Mama to Chatham.

Lydia exhaled with what might have been relief. "I have heard of Mr. Hallett's visits," Lydia said. The edge of her mouth twitched. "But I wouldn't worry for Elizabeth. She loves you well. You and the attention that flocks in your direction instead of hers."

Maria blinked. "What—"

"Goody! Are you in here?" Papa's harried voice barreled into the kitchen. He surveyed Maria and Lydia. His eyes crinkled with affection, that soft spot toward Maria she'd always sensed from her father. "I'm headed out. Do we have a decent menu for the evening?"

"Only pease porridge, Papa."

"Might we do a little better? Mr. Hallett will be joining us again after town council." He pulled a pocket watch from his coat, muttering about the time before abruptly exiting the room.

Maria felt the blood drain from her face.

"Goodbye, Maria," Lydia said, leaving the lavender on the table and inching toward the door. "Perhaps I'll see you next time, once Elizabeth returns." Without another word, Lydia was gone, too.

CHAPTER 10

Sam knew himself as a person easily provoked, sensitive to how others viewed him, and too outspoken. His back, etched with layered scars, proved that much. His skin prickled at feeling less-than, the target of scorn or mockery.

And yet, here he sat—spending precious hours he didn't have—his hands working knots down the length of the raft, ready to apologize, to make things right when she came.

If she came.

The caw of a lone bird overhead reminded him of his father, the scent of his gray shirt with the patches in the elbows. Sam recalled the two of them kneeling in the wheat field beside a razorbill with a broken wing. Black silk feathers, the white breast, the cries of the poor beast.

"What do we do?" Sam had asked, looking away, eager to escape from the shrieks and fragility of the bird.

Sam's father picked up the twitching creature and stroked the back of its neck. He whispered coos.

"Father?"

The creature calmed. His father stood—impossibly tall—gently wrapping the bird in the front of his tattered shirt.

"Should we shoot it?"

"Samuel, listen first. *See* before you act, otherwise you'll miss what's right in front of you. Patience is the mark of a true man." His father took a deep breath, then closed his eyes. The corners of his mouth turned up in an evergreen, contented smile. Sometimes, Sam resented him for that smile.

Young Sam trailed after his father toward the house, peppering him with questions about the bird, the landowner's recent demands, the dwindling harvest, his sister's cough. His father chuckled, then ruffled Sam's hair. "We'll just have to wait and see, won't we? If only your mum were here. Then maybe I could help you understand."

A strong gust blew from the bay, and sand flew into Sam's lap. He cringed to remember his behavior with Maria, not only his forward ask, but his other questions and—as his crewmates were fond of calling it—his "blustery" speech. He'd been too forward and spoken too much, burying her with his own beliefs and burdens. He would do better if given another chance. One more chance . . .

Please come.

"I can't swim today."

Startled, Sam jolted and stood. "I didn't hear you."

Her arms were folded tight against her bodice. She looked askance, gaze fixed on the ocean.

A silence.

"I'm sorry for what I said yesterday—everything," Sam started, removing his tricorn. "I understand. I'll finish up the raft for your use in my absence. I won't trouble you again."

At this, Maria snapped her attention back. Red rimmed her eyes. Those eyes, emotion high as a springtide. "Oh, I didn't mean that. I'm not finished with our lessons. In fact, I have something for you." She searched through the pocket strapped to the belt around her waist and pulled out a cake of soap. "Lavender," she said.

Sam took the bar and brought it to his nose. Lightly sweet.

Earthy. A smell just out of reach—a scent of the upper class. A reminder of what he'd already determined in the hours since their last encounter: He couldn't afford to entertain this dangerous dream. But more importantly, neither could she. Maria risked enough, coming here to swim.

Restraint would be best for both of them.

"So, this is a thank you, not a goodbye gift?" he asked.

"No," she said, startled. "Not goodbye. Not yet."

Damn his selfishness, he couldn't deny her that. Even if he should say no. Even if he'd venture no further and never make another advance.

He dared a step closer. Her emerald eyes flashed like a summer storm, her feelings a pent-up gale.

"Maria," he asked. "What's wrong?"

CHAPTER 11

To her own shock, she fell into his chest, sobbing. Her felt hat tumbled off. It was all unseemly. But in response, he wrapped his arms around her and said nothing, his chin buried in her hair. Maria wasn't sure which was worse: the sin of crying in public, or crying in public in front of *him*. The thought only made her cry harder.

"I can never be free," she choked. "I don't know what freedom means, but I do know I can't manage even a few hours to myself to make good on this childish, ridiculous dream of swimming."

He held her by the shoulders, black eyes blazing. "If it's what you want, it's not ridiculous."

"No? In what way is it responsible then?" She told him about her family, the daunting chores, and even Mr. Hallett and the un-made supper.

"I'm sorry," he said, affirming what she'd said and apologizing again about yesterday. "I didn't mean to belittle your beliefs or pretend to know your experience. I was insensitive. I have no right to meddle in your life. You're very brave to come."

She wiped her remaining tears on her sleeve. "There's so much I don't know anymore." Maria felt a stirring, a hunger. One she knew she should ignore. A door she should never walk through.

What if God gave you a heart full of desires you could trust exactly as they are?

She raised a shaky hand to his cheek. It felt hot to the touch. She tucked a wavy strand of his black hair behind his ear that had come free from the tie. He smelled of fresh-cut timber and sea.

Then he took a deep breath and pulled away.

"Miss Brown . . ."

Her stomach hit the ground, and she angled away.

Sam must have seen the sting of his words on her face. He cleared his throat, his bright eyes eager to return her gaze. "Maria," he corrected softly. "We could talk all day. And believe me, I *want* to. But this won't solve your immediate problem about swimming and supper."

As if she needed her problems counted, she thought, wondering why, again, she'd wanted to come.

"I have an idea," Sam said, reaching for her hand and catching her eye to draw her out of her whirlpool of thoughts. Her fingers tingled in his grip. "A way so you can practice your lessons and still get something on the table. I know a recipe, a port special."

"You cook? As a man?" She gaped, her attention reluctantly pulling away from her shame and onto his words.

"I was a cabin boy for many years, remember?" he grinned, letting go of her hand as her heart thumped. "This beach is full of clams, as you know—all those bubbles in the tidal flat. Boil some with potatoes, then throw in a heap of salted butter and herbs. Cream too, if you have it. You'll get a fine stew without much labor."

"Are clams not a poor man's meal?"

"I think you've already made a favorable impression on the dear Mr. Hallett." Sam grimaced as he stooped for the last untethered log. He seemed to have more to say, but swallowed hard instead. Sam handed her the plank. "You tread water. Don't go too deep. I'll be here, combing the sand for clams. I'll even shuck them for you." The smile returned. "You're welcome."

Much as she enjoyed his teasing and this offer, she couldn't make sense of his motivations. She wanted to claw out the sadness lurking beneath that sly expression. What did he intend with her? Maybe she was naïve to wonder or hope for more. She'd overheard enough lewd conversations at the docks to know how sailors behaved with women, never binding themselves down after a night of fancy. He was one of them, after all.

And she was a gentleman's daughter, with no real desire to attach herself to a man. Wasn't that the point of these lessons? To do something for herself, something that had nothing to do with the game of matchmaking?

"But why? Why are you helping me?"

"So you can come back again tomorrow, and the day after. To catch freedom in tiny snatches." Before she could pry, he beamed in a way that left her dizzy. "Go on now! I'll keep watch. You'll do fine, I trust you."

Maria studied him, his face radiant with a look no one had ever given her before. It made her queasy and fluttery, like he could see right to her core.

She didn't share his blind trust in herself. Trust what? Or should she say, *who*? The person here in secret, or the person the world knew her as?

CHAPTER 12

The Great Island Tavern reeked of fish and damp leather. Sam stared into his ale, which he swirled absently in the cup. The rim had a faint taste of dirt—something he would bring up with the owner, Israel Cole, if Sam wasn't so afraid of that bastard and his cronies. Cole was a black-market dealer and merciless money-lender. Aunt Lamb had explained the family relation, some cousin of a cousin who sometimes directed lodgers to the Higgins.

The hearth behind him crackled. Sam ignored the snorts and laughter coming from the whalers camped at the other end of the smoky room.

Damn, John Hallett.

He'd heard the surname before. But after a few queries—including some hearsay from Aunt Lamb—the man's portrait emerged:

A rich fellow with no children, overdue to settle again . . .

. . . Hopes to become sheriff . . .

Sam put down his cup decisively. He noted the narrow cut along his palm where his knife had grazed the skin that afternoon while shucking clams. He'd hidden it from Maria. It wasn't serious and, much as he wished or pretended otherwise, he had a nasty streak of pride—something his father had never had.

A blast of laughter from the table to his right interrupted Sam's thoughts. He took a swig of ale, then studied the red wound across his palm and the problem still at hand.

Respectable family, those same Halletts out of Yarmouth . . .

A mind for politics and little else . . . Putting up funds for the second meetinghouse . . .

Of the Browns, Sam had already gleaned as much as he could without drawing notice. Eastham was a small enough town. Mr. and Mrs. Brown wanted the best for their remaining daughters at home. There was some sort of incident with the mother, a midwifery birth that went wrong that put her at odds with the town for a few years. Mr. Brown's position in the community seemed to smooth over the damage.

Everyone knew Goody as the town beauty. No wonder the ambitious, opportunistic Hallett wanted to claim her like a hunting trophy, another reform project to show off his great leadership abilities. Sam bristled at the clichés the gossipers hurled: unruly, haughty, a temptress always out of reach. They knew her by sight only, he tried to reason. Or sometimes by her unparalleled weaving skills. Nothing compared to how he knew her—brave, passionate, bursting with aliveness.

Even with Mr. Hallett haunting his thoughts, it was difficult to stay upset for long as he relived the rush of being with her in secret. His pulse skittered, and his muscles tensed with desire.

Calm down. Think, you fool. Plan.

Sam gulped the ale, bitter laced with sweet. Earlier on the beach, it had taken every good angel in him to not show more dissatisfaction than warranted over Hallett or default to his typical speeches—his selfishness was not Maria's problem. He'd learned his lesson. Even if she felt about him the way he felt about her, they both knew she had a future to consider—never mind his big talk of freedom. Ideas alone did not change the world, or his place in it. Sam meant what he'd told her earlier: He didn't have a right to meddle in her life. He tried not to think about the supper, what Mr. Hallett might have said or not said. Sam's jealousy boiled again at the thought. All he wanted to do was storm down the street, approach Maria's father, and . . . and then what?

Build a life here?

Take her away?

Say, "Honorable sir, I know you have the highest expectations of securing an advantageous marriage for the most-sought-after girl in Eastham. Might I offer your daughter the hand of an unemployed, nonbelieving orphan?" He continued drafting this internal speech until someone knocked on his table.

"You must be Samuel Bellamy."

"Depends on who's asking," Sam said, not looking up. He'd come to these remote bluffs instead of the Higgins Tavern, where he was lodging, to be alone.

The man slid into the chair beside him. "Your aunt said you might say that. She also said I'd spot you easily. The only one to eschew a wig."

The man held out a hand, and Sam took it.

"Name's Williams. Paulsgrave Williams," he said. He had dancing eyes, a mirth Sam rarely saw in a middle-aged man. He wore several rings and a brass-button waistcoat. "I'm an old friend of your relatives."

"To what do I owe the pleasure?"

"I hear you need work."

Sam clenched his jaw. "Yes. Like thousands of other sailors, tossed aside now that the Spanish Succession business is over." Despite all his efforts to find a position whenever he wasn't out with Maria, he'd struggled to find a single lead with the navy.

"You're not at all like thousands of other sailors, from what I hear." Williams glanced around to check for potential listeners, then lowered his voice. "What if I told you I know a way to better fortunes, better than you'd make in a lifetime with the navy?"

Sam considered him with skepticism as Williams signaled for a drink.

"Do you have any idea how many ships have gone down on

the Atlantic Coast over the century? Countless." Williams leaned forward and took off one of his rings, which clanked on the table. "Galleons loaded with silver, bars of gold. Coins from every nation. Gems the size of fists." He snatched the ring and slipped it back on. "Riches waiting for someone to claim them."

"Treasure hunting, then?" Sam said in a monotone.

Williams's eyes glinted, the corners crinkling. "Oh, come now, boy. No one is above a little treasure. Even the locals here. They scorn any plans to build a lighthouse. And why? Because they like to plunder whatever washes up, same as anyone else. They call it 'God's will,' then collect on several shipwrecks every year in Eastham. Haven't you heard their prayer? 'We pray Thee, O Lord, not that wrecks should happen, but that if any shall happen, Thou wilt guide them onto our shores for the benefit of the inhabitants.' Bah! This isn't piracy. Merely a good ol' game of finders keepers."

Sam had to admit he could feel excitement mounting. As a boy, Sam dreamed of wealth and all the liberties it afforded. During the long, grueling hours at sea, he used to imagine bringing enough money home to save his family, to help them live for something other than survival. But the older he got, the harder the work and the scarcer regular pay became. He stopped indulging these fantasies. Williams's words brought them back to life, and the thought of the freedom he'd have with money was enough to start his heart beating heavily in his chest. That old ambition of getting rich, tinged with new anger, taunted a surefire way to tower above his superiors and demand the respect he'd never received. A respect he and his family, and countless others, had deserved.

Then Maria's eyes flashed before his. That bold look she gave him in the water, the first time they'd met. He couldn't deny the softening change in him, still rooting its way through his consciousness.

See before you act . . . otherwise you'll miss what's right in front of you.

This wasn't the kind of thing fellow sailors bragged about after dark. No. What he felt for Maria didn't narrow his world, it exploded it. Feelings and possibilities he hadn't considered before. A settled life with someone else? To feel content? Satisfied? To have a home to call his own? He'd never entertained it. Tempting as an offer like this might have been to his former self, he knew in his bones he didn't have the grace to let Maria go so easily.

"I'm afraid I've run out of time for frivolous dreams," Sam said, raising his empty cup.

"Spoken like a man twice your age."

"You seem established enough." Sam gestured to his companion's dress. "What's in this for you?"

Williams laughed, a full-body laugh that made the chair groan. "You sound like the Mrs." He recovered himself and continued. "Adventure? An escape from the tedium? Call it what you will. I'm a jeweler out of Rhode Island. The shop runs itself, but this would be good for business. I'm here to collect a crew. I have twelve or so ready at my signal, but we could use a leader who can sail. And a sloop . . ."

Ah, the catch. If Williams didn't have a decent ship, he didn't have a chance.

"We'd split the profits, of course. I have the funds to finance half the expedition. Folks in these parts," he said with a jerk of his head in the direction of the backroom, "can lend the rest under certain conditions. I just need someone to navigate. The best of the best."

Sam returned to drafting that internal script addressed to Mr. Brown: "Dear Honorable Sir, not only do these features recommend me, but I will *also* be running away to heaven knows where, for an unstated time, in search of an unlikely stash of foreign objects of unspecified value."

He liked Williams's spirit. He really did. The plan might have appealed to him before, but he didn't have time to waste on schemes. He needed something steady, something local and respectable. And quickly. Only then could he approach Maria and her father.

After drinks and some friendly conversation, Williams rose to go. His velvet waistcoat looked dashing in the firelight. For a moment, Sam was seized with envy.

"Think on it," Williams said, slapping Sam on the shoulder. "I'll find you when I get word of an opportunity."

CHAPTER 13

Maria and Sam lay with their backs against the now-completed raft, rising and falling with the mild swells in the bay. Their feet dangled off the edge, dipped into the brisk water. Sam had his eyes closed, his hands behind his black hair as he dried off in the sun after the day's swim lesson. Maria stole the chance to study him.

She'd never examined a man this closely before. Her eyes trailed the pink curl of his inner ear, the dark of his lashes, the hard line of his jaw. His tanned skin was paler on his wrists, soft with green veins that forked like a river delta. Today, his lean torso showed through his wet shirt, and his breeches hugged the muscles of his hips and thighs, causing her insides to stir.

When Maria leaned in closer, she lost her balance, and the raft teetered.

"Easy," Sam said, one eye opening as he rolled onto his side to steady them. Their hands brushed. It was the only intimacy they'd allowed each other—this occasional, daring dance during lessons. He looked at her for a long moment, smiling lazily. "If we aren't careful, we'll tumble in." He squeezed her fingers, causing her stomach to flutter.

But Maria didn't let go when he tried to pull away. Instead, she laced her fingers between his, feeling the calluses on his palms. She felt him freeze, though heat passed freely between their skin. That small gesture made every nerve tingle, every inch of her glow.

For once, neither of them had words to say. For a long time, they said nothing.

"I think my mother will return tonight," Maria said, reluctant to break the trance. But she had to tell him.

"Oh?"

Maria gazed off toward the horizon. In the passing days, she'd been surprised how natural it felt to be together, how quickly he'd become her closest friend despite their frequent debates. Fighting for time together proved to be a challenge, and more than a few days had passed between some lessons. But he was always honorable. Infuriatingly honorable. He said he stood on the beach at the same time every afternoon, just in case she arrived.

Conversation with Sam was like talking to Elizabeth, but easier. He countered with challenge and questions, not rebuke. He did not hold back the way Elizabeth did, the way she retreated into her novels and private thoughts or whispers with Lydia. And for once, Maria's ideas weren't the most scandalizing in a discussion. She'd told Sam about schoolmaster Miller, her teacher from reading school, and her frequent praise and punishments, of when she cut Elizabeth's tresses too short, and of the time she fell and slashed open her knee—how her father doted on her night and day despite Mama's protests. In turn, Sam had told her about the unpleasant task of swabbing a deck using salt water and gritty holystones to keep the timber clean and smooth, his vow on his father's grave to never become a farmer, and of the kindness of a certain man called Evans who'd taught him to read as a cabin boy—one of the few acts of kindness he'd experienced from a superior in his career. She'd swooned when he described the streets of London. London! Cobblestones and fog, crumbling castles and the bells of spired cathedrals. She'd made him slow down and tell it all again, in more detail, swallowing hard the impossible ask of *take me with you.*

But that would be out of the question, beyond the realm of possible. There were two very real subjects that she didn't mention at length, two he didn't ask her about in return: Mama and Mr. Hallett.

"How do you know?" Sam asked, still holding her hand. "I thought she wrote to say she'd be gone for an additional week."

Wispy clouds dragged across the blue. Maria sat upright as the raft wobbled. They hadn't drifted too far from shore. "I don't know. But somehow, I know. It's hard to explain."

"Try?" Sam said, tracing the outline of her knuckles. Her skin blazed. She felt like a heroine in a story from the docks, but the story was hers. And better.

She sighed, surprised at her instinct to tell him. "I get these . . . whisperings, is what I used to call them. It's a burning feeling of sorts. What people are thinking, and—don't laugh—sometimes things before they happen." She told him about the spoiled milk, the pangs before a storm, and of a barn fire she could smell before anyone else.

"Where I come from, we call that intuition," Sam said. "Inspiration."

Maria balked. "And where I come from, we call that 'of the Devil.' Women shouldn't be mixed up with any of that. People cry witch."

Sam brought her hand to his lips. The world came to a halt.

"It is not a curse to be so feeling," he said, so quiet she could barely hear. "Sensitivity is a form of intelligence, no? Father always told me the most foolish thing men do is ignore the sense and minds of women. But tell me what you think before I run away again with one of my speeches."

Maria forced herself to focus as need awakened in every corner of her body. "I think my stirrings, these 'whisperings,' are often right. But I've been wrong before. They are dangerous to mention and scare me sometimes, and yet, I can't ignore them."

They locked eyes, and she felt a swift rush to her head. For some inexplicable reason, she knew he wanted to know if she'd felt something, anything like that, as it related to him.

No. That was wishful thinking. He'd had every opportunity to state his intentions, and he was—if anything—a man unafraid to speak his mind. His silence spoke louder than her foolish hopes. She'd made peace with that, difficult as it was. Though Mr. Hallett had made no further advances, the stage was set. This adventure with Sam was always temporary. Beautiful, but temporary.

And *hers.*

His face softened. "It is difficult to trust oneself, isn't it?"

"Difficult. And then there is the problem of which self." Lately, Maria felt split into two, irreconcilable people. The woman at home, worried about chores and what her family thought—a woman who bit her lip during dull dinners and let her mind drift far away from her body stuck in the chair. Or the woman here, growing and changing faster than a cherry blossom in the spring into someone she didn't recognize but who also felt deeply familiar.

Sam grunted in agreement. "What does this mean for swimming lessons? There's one more foundational technique."

"*Another* one?"

"This one would give you more distance. But I have to teach you on land. It requires . . . well, a lighter wardrobe in the ocean. You can try it in the water later. By yourself."

Maria raised a brow. "You mean less clothes?" A thrill seized her.

"Frankly, yes. Your skirts fight you every step of the way. Surely you've noticed."

"I can do that."

Sam's eyes widened.

But she was already on her knees, tugging her dress over her head.

"Maria!"

She tore it off, then began undoing the laces of her stays.

He looked away, trying to stabilize the small raft, his cheeks pinker than she'd ever seen them. "Maria, you've already been swimming today. You're tired, this is—"

She felt a wellspring of pure confidence she didn't know she possessed. Who was this person, so delighted with the raw joy of herself—this energy surging through her, the feel of bright sun on bare shoulders, the shyness of the man inches away? A man who understood her, who cared for her in a way nobody had before. For this precious, fleeting moment, what else mattered?

She stopped when she got to her sleeveless cotton shift. "Don't worry, I left something on."

Sam cursed and shook his head, still facing the opposite direction.

"You promised you'd teach me how to swim."

He grimaced and muttered something that sounded like a prayer. She felt lighter than a blade of switchgrass. A breeze rippled across her skin as she slid into the frigid water, which covered her entire body in goose bumps. She rested her elbows on the raft.

Finally, he turned. For a moment, he just stared. She felt him searching the planes of her face. Seeing her. Truly seeing her, in a way that had nothing to do with what she was wearing.

Or rather, what she was *not* wearing.

Speechless, he moved closer, his abdomen now resting against the raft as he propped himself on his arms. He paused, then lifted her chin with a finger. He was close enough for Maria to hear him swallow.

"Ask me again," Maria whispered, sharing his breath as she remembered the first time he'd asked to kiss her.

Sam didn't need a reminder. He pulled her lips to his. Hard. Her eyes flew open. The initial surprise was overwhelmed by the lightning that shot through her—a bolt stronger than a first dive into the sea. She closed her eyes.

This was what she'd been missing?

What else did her body know?

Shutting her thoughts out, she leaned in deeper. His mouth on hers. Hot and soft and sweeter than honey. She gripped his shirt, overwhelmed with the desire to pull him nearer.

"Maria," he panted.

"Oh no. Was it bad?" Her insides knotted. *What* was that? Or rather, *who* was that who'd kissed him back?

"Quite the opposite," Sam gasped, and his face flushed. But Maria thought she detected a faint sadness mingled with the happiness. "You are the strangest, boldest person I have ever known." He beamed. "I've never done anything like this with a half-clothed woman."

Maria's jaw fell open. "But you're a sailor."

Sam shook his head. "I see we are both still unlearning stories we harbor about each other." Shifting onto his knees, he reached for his shirt. "May I?"

Maria nodded, careful not to blink. "It's only fair."

He ripped it off and braced himself before jumping into the bay. She held up a palm against the splash. When she opened her eyes, he had one hand in her hair, the other on the raft.

Maria could feel heat radiating from his bare chest. She reminded herself to breathe. "Don't flatter yourself. We're only swimming," she said, flinging water into his face. He laughed, then returned fire. Maria didn't know what she felt or believed about a great many things. She didn't know what Sam wanted, or if he was tempting enough to sway her heart toward something more. But maybe uncertainty was all right.

When the battle was over, he swept one strong arm around her waist to embrace her, keeping them both afloat.

She held his head between her hands as beads of water fell down his forehead. His dark eyes burned as if with fever.

"Maria."

He longed to say something, she could see. Maybe pull away, or say the obvious:

We can't.

We shouldn't.

She touched her nose to his, felt him exhale, felt the protests dissolve. This much she knew with unshakable conviction: She needed to kiss him again, and somehow it would be even better with them both in the ocean.

CHAPTER 14

Sam was back at the Higgins Tavern, sharing drinks and clearing tables for Aunt Lamb for meager tips as he listened for useful gossip—updates on the cod market, potential positions on incoming vessels, anything—when he looked out the window and spotted a figure in the apple orchard across the way. He blinked.

Maria?

"Never enough coin," an old, jobless fellow was complaining about haddock fishing. "But better'n some of the small farmers' lot, I tell ye, I was just saying to Abbott—"

Sam stood up abruptly. The cluster of other unemployed listeners stared. "My apologies," Sam said, straining to keep his face neutral. "I . . . I just remembered something urgent."

The old man continued to drone as Sam made for the door. Sam scanned for observers before darting toward the orchard.

Sure enough, there she stood with her arms folded. A golden light shone through the branches, and a waft of white blossoms perfumed the air.

She turned as he approached. "Finally!" she cried, relief thick on every syllable. He'd never seen her eyes so wide, so terrified. "I worried you'd never look out. I didn't know what I'd do if you didn't. I had to find you—I *had* to. But I can't go in a place like that."

Sam glanced over his shoulder to ensure no one had followed, then pulled her into a thicker part of the orchard. He should hesitate, exercise caution, protect his runaway heart.

Instead, his mouth found hers and they spoke without words. His body burned for her. She sighed with audible pleasure and relaxed in his arms, letting out a breathy noise. His own breath hitched. He felt the press of her thighs through her dress as she leaned into him. They were fools. They were out of their depth in this world. They were their own world entirely.

But as he tugged at the string on her bonnet to let her hair fall, to smell that delicious scent of soap and wool and summer air, of her, he felt her rip away.

"He's coming. Tonight, in an hour. Papa told me to prepare for an important conversation."

Sam clenched his jaw with enough force to snap his teeth. Mr. Hallett had been dining regularly, especially since the return of Mrs. Brown and Elizabeth and the spike in political debates. Sam had heard grumblings at the tavern regarding soil ruin and common land divisions. Swim lessons had occurred less frequently, whenever Maria could sneak away. He knew this day would come, but he'd hoped not so soon. So much for the colonies being the land of opportunity. He still didn't have a plan worthy of Mr. and Mrs. Brown's daughter. He cursed.

"Sam," Maria said, struggling to steady her voice. "You once asked me what I wanted. I'm still not sure I know, not really."

He could see her wrestling, fighting herself, grasping for the right words as she stared at the ground. His chest thudded, each heartbeat like cannon fire as he waited for her words, her thoughts.

Then, finally, she took his hand and placed it to her cheek. He could feel the warmth from her rush into town.

They'd spoken boldly before. Damn, they did nothing *but* speak boldness. But never about this. Never about the invisible weaving that seemed to bind them together despite the impending end to their meetings. But the brazen truth of her stated love, a truth he craved like a drunkard for the bottle? That would light every shadow of his mind ablaze, dispelling every self-doubt with bonfire.

It was entirely selfish to hope. If this was goodbye, he would brave it stoically, with everything she deserved—anything to make it easier on her.

"I won't ask for your pity," Maria continued. "I never expected more from our encounters. But to marry him, after knowing you." She shook her head. "Have you considered such things?" Her blush deepened. "I have to ask, just in case, have you ever thought—"

To hell with self-control.

Sam kissed her, hard, then dropped to his knees.

"Night and day, since the first moment I saw your raw courage, that wild heart of yours when you jumped from the dock." He pressed his lips to her shaking hands, the words flooding out of him like a burst dam. "Will you marry me, Maria? I've spent the past weeks looking for work as a sailor, now as a fisherman. I haven't a shilling to my name, no land or home to give you, and little family to speak of. But God help me, I love you. You make me feel the way my father always said I would, when the time came—like I want to be a better man."

He watched her gemstone eyes well with tears. She pulled him up and threw her arms around him so tight he thought his ribs might crack.

"Surely you've always known," he whispered into her ear.

"Then why didn't you say anything?"

"Believe me, I wanted to." He laughed. "But I wanted to improve my chances first."

They pulled apart, and Sam met her gaze. They both knew what he meant.

"Will you lead me to your home?" Sam said, feeling slightly nauseous. He checked his breath for alcohol and smoothed his coat. He wished he had time to grab a comb.

* * *

As Sam and Maria walked down the road, passing the old East-ham cemetery and conscious of every glance, Sam caught sight of Paulsgrave Williams hurtling toward them in that green velvet waistcoat.

What now? Sam groaned.

"Bellamy! There you are," he wheezed, hands on his knees. He gathered his breath and wiped his dusty forehead with a lace hanky. "It's time. Eleven galleons sank off the Florida coast in a hurricane. A Spanish fleet loaded with gold and silver—pesos lit-tering the sandbars."

Eleven ships? His heartbeat quickened. The thought made Sam's mind spin, but he had to focus.

"Mr. Williams, I'm busy at the moment," Sam interrupted, nodding toward Maria, whose jaw hung open.

Williams bowed slightly in acknowledgment, then continued, spittle flying, all pretense of secrecy gone. "I've secured the sloop and crew. We can't wait, or others will claim our opportunity. The time to talk is now to secure Cole and his investors."

"As you can *see*," Sam emphasized, "I can't at present."

Williams shook his head and growled. "Fine, tonight then. Meet us at the Great Island Tavern." He hurried away until Sam called after him.

"Williams?"

"Yes?"

Sam had spent a lifetime studying the ways of the upper class, modeling their speech, watching their behaviors, attending to hy-giene. But he had to also look the part.

"Might I borrow your wig and coat?"

Blood pounded in Sam's ears. The wig itched, and his armpits gathered sweat in Williams's coat. He sat up straighter in the ma-hogany chair, facing Mr. Brown, keenly aware of the terse words exchanged between Maria and her mother outside the door.

"What is it I can do for you, Mr. Bellaby?"

"Bellamy, sir."

"Ah. Right." Mr. Brown had eyes clear as a tidal pool. They quivered under the tension, and he stared from the clock to the desk in front of him, papers and ledgers groomed into neat piles. "I don't believe I am late on any payments. Who do you work for?"

When it became clear Mr. Brown would not make this any easier for him, Sam cleared his throat and began. "Mr. Brown, I have come to introduce myself and make my intentions clear. I seek the hand of your daughter."

Mr. Brown frowned. "Elizabeth?"

"Mehitable," Sam said, keeping his hands as calm and steady as he could manage.

At this, Mr. Brown's eyes flared. "I'm afraid that's impossible. She is already claimed. In fact, the man in question is coming to talk to my daughter as we speak."

His throat tightened. Sam would need to channel years of persuasion and confidence to redirect the conversation. "Not formally claimed, from what I gather. If you'll allow me, Mr. Brown, I know you to be a kind sort of man. A reasonable man. Maria has told me so herself—she admires you greatly. I know how much you care for your daughter—*love* your daughter. I believe her best chance of happiness would be with me, and I know she feels the same."

"Good heavens, what have you done?"

"No, nothing like that, Mr. Brown," Sam stumbled. "I assure you. My feelings are honorable, as are hers."

Mr. Brown leaned back and assessed him.

"I've served faithfully in His Majesty's Royal Navy, and I've come to the colonies in search of work. I'm staying with my aunt, where I help out at the Higgins. I'm a skilled sailor, and I believe I can secure a position as a fisher in the area, at least until my next commission."

"And what kind of life is that?" Mr. Brown said, arms crossed across his gut. "My brother was a ship captain. Went out one day and no one heard from him again. And as far as the Higgins, well, is that really the sort of place for a gentleman to spend his time?"

"I understand and appreciate your concerns, sir. I assure you, I know how to work hard, and I will do anything—everything—it takes to support your daughter. I'll find suitable work. I can learn a new trade. Might we bring her in? Wouldn't it best for all of us to talk together, with Mrs. Brown, too?"

The man's face reddened. "You insult me."

Numbskull. "I didn't mean—"

At this, the door flung open.

"Papa, please listen to him! For me."

Maria stood tall before coming to Sam's side. She must have been eavesdropping, along with her rigid mother who remained a few paces back. Maria placed one hand on Sam's shoulder. Mr. Brown's eyes shifted between the two of them, a scowl smoldering.

"I want this. I want to marry Mr. Bellamy."

Sam froze. Her words had an effect on her father, visible in the brief hesitation in his eyes. But Sam knew a lost battle when he saw one. Mr. Brown stood and shook, placing both palms on his desk to steady himself.

"Get out."

Maria clapped a hand to her mouth.

"Mr. Brown, if you'll please listen—"

"Only Satan works in secret, and here at the eleventh hour. I know what's good for my daughter. I said, get out."

Sam felt as though his legs were doused with molten ore. He couldn't move. Hadn't he known this is how it would go? *Known* he never had a chance, no matter his feelings, his intentions, or what he might have to offer? No matter how sincere, how patient and careful he could act in speech and dress and ways? Some chasms couldn't be crossed with respect alone. His pulse thundered with rage. In what sick world did he and Maria need permission to build their lives together anyway?

One worth ripping apart.

I'm sorry, Father. But you were wrong.

"And would it have made a difference, had I come sooner?" Sam snapped. "Or if I came now, as I am, bearing rings and land

and connections that suited your own interests? A title, perhaps? If I wielded the kind of power people like you worshiped?"

"Why, you impudent—"

Sam tore off the wig. "I care for Maria in ways you could never fathom. You don't know or appreciate the half of her. Shame on you, on all of you. When I return—and I *will* return, rich enough to make you eat your words—you'll regret this moment."

"No," Maria said, her father grabbing her wrists and yanking her behind him.

Sam found her eyes. "I love you, Maria." *We'll find another way.*

Mrs. Brown, the glowering woman in the background, pointed to the open door. "Leave."

As he stormed out, ears ringing, Sam heard Mrs. Brown yell after him, "Never come back."

CHAPTER 15

Maria flinched at every sound of the night—the cry of a raven, the wind through the apple orchard, the snap of a twig as she stepped. The rasp of her own, uneven breath left her uneasy. Her heart raced, and the lantern she hid beneath her cloak sat warm against her leg.

I could die for this, Maria thought, pushing away the thought.

I'm hardly alive if I don't *do this.*

She crouched against a tree, peeking out of her hood at the Higgins Tavern across the way, windows lit with candles. He had to come back tonight. He had to.

She didn't know how much time she had. Borrowed time. Elizabeth—furious as she was—might have woken up and ratted her out already, told Mama and Papa she'd snuck out of bed. They'd certainly know where to look.

Where was he?

Then she saw his silhouette make for the wooden door.

"*Sam*," she hissed. "Sam, it's me."

The man stopped, straightened, and reached for something on his belt, but did not turn around.

What if it isn't him?

Maria held her breath. The figure took a few steps back, glanced in both directions, then hurried toward the orchard.

"Maria," he whispered, fumbling to where she crouched.

She flooded with relief. "Over here." She pulled her cloak back just enough to signal, then covered the lantern again.

His hands found hers, and she kissed him. Softly, slowly. They stayed like that for a long minute, then pressed their foreheads together. His hair smelled of pipe smoke rather than drink.

"Are you all right?" he said. "I worried I'd never see you again. That maybe you wouldn't want to see me."

Maria snorted. "I'm not that easy to spurn. Though my family might be."

He tensed, but sat beside her, resting a head on her shoulder with a heavy sigh. "I'm sorry." The hot anger she'd heard earlier had abated completely, replaced with a cold note of despair. The shift scared Maria, extinguishing her own anger at his foolhardy threat.

"What for?"

"Everything. The mess I've made of this. I've been wrong about everything."

She swallowed, then gripped his hand. "I hope not everything."

"No, not about you, of course." He squeezed her palms.

The silence hung around them like a fog. Anxious questions pelted Maria like arrows in the dark.

"It isn't safe here, if my family comes looking for me," Maria said. They stood. "Will you walk with me to the dunes?"

They lay side by side between patches of beach grass, their bodies imprinted in the fine sand, fingers laced. Maria's abandoned cloak covered the lantern light, and the waves crashed somewhere below. The stars overhead seemed impossibly bright, like a taunt from on high.

"You'll go then?" Maria said, tears beading at the edges of her eyes. "To Florida with that man Williams we saw in the street today?"

"What choice do I have?" Sam said, telling her about the meeting at the Great Island, the money Israel Cole and some other black-market merchants pledged to match Mr. Williams's funds. But Maria had never heard Sam sound so unsure.

"You have choices," Maria said, nuzzling in closer. "We always have choices, a chance to change things. Remember everything you told me? Besides, you'll get a job as a fisherman. Perhaps study a new vocation—you'd be an excellent carpenter, or a merchant. If you give Papa time, he might understand."

Sam laughed—a bitter, broken laugh. And Maria knew he was right. It wouldn't be enough. They couldn't continue as they were.

"Fine. So you'll go then. Be one of those fortune-seekers." She wiped her eyes. "Carry on with that free life you always spoke of, leaving me here with nothing more than memories while you return to Devonshire and—"

"Maria," he said, turning to face her. His somber face shone with moonlight. "You've said nothing of what happened with Mr. Hallett after I left."

"Oh," she said. "So that's what's got you down? Nothing, that's what happened. Mama said I was sick—how could any of us recover after a thing like that? I'll get a horrible beating tomorrow once the shock wears off, that's for sure. When he comes again, I'll tell him no. Papa won't force me. He won't allow me to do a great number of things, but he won't force me."

At this, Sam grabbed her head and kissed her. "So you're not engaged?" he said, a smile back in his voice. "You'll not marry the old man?"

"No," Maria said. "So long as I have you."

He pulled her into a hug and they rolled down the dune, tumbling and giggling like children. When they landed at the bottom, Sam hovered over her, his black hair speckled with sand that rained down on her. She dusted away the grains and felt his torso tighten.

He ran his finger down her nose and parted lips. She sighed with pleasure, relishing the tingle of his touch.

"Come with me," he said.

Her stomach clenched. *I can't. He knows I can't.* As romantic as that sounded, leaving would be impossible—the stuff of a story life, not a real life.

"Women aren't allowed on those ships," she said. She'd gathered this knowledge from the docks.

"Since when do we follow the rules? I'm in earnest."

The burn of a whispering tried to swell, but Maria stifled it, dusting it away like a cobweb. Leaving with Sam would mean abandoning everything and everyone she'd ever cared about before him, a price too great to bear.

"You know I can't. This is my home," she said firmly. "I'm sorry."

She felt his body exhale with disappointment.

"Then I'll be back in six months, ready to fulfill my promise," he said. "I'll bring back a ship full of gold and marry you. Properly. With a ring in the meetinghouse before Reverend Treat."

"A whole ship full of gold?" she taunted, then gripped him closer. His hips pressed against hers.

"Whatever it takes."

"You promise?" she chided, desire surging through her veins.

"Does the sun rise? Does the tide turn?"

Maria's eyes met his. "Give me something to remember you by," she said. "While I wait."

"Like what?" His breathing felt warm and fast against her exposed neck. Her skin burned despite the chill in the late August air.

The rule about women aboard ships wasn't the only thing she'd learned from the docks.

Maria leaned up to kiss him. He tasted of salt and the elusive hope of happiness. With a deep, assured inhale, she gently removed his coat, then guided his hand to her chest, cupping his fingers around the curve of her breast.

"You," she whispered. "All of you."

PART 2

FALL 1715

CHAPTER 16

Sam gazed from the listless salvage boat at the endless horizon of blue—blue upon blue upon blue. No other color existed anymore, and the sight left him nauseated. The sun blistered near the Tropic of Cancer. Autumn brought with it choppier waves and seasonal churns, the threat of winds from the east. He wiped his brow and re-tied his hair. Each dive left the texture feeling more like straw.

"Another waste of a day," spat John Julian, a thin, seventeen-year-old Miskito boy from Nicaragua who'd been more than eager to join Williams's expedition of thirty men weeks earlier. Julian had a head of thick hair and a scar running along his eyebrow. He'd worked his way on various merchant ships—getting by with proficient English, German, Spanish, and Creole, in addition to his native tongue—to join the fortune searches in Florida. Sam had never met a cleverer boy his age, nor one so opportunistic and skilled at navigation.

Paulsgrave Williams sat across from them. He waved a hand against the sweltering heat.

"Hey, Williams," Julian shouted.

"Mmm?"

"How much longer will we pretend there's a single peso left in this godforsaken patch of water?"

Williams cracked an eye open. "When the funds run out, which I suspect was last week."

"Meaning?" asked Julian.

"Most of us aboard have a debt to make up in addition to a fortune to find."

Sam frowned, glancing around at the crew. The pinched-face, desperate men looked none the better for wear. Day after wretched day they'd grappled the sites, scraped the sandbars with rope suspended between boats, and sent down divers, but no one in the party had found a single coin since they'd arrived.

Not one. Single. Peso.

Sam clenched his fists. He shared Julian's impatience. He didn't have time to sit here like a plump turkey ready for slaughter. He swore he'd return to Maria rich, not as a town laughingstock and indentured man—slumped over a plow, prey to the whims of Israel Cole and his investors. Sam had known the risks, they all had, when pledging bond service in exchange for an advance, one they'd pay back in full with interest from the profits. A gamble, yes, but it was a bet Sam was willing to risk. Now, he shuddered to imagine the back-breaking field labor, the kind he'd promised his father he wouldn't repeat, sweating away another decade of his life he couldn't call his own. Under such circumstances, Sam would never convince Mr. Brown to let him marry his daughter. Sam's chest ached at the memory of Maria, her sea-glass eyes, their conversations and afternoons swimming in that cold, empty bay.

The night on the dunes a month ago.

A ripple of pleasure washed over him. Sam had to make good on his promise, no matter what it took.

Three divers returned to the surface and heaved themselves back into the boat among the grappling hooks, long-handled rakes, and coils of line. The longboat wobbled in response. Pools of water gathered around their feet on the musky boards as they dried themselves.

"Well, look at that. It's your turn, Julian," Williams added with a wry smile. Only Williams among the crew had enough energy left for banter.

Julian sighed, then tore off his clothes before plunging stark naked into the ocean. The spray hit Sam's sunburned cheeks.

He moved beside Williams. Then, Sam picked up a waterskin and splashed the man he'd begun to call a friend.

"Thanks for that," Williams laughed, wiping his face on a tattered shirt and readjusting his wig. Most of Williams's extravagance from the Eastham days had gone, but his good nature and optimism remained. Sometimes, Sam swore he was enjoying this. But with a father who'd once served as Attorney General of Rhode Island, Paulsgrave never had as much at risk as the rest of them.

Sam leaned forward. "Would you wake up? Williams, the boy's right. What are we doing?"

"What we can," Williams shrugged. "What else would you have us do? I brought you here for your sailing skills, but also your smooth tongue and quick wit. Might you motivate the boys? Lead us better?"

"Toward what?" Sam said. "You said we were in this together, but we're too late. The waters are overrun with seafarers who had the same bright idea, but earlier. Spain takes the lion's share." Rumor had it Spanish nobles had hired local natives to do the risky diving for them: Two men had been crushed lifting heavy chests, a third met his death in the jaws of a shark.

Williams tapped a finger on his chin. "As it happens, I do have an idea. But I don't think you'll like it."

"Try me."

"You want us to *what*?"

"Are ye mad?"

"Fancy a dance at the end of Jack Ketch's rope, do ya?"

"Listen here, lads," Williams said, palms raised in a gesture of surrender now that they were back on land. "Hear us out first. Each of us wants to walk away from this expedition with some gold to our name. Each of us has put in the sweat worthy of a payout. No?"

A muffled grunt rang out from the camp. Palm fronds swayed in the welcomed breeze from the gulf as Williams shared the recent news about Henry Jennings, an English privateer out of Jamaica who—along with a crew of three hundred—had successfully stormed a Spanish fort serving as a storehouse in Barra de Ays.

"Moral of this story? They sailed off with sixty *thousand* pieces of eight. Imagine it!"

Sam had no problem imagining it, going one step beyond: trying to picture Jennings's smug face and loaded ship.

Where Jennings and his shiny loot might have gone next.

Sam scanned the faces of the crew along the beach, then moved to the front. "There's treasure aplenty here," Sam said. "We know that, have *seen* that—fine sloops casting ripples at us in their wake, Spanish ships reclaiming the losses for their own government." He huffed. "But when has any bloody *government* treated you fairly? Is it not the government's failure to provide a means of an adequate living that sent us here to begin with?"

Sam spotted Isaiah Abell, a mop of blond hair and sun-scabbed lips. "Abell, where was the government when your farm's soil turned to sand, thanks to the sand plague caused by your neighbors?"

This was met with a nod.

His eyes fell on young Timothy Webb's vacant stare, then gentle Caleb Dixon's sunken cheeks and deep wrinkles—easily the oldest person there. "And, Webb, when your leg got mangled on the whale boat, who covered the costs?" He paused. "And who could forget our Dixon, here. You'll tell me that after decades of serving the crown in the navy, our good man still can't afford passage home to see his growing children? His dying mother?"

The listeners exchanged mutters and glances, but Sam could tell he had their ear. Williams gave him an encouraging wink.

"We're proposing a short-term solution, a way to get back the gold we worked for, from those who need it least."

"Precisely," Williams broke in. "If we sell the salvage ship for two pirogues—"

"*Periaguas*," Julian corrected.

"Yes, same thing," said Williams. "Smaller rowboats, flat-bottomed and slick as fins in the water. With two, we could strategize—take a few modest prizes by flanking them on each side when the winds die. Let them hand over what they've got. This is small-scale risk, enough to put us back on the map and get us home with a little coin to spare. Enough to pay back our pledge and avoid indentured servitude of any form."

"Piracy," Julian interrupted again, his brown arms folded across his chest. "Call it what it is. Even if the proposed vessels can barely handle the sea."

All focus locked on Julian. Sam's stomach lurched.

"You heard me," Julian said.

"Calm down, boy. No one's forcing you to go on the account," Williams said, stepping up beside Sam and placing a hand on his shoulder. "Anyone is free to leave. But at the same time, no one's proposing any serious theft . . . if it can be considered theft at all. Just enough to be on our way."

Those words might have been true for the others, but not for Sam.

Sam's and Julian's eyes met. Julian raised an arched brow, as if detecting Sam's personal plan and motive. Julian's strong cheekbones appeared sharper in the fading light. He knew Sam had designs to get rich. But didn't they all? Under what means, and to what end? The gaze unnerved him, but Sam's plan to hunt down Jennings's loot wouldn't impact anyone else but himself, he reasoned. Not if he could help it. His father might not have approved of treasure stealing, true, but Sam had also vowed to the dead man to forge a better life for himself and the family name. Change *must* be possible. He steadied himself and continued.

"If any man here pities King Charles of Spain over a fistful of coin he'd scarcely notice, I wouldn't begrudge the man," Sam said, his voice growing louder. "But I'll not go home with my tail between my legs like a cowardly whelp, giddy for bond servitude, to protect the honor of tyrants. Not while sloops, galleys, and even rowboats sail by, laden with riches they aren't any more worthy of carrying." He paused, the vein in his neck pulsing. "Who's with us?"

Almost all the men stepped forward, showing more energy than they'd exhibited in months. They shook hands with Williams and then, to Sam's surprise, with him. It wasn't so long ago that he was a cabin boy, and even more recently that he was an unruly sea hand—lowly and disposable. Sam tilted his tricorn against the sun's glare as he struggled to take it all in. What did this make him now?

After a long moment, Julian exhaled and put out his hand, cursing in languages no one else could understand. "To head south, you'll need me as a guide. I'll be your pilot."

CHAPTER 17

Maria finished setting the four-post loom, the white strings of the warp stretched in long, tight lines before her.

Linear. Orderly. Strong. So her thoughts should be, Maria reasoned: focused on a sure, if unseen, future outcome.

She gathered a basket of freshly dyed wool with a strong scent of leaves, then stooped to pick up the carding tools before taking a stool beside the spinning wheel. She no longer felt the ache of the lashes left by the hickory rod weeks ago, the bruises turning from purple to green, pale yellow to invisible.

This red will make a nice accent color in the weft, she thought, keeping her mind stubbornly centered on the immediate task, and *only* the immediate task, at hand. To do otherwise, to let her active imagination wander, ripped open a terrible hollowness almost unbearable since Sam's departure and the abrupt end to their conversations, an emptiness and longing that gripped her most in the dead of night, shaking her awake in cold sweats. Elizabeth ignored her, no matter how much Maria tossed and turned. During the day, whenever Maria tried to explain herself, Elizabeth held up a hand or left the room. The compounded loss of her sister's confidences knocked the breath right out of her.

She took a small batch of wool and began carding when she heard a knock.

"What now, Mercy?" Maria said without looking up. Little Mercy, the only person in the family on speaking terms with Maria—with no real understanding of the fuss—had approached the weaving room every few hours with all kinds of pranks or creative excuses to distract Maria from her isolating work. Sometimes, she left a plate when Maria declined invitations to supper.

When Maria got invitations to supper.

No matter. Maria had little appetite. At first, Maria wondered when her family would demand help with the other chores—especially from Elizabeth. But so far, this silent battle line seemed to suit everyone. They could profit from her weaving while not having to endure the sight of her, and Maria could work, wander, and even swim without anyone reprimanding her.

The hinge creaked, and Maria blanched.

"Mama," she said. Her fingers froze midmotion.

"Mm-hmm," Mama said, her jaw firm as she scanned the room. She had dark circles under her moss-green eyes and strands of graying hair poking out from the bottom of her bonnet. She looked tired. Older, as if overnight, and the sight gave Maria an unexpected surge of tenderness, a feeling she hurried to swallow.

Speechless, Maria forced her hands to continue the rhythmic motion of combing out the fibers.

"Another coverlet?" Mama asked.

"Yes." They sold well at the docks, as Mama well knew, being the one who encouraged this one, useful talent Maria seemed to possess. It was the only thing the town knew her for other than her unseemly behavior.

But did Mama do more than approve? Did she admire—or even notice—the design, the subtle elements Maria added to make each piece unique? To Maria's continued surprise, Mama pulled up a second stool beside Maria and dug out a wad of wool.

"You spin, I'll card."

A pit lodged in Maria's stomach. She didn't know what to make of this intrusion. Her mother hadn't helped her with the weaving since teaching her and Elizabeth when they were girls. She handed her mother the brushes and turned to prep the bobbin.

"You're too old for beatings, darling," Mama said. "You're a woman now."

Maria bit her lip. "Then why don't you and Papa treat me like one?"

Mama ignored her brash reply and handed Maria a batt, a fluff of cloud. "There is so much you don't understand."

The two worked side by side. Maria pumped the foot pedal and watched the wooden wheel spin. *Focus on the spokes*, Maria said when she felt her eyes burn. *Count them. Watch how they blur together.* She was determined not to cry. Why did she always have to cry? She wanted to suppress all outspoken impulses until her mother apologized.

The problem: Maria had never known her mother to apologize.

"I never told you everything. About the accident."

"I already know. Everyone knows." The birth that went wrong. The horrible, fatal defect that reflected poorly on both the baby's mother and the midwife, Mama.

A sign of the Devil.

Her mother laughed, an echo of the rich music of that laugh from many years earlier. "I'm sure you think you do. You seem to know everything these days, more than the Almighty."

"Not everything. But I do know some things," Maria said as she pinched, pulled, and twisted the yarn, the wheel circling. "More than you give me credit for."

"That might be, but there are some lessons I would prefer you never learn for yourself."

Mama handed over a fresh batt of wool, and Maria paused the wheel, taking it from her.

"When I was growing up, I wanted more for myself," Mama said. "To become a doctor," she smiled. "But ambition, as you know, does not flatter a young woman. And unlike you, I didn't have a prosperous father. I am lucky to have met your Papa when

I did. It was a suitable match, both our families agreed. We had complementary strengths—my practical mind, his generous character, our shared work ethic. We've built a life together of quiet companionship, one that allows me satisfaction as a wife, mother, and midwife. Without the support of family, of community and God, I'm not sure what would have become of me after . . . well. That birth."

Maria worked the pedal.

"Love wears many different faces, Goody. And not all speak the truth."

What did her mother possibly know of love? A duty-bound love. A small love. Maria didn't care how haughty it sounded. What her parents had was nothing like what she and Sam shared.

Right?

Maria stopped, tears forming despite the shame her mother might feel and express at the sight of them. She finally met her gaze.

"Oh, the truth then, is it? Here's truth for you, Mama: I love Samuel Bellamy. I know he loves me. And I know you and Papa stalled the match because . . . you're afraid. Maybe your good intentions blind you. Maybe you can't imagine a different life than the one you've lived and don't believe in change. Or maybe you're angry—punishing me for not being the daughter you want me to be."

Mama put the carding brushes down and took Maria's hands. The rare gesture caused Maria's lips to tremble.

"Life is not kind to women who are different, Maria. The townspeople took me to the square, after the birth—me and the mother. They rent our dresses and exposed our backs to a whip for anyone with eyes to see. They thought me a witch and threatened to cast me out of town. They still watch me with a thin veil of suspicion, no matter how many healthy children I deliver into the world. Some make an effort to read the Bible in my presence, knowing witches recoil from the goodness in that book. Now, I must act twice as carefully. That is my burden, the cost of whatever sin I committed."

Her eyes showed no embellishment. Mama never embellished. "You did nothing wrong."

"What if I did? Only God knows, punishing how He sees fit. My election is not made certain."

"But you're not a witch."

"It doesn't matter what someone really is when others think them to be another," she said, smoothing a thumb over Maria's knuckles. "And you, daughter, already have a reputation to mind. A headstrong disposition. A dangerous tongue to fight. Despite it all—count your blessings—Mr. Hallett is still willing to marry and reform you. He praises your well-regarded beauty and is not a man used to 'no.'"

Maria yanked away and scrubbed a rogue tear with her sleeve. The things that so displeased her mother were the very traits Sam believed to be her strengths.

"Eastham is not Salem, I'll give you that," Mama continued. "But your soul is in peril. Your feelings deceive you, distract you from eternal matters. A woman without connections and a support system is the most vulnerable creature in the world. And you, Maria, are vulnerable."

Vulnerability? Was that really *the worst* thing imaginable? Risk, courage, and vulnerability had led her to Sam. A fire burned in her at the memories: the sun's reflection on the tidal pools, the way he cocked his head of black hair when he listened to her, the thrill of swimming half-naked in the bay as if no one else existed. Despite everything she'd been taught, every rule she knew she'd broken along the way, she regretted nothing. Sorrow for her deceit and the family rift, yes, but what other option did she have? They'd never have approved. They would have forbidden them from courting. Maria would do it all again if given the opportunity. "Ye shall know them by their fruits," the Bible reads. "A good tree cannot bring forth evil fruit, neither can a corrupt tree bring forth good fruit." She'd never felt so alive, so herself, and drunk on the thrill of it. She couldn't possibly explain. And as for her soul?

I'll take my chances.

"I will marry Samuel, Mama," Maria said, recovering herself. "I'm sorry for the hurts you've suffered, I am. But they are not mine. When he returns, I hope you and Papa will open your hearts, regardless of his circumstances."

Mama sighed. Maria thought she might say something else, and hoped she would. Strained as their relationship tended to be, she longed for her mother's company, her full attention, if not her affection. Even if they disagreed. She wanted to lean into her chest and sob without fear of her own enormous feelings, to be seen, to sense the tight embrace of arms around her with unrestrained acceptance. If Mama couldn't apologize and never would, might she offer that much?

And couldn't Maria do anything to meet her halfway?

But instead, Mama shook her head. "Then, my child—my dear, grown child—I'm afraid you're on your own." She stood, picking away the stray fibers stuck to her skirts. "The first and greatest commandment tells us to honor God above all, even other loves." Her eyes became glassy, and she blinked back the emotion.

"Mama?"

"I can't protect you anymore, Goody. The Lord alone grants salvation or damnation, and I will not jeopardize my own precarious standing before Him." Her mother kissed her on the top of the head, lingering there for a moment before leaving. "May you repent and God show you mercy so long as you live under my roof."

CHAPTER 18

I'm not a pirate, Sam told himself as the periaguas sliced through the opal waters of the Yucatán Channel. Their rowboats were being towed by a sloop commanded by a blithering Captain Young. The surrendered captain had no choice but to haul them, when asked, to a place west of Cuba with heavier traffic and more opportunities to plunder.

And more news, Sam hoped.

"Did you see his face?" Julian mocked, pinching his expression to imitate the sour Captain Young after boarding their ship earlier. The crew laughed heartily in response, but not Sam—even if Young did remind him of far too many sniveling officers in the Royal Navy. These wins were minor victories while Sam pursued his secret hope of finding Jennings. They passed around a bottle of brandy snatched from the captain's quarters. Waves sloshed against the balsa wood periaguas.

"No, like this," shouted Paulsgrave Williams from the other rowboat as he mimicked the stern scowl of a preacher waggling his finger.

It had been Julian's idea to attack in the buff. To look like madmen wielding nothing but a few cutlasses and five pistols. The tactic worked. Intimidation over violence. So far, thankfully, they hadn't needed to resort to serious violence. They'd slipped back into their clothes and continued on as before, overly boisterous as if to mask the surprise and unease of getting away with another raid.

Sam was certainly not a pirate. And yet, the evidence mounted.

Charge number one: Sam had led them there, his heart hammering in the thick of the fight before Young's near-immediate surrender. He could still taste the sulfuric gunpowder.

Charge number two: Thanks to Julian's expert knowledge as a pilot, their novice fleet had managed to overcome a handful of small boats in the shallows of Honduras and succeeded in another raid off Portobelo, Panama, leaving the crew with a handful of provisions, some initial weapons, and a whetted appetite.

Charge number three: Peter Cornelius Hoof—a Swede who'd joined them in Belize, a man with seventeen blessed years of navigational experience in the Spanish Main—had talked about sewing a makeshift Jolly Roger to raise. A black one, of course—to signal mercy to those who give up their goods and ships. Not red, which would threaten a fight to the death.

But still. A Jolly Roger.

Despite it all, Sam still hadn't heard of Henry Jennings or the whereabouts of his stolen stash. In his dreams, he heard the clink of pieces of eight and held the chill of them in his palms. But in the mornings when the sun cracked over the blood-orange horizon, he felt no closer to his goal than when the crew agreed to go on the account in Florida.

If he wasn't a pirate, he certainly looked like a pirate. Acted like a pirate.

Well, I'm not a real *one*, he reasoned, imagining what his father would think. What Maria would think.

I'll be back soon. With a ship full of silver, if not gold.

Growing up near the bustling docks of Plymouth, England, Sam had heard plenty of tales about pirates. Homegrown sea dogs, most of them disturbing. John Hawkins made his career by selling hundreds of slaves to Hispaniola, all backed by Queen Elizabeth.

Francis Drake soon followed with his own despicable career in slave tradng and a personal vendetta against Spain, which somehow granted him a title of "Sir" and "gentleman" privateer. Even more recently, not twenty years ago, was that local Plymouth man, Henry Avery, who preyed on spice merchants—the one known for spending three days raping and torturing a Mogul's daughter and her attendants.

The thought made Sam shiver with disgust.

In all likelihood, Sam probably met dozens of lesser-known pirates as he crept along the docks, the place where he searched for bread scraps or bits of salted fish to fill his growling stomach as a lad. Those damned sumptuary laws in England prevented lowly folk like him from dressing higher than their station. The young, barefooted Sam—garbed in shabby linen—knew it well. Yet, Sam had a sharp memory of a foggy afternoon at the pier, of a sailor wearing an embroidered vest stiff with pearl buttons, a red sash around his waist, a man who seemed to strut down the wharf. He wore a cocked hat with a feather and held his head high, as if begging the world to look, to dare question his authority. He appeared nothing like the skinny, weathered mariners of the day, though his eye had the same hunger for sea and a glint of something more.

Freedom.

Sam caught his gaze for a few moments before the dapper man laughed, then swaggered onward, with Sam's stare not leaving him until he disappeared from view.

One of the men showed off a minor foot wound to Julian, and Peter Hoof flexed his pale Swedish arm for two others while recounting an alleged pummeling during a raid. The courage and almost boyish excitement among the motley group both warmed and troubled Sam. They had twice the heart of men like Captain Young. He'd meant every word of his earlier speeches: Tyrant kings, queens, nobles, and landlords governed their lives from unreachable heights. Perhaps radical actions were the only way to create radical change. Still, outright piracy gave Sam pause if it resembled the actions of the famed names of history. He couldn't wait until his crew had enough to sail back to safety, to pay off the debt to Cole and his cronies at the Great Island Tavern.

Back, that is, before the crew forgot their plan and got swept up in a buccaneer's life. Even if Sam had his own plans to get what he wanted, faster.

"What's that?" Julian said, shielding his eyes at a ship surrounded by three others off a white shore in the distance.

Sam stood and squinted. The periagua wobbled, and his pulse galloped at the sight.

A sloop with a single mast raked backward like a swordfish— Bermuda-made, no doubt. Eight guns. Maybe forty tons. Flying the British colors, exactly as described.

The *Bersheba*.

"Henry Jennings's flotilla," Sam breathed, taking in the group of ships. He groped under the seat for a pistol and aimed it to the sky. A crack rang out.

"Captain Young!" he yelled. "Make ready to tack."

But it appeared Captain Young had the same idea, for opposite reasons. Clearly hoping to be saved from Sam's crew, Young veered right, making all due haste toward the beaches of Cuba. The spray hit the men without warning, and they lunged for their paddles.

"Bellamy?" Williams said, rowing at his right. "You know what you're doing?"

"We'll make friends with Jennings," Sam said, turning to face the now-quiet crew in both periaguas. "Give him Young's ship and trade whatever we can spare. Lend him a hand, split the booty." He grabbed the half-empty bottle of brandy and stoppered it. "Let him teach us what he knows."

All he knows.

Sam pressed his lips into a tight line before adding: "And not a word about the silver taken from the fort."

* * *

"I don't *care* what I said before," the red-faced Henry Jennings screeched at his quartermaster. "Bring me another flask. And do something about the captured sloop."

"Commodore, what would you—"

"You figure it out!" He stamped his boot into the sand with such force that his enormous black hat threatened to topple off his wig. "I will not be pestered with the problems of rogues."

Sam, the likely "rogue" in question, did his best not to stare at the piece of meat stuck between Jennings's teeth. The quivering quartermaster clutched his side, as if suffering from digestive cramps. His leader didn't notice, or preferred not to.

Williams kept clearing his throat and elbowing Sam in the ribs. Their crew of thirty stood behind them. Sam didn't dare look at his friend, fearing he'd lose all composure in the presence of this man-child.

Aristocrats. They reek from a mile away. What would a man like this be doing out here? Fortunately, Sam knew his way around their brittle egos.

"Sir," Sam began. "We've heard of your skills on the high sea. We've come to offer you our services, for a time."

Jennings recovered himself and strode forward, his beaked nose inches away from Sam's face. His red coat jingled with decoration. His breath smelled of rot. Jennings looked at Sam, then at Williams.

"I already command a fleet of four vessels. So who are you?"

"Paulsgrave Williams. Delighted to make your acquaintance," Williams said with exaggerated politeness.

"Samuel Bellamy, sir, at your service." He offered up the half-full bottle of brandy. "Fought for the king's cause during the Spanish Succession, same as you."

A spark lit in Jennings's beady eyes and he relaxed his stance, taking the bottle.

"You captured that sloop out there? With nothing but what I see before me?" Jennings's lip twisted with revulsion as he studied their shabby garments.

"Yes, sir," Sam said, ignoring the condescension. "We're a small but strong crew."

"Pirates?" Jennings asked, examining the brandy.

Sam and Williams exchanged a look. Were they? Was there a *correct* answer to further their present cause? Sam could make out a few mumbles in the crew behind them.

"Whatever you need," Williams offered, his voice smooth as honey. "But we're not typical rogues, as you put it."

Spoken like the son of a politician, Sam thought.

Jennings pulled a piece of well-worn paper from his coat and unfurled the yellowing document. He held it up for all to see. "This here is a commission from Governor Hamilton of Jamaica, declaring me an official privateer of these seas." He puffed out his chest. "Plundering in service of the king. Taking back what is owed. I'm a gentleman of honor."

Something about this speech felt rehearsed.

"We share your . . . passion," Williams said, one brow raised at Bellamy—a look that said: *What the hell are we doing?*

At that moment, the quartermaster returned, sprinting toward them. Sweat poured down his forehead and he clutched his stomach, then doubled over. "Commodore!"

"Not again. I told you—"

"Sir, a ship! French. A merchant vessel anchored up the bend at Bahia Honda."

"Did they spot us?"

"I think not, Commodore."

Jennings paused, and something like a smile crept up his unshaven cheeks. "Lads, you've come just in time." He surveyed them again, then grunted at their threadbare attire. "Show these men the stash of pilfered clothes," he told the quartermaster. "They'll need weapons."

"And our share?" Sam asked.

"Prove yourself first, then we'll talk." He waved them away. "But we take no English ships, mind you."

* * *

As Jennings gave his flotilla instructions to dispatch a canoe to investigate—all while ignoring Captain Young, beached until anyone had time to deal with him—the unwell quartermaster led Sam's crew to the hold below deck. The dim air smelled strongly of rot and damp cedar. Sam scanned for any sign of the Spanish plunder in the lantern light.

"We'll launch an attack in the morning," the quartermaster said, hand pressed against a pain in his belly while Sam's men rummaged through the stores. "*If* we raid. That ship's got a lot of firepower. The commodore is . . . how to say it? Protective of the *Bersheba.*"

"Look at this," shipmate Abell said, holding up a wrinkled white shirt with brass buttons from an opened barrel. Webb limped over to have a look. Dixon inspected a coat and a new pair of breeches, while Hoof pulled at some faded boots buried under a pile of raiding pikes.

"Where did all this come from, if you don't mind my asking?" Williams asked, turning over a rapier with a rusty knuckle guard. He stepped a few feet away to test out the long, narrow blade, flicking it with deadly precision. Sam gaped with awe. He shouldn't have been surprised: Someone like Williams, of the upper classes, would have been trained for years to wield such a sword. Types like Sam were groomed for weapons requiring little more than strength, expendable men on the frontlines armed with knives and cutlasses.

Thank the Lord that Williams was nothing like Jennings.

"The commodore likes taking the victims' clothes when he plunders. It's a whim of his."

"A whim?" Sam balked, considering an old, sawed-off musket. Though out of order, a gun like this could blast like a shotgun at close range. Maybe Jennings kept an armorer in his company to make it serviceable.

"Common enough for plunderers in need, but Jennings suffers

for nothing," the quartermaster said, going on to describe, at great length, Jennings's sprawling plantation estates on both Bermuda and Jamaica.

As the crew rooted through the stash and half listened to the conversation, they wore expressions ranging from glee to terror to irritation. Webb grinned like a blunderbuss under a wide-brimmed hat as the younger and more agile Abell swiped to take it for himself.

"Not a large hold area," Sam commented with as much neutrality as he could summon while examining the musket's stock. "What does your commodore do with the other loot?"

"Oh, he takes it safely back to Port Royal or Nassau when he can. We plundered a Spanish fort a while back, enough to know we had to shed it quickly. Now the Commodore has sights on . . ."

But whatever else the quartermaster had to say, Sam didn't hear it. He clamped his jaw together so fast he bit his tongue.

Of course Jennings would have disposed of the risk. How could I have been so naïve?

Julian fixed his attention on Sam, black eyes watchful as a cat's.

He knew, Sam figured. He'd always known Sam had sights on finding Jennings and stealing the silver, even if most of the crew seemed content with chasing small prizes. They could go on with Williams, pursuing their tiny wins to cover the basic debt or to try their luck as privateers. But Sam's path required a swift windfall, even if it meant acting alone.

So what if Julian did know the truth of his full ambition? What would they do now? Joining Jennings had never been part of anyone's half-formed plans. They'd all need a way out of here soon.

It couldn't be soon enough.

CHAPTER 19

"I thought I might find you here."

Maria, who'd been wringing the water from her hair after a brisk swim, whirled to see Elizabeth standing behind her on the beach. Maria couldn't breathe. These were the first words Elizabeth had initiated since the night Sam proposed over a month ago.

"You've improved a lot. I watched you for a while."

"You're speaking to me!"

"We can't go on with this silence forever."

A knot formed in Maria's throat. Before she could stop herself, she threw her arms around her sister—wet shift and all.

"Careful," Elizabeth said, pushing her back and examining the imprint left on her apron. "I didn't say you're forgiven yet."

"You didn't have to," Maria said, smiling for the first time in weeks. "I missed you." Both her *and* Sam. Swimming kept Maria tethered to those exhilarating summer months and anchored to that still-alive dream of fending for herself in the water. She'd grown stronger, more confident in her strokes, more sure of herself. Still, Maria loathed the crush of loneliness, the feeling of being left behind like a crab husk, tangled in seaweed at low tide.

"Come on," Elizabeth said, presenting a basket. "Get dressed and let's buy some oysters. I brought some of your weaving to sell."

Maria stumbled to get back into her petticoat and stays. As she bent, the whale bone support dug into her ribs. She balanced on one leg to slip on her shoes and stockings while scraping away the sand.

"I'll summarize all the ways you've done wrong as we walk," Elizabeth said. "But I'll try to keep it brief."

"I'm sure you will." Despite the threat, Maria heard relief tinged with joy in Elizabeth's tone.

At least now I'll have my sister again.

They took the long route to the docks, ambling along the marshy shoreline. Maria's nostrils flared at a whiff of whale blubber over try-pot fires in the distance.

"I'm sorry for ignoring you," Elizabeth said. "I was angry, and I didn't want to get crossways with Mama and Papa. I knew you wanted those swimming lessons, but how could you let it go so far?"

Maria exhaled and did her best to explain all that had happened without revealing the most scandalizing details. To Elizabeth's credit, she didn't interrupt. Ever since Elizabeth returned from Chatham, Maria had exercised caution when it came to discussing Sam—for Elizabeth's sake, or so she believed. Though she'd never lied outright to Elizabeth about where she was going on days she managed to slip away, she also hadn't been forthright, knowing her actions had crossed a line. The guilt festered. Elizabeth, in turn, never pressed her for particulars. On purpose, Maria suspected. Why else would Elizabeth not bring up the subject of swimming lessons when it had been such a risk before Elizabeth went to Chatham?

"I'm sorry, too. When you didn't ask, I assumed you didn't want to know," Maria said. "Besides, I didn't want to keep endangering you. The less you knew, the safer you'd be."

And the safer I'd *be*, Maria thought. The impression pierced her heart like a hook she longed to yank clean out. She wasn't used to hiding anything from Elizabeth. But how could her sister possibly understand? How could anyone at home understand? Maria struggled to articulate the magnitude of her inner shift, even to herself. A part of it felt private, too personal, even sacred—as blasphemous as that sounded.

"Since when is 'safe' your strategy?" Elizabeth teased Maria, knocking into her with the basket. "I'm not sure which was worse: not hearing the story from you until now, or knowing you didn't want to tell me."

"I did want to," Maria said, "but I worried you'd try to stop me. I apologize for keeping something this big from you." She swallowed. Could she tell Elizabeth *everything*, even the starlit night on the dunes? Should she?

"Sorry" was not the same as regret. The sisters halted and looked at each other, assessing the length of shadows in the remaining silences cast between them. Maria suspected Elizabeth had her own secrets. Could they put it all behind them? Trust each other enough?

"Why talk to me now?" Maria asked. "What changed?"

Elizabeth's freckled cheeks glowed redder than the tresses under her bonnet. "When Mama had the bright idea of foisting *me* onto Mr. Hallett."

"She didn't!" Maria said, gripping her sister by the shoulders. "What happened?"

Elizabeth waved her away. "It was never a serious consideration, merely an idea Mama brought up during soap making. Lydia was there and . . . Oh, Maria, it was awful. I don't think I fully appreciated your situation until facing it myself. Even the thought of it felt like staring into the barrel of a rifle." She shuddered. "I told her no, outright, that it wouldn't be appropriate. I'm too young, and Mr. Hallett made an offer to *you*. Mama didn't press the issue."

They resumed walking. Maria pursed her lips. Sam couldn't be back soon enough.

The noise of the dock neared, and Maria sensed Elizabeth tense.

"What is it?" Maria asked.

"It's just . . . never mind."

"Please?"

"Forgive me. I think a part of me wanted you to ruin yourself, and both of our chances of marriage." Elizabeth stared hard at the ground. "I didn't fully realize it before, but the thought of marrying Mr. Hallett, the *reality* of marrying any man." Her flush deepened, and she shook her head. "You and I might not be so different after all."

"Elizabeth—"

But her sister had no more she was willing to say. Elizabeth thrust the basket at Maria and stepped aboard the pier with hands on her hips, eyes fixed on the oyster stands.

"The Brown girls!"

"Mr. Abbott, what a delight," Elizabeth said, her pitch a few notes higher than before. "Who's got the best catch today?"

As Elizabeth chatted with the fisherman, Maria replayed her words. Her stalwart sister *wanted* ruin? She wasn't "so different" from the very person Elizabeth censored most? Maria stepped back and caught her breath amid the clamor and excitement of the docks. She had no taste for gossip or news today, and no interest in questions from anyone who may have heard about Sam's proposal. She pressed a hand to her temple.

"Is that for sale?" came a voice from behind.

Maria opened her eyes with a start, then jerked around to see a Wampanoag woman wearing a gray dress with her hair pinned atop her head according to the latest style. Though Maria had seen Wampanoag people at the docks and with Reverend Treat at church, she'd never been addressed directly before.

"This?" Maria asked, pulling the cloth from the basket. "Yes. Homespun linen."

The woman set down her bundle of herbs and gestured to pick up the fabric. Maria handed it over with a tremor of curiosity. The woman held up the cloth, unfurling the sheet in the breeze and scrutinizing every stitch. She looked almost displeased. "How much?" the woman asked, rubbing the fibers between her fingers and gauging the thickness against the bright sunlight.

Maria told her.

"You aren't charging enough," the woman said flatly, considering Maria.

Maria blinked. It was the same price she'd always asked for her work.

"Your people call you a master weaver behind your back. Yes, I've heard of you, even if you've never heard of me." Her eyes narrowed. "They take advantage of your youth. But it pulls down the prices for all fine weaving—including supplies made by my people. Learn to negotiate, and charge more."

But before Maria could ask more questions, the woman was already shouldering her bundle and moving on.

"Who was that?" Elizabeth asked Mr. Abbott.

"Ah, that'll be Abiah Sampson," the fisherman said, shaking his head with disapproval. "A savvy woman, that one. Fancies herself a trader and behaves like a man doing business." At this, Mr. Abbott spat. "Something ought to be done. Making the Indians dress and talk like Christians doesn't *make* them us. She's got no right to speak to me, or to upstanding girls such as you two."

Elizabeth squeezed Maria's hand to silence her. But before Maria could retort, another fisherman—busy mending his nets— interjected. "I don't know, Abbott. I've heard she's a great healer," he said with admiration. "Some say she used a poultice to save an Eastham woman suffering from tumors. I heard it straight from the survivor's daughter."

Mr. Abbott reddened. "She's a political meddler and . . . well, other names I shouldn't like to repeat in the presence of ladies."

Maria watched as Abiah moved from sight, the hem of her skirt fluttering in the salty breeze.

Maria, you'd love the color of the sea here, Sam thought as Commodore Jennings's captains squabbled over the ransack strategy of the French ship.

"Our scouts discovered they're selling to the Spanish locals," someone said.

"*Illegal* goods. Smugglers."

"Fair game!"

It's pale green in the shallows, then the most luminous turquoise you could imagine—darker in spots with patches of coral reefs. Sand fine and white like sugar. Fish the color of ripe fruit.

"But they've got *sixteen* cannons!" Henry Jennings countered, face twitchy in the blinding light. He kept a hand on his pistol.

"Plus a crew of forty-five," one quartermaster added. "This is madness. If we lose, they'll hand us over to the Spanish."

Maybe we could come back, together. Under different circumstances. After we see Boston, then London. Imagine an ocean warmer than a bath and clear as a mountain spring. We could swim until our muscles dissolved. Reminisce about the time I fought under the command of a despicable human for a bit of gold.

"Where's your courage, Commodore?" another quartermaster shot back.

"Yeah, what've you come out for, if not for this? To look and then retreat with your fingers in your mouth?"

Jennings glowered.

We could laugh away the details. Exaggerate or minimize as needed. Because we'd know how the story ended—happily, the two of us together, with no harm or injury or permanent loss to me or anyone I came to care about, the men who trusted me.

"Riches for all," a single voice yelled.

"Aye, riches for all!" came another, until it became a chant of solidarity.

Jennings flushed with silent rage under his broad hat. Sam saw that the commodore had no choice but to wage a siege. Sam's shoulder muscles tightened. He felt torn between fear and relief— trepidation for the fight, but eager to be one step closer to a quiet, comfortable life with Maria, with this all behind him.

"Fine," Jennings said. "We'll trail them out of port. Get them within cannon range under the cover of nightfall." Then his beady eyes fell on Sam.

"Bellamy, Williams," Jennings barked. "You'll take the lead."

As soon as the French ship pulled out of Bahia Honda, Jennings's flotilla followed. For good measure, they'd added the defeated Captain Young's sloop to the mix, sailed reluctantly by Young himself. Sam and Williams, as instructed, paddled ahead in the periaguas—the quickest vessels in the fleet, but also the most vulnerable.

"How long do we have to wait for the signal?" Julian asked, chin resting on his fists as he stared at the French sails bathed in the light of a full moon. Stars glinted like a knife on the water.

"Until our flotilla gets within cannon range," Williams said, ruffling Julian's dark hair—an action met with marked annoyance. "Not to worry. We'll have the element of surprise."

"And the protection of night," Hoof added.

"Bellamy, you're awfully quiet today," Williams said.

"Staying focused," Sam said. Not many of the men had seen actual battle before. As he rowed, he craned his neck to watch Jennings's men behind them, the *Bersheba* safe in the back of the line.

Cowardly bastard.

Maybe a few raids with Jennings would be enough.

Maybe this trip alone would send them all home with heavy pockets, if Jennings was feeling generous.

"Will we attack in our skins again?" someone asked.

A few hooted, and others groaned. Sam glanced around. Abell wore his new shirt with brass buttons. Dixon sported a coat a few sizes too big for his hunched, aging frame. Hoof ended up with the coveted hat—a fact that the Swede had no problem reminding everyone about. These were not soldiers, but they were brave men.

Why were they all looking to him, Williams included? When had Sam become their leader?

"Whatever you boys want," Sam said.

Julian stood up and ripped off his shirt. "This is the uniform of the undefeated!"

A few others cheered, yanking off their garb and pounding their chests. The crew had spoken. But Sam noticed how they clung to their boarding pikes. The tapping of fingers after inspecting their weapons for a fourth and fifth time. Webb drummed his bad leg. For a while, Hoof and Julian rattled on about the constellations, debating the names, shapes, and legends across half-a-dozen languages. The great lion seemed the only one they could agree upon across Swedish (Lejon), Spanish (León), and English (Leo).

"I'm cold. Whose idea was it to get naked?" Julian said.

"Yours," Williams grunted.

"Look there," someone whispered. A man aboard the nearest sloop waved a flag.

Jennings's flotilla was in position. Sam took a deep breath.

"Let's move," he said, and everyone gripped an oar. "When we hear the others cheer, we'll row like the devil. Understood?"

The silhouetted figures in both periaguas nodded.

"Let no one forget—whatever we find on that ship, they came by it illegally," Sam said. "If we fight with half the heart we've shown these past few months, they'll surrender within minutes." Just like all the other times.

Not like Jennings, who robbed for pleasure. But like men who needed the money.

"Take control before either side has a chance to fire a cannon. Intimidation is enough—no one needs to die tonight."

The sentence lodged in Sam's throat as a cheer rang out from Jennings's fleet. His pulse quickened.

"Now!" Sam bellowed as the rallying call crescendoed into a roar.

The periaguas cut through the water swifter than a falcon after prey. Ocean spray slashed like needling blades against Sam's face. The air tingled with raw determination. In a frenzy, they closed the distance. Sam saw a French lookout, who gaped down at the commotion below.

The lookout leaned over and shouted, in clipped English, "Where do you go?"

"Aboard, where do you think?" quipped Williams as the first periagua met the ship. Williams pulled out his rapier and led the first rowboat with pikes and axes as they scaled the ropes and ladders, hollering and brandishing their weapons to announce their intentions. Sam and his men in the second periagua were about to climb after them when he heard Williams call out from above.

"Bellamy, to your left!"

Sam whirled to spy a French runaway clambering down the other side of the vessel to escape. The man, hiding a parcel under his arm, was hastily sawing at a canoe hitched to the ship.

It didn't look like any old parcel either.

"After him," Sam said, and the crew on the second periagua picked up their oars again. They paddled with fury to intercept the runaway.

That's when a cannon fired overhead, loud enough to make Sam's ears ring. The haze blanketed the stars.

"Who fired?" Hoof yelled, though the smoke gave the culprit away.

"It was an accident!" bellowed one of Jennings's shipmates from the nearest sloop.

Sam gritted his teeth and cursed. *Great strategy, Jennings.* He risked a glance up at where he'd seen Williams and the rest of his crew disappear. He'd hoped they could get through this ordeal without spilling blood. Needless blood—if the concept had ever occurred to Jennings. Experience had taught Sam that captains were more likely to immediately raise a white flag if they weren't spurred to kick back. Demoralized, underpaid crews didn't value cargo over their own lives. The last thing they needed was for the French ship to let loose its fire power in defense. Most sailors in the Spanish Main knew they could expect fairer treatment during a siege by not making a scene. But spur them to self-preservation?

Chaos.

The deserter hacked the last lines tethering the French canoe. It fell into the sea with a splash, and the man dived after it, clambering inside with his parcel, then lunged for the paddles.

"Stop!" Sam cried. His periagua blocked the canoe from moving. Sam reached out to grasp the shaking man by the front of his wet shirt. He refused to let go of the leather-wrapped package.

"Cease fire!" came a voice above.

Sam loosened his grip and listened.

"*Nous nous rendons.* We surrender!"

That's more like it. Quick and efficient.

Sam exhaled, panting, then pulled the deserter closer.

"You speak English?" Sam demanded. He reached for the package, which the man again refused to relinquish.

"*Qu'est-ce qu'il y a sur le bateau?*" Julian asked, this time in French.

The man jerked with recognition toward the speaker. His eyes widened as Julian continued his speech, cutlass raised.

"What'd you tell him?" Sam asked.

"That, if he values his life, he should know that *we* know that what he carries outlines the true contents on the ship, not whatever his captain is groomed to tell us."

Sam furrowed his brow, then gave a curt nod of shared understanding.

With that, the French runaway unwrapped the parcel and offered it to them. Sam reached out to take it.

In his hands, he held the merchant ship's manifest.

By dawn, Jennings and his men had boarded the captured ship to interrogate Captain L'Escoubett. The hold, stocked with little more than fine linen, put everyone in a bitter mood, until Sam and Julian scoured the ship's manifest for answers. The ledger declared thirty thousand pieces of eight.

Unfortunately, somehow, the silver was no longer on board.

Jennings stomped around the deck. "Separate the crew," he said. "Find out where they stashed the treasure." Then, to the larger group, a threat: "Lie, and there'll be no mercy, you disgusting rats."

Sam and Williams exchanged a groggy glance. Thankfully, none of their own men had been harmed during the night's raid. But had there been a point to the battle?

Thirty thousand pieces of eight, Sam thought. If found, Jennings hadn't exactly promised them a cut. Sam and Williams's men had certainly proved themselves, but would a man like Jennings act with honor?

He winced at the tortured screams of the French captives as Jennings's men set upon them with their questions and sharpened knives. Julian covered his ears, and the unflappable Williams puffed out his cheeks. Sam had wondered how a man as vile as Jennings could command the respect of so many. Now he knew. Cruelty. A poor substitute for strength. His lip curled with the realization.

The door to the captain's quarters flew open, and out came Jennings, throttling Captain L'Escoubett. Jennings threw him to the deck, where he writhed and wheezed for breath.

"They stashed the coins ashore."

Within hours, L'Escoubett pointed to the spot where he'd buried the treasure the night before. Suspicious of Jennings's spying canoe the afternoon prior, L'Escoubett had made plans to protect the profits from their illegal sales.

A shovel hit the chest with a dull *clunk*, and Jennings's men cheered as L'Escoubett shrank into the background. Six men heaved the first of four chests from the sand, grains spilling over the edges, then sprang it open.

Sam's heart leaped at the sight.

Silver. Bright as a mirror. Shimmering with light like waves reflecting sun. More riches than Sam had ever seen in his life.

His fingers twitched, and he repressed the urge to touch the coins.

Jennings kicked the lid closed with a smack.

"Load the chests for transfer," he ordered. "Get ready to make way."

Sam couldn't peel his eyes from the wooden trunk stowed in the nose of his periagua. He floated at the back of the line while the rest of the loot was being shuttled to the *Bersheba.*

At the height of triumph, another surprise snuck around the bend: a lone canoe with a handful of frazzled passengers. Inside, a man stood, pinwheeling his arms for attention. *"Aidez,"* the man yelled. *"Aidez nous!"*

Sam groaned. *Another* French boat? Between his and Williams's two periaguas, the captured French merchant ship, and Jennings's *Bersheba* leading the fleet of sloops—including the still-captured Captain Young's vessel—things were feeling cramped and absurd.

"What now?" Hoof said, eyes bloodshot with fatigue under his wide hat.

"Row hard," Sam directed Williams, who captained the second, faster periagua that was unburdened from carrying a heavy chest. Within minutes, Williams caught up to the floundering canoe with Julian to translate.

"Pirates!" Williams yelled back. "Just east at Porto Mariel."

"Who leads them?" Jennings crowed from the *Bersheba*.

"One called Benjamin Hornigold, sir."

Sam, near enough to Commodore Jennings to make out his wide-eyed expression, watched with curiosity. A shadow of fear crossed over him, then his jaw hardened. Pink blotches formed around his mouth.

Sam knew that look. *Revenge.*

"Commodore?" one of his quartermasters asked with trepidation. "Shall we make haste before he finds us?"

Jennings bared his teeth, then stood. "Not this time! If we can take a ship mounting sixteen cannons, we can defeat that rotten Dean of the Buccaneers." The commodore straightened his hat and shouted orders.

"Intercept that canoe. All sloops, make way for Porto Mariel!"

"But, Commodore—"

"Who's Hornigold?" someone whispered behind Sam. This was met with shrugs.

"Periaguas, stay and stand guard," said Jennings. "Watch the French and Captain Young."

Focus, Bellamy, Sam told himself, taking stock of his crew in the periaguas, never forgetting the silver that seemed to burn through the toes of his boots. In a matter of harried minutes, Jennings's fleet bore east as the harbor cleared out. This time, the emboldened *Bersheba* took the lead. The flotilla's sails unfurled and caught the wind as an idea lodged inside Sam's mind.

He scanned the scene.

Two periaguas.

One captain-less French merchant ship.

One unarmed sloop belonging to the pitiable Captain Young.

One chest of the treasure sitting at his feet.

No Commodore Jennings.

God help me.

Sam cursed, acting before he had time to think. He sprang for an oar and called for Williams.

"What is it?" Williams asked, rowing the second periagua toward him.

"I'm leaving," Sam said, frantically rummaging through the supplies and tossing a line to Williams to rope the periaguas together. "Transfer the men. You and the others carry on without me. Demand your share of the silver and tell Jennings I slipped away. You can shoot after me, if you'd like, but I'm taking this chance."

To Sam's irritation, Williams laughed, a laugh caught by the rest of the crew.

Sam glared. "I'm in earnest. I don't have time for—"

"And how far do you think you'd get alone?" Williams said. "Fancying that no one else can fathom what you've got a mind to do?"

Sam stiffened.

"Fool," Williams smirked. "We're going with you, lad."

"Yeah. We *hate* that bastard," Julian added.

A grunt of unified agreement rang out, and Sam peered around at their intent faces: Hoof and his ridiculous hat, Webb massaging his bad leg, Dixon with his deep-set wrinkles and gentle gaze, Abell—who had no business being left in the sun—with that chapped face and youthful confidence.

"You understand the risk?" Sam asked. "Jennings will stop at nothing to punish us."

"Aye, Bellamy," Hoof said with a salute in his Swedish accent. "Julian and I can navigate us to safety. We're faster if we all row together in a single vessel, even with the booty. There's no time to intercept the other chests."

Sam's mouth hung open, but Williams was already ushering the crew into Sam's periagua, tossing out the empty cartridge boxes, and letting the second periagua drift away.

"Belay there," came a high-pitched shriek in the distance. "Stop this instant!"

"Ils s'en vont!"

Hoof, the last one to scramble into the periagua, waved his prized hat in the direction of Captain Young. A few bullets whizzed by, but the crew dug hard, paddling for their lives.

CHAPTER 21

Maria concentrated on the reddish glow behind her eyelids as she floated on her back, every limb and muscle buoyant. The smell of salt water brought Sam closer and kept him near. The bay's chill felt refreshing after jogging to the beach. The sickle-leaved golden aster, ablaze at the height of August, had dropped its starry petals. The groundsel tree's ivory blossoms had bristled into feathery seeds, the miniature dancers ready to throw themselves into the wind. Autumn now reigned. She didn't know how much longer the weather would hold for swimming.

Her hair fanned out as her hands rested on her stomach.

She was late. More than late.

What are we going to do, my love?

Maria didn't know which "we" she addressed in her thoughts anymore: Sam or their baby. Her "whisperings" had tried to tell her—in a fleeting dream she couldn't quite remember, a heightened sensitivity toward a newborn calf on wobbly legs, the quality of light through the open window when she stopped her weaving to look out. Instead of heeding the message, she chose to ignore her first missed monthly, attributing the delay to distress or grief, maybe both; her parents still refused to speak to her, and she'd heard no word of Sam. Then another moon passed. But with a mother for a midwife, Maria could no longer repress the signs. Tender breasts. Sudden fits of exhaustion. The stench of fish nets when visiting the docks, followed by the occasional upsurge of bile to swallow or spit.

Maria breathed deeply, her mouth a relaxed smile.

She knew she *should* feel afraid. Ashamed. Angry. Maybe sorry.

But at present, alone, Maria felt none of those things. Anxious, sure; she'd never known such a huge responsibility before, and women risked their lives giving birth—women who were in far better situations than hers. But those other tired scripts didn't come from her. While this pregnancy remained her secret, her hidden world, she let her honest thoughts and impressions rise to the surface before others could stamp them out.

Radiance. Joy.

Excitement.

Would the child have Sam's strong hands? His black curls and thick lashes? Or would the baby resemble her, in body and in temperamental spirit? Heaven help them all if so. She imagined the moment Sam stepped ashore, telling him, the look on his face and the crease of his eyes before sweeping her up into his arms.

Maria knew the consequences of sex. She'd grown up on a farm and near seafarers, after all. Sam had also warned Maria this could happen if they didn't take precautions. They'd taken one, a supposedly sure-fire tactic he'd heard from sailors who visited brothels. Sam had asked her multiple times, before they made love, if she was sure, and she had insisted yes.

She put her arms out and balanced her body through a swell, then sighed at the memory of his touch and thoughtfulness. She was sure then. She was still sure now. Though she wished, with burning regret, that she had gone with him when given the chance—however impossible it seemed then.

Maria wasn't the first young person in town to find herself pregnant out of wedlock. Yes, preachers warned about fornication, and the law threatened punishments—but it wasn't as severe as adultery. What was done often differed from what was taught. Everyone in Eastham knew that couples regularly appeared before Reverend Treat before the bump showed. The reverend baptized children born too soon and welcomed back the parents, so long as they confessed their sins to the public. In Billingsgate nearby, Pastor Josiah Oakes and Margaret Hough had a baby six months after their hasty marriage. Mistakes happened, even among the most righteous.

But you, my dear, are not a mistake. And I have no ambition to be righteous.

Maria meant it with every inch of her being while also recognizing her situation was far from ideal. She thought of little else. Unlike these other couples, Sam was not here for them to rush to Reverend Treat, and he wouldn't be for months. Rich or not, Maria thought this news might incline her parents more to their swift union. The hope warmed her, though an opposite outcome was more likely. Maria needed a plan for the meantime.

Should we run away?

You're right. No money.
And how would Sam know where to find us?

We could go away for a while.
Maybe see Aunt Ruth in Chatham?

No, we'd bring her shame.
And I'll protect you, darling, from any shame.

Hide you?

Under how many layers? With what new clothes?

We could ask Mama what to do.

Impossible.
She'd race us to marriage like a horse to marsh hay.

Tell Elizabeth?

Maria blinked away beads of ocean from her stinging eyes and stared up at the gauzy sun. She could tell Elizabeth. Though she feared her sister's judgment and initial wrath, Elizabeth had proven worthy of trust and had asked for honesty. She might have better ideas. Elizabeth had listened to Maria, loved her as best she could. And she knew Sam, if not as well. Maria could carry this child with strength, somehow. Some way. But not alone.

The blues overhead extended forever, making it impossible to focus on one spot for long. The edges blurred until her vision pulsed.

Yes. She would tell her sister.

And if that doesn't work, we'll find another way, Baby. You and me. You, me, and Sam.

Maria swam ashore in her wet shift and dried her goose bump–covered body. After dressing and rebraiding her tangled tresses, she caught sight of the raft stashed away behind a thicket of scrub oak. A pang gripped her heart, and she went to inspect the wood. Still strong, ropes taut and sturdy. A sweet smell of pine, the bleeding auburn sap.

Maria traced the clove hitch knots, then her ring finger, pink with cold.

Bare.

Clouds closed in quickly over the house by the time Maria returned home. The heavy air smelled of seaweed. The door to the chicken coop had flung open. A horse from the barn whinnied, and wind yanked at the clothes on the line. Maria rushed to retrieve the sheets before the rain came. That's when she saw Elizabeth approach at a run, clutching the bonnet to her head.

The sight gave her pause, making her blood run cold.

Something about her face, determined but soft with worry. No, not quite worry.

Pity.

Did she know?

How could she know?

Maria gulped as Elizabeth caught up, bending over to catch her breath. She straightened, her copper hairs wild around her face.

"Maria . . ."

"Tell me," Maria said in a whispered monotone.

"I'm sorry. I had to warn you. Before you went inside. Before you went into town. Thank heavens you weren't in town." Elizabeth pulled a folded-up newspaper from her pocket. She resisted, then handed it over.

Maria took the paper without looking, without seeing.

Let me have a few more seconds of my beautiful world, she thought. Her heart thudded. *See the big sky. Hear the rustle of grass. Feel the heat of his name spoken in every corner of my mind.*

Sam.

Samuel.

My love.

My best friend.

Then she unfolded the newspaper and read.

Her legs buckled, and she fell to her knees. The parchment blew from her grasp.

"Maria," Elizabeth cried, joining her on the ground, kneeling across and shaking her by the shoulders.

Maria swept up her own body into her own arms, hands tight to her abdomen. She rocked, suppressing a noiseless sob.

"Sister . . ." Elizabeth said with all the gentleness she could summon, prying Maria's hands away from her stomach. Elizabeth gripped her elbows. "What have you done?"

CHAPTER 22

Sam's crew camped on an uninhabited island, a snatch of land not included on any maps Julian or Hoof had ever seen. A few men took the periagua out to catch fish and turtles for supper. Others dragged wood for the fire, while Dixon fanned the weak flame with a palm frond. The rest of the men watched as Sam and Williams counted the coins once, twice, then again for good measure, while Hoof—skilled at math as well as navigation—scribbled totals in the damp sand with a dirk.

They'd made off with ninety-five hundred pieces of eight. Just shy of eight hundred and ninety Spanish *reales*, or about twenty-four pounds sterling.

"We still have the debt to pay," Sam said, biting his brittle nails. Though he'd never seen such a fortune, it somehow wasn't enough. They'd sold their first sloop and salvage equipment for a fraction of the purchasing price. Now they had one periagua, no provisions, and no safe way of exchanging their plunder at any port they might encounter. Not with Henry Jennings on the loose.

"Let's stay positive," Williams said, placing a hand on Julian's shoulder. "If we split the profits, what's left?"

Hoof did some calculations, then winced beneath his wide-brimmed hat. "When we have profits, I'll let you know."

Sam felt light-headed. After all that, and still little hope in sight? "I need a minute," he said, standing to walk toward the surf.

He paced the pebbly cove, ripping at his tangled hair. His skin felt as dry as leather. His armpits reeked, and he could feel the ribs beginning to protrude beneath his shirt from want of decent food. Again.

Rich. Not starved. Not stranded. Not stupid. Rich was what he'd promised Maria, but also himself. The world. He ached to go back to Eastham, to find honest work as a shipwright or black-smith. Anything, for all he cared.

But he *did* care. More than he dared suppose. Enough to dread the thought of taking up any form of disrespected labor. The daily fear of how to scrape together another meal.

Besides, he'd promised more, and Maria deserved more. He'd have to come back rich, or not at all. And "not at all" wasn't an option.

Then Sam froze.

A fleet flying the British flag had crossed into view.

"Ships!" Sam yelled, hurtling back to camp. "Sails on the ho-rizon."

"Not again," Julian moaned. The crew rose to their feet, hands clasped on their weapons.

"Hush," Williams said, the deep creases of his forehead fur-rowed. "It isn't Jennings."

The ships threw down their anchors, canoes making ready for the shore.

"Hide the silver," Hoof said.

"How?" Sam asked. "A trunk we can barely lift and a missing periagua? They've seen enough already." He grimaced. "We'll have to win their respect with kindness and a tale of woe." He loosened his grip on the knife at his side, but he wouldn't hesitate if the moment came.

He turned to Williams. "Any chance we've got another bottle of brandy?"

*   *   *

"Which one of you is Black Sam Bellamy?" a barrel-chested man asked when the strangers stepped ashore, a man with a blue waistcoat trimmed in silver who Sam assumed must be the captain.

Black Sam Bellamy?

Whoever this was, Sam decided to act fast if he had any chance of saving his crew.

"I am," he said, stepping forward with his heart thumping. "I forced these men into my company."

The leader grinned, brushing back a sandy-brown ponytail and looking at his second-in-command. "One against thirty. What do ya think, Teach? Is he man or demon?"

"Demon," the second said with a toothy grin as he twisted a dread of his grizzled beard.

"We already picked up your men and the periagua, you see," said the captain. "Come! Join us aboard. We have food and drink aplenty. We mean no harm to you or your plunder. Shall we help you load the trunk? Yes, yes, we know. It's our business to know these waters. And their news . . ."

Sam glanced at a bewildered Williams, who offered a small shrug.

"What do you mean to do with us?" Sam asked, turning back to the captain.

"Do with you?" the captain laughed, slapping his leg. "Did you hear that, Teach?"

"I heard 'em."

"We mean to celebrate you. It's not every day you meet a man and crew bold enough to double-cross the pissing Henry Jennings."

"We hate that bastard," said Teach.

"Us too," Julian mumbled from behind before someone elbowed him into silence.

Sam stuttered. "How did—"

"Benjamin Hornigold, at your service." He gestured toward the black-bearded man. "This here is Edward Teach. We met up with the bonny Captain Young. Quite a sniveling numbskull. Seems Jennings sank your other periagua, then set Young's sloop ablaze before vowing he'd hunt you all down and skewer you alive."

Sam didn't doubt it, remembering the tortured screams of the French.

"Soon as we heard, we knew we had to find you," the bearded fellow said.

"Help you," added Hornigold, extending a hand.

Sam paused, then took it.

"Now, will you join us aboard?" asked Hornigold. "We have lots to discuss, and I'm parched."

Everything about Hornigold's flotilla made Sam reel. Aboard the flagship, they wined and dined on individual pewter plates paired with engraved utensils—nothing like the maggot-infested biscuits and watery sludge Sam had endured on countless navy voyages with nothing but a knife and shared bowl. The men had shorter watches, giving them time to clean their weapons, relax, or listen to music and song. They even had a playwright who created skits for the men to perform. Hornigold's crew enjoyed blatant luxury: Jacobean candlesticks, Queen Anne teapots, and fine clothing dripping with brass buckles, silver cuff links, and glass and silver buttons. He'd never seen so many hues of skin or heard so many languages at once, a crew working together and alongside each other without rancor or shadows of fear, a crew without a clear upper class. Anyone could enter the modest captain's quarters or take a nap on the carpeted floorboards.

Later that night, head dizzy with drink, Sam stood at the rail as stars emerged into stark view. A gentle breeze traveled across his cheek, clearing the fog from his mind. The rum had a sweet aftertaste, and he tried but failed to remember the last time his stomach ached not from hunger, but from feast. Sometime at the Higgins with Aunt Lamb, no doubt—a world away, a world with Maria in it. He closed his eyes, as if to summon her: pink lips, curious eyes, her brave, sparring conversations.

Can you hear me? Feel me?

"It's a lot to take in, isn't it?"

Sam turned to find Ben Hornigold standing beside him. The captain removed his cavalier hat—complete with what looked to be an actual ostrich feather—then took a deep breath, inhaling the sea.

"You could say that."

"It was for me, too. At first," Hornigold said, clearing his throat. "I hail from Norfolk. From what I hear, you and I grew up not so different: poor folk, nobodies in the eyes of the king and country. Served in the war myself, you see—as a privateer for the crown. I've got a few more years of maltreatment under my belt, but we are men of the same cut."

Sam wasn't at all sure about that. "I'm not interested in a piracy career."

"I prefer the term *privateer.*"

So did Jennings, Sam noted. And what a specimen he turned out to be. Privateer. Pirate. What difference did it make?

"How did you know those things about me?" Sam asked, eyes fixed on the dark, glassy water.

Hornigold chuckled. "Your men talk. Other men talk. Word spreads faster here than driftwood on a riptide. By now, everyone in the West Indies will've heard of your double-crossing. You might've considered that before letting others brand your preying self with your Christian name, 'Black Sam Bellamy.' Or should I say 'Black Bellamy,' the form others fancy?"

Sam buried his face in his palms. "I wasn't thinking." It couldn't get back to Maria before he did. But how could it? No one there had paid him any notice before. Besides, he would be out of this mess soon enough, with his old name intact or with a new name if required.

"Nonsense. Be proud!" said Hornigold. "I've done the same. No sense in hiding. There's no shame, Bellamy, no shame in plundering the seas."

Sam gripped the rail harder. "No?"

"You know as well as anyone how governments gorge themselves on other people's lands and treasures. Spain especially. Thieving, exploitative tyrants. By what authority do they come by power? And who gives them that authority? Thousands of supposed nobodies like you and me who make their self-interested lives and corrupt systems possible. And what do we get for it? How do conquered peoples benefit?"

Sam couldn't argue with that.

"Some might call me a rat, a criminal, a pirate. But they are the true thieves, not me. I have my own crusade: to take what they stole and to give it to better men. To invest in building havens, like Nassau in New Providence. A place for rogues, renegades, seafarers, freed peoples, and buccaneers alike. Away from the grasp of greedy nations." He paused. "I'd like to make something of you, and I believe you can be of use to us, too."

Sam's pulse quickened, similar to the way he felt when talking with Maria. That tingle of possibility that came from imagining a better world.

He let go of the rail and stood tall, arms across his bony chest.

"Why me?"

"Why not you?" Hornigold asked. "You've got fire in you, boy. An ability to lead, and an unquenchable hunger in the marrow. No sense denying it—you're forged that way. I've seen it in dozens of others. Edward Teach, for example. We'll plunder more, and faster, as a team."

Sam studied Hornigold, who leaned his back against the rail and thumbed the brim of his hat. His gaze remained intent and sincere. To his credit, Ben Hornigold seemed the opposite of his rival, Henry Jennings. Something about the self-made captain—commodore, he corrected himself—put Sam's suspicions at ease. His shoulders relaxed, releasing the knotted tension along his spine that had been accumulating since Florida. Sam swore he'd return to Cape Cod with a fortune, and Benjamin Hornigold seemed as good as any to teach him how. For Maria, yes, but also for Sam himself. For his family name, and the memory of his father. To shatter, once and for all, the vicious cycle of oppression. To never beg for another pitiful commission. To never pine for a crust of bread again. To never suffer like a dog under the whip of another man.

For freedom.

"And when I want to break away? Return home?" *Home.* His lip turned up at the slip. Devonshire was home no longer.

"Oh aye," Hornigold said. "Anyone can break once each man has a share of one thousand pounds. It's all outlined in the Articles."

"The Articles?" Sam asked, wobbly at the word "thousand."

"There'll be time enough to explain all that." His eyes danced with starlight as he returned the cavalier to his head. "See that sloop there? The *Marianne*? She's been among my favorites. Built for speed, easy to maneuver."

Sam squinted at the outline of a vessel off the port side. "I do."

"She's yours. The crew votes on it tomorrow . . . *Captain* Bellamy."

CHAPTER 23

Better that he were dead . . .
 Better that he'd never been born at all . . .
  . . . Black Sam Bellamy

"Maria, are you even hearing me?" Elizabeth asked, stopping under a cluster of white pines.

Maria blinked, ripping her thoughts back into the land of the dreary present.

They were on the path into town, where they would purchase fresh game for the wedding feast and spices for the sack-posset wine. Elizabeth braced a basket against her woolen cloak. Her freckled nose appeared chafed in the early December air.

"You were thinking about him again."

She flinched. "No, not exactly," Maria said, tugging at the hood of her own cloak. She'd done her best to hide how much she thought about Sam since news of his turn to piracy. "More about the cruel things people are saying about him." She shuddered, placing a palm on her stomach. "It isn't fair. Something isn't right . . ."

Elizabeth frowned and pulled Maria's hand away, glancing around to ensure no one saw. "We've been over this," she whispered. "You mustn't speak of him. Mama—"

"I know," Maria sighed. Thanks to the newspaper, the whole town knew Sam had gone on the account, and they had nothing else to talk about. A smaller sect suggested Maria's influence had poisoned his mind. His own aunt vowed to never speak his name again. Even if Sam did return, he'd be hanged. Possibly without trial, with his swinging corpse left to rot as a warning to others. Pirates, lower than criminals, had no rights in the eyes of the law.

What if he did it for me, because of my family?

What if this is my fault?

"You're paler than a wraith the Scots go on about."

Maria picked up her skirts. "Come, let's get this over with." Tomorrow, she'd prepare the wedding gloves, put on finery, join the procession toward the meetinghouse, sit in the most prominent seat in the gallery, listen to the benediction, hear the drawling performance from the Bay Psalm Book, and consent to become a wife. Tomorrow, she'd marry Mr. John Hallett, not Sam. For survival, not love.

All of Maria's half-formed plans and fantasies for waiting out the pregnancy until Sam's return had burned up with the gossip, followed by shock punctuated with anger. She'd always believed her life was a real life and not a story life, and now she knew it well. She had another person to protect. Blinded by despair and few alternatives—for she had been right in her words to Sam: What choice did women in such circumstances have?—Elizabeth had convinced Maria to tell Mama that she was with child. Maria recoiled at the sting of memory: disgust churning with agony in her mother's narrowed eyes, a slap across the cheek, a terrible silence. Mama demanded details, private details that made Maria squirm, then said she'd arrange for the swift union on three conditions:

Maria could not tell Mr. Hallett, or Papa, or anyone, about the pregnancy.

She could never speak of Mr. Bellamy.

And last, if anyone learned of Maria's disgrace, Mama would deny the knowledge, renounce her without hesitation, and never see her again.

"I did my best," Mama had said, her gaze harder than a grindstone. "You know I can't endure the risk you heap upon me, or this house. Neither can your sisters."

Maria said little, then nothing. She became a husk, numbing herself to emotion, those troublesome feelings that had landed her in this mess and endangered Elizabeth and Mercy. Resigned to facts, and the only fact that mattered—her being three months pregnant, and the father being a fugitive—plans moved forward. They had to. She had a child to think of. *His* child. The knowledge scraped the lacerations on her heart. Worse, she couldn't bring herself to hate Sam. Not even close.

As they passed the old cemetery near the Higgins Tavern, Elizabeth counted the coins as Maria stared past the bare apple orchard where Sam had proposed.

"We might pick up the sugar, for the bridecake," Elizabeth said. "Save Mama the trip. Papa is so looking forward to the cheese."

"Mmm."

"Don't worry," Elizabeth said, putting an arm around her with an encouraging shake. "I'll take care of everything. Things will turn out. You'll see."

Maria squeezed her eyes closed. Pried them open again.

"There's somewhere I want to go first. Before we return."

Before my wedding.

"All right," Elizabeth said, squeezing her stiff fingers, allowing Maria to take the lead.

A gauzy sky blanketed the gray of the sea. A gale blew in with a spray of salt. Beach grass whipped at Maria's ankles, her scarred boots sturdy atop the dune.

"Here?" Elizabeth said.

Maria nodded, then stepped forward a few paces. She clutched her elbows, letting the wind lash at her cloak. Her eyes brimmed with sudden tears, at all the memories she'd suppressed.

Fingers tangled in the black of his hair. His smooth skin. Her breath quickening. His mouth, sweet on hers. Her urgent fumbling. The sharp pain. Their tender words, big enough to break the world.

What had she told him? Promised him?

That she wouldn't marry the old man.

So long as I have you.

Her chin quivered. *But I don't have you, Sam.*

If she had anything to throw into the ocean, she might have done so in a dramatic, parting gesture. Or rather, her logical mind might have done so. Had she not reaped enough shame for herself and her family?

But then a pang hit her. A whispering. A current of brimming warmth. Slow at first, then overwhelming: a springtide rising from the tip of her toes to the ends of her golden hair snapping in the wind.

A child was growing strong within her, even if she couldn't feel it yet. Maria's intuition, stirrings—whatever she called them—all rallied to confirm the very thing she and everyone else had fought to shield her from.

A maddening, bone-deep knowledge that Sam loved her, as she loved him. He had not betrayed her, and never would. He'd return, somehow, some way, and—together with their child—they'd escape from this place and create a better world, the one they'd imagined. And if there was anything that Sam had taught her, it was how to start trusting herself.

A loud gale rose as a peace settled into her chest. He'd made his impossible choices; now she must make hers. They would understand each other, as they always had. She channeled her mind across the horizon.

Find me.

I'm still waiting.

No one else will know.

Elizabeth stepped to her left, clearing her throat. "Do you have any sense of the weather tomorrow?"

Maria managed a weak smile as the new energy took hold. "Fine. Just fine."

"Have you thought of the scripture you'll choose?" Tradition allowed the bride to select the text for Reverend Treat's sermon following the ceremony. Maria hadn't forgotten. She'd considered a few vengeful selections in bitterness, aimed at judgmental listeners: Deuteronomy 32:35, Hebrews 10:30, Mark 11:25, for example.

"Proverbs 10:12," Maria said, yanking up her hood and spinning on her heel. She took Elizabeth's hand and squeezed it with affection. She'd meet her future with eyes opened, on her own terms.

"Hatred stirreth up strifes: but love covereth all sins."

PART 3

1716

CHAPTER 24

"Now *that's* more like it," Benjamin Hornigold said, appraising Sam in his new clothes as Hornigold held up a looking glass.

Sam wished he had the wherewithal to speak. In truth, he'd never worn such finery: silver-buckled shoes, silk stockings, new breeches, a lace-trimmed shirt, and a black velvet coat. Sam brushed the deep-cuffed sleeves. He caught his reflection, blinked, then looked away, shaking his head as if to shake away a dream or a nightmare. He wasn't sure which, given the kinds of gentlemen he knew to wear such expensive attire.

Sam hadn't seen a mirror since leaving Eastham four months earlier, and something about his own gaze unnerved him. But he also recalled his memory of the dandyish man he'd seen as a child, the likely pirate who'd strutted down the wharf on the docks of Plymouth, England, with that haunting air of freedom.

Sam didn't hate his transformation.

Quite the opposite.

He ran a thumb along the soft hem and grunted, remembering the coat and wig he'd borrowed from Paulsgrave Williams before speaking to Maria's father.

What if Mr. Brown could see me now?

Sword at his side, and not one, not two, but *four* dueling pistols in his sash. He'd tamed his hair by pulling it back with a tidy satin ribbon. His tresses had grown longer, wilder, and wavy with humidity.

No wig. Never a wig again. His hair would be his boundary, the thread back to his former self, and a reminder of what set him apart, no matter how rich he might get. This would be his way of rebuking gestures and status while still signaling confidence.

He traced a waistcoat button with his finger.

Impressive . . . worthy . . .

Except for the part where I'm a pirate. Privateer. Whatever. His thirst for approval made him cringe. He'd rather Maria see him now.

Would she *approve? If he could explain?*

He'd tell her, of course—something that could be their secret, something she'd have her own opinions about. Maria deserved the truth, and he trusted their unique ability to communicate about difficult things. But first, he'd put this shrouded past behind him. He imagined the thrill of first knocking on her door in the nearing months, ready to make good on his promise, to hear the squeak of the hinge and the rush of her in his arms again. To smell the wool and soapy scent of her hair. Hear the laughter in her voice.

"Best to look the part, aye?" Hornigold said, thumping the table and rising.

Sam recovered himself and started to thank Hornigold when Edward Teach burst into the captain's quarters.

"Prey ahead, a merchant ship off the starboard."

"Any cannons?"

"Nay."

Hornigold nodded. "This won't take long—we'll capture it with one vessel. But all the same, you two best return to your own sloops and follow."

Sam returned to the *Marianne*, flinging himself over the rail. He landed on his feet with a smack, happy to be back on his own ship—*his* ship. The shock and surprise of that phrase always made him smile with a pride he couldn't suppress. Even as a cabin boy, he'd never dreamed up such a fantasy: a large sloop that could carry well over a hundred men—all outfitted with gleaming oak planks, a headsail and mainsail aft of the mast, mounted cannons, and a crew who respected him and called him brother, as well as captain.

The irony that the *Marianne* had a name similar to Maria's was not lost on him.

A few members of his original crew, wearing their own improved garb, looked to him for instructions now that he'd returned.

"You clean up well," Williams said, offering a hand. He jabbed a finger into Sam's black coat and swooned over the pistols. "Got enough firepower to last until the resurrection."

Sam laughed, but flushed despite himself.

"Captain Bellamy?" Julian asked, still their faithful pilot, alongside Peter Hoof as navigator.

"Follow Hornigold. He'll cover the raid. Teach will go left and we'll go right of the merchant vessel. Likely no action or fighting for us today."

The men assumed their usual posts as Paulsgrave Williams shouted orders. Williams had been voted in as quartermaster at the same time they'd voted for Sam to be their captain. They'd been joined by some of Hornigold's crew: a sailing master, a boatswain, a few gunners, and Dr. James Ferguson—a political rebel fleeing punishments from the Scottish uprising—serving as surgeon. All had been elected by the crew, a democratic process that stripped away all Sam's prior notions about hierarchy at sea. Or anywhere, really.

While the boatswain saw to the rigging, the ship veered north, tailing Edward Teach until the formation broke. A pair of dolphins leaped along the port side as Sam walked to the bow. *A sign of good luck*, Sam beamed, taking in the sight of their fins. Spray hit his cheeks, and he savored the sound of the able crew behind him, a crew he, Sam Bellamy—a poor cabin boy from Devonshire—somehow led.

He couldn't believe his good fortune.

The *Marianne* turned out to be a fine sloop, the finest Sam had ever seen—though he couldn't be more biased. In the month since he'd joined the flotilla, Hornigold had been a masterful teacher, covering everything from swordsmanship to cannon care, to types of grenades and how to lob them to encourage surrender before bloodshed, to attack strategy, to the art of recruitment. Recruitment was a captain's responsibility after every raid. Abysmal as conditions tended to be on government or merchant ships, a handful of sailors from every prize inevitably joined their flotilla for the same reason Sam and everyone else had gone on the account—in pursuit of a better life. One with dignity.

The Articles, also known as the Articles of Agreement, surprised Sam more than anything. Sam had believed all pirates to be disorganized, selfish fiends, but the Articles proved otherwise. Hornigold had them memorized, uttering their terms with reverence. These governing rules, drafted decades earlier in the West Indies, fostered more egalitarianism than any nation on earth. They ensured every person—regardless of status, age, nationality, or race—had an equal vote. Everyone enjoyed equitable divisions of loot, access to provisions, drink, and space aboard—unless scarcity required a vote to do otherwise. A captain couldn't overturn a vote made by the crew, keeping powers checked, and Sam could be ousted at any time outside of an active battle. The Articles spelled out strict punishments for breaches—such as robbery, gambling, desertion, quarreling, disobeying orders, abusing prisoners, or violence against another crew member—and other particulars, such as the rules that all candles had to be snuffed out by eight at night, and that musicians could take the Sabbath day off. Though initially worried that another governing system might stifle his attempts at gaining freedom, Sam felt he could consent to the new demands. He'd never been invited to participate in the laws of England. That cruel world had been thrust upon him with-out invitation. Sam especially appreciated how the Articles took care of their own: Any man wounded in the line of work would receive as much as six hundred pieces of eight, and any crippled or maimed crewmen could stay aboard for as long as they wanted thereafter.

There was one wrinkle Sam might not have noticed prior to meeting Maria and learning more about her experiences: The Articles did not allow women to join. She'd been right about the limitations she encountered, and that sensitivity made his insides ache to be with her, to discuss her thoughts on the matter before officially joining Hornigold.

Sam remembered that night well. Hornigold and Teach had hosted a candlelit celebration in the Great Cabin for the men sign-ing the Articles. Anyone who couldn't read or write pledged their allegiance through a custom-made seal forged by the armorer. Be-fore signing—or stamping—each swore to abide by the rules over a Bible or an axe.

Sam went last. Peering at the objects, he saw little of himself in either. "Can I swear over my own heart?" Sam asked, which was denied. Then, "What about the name of the woman I love?" Hornigold surveyed him with annoyance, then offered his gruff assent and Sam spoke the oath. Once everyone signed, they fired off cannons amid the clink of glasses and the hollers of cheers.

Training was going well. Hornigold recently encouraged Sam to take his crew alone to conduct a smaller-scale raid, which had proved an easy success—even without taking up Edward Teach's strong recommendation to terrorize people with fire. Sam mar-veled every time Teach prepared to board a ship. The bear-like specimen tied candles to his beard or tucked pieces of fuse into the base of his hat as an intimidation tactic, smoking like the Devil himself. The aura suited him, but Sam decided to pass. The acrid sizzle made his nostrils flare.

"Bellamy?"

Sam turned to find a rosy-cheeked Paulsgrave Williams beside him. How he kept that boyish look and cheery disposition well into middle age, Sam would have to ask someday. "Mmm?"

Williams tilted his head toward the raid a few yards off the port side. "I spy trouble."

Sam peered ahead at Hornigold's crew already aboard the merchant ship. Not a single shot fired. No bellows of retaliation.

"I fail to see how it could go any better."

Williams clicked his tongue. "Listen."

Sam rolled his eyes, but perked his ears.

"See the flag?" Williams said. "Portuguese. But yon captain there seems to be shrieking in English like a man straight out of Bristol."

Not long after, Hornigold signaled for Teach and Sam to join him on the prize vessel. The surrendered sailors hunched as Sam walked past them on the slick planks, and he did his best not to meet their glowers. He felt keenly aware of his new coat. Hornigold's own crew appeared out of sorts: grumbles and huffs of impatience.

"Bellamy, Teach," Ben Hornigold signaled. "Help me settle this matter."

Teach—with his long hair notably not ablaze—crossed his arms and peered down at the puffy-faced captain.

"Hidden the loot, have you?" Teach asked, sharp nose inches from the captain's face. The captain cowered in response.

Hornigold tugged him away. "The manifest says there's nothing but a pile of logwood in the hold. But that isn't the concern." Hornigold gestured for Sam and Teach to follow him out of earshot of the others.

"I don't attack English ships."

"Aye," Teach said, who'd pulled out his cutlass and was checking his teeth in the reflection.

"And though the ship is Portuguese, the captain is English," Sam added matter-of-factly.

Hornigold sighed. "Aye."

"Sir?" asked Sam.

"Bellamy?"

"Why does it matter? So what if the ship or captain or crew are English?"

Teach snorted but kept silent. Hornigold stiffened.

"I'm a privateer, Bellamy, if unofficial—not your run-of-the-mill pirate. I fly the British colors, and there are some lines I won't cross."

"But why?"

Hornigold scoffed. "You've still got a lot to learn."

Sam's chest tightened. A student he may be, but unobservant he was not.

An excuse, maybe, but not an answer.

Teach exhaled, then put his cutlass away. "With a hold full of a bunch of rotten logs, why are we wasting our time here anyway?"

Hornigold nodded. "Nothing for us here."

"And the recruitment speech?" Sam asked. "Do we still deliver that?"

Teach and Hornigold shrugged, already headed toward the rest of the crew.

Sam clenched his jaw. He was new to this, sure, but didn't these sorry men deserve as much of a chance at joining their flotilla as the rest of the ships they'd attacked? He strode back to the onlooking men, their absent gazes and bodies gaunt, ragged garments hanging off their limbs. He wondered how many might understand his language, but wanted to try anyway.

"Brother sailors," Sam said, beginning the speech. "I've been where you are, sweating for a damn pittance, the fever dreams after a cruel thrashing, eating only at the whim of supposed gentlemen officers."

A few looked up, eyes widening in recognition.

"You might fear us, fear what might happen if you went on the account. But that fear is stopping you from snatching the freedom to truly live." He described life aboard, giving a summary of the meals, vote system, shorter watches, and the benefits outlined in the Articles—including the provision about an opportunity to break at one thousand pounds per share. Teach and Hornigold paused long enough to hear the rest, then began the transfer of men back into their own ships.

"Did you say one *thousand* pounds?" came a voice from the back.

"That's right," said Sam. That number had solidified in his own mind—the moment he would be able to pocket his share, or send some to Maria in the meantime. "Though most brothers will stay on longer and earn even more. We are in earnest about our mission."

A ripple of murmurs.

"Will anyone here join us?" Sam ended.

After a few glances and the nervous crumpling of skull caps, a black man with a winning smile stepped forward.

"John Brown of Jamaica, ready for a proper meal with sweet meats, if you have any. Oh! And don't skimp on the drink, you hear? I'm partial to grog. Have you got any wine? Claret? And I could use a new pair of shoes, like those." He pointed at Sam's feet.

"I think we can manage that," Sam grinned, reaching out to offer his hand. "Welcome, shipmate, to the *Marianne.*"

CHAPTER 25

Maria's new house smelled of smoke from the constant hiss and snap of frozen logs. Among several properties, Mr. Hallett kept a big, drafty abode on a parcel in the farthest reaches of Eastham. He'd dismissed his servant weeks before Maria had arrived. The cellar stuffed with root vegetables provided the only food for the household.

Maria paused in her morning chore routine to stare at her fingers. She'd been married for a month, the longest month of her life. Her gloves bore tears from hauling pinewood daily in the dark, January mornings. The tips were pockmarked from the embers of tending the cooking and fireplaces. She often placed her palms too close to the flames. No matter what she did, she could never keep warm, as if struck with fever. Not even pregnancy seemed to help the matter.

She placed a hand on the tiny arc forming along her stomach. She often did so when no one was around to scold her or when she wasn't covering herself with baggy layers—a blessing of winter. She spent almost all of her days in solitude.

Too much solitude, she thought as she scanned the empty, echoey room.

"You know, Baby, you could say something. Your father always has plenty to say . . . Or you could move, do something in return for me. Must be nice, having such a warm, comfortable home."

Home. This wasn't a home. She cringed and the memories returned. She didn't recognize this withdrawn, absent Mr. Hallett from the man at suppers around the Browns' family table: that awkward, business-minded fellow, shy but not unpolite—especially toward her father. Not unfeeling, not unkind. From what she'd gleaned of this stranger, her actual husband, he had no tolerance for extra costs and even less tolerance for anything beyond his fields and local politics. He spent most of his time in meetings, suppers hosted at strategic homes, or traveling to visit relations in Yarmouth, overseeing family affairs regarding the farm. When home, he kept to his office, where he scratched calculations with a swan-wing quill. He enjoyed pickled eggs and silent mornings. He carried a ledger under his armpit and had patches of wispy white hair he hid beneath his wig. His mind had little room for anything beyond work. His heart pulsed to a one-note beat of bland ambition. A few weeks into their marriage—shaky with boredom and sequestered from everyone Maria knew—she asked Mr. Hallett if she could join him on his travels. He hadn't yet allowed her a horse and, without explanation, instructed the stable lad—who worked between this property and his horse breeding estate in Yarmouth—to obstruct her attempts to get to town.

He dismissed her request outright.

"No place for a woman."

"No place for a wife, you mean?" she asked with a forced, best-behavior smile. *A second wife.* "Where is my place then?"

Why keep me here alone?

Do you somehow know?

Mr. Hallett met her questions in two ways. The first, with excuses: telling her she would not enjoy the company, that she looked too pale for an outing, that it would be an imposition to the host, or that the event was a gentlemen's discussion of politics. The second, and most frequent response, was silence, sullen or sometimes with a hint of triumph, like ignoring a child. She was young enough to be his child. Maria used to think Mama's verbal lashes hurt more than the rod. Since Sam left, she now knew a worse insult: utter indifference.

The apathy might have suited her, in another situation. She didn't care for his company. How opposite he was to Sam: cold, calculating, and quiet. But this was temporary, for the baby. A safe arrangement for her and the child until Sam came back in a couple months. They'd have to discuss this distasteful piracy rumor. With time, she'd recovered from the shock of it. If true at all, which she doubted—knowing his mind and commitment to goodness. Sam would have a reason, she decided, an excellent reason that probably had something to do with his promise. They'd have to run away now, regardless. But no matter. They'd sort it out together. Mr. Hallett's controlling behavior lessened the guilt she might have felt in deceiving him, at Mama's demand.

But she needed the old man to sleep with her again.

After dusting the cobwebs and mopping the floors, Maria sat on a stool to knead the splitting tension between her brows. Her nail beds smelled of resin. The night before, Maria had approached Mr. Hallett's room for the fifth time since their marriage. She shuddered to recall another humiliating rebuff. Barefoot in her shift. Choking back her disgust. His scornful "no."

"Why did you marry me?" Maria had blurted, her docile performance crumbling.

Mr. Hallett removed his spectacles and placed them on the bedside table before blowing out the tallow candle. She stood in the lightless doorway.

"Tell me. Why? You can't stand my presence. I've tried to be kind, I've done as you've asked. Why do you despise me?" He had from the very first night. She'd sensed it, like ice slipping down her spine. He breathed through his bared teeth as he fumbled for what felt like an hour to ready himself while Maria braced herself in the dark. They'd barely consummated the marriage. Just enough. Enough to make it a legal marriage.

Enough to make a child?

Doubtful. But soon, Maria would tell him about her condition. She couldn't hide it much longer.

"I need rest," Mr. Hallett had finally said, then nothing more.

Maria shivered. She stoked the fire in the makeshift weaving room she'd fashioned to pass the days. Her clothes and this loom were all she'd brought with her from her former home. Taut columns of yarn splayed across the broad frame with a piece halfway complete. She coughed on the smoke, and a spasm shot across her stomach and down her leg.

"Ugh!" Maria cried, steadying herself with one hand on the wall, the other gripping her lower abdomen. Her vision blurred to stars, and she squeezed her eyes shut until the pains subsided. When it passed, she checked for blood.

Spotting. Again.

She let out a whimper, her short breaths visible as tendrils in the air. A tight urgency gripped her airway. "I'm sorry, Baby. I won't speak harsh words to you again. Just stay with me. Don't leave me here alone." Her eyes watered. She needed to see her mother, even if Mama hadn't forgiven her yet.

Maria had to be careful, yes. But she also couldn't stay here worrying. She had to do something. A knot formed in Maria's throat. She clenched her fists, then stood. Mr. Hallett had taken the mare down the oak-lined trail that covered the miles into town. She would have to walk, very slowly, taking a route through the marsh so the stable boy wouldn't see her.

"Baby, we're going out for the day. Even if we don't get back before nightfall." *Even if we don't come back at all.* She didn't have a plan, just an impulse. She stuffed a basket with her weavings and a lump of rye bread, put on every layer she could manage, and laced her boots, boots that could lead her to her former home. Her family.

Before leaving, she paused at Mr. Hallett's office, the door ajar. The air buzzed, and her skin prickled. Without thinking, she entered.

A Cromwellian chair made of cherrywood. A dirtied handkerchief. A walnut clock with large black hands. She hesitated, then thumbed through the papers on Mr. Hallett's desk.

What does he do all day?

Do I need money?

Answers?

No sooner did the latter word appear in her mind when she caught sight of a letter written in a familiar hand. Papa's hand. Dated two months earlier.

Mr. John Hallett:

I understand your conditions and look forward to a strong, mutually beneficial alliance between our families, especially in light of these recent threats to property. If—by God's good will—common lands are to be divided, the founding families shouldn't have total claim and power, not when men like us have toiled and served the community for decades, same as them. Those supposed 'Proprietors' have property enough. I've thought long and hard about your advice to band together in the face of these changes. I thank you for your alliance and protection. I agree that your standing in town council will improve by taking a wife again, and the best-known beauty at that. A gesture that signals strength and an investment in the future.

After much consideration, I am including our southeastern parcel in the dowry arrangement. The soil is strong against this wretched sand plague, and it will yield a strong crop. As soon as one of my daughters agrees, we are prepared to move forward with an engagement. I am confident Goody will come around to the idea . . .

Dizzy with sudden nausea, Maria flipped to a second letter, dated a few weeks before her wedding.

> *. . . I am fond of Goody, but her mother and I fear she has become spoiled from that affection. Treat her well, but know she has much growing up to do. Away from the familiar comforts of family, as much as possible. I trust you understand my meaning. Her mother insists it will do her good.*
> *With sincerity and respect, your faithful and obliged servant,*
> *George Brown*

Maria didn't so much walk to town as stumble there, her mind circling high above the ground, like a northeast windstorm. The skin on her heels had rubbed off. A cold damp burrowed into her bones. Her cheeks burned from the chafing wind. She wanted to collapse with exhaustion, but she couldn't afford to. She had to keep moving, anything but stay put. She had to confront her parents about the letters buried in her basket, beg Mama for help, get away from Mr. Hallett, secure some money, find Elizabeth—

Yes, *find Elizabeth*. She always knew the sensible thing to do.

When Maria reached the meetinghouse on the outskirts of the Town Cove, she paused and lowered the hood of her cloak. Her teeth chattered. Reverend Treat stood outside with a small crowd of Wampanoag followers, folks he called the "Praying Indians." Among them, she sighted the woman she'd met at the docks— Abiah Sampson.

Without pausing to think, Maria approached Abiah, who turned in recognition. She said something to her companions in her own tongue, then faced Maria with an unreadable expression.

Maria pulled some woolen homespun from the basket. "Abiah. Do you remember me, the weaver from the docks? Can you say how much more I could sell this for? I think I might need money. For my . . ." Maria's words snagged as unwelcomed emotion bubbled to the surface.

For a long time, Abiah said nothing. At last, she sighed, tugging Maria by the elbow out of earshot behind a snow-dusted juniper.

"Maria Hallett, do you have any idea what's going on here? What your husband is organizing at the other end of Eastham, likely as we speak?"

Maria blinked back tears. "What has he done?"

Abiah studied her carefully, one eyebrow cocked with suspicion.

"His rallying vote to carve up the common lands shared between us? The division of Great Island? The 'special' parcels surveyors are now putting aside for my people, away from yours and onto the land plots they already turned to sand?"

A chill ran down Maria's neck. "I'm sorry. I don't know what you're talking about. What parcels? Where?"

Abiah snorted. "How fortunate, to never have to know." Her expression shifted to a frown. "And you? His wife. I shouldn't be speaking with you."

A sudden nausea rose in Maria's gut. She clutched her stomach and then, to Maria's surprise, Abiah placed a wrist against her forehead.

"You look awful. Your eyes are glazed, and you're burning up." Abiah made a noise of disapproval in the back of her throat, then reached into a bag at her side, pulling out a fistful of bark.

"Steep this in hot water. It'll help with some of the pain and reduce the fever."

Maria nodded vigorously, taking it with gratitude as the nausea passed. She offered up the loaf of rye bread in return.

Abiah stared hard at the gift before accepting it with a nod. "You need rest," she said. Her gaze drifted to Maria's abdomen. "For the child."

"It isn't his."

Why did I say that? I promised! I promised Mama I wouldn't tell a soul.

Abiah exhaled. "All the more reason to stay strong. And more attentive, if you can manage it."

As Abiah turned to rejoin her companions, Maria reached out an arm.

"I'll watch him," Maria whispered. "I'll . . . I'll learn what I can. If it can be helpful to you."

Abiah's eyes flared with astonishment, then narrowed. "You offer this freely?"

Maria's throat bobbed. "I do." Anger toward Hallett flooded her veins, and her skin needled with the impulse to do something about it.

"And you understand the danger, to yourself but also—especially—to me?"

Maria nodded, hoping that she did. She would ensure no one got caught.

In hushed voices, they arranged for a time to meet in the forest the following week.

Maria placed the two letters faceup on Papa's desk. Her father and mother stared at the papers, then at her.

"What is this?" Maria asked, dimly aware of her disheveled appearance.

"Dear child, where did you get these?" Papa began with a look between concern and shock. "The insolence! To read another's correspondence? Your husband's—"

Maria refused to answer or deflect. "I may be a bargaining chip to you, but I deserve the truth," Maria said, her voice hoarse but firm. "Tell me about the common lands. Tell me what you promised Mr. Hallett."

"Goody," Papa said. "This may seem confusing to you, but politics are not for women."

"We wanted to keep you *safe*," Mama said, a bite in her emphasis. Her eyes shot daggers.

"Am I safe?" Maria asked, gesturing to her mud-crusted dress and torn gloves. She told her parents of Mr. Hallett's change in character and of his cold neglect. "He won't let me visit the docks or pick up supplies, even for food, insisting we have sufficient for our needs when we don't. He avoids the house and ignores me outright. He isolates me at *your* request."

"If your problems are there, why are you here, Goody?" Mama said with exasperation. "Oh, foolish girl, don't you see how blessed you are? To have a secure future with a successful man, despite your unruly nature? Don't be selfish. Not after everything we've done for you. As Genesis instructs, 'Cleave unto your husband and *none* else.'"

Maria caught the emphasis and clenched her teeth, swallowing her retort. What was wrong with her? This wasn't the way. She needed to focus, to remember why she'd come in the first place, the urgency of her situation—even if her bleeding had stopped. Her vision blurred at the corners, erasing the room. It was the same room where Sam had stood and proclaimed his love and his intentions to marry her. The same place where he vowed to return. The memory infused her with a warm strength.

She turned to her father, softening her approach. "May I talk to Mama alone?"

Papa wiped his palms on his breeches and straightened his coat, though he slouched with shame. He seemed more than eager to leave the room.

The door clicked, and Maria's eyes found her mother's.

"I know you're angry, and I'm sorry. But I need help, Mama. The baby. I fear something's wrong." Maria described the symptoms and sudden pangs, the traces of blood.

As Mama listened, a look like relief swept across her face.

"Mama?" Maria said. "Are you hearing me?"

Her mother opened her eyes, the furrowed line between her brows returning.

"Have you told Mr. Hallett you are bearing his child?"

"No, not yet."

"Then why should I help? Take this as a sign. You have sinned, Goody. The wicked reap their reward."

Maria's hand flew protectively to her stomach. Her eyes hardened. "Mama, this is my child. *Your* grandchild. I know we have our differences, but surely we can agree on that much. There's no better midwife in Eastham. You helped Aunt Ruth when she needed you. I know you can help. I beg you . . ."

"I will not intervene. I told you, Goody. I will not—cannot—protect you any longer. Your situation is nothing like Aunt Ruth's, a properly married wife and a God-fearing woman. Don't you understand what I risk? Don't you appreciate my precarious position? The Lord's will shall be done."

Maria placed a palm on the desk to steady herself. She felt like she'd been kicked in the gut. Why, why was she surprised? Hope and the need for love were blind, inexhaustible impulses. Though she longed for her mother to soften and change her mind, a deep stirring told her otherwise.

In the doorway, Mama shouted orders for Papa to get a cart ready to take Maria home. Her cheeks flared red. Amid the noise, Maria could hear her own pulse pounding, like the exaggerated distortion of being underwater. She watched her mother as if in slow motion: calling out directives, assembling the basket, scrutinizing the bark, returning the letters to the bottom quickly as if they burned to touch.

"I want to see Elizabeth before I go."

"She's away."

"Where? I can wait. Just a few minutes, at least?"

Her mother shook her head. "Go now, Goody. And do not try to come back."

"Mama—"

"Please, Goody. If not for me, think of your sisters." She held out the basket with trembling fingers and gestured toward the door.

Maria paused as if struck, then put on her cloak with frozen movements before taking the basket. Fury coursed through her veins—a fierce protection for the life inside of her—as a terrible whispering seared through her, a feeling she would never speak to her mother again.

CHAPTER 26

Sam rested on his back in the sand, covering his face with a musty tricorn. He found a semblance of comfort from the hat, one of the few objects left over from his past that served as a reminder that he was still the same person. That physical evidence kept Maria near.

Despite the loud voices from the crew and the general commotion of cleaning barnacles off the ships, all careened in Samaná Bay off the coast of Cuba, Sam could tune it all out and enjoy this private moment of quiet. With Hornigold's flotilla, he'd managed to secure a small portion of the ever-increasing amount of plunder. With each passing month, he improved his circumstances. Not enough to live independently, but enough to pay off his debts and to have a modest beginning.

It wasn't, however, enough to return. Not yet. Not enough to start a respectable trade while supporting a wife. Not enough to afford a new life his father could never dream of for himself.

But I'll have it for us soon, Maria.

Sam tore away his tricorn in frustration and focused on the cloudless sky. A gull flew overhead. He could only imagine what a few more months with Hornigold might afford his future.

He'd also promised Maria he'd be home within six months. Any day now. His stomach knotted with guilt and impatience.

Would you understand, Maria? Can you feel me, reaching for your hand from this patch of beach in the middle of nowhere?

He would find a way to tell her. Mutual trust defined their relationship, and he believed she would hold true to her word to wait for him. Neither of them could deny the unbreakable connection they shared. Life at sea, especially in his precarious situation, made usual means of communication all but impossible—no matter how much he'd fantasized otherwise. To attempt contact violated the Articles. All writing, however rarely done, had to be tacked to the mainmast for everyone to scrutinize. This practice ensured no crewmember, or recipient, could accidentally put the crew in danger. There could be no evidence. He had to consider the risk to her, as well as to his brother sailors. Still, given this unexpected delay, he *had* to find a way to send news to Maria. Somehow . . . As foolish as the task sounded for a man who spent all his days avoiding land and law enforcement of any form.

"Bellamy?"

Sam sighed, his thoughts ripped back to the glare of heat. He squinted at Paulsgrave Williams standing over him.

"Mm-hmm?"

"Sorry to disrupt your little holiday, *Captain*," Williams mocked. "But you're needed at camp. Hornigold is asking for you."

Though a part of Sam was getting used to the name "Captain" and secretly enjoying it, other parts of him questioned his authority to be in charge. Though the Articles outlined structures that kept power in reasonable check, Sam's suspicions tingled at how much he enjoyed leadership—a skill that seemed to come naturally to him. Maybe too naturally for his own good.

Sam sat up and shook the sand from his black hair. He dusted stray grains from the brace carrying his pistols and cocked his head toward the shapes of people who appeared to be in the middle of some dispute. Not the most uncommon scene, especially when beached with rum exchanging hands. Minor arguments. Nothing a quartermaster or a boatswain couldn't handle.

But uncommon to make out Hornigold at the center, marked by his feathered cavalier hat.

As Sam and Williams approached camp, he could feel a dozen eyes trailing after him. Sam smelled the tar layers applied to the hulls of the sloops to protect them from barnacles, each vessel tipped over onto its side. He glanced with affection at the *Mari-anne*, then back at the commotion.

"Ah, there you are," Hornigold said between gritted teeth.

"It's this business about English ships again," Edward Teach added with boredom.

Sam heard a snort from the gathering crowd. Someone taunted Hornigold in the distance. Sam's shoulders tensed. He still didn't fully appreciate the line between privateer and pirate, but the issue of the logwood vessel hadn't been an isolated incident. A few days ago, they'd run across another English ship. They'd let the cargo alone but pilfered the liquor before sending the plump-with-goods ship on its merry way.

Many of the men struggled to understand why. Sam, admittedly, was among them, though he kept that to himself. Hornigold was not a paper-carrying privateer and likely would not, along with the crew, escape the consequences of plundering if caught, regardless of this precaution.

"Business is business," someone shouted at Hornigold. "Free plunder for all."

"Aye!"

Hornigold glowered, raising his arms in a futile attempt to stop the growing shouts. Even Edward Teach appeared unnerved by the mounting energy as he glanced at the shipmates' rioting. Someone threw an empty bottle. The noises made Sam's ears pulse. He pulled out a pistol and raised it toward the sky, letting it crack.

"Enough!" Sam yelled. "We won't settle anything if we can't listen to each other with respect. One speaker at a time."

To his own astonishment, it worked. Silence fell over the camp. Hornigold straightened his coat.

Then John Brown, the talkative, recent recruit—outfitted with his own silver-buckled shoes—came to the front. "Why give the English special treatment? I didn't join this brotherhood to shy away from the best prizes. I've sailed under a dozen captains, and the Brits are none the better—arguably some of the worst . . ."

As Brown continued, along with a few other contributors, Sam scanned the combined crew of two hundred strong and caught Julian's gaze across from him. Julian folded his arms and stared, reading his expression the same way he did back in Jennings's hold when Sam had learned that his foolish plan to steal the Spanish silver had been foiled.

But this time, Julian didn't just watch. Julian gave a slight nod in the direction of Hornigold.

Then Sam understood. While others joined the debate, he kept an ear on the speaker and one eye on their commodore. Ben Hornigold. The Dean of Buccaneers. Courageous. Generous. A self-made leader.

And *afraid*?

A vein throbbed in Hornigold's throat. His brow glistened with sweat below his cavalier hat. His forehead knitted with concern as the debate heightened.

Honor was one reason for the ban on British ships. But fear was quite another. Hornigold, with no official letter of marque as a privateer, had no real claim to safety. None of them did. Fear reigned in the hearts of the rich, their white-knuckle grip on their own sense of power that prevented them from seeing the larger world around them. Fear blinded people like Maria's parents, unable to see the benefit of change or the bravery brimming in the daughter right before their eyes. Fear had stopped Sam himself on too many occasions, all the times he found himself complicit with an unjust system, all the times he toiled with rigging or fought the whip or ached from hunger—all the times he'd kept his head down rather than try to tear down that broken world.

And he wanted a better world. For him. For Maria. He needed to be brave, like her. Willing to risk it all.

"Commodore Hornigold," Sam began, saying something before he could stop himself. "You once told me that governments gorge themselves on other people's lands and treasures, that you make it your personal mission to take those stolen goods to give it to better men."

What are you doing? Sam thought. This is Ben Hornigold. A godsend. A teacher.

A friend.

Sam caught his breath, then continued. "Can you say, in good conscience, that England is innocent of these crimes? That England is not, in fact, behind much of the despicable slave trade to the Gold Coast? That England does not exploit the colonies and ravage the locals in the same fashion of Spain? That England truly takes care of its own? Or is it the king's large navy, that gives no wit about us living, that gives you pause? After all—you do not have a letter of marque making you an official privateer. What makes you think they will spare you, or any of us, regardless of what you call yourself: privateer or pirate? What difference did that make for Captain Kidd when he failed to produce his marque for the London court?"

A muttering of agreement rippled over the men. A few gasped. If caught, nothing would except them from being hanged or gibbeted by the navy at this point—it wasn't as if they were reporting their stealing, or giving any back to a sponsor. Was now the time to exercise caution, when time was of the essence?

And time, for Sam, was of the essence.

Hornigold blanched, but his flinty pupils never left Sam. Then Sam made out something peculiar: a slight pull at the corner of his mouth.

A smile of contentment. Something like that look his father used to give him.

"We could plunder twice as much if we took on England," someone shouted.

"We bow to no nation," hollered another.

"Let's put it to a vote," Julian said, stepping forward along with many of Sam's original crew. "Who here believes Sam Bellamy would make a better commodore of our brotherhood?"

Sam froze. "I didn't say—"

"Aye," said another.

"Aye!"

Edward Teach groaned and stepped into the center of the debate, pacing in the sand. He scratched his grizzled beard, glancing between Sam and Hornigold with a pained expression.

"Commodore, do you have anything else you'd like to add?"

Hornigold exhaled. "I stand by my title as privateer, official or not. I cannot and will not attack any ship flying the Union Jack. Not after serving the crown in the war."

Sam heard the words, but not the heart. He saw the defeat in Hornigold's stance, and perhaps some wisdom—a chance, however slim, to escape at least one powerful nation's noose.

"And you, Bellamy?"

Sam opened his mouth. For once in his life, no words came.

Teach held up a hand to tame the uproars.

"Then we'll have a vote," Teach sighed. "All in favor of continuing under the command of Benjamin Hornigold?"

A couple dozen raised their arms. Teach rolled his eyes, looked to Hornigold, then raised his own hand.

"And all in favor of making Black Sam Bellamy leader of this flotilla?"

Sam lost feeling in his feet. Up shot Julian's hand, then Williams's. Hoof the Swedish navigator. Brown the new recruit. He saw the hands of his original crew members—such as Abell, the uprooted farmer; Dixon, the aged and displaced sailor; and Webb, with that limp remaining from his whaling injury—and the hands of many others whose names he knew and many whose names he had not yet learned. Men, like him, who held no more respect for England than it had earned.

The vote was near unanimous in his favor.

*   *   *

"I'm proud of you, Bellamy," Hornigold said when they finally found themselves alone in the dim hold of the flagship. "Strange as that sounds. Pained as I am." After careening to clean the hulls, they'd divided the plunder into neat, equitable distributions to split among the faction leaving with Hornigold. Now that some were parting ways, the whole crew could divide up the loot according to the Articles—an option unavailable to Sam before now. The bagged piles surrounded them in the hold.

Sam buried his face in his fingers and stared at the floorboards. Who was Sam fooling? Not only was he a pirate, he was now a captain of pirates. A *commodore* of a flotilla. How had it come to this? Now it would be several more months at least before he could part ways with this fleet and sail back to Maria. But hopefully, with his new policy in place, they could plunder even more for that triumphant day when Sam could return to Eastham.

"I'm sorry, Ben," Sam said. "I meant what I said, I did. You're wrong to grant England special privileges. But I didn't mean for . . ."

"I've trained you well," Hornigold said, smacking him with his cavalier hat. "The men chose you. A peaceful transition for everyone. I am sorry to go, sorry to see you all go." He cleared his throat. "Teach, of course, agrees with your stance. But he is loyal. He'll sail off with me and our portion of the loot."

"I understand," Sam said. A wave of guilt knocked into him like a brick. Teach, that feral man, at least had loyalty. What anchored Sam now?

Instinct.

Courage.

Friends.

His wife-to-be, waiting for him, a whole future ahead.

But also:

His hotheaded speeches.

An insatiable thirst for approval.

A growing appetite for wealth.

And beneath all of that, his deep-down satisfaction at having taken command, challenging every lowly expectation anyone had ever had of him before he'd set out on this unthinkable adventure.

Sam stood up and gazed one last time at his mentor. But instead of seeing the figure before him, he became conscious of his own form: better-fed, well-armed, dressed to dine with nobles in his black velvet coat.

"I don't deserve it, but I do have one more favor to ask—an important one. As a friend."

"What is it?"

"I need to send a letter to Maria."

Hornigold grunted with understanding.

"I'd also like to send her my portion." Sam moved to the other side of the hold, retrieving his bag. He returned, then pulled out a necklace with round, pearl-size beads made of gold. They glowed like the last beam of light before dusk. Before this enterprise, he'd never touched a speck of gold. Rather than cradle them in his palm, he returned the string of beads to the small sack without hesitation. "Your armorer made it for me," Sam said.

"*Your* armorer now." Hornigold huffed. "You know what the Articles say. Nobody can write a word without nailing it to the mainmast for all to read and scrutinize."

"That rule only applies to crewmembers, of which I am no longer." Sam removed a folded piece of parchment from his coat, then passed it and the bag to Hornigold. Since Sam had written the letter while on land and was no longer a member of Hornigold's band, he felt he could justify his action under the Articles.

"Most of my men dislike the thought of you," Hornigold said. "Especially making off with our *Marianne*."

"Yes. And they'll like me less if you let them read my pitiful writing. But maybe, with your vast network of connections in this region, you could ensure that it finds its way into the right hands. Not directly to her home. No. Too risky. But I know a man by the name of Israel Cole who runs a Cape Cod inn called the Great Island Tavern. They won't make a fuss, not those black-market types. I'm including a second note with directions, one addressed to Cole along with the last of my coin, letting him know we plan to make good on our word of repayment soon."

Within the year. No longer.

The plan promised risk, Sam knew. He didn't have much optimism that his gift would make it to Maria, and if it did, she'd need to convince her parents it came from his original treasure-hunting scheme. But the letter, through Hornigold, at least stood a fair chance of arriving. He had to believe it. He had to try. He couldn't let her think, even for a moment, that he'd forgotten her.

Sam had taken great pains to write this letter in his cramped handwriting, but with Paulsgrave's help, he'd managed: renewing his vow, explaining his plan, describing what it meant to go on the account as delicately yet honestly as he could, and offering Spanish Town as a place he could receive a reply in the coming months before his return. His heart leaped, anticipating her thoughts, but he hoped she'd understand, seeing the investment in their future when they could step away from this life and into another.

Hornigold laughed. "Always a schemer."

Sam held out his hand. "I learned from the best."

Hornigold took it, shaking a little too hard. "I'll do what I can for you, lad. I hope our paths cross again under better circumstances. Come visit Nassau, when you can. New Providence is a fine place, safe for the likes of people like you and me. You'll always have a home there."

"I appreciate that," Sam said. But he knew his home was elsewhere. "Thank you, Captain Hornigold. For everything."

After waving off Hornigold and Edward Teach's small but loyal crew, Sam's men made ready to sail. In the background, fire reds shot from the angry orb of the setting sun, sending pink and orange ripples toward the *Marianne*. His newly elected boatswain positioned the sails against the wind and called for the men to tighten the shrouds of the rigging. The men worked hard, despite the heavy atmosphere. Sam watched in a daze, taking stock of his new position. Ahead he saw the new sailing master working with Julian and Hoof on navigating them east, away from Hispaniola. They hunched over a chart, using a ruler and a brass ring dial to work out the latitude. Paulsgrave Williams, voted Sam's quartermaster again, squinted at the equipment with interest.

"Captain, I mean . . . Commodore Bellamy?" asked a tentative voice from behind.

Sam laughed. "Captain is fine. Sam too."

The shipmate recovered himself. "I thank ye. That is . . . well. With Hornigold and his snatch of boys away, it seems we've run out of hammocks somewhere in the shuffle. We're short seven. What would you have us do?"

Sam leaned against a beam, thumping a finger against his leg.

"Until we secure enough hammocks for everyone, we'll all sleep on the floor. Me included."

CHAPTER 27

"I'm leaving for Yarmouth to oversee a family affair," Mr. Hallett said one early spring morning as he loomed in the doorway. "Nothing significant. I expect I'll be back in a few days."

Maria nodded, but did not look up from her weaving. She did not question or challenge his business, nor did she ask if she could come as part of the supposed family. Not anymore. In the four long months that she and Mr. Hallett had been married, she'd learned their proper roles. She spent their first "honeymoon" month in isolation as he traveled. After that, when he was in Eastham, Mr. Hallett at least allowed her to attend church services with him in public, though he ensured that they left immediately after the sermon—unless Maria and Elizabeth could get to each other first, the sisters hugging while whispering discreet updates if either of them could manage it. On non-Sabbath days, Mr. Hallett tended to his lands or went into town for meetings. At night, as his letters revealed, he dined with every prominent head of house he could persuade to support his causes for further dividing the common lands, while his pregnant, "fragile and easily excitable" wife stayed home. Though it had taken Maria three sleepless nights to work up the courage to tell him of her condition, Mr. Hallett's reaction proved uneventful. He took a few heartbeats to respond, blinked, then removed his spectacles. He congratulated her with stiff acknowledgment, raking his eyes over her body for signs. "I confess I know nothing about this female matter," he said. "My first wife could not bear children." He tapped a finger on his desk while Maria wondered that he'd mention his first wife when he, clearly, struggled to participate in conception. Had this always been the case? Did he prefer not to admit his own impotence by challenging Maria's condition? He'd gone on to verbally note the benefits of this development, namely, having an heir to inherit his work. "We'll pray for a son," he concluded.

As far as Mr. Hallett was concerned, Maria stayed home and out of sight, out of trouble, busy with the chores, without a thought or plan of her own.

"Have a safe journey," Maria said, glancing up at last with a thin smile. She set the shuttle down on her lap.

Mr. Hallett grunted, then he was gone.

Maria sighed with relief. She glanced out the window, holding her breath until she saw the mare and cart creak down the road and out of sight behind a copse of winterberry trees. As soon as he disappeared, she sprang from the stool and made for his office, where he kept his documents.

In the passing months, Maria had studied Mr. Hallett's various papers and proposals, his meeting minutes and letters, teaching herself snatches of the problems Abiah had alluded to: rampant misuse of soil at the hands of irresponsible farmers; unprecedented tree loss; population increases in the settlement; threats of food scarcity; controversial council votes; and the valuable, vulnerable common lands shared between the Wampanoag and European families. The "Purchaser" families—those Old Comer, original English settlers—as well as the newer arrivals, coveted to control the land for the security of their own futures and private interests. Everyone wanted a cut. Maria read that they'd debated owner- ship and land succession rights since 1694, then again in earnest in 1711, voting to divide up various portions of common lands.

But how could these Purchaser families—as well as families like the Halletts and Browns, second-generation settlers—claim to be entitled original founders when Cape Cod had long been inhabited by others? She longed to talk with Sam about what she'd studied and sometimes visited the docks in a well-concealed cloak to over-hear news of him whenever she could. But no updates came, so she trusted she'd be able to discuss the common lands with him soon enough. He was only a month later than they'd planned, *just one month*, Maria reasoned. He likely needed a way to reach her with-out giving away his position of safety, and he'd need to be extra cautious if he'd heard news of her marriage. Would that stop him?

No. Maria wouldn't entertain the thought. How would he know anyway? For now, Maria made a habit of committing Mr. Hallett's notes to memory, sneaking away once per month to share her find-ings with Abiah in the forest outside the Town Cove. Abiah, Maria had learned, could not read English despite her spoken fluency. In return, Abiah—a community leader, as well as a respected healer among her people—often supplied herbs and advice about Maria's risky pregnancy. Maria had a reasonable knowledge of midwifery, she reminded herself, refusing to think of Mama. Cruelty to Maria was one thing, but toward her baby was another.

"You're sure the father is returning?" Abiah had asked at their latest encounter.

"As sure as I've ever been about anything. Yes."

Abiah hesitated, then pressed, "And if he doesn't?"

"He'll come for me."

He'll come for me.

If Mr. Hallett were only visiting Yarmouth to tend to something regarding his extended family farm, chances were good that he'd left behind his recent political plans.

As Maria reached for the door of his office, a bolt of pain hit her.

She yelped, collapsing into the wall, clutching her lower stom-ach. She squinted, grinding her teeth until the ache stopped pulsing. Though she'd experienced warnings throughout her pregnancy, this was not a pain she'd felt before. And she knew it immediately.

"Sam . . ." Maria cried, gripping her abdomen. He'd been gone seven months. Too long. But for their child, much too soon.

Pushing against the wall, she braced herself and waddled toward the warm cooking hearth. If she could only relax for a while. Rest. Maybe it wouldn't come back again. But several minutes later, another pain pummeled her. She gasped, then doubled over as the agony washed through her.

Mama.

Though Maria had avoided thinking of her mother since being turned away from her parents' house, she couldn't stop herself now. She lay down, hoping to halt the progress. But five minutes later, a cramp pounded through her, then ceased. Maria could no longer pretend they wouldn't return. She'd attended enough births with Mama to recognize the signs. She had to get to Mama. No, not to her. To Elizabeth. To a woman, any woman.

Another shock through her pelvis.

And I have to get there now.

She stumbled to the window and tried to catch sight of Mr. Hallett. By now, he'd be too far gone. Fine. She didn't want him near, not for this. He wouldn't want to be around either. But she'd find the stable lad. Yes. He'd call the midwife. He'd call for her mother, and then Mama couldn't refuse.

Between waves of body-ripping cramps, Maria did as she remembered her mother telling so many other women. *Breathe . . . In . . . Out.*

In.

Out.

And think, Maria also told herself. *Stay calm.* She knew to count the time between the pains, gauging for a steady, sure pattern. She reached for her wool cloak, packed a basket of clean cloth and, at the last minute, returned to the weaving room.

Her fingers shook as she reached out for a needle and thread, *just in case.* Then the shears. She tucked them into the pocket at her side before another cramp seized her.

One. Two. Three. Four . . . Maria began, teeth bared and counting the time between contractions. She channeled all of her energy into moving. One boot in front of the other. Yes, like so. From the house, to the path, to the barn.

The stench of animal tang from the absent horse. A leather harness. A bucket of half-frozen water. But no stable boy.

Weighing the risks of traveling and hastening the process against staying put, an emotional pang beneath the physical answered for her. Something was wrong—desperately wrong. She refused to risk her child, or bleed to death alone, here in this godforsaken home.

Another spasm, and Maria screamed loud enough for anyone within a mile to hear. When it was over, she stared down at her feet, the gush of pale-yellow fluid pooled on the dirt, a strangely sweet-smelling water that signaled the point of no return.

The baby was coming.

"Help!" Maria yelled as she followed the bramble path. "Is anyone there?" She kept a firm hand on her bulge of stomach and her ear perked. But no one answered. Only the whistle of wind and the high-pitched cry of an osprey somewhere out of sight. She could hear her frantic heartbeat like a fist beating a drum, could see the steam rising from her panting breaths.

"Stay with me, Baby," Maria said. *Stay strong. Stay brave. I'll get us to town. I'll take care of us.*

Maria walked as far as she could between spasms, counting the even intervals between. The rhythm unnerved her. Surely she had more time, hours and hours. She'd made it halfway to Eastham already but couldn't believe how suddenly the pains came on, especially for a first pregnancy. Mama taught her otherwise. Maria had *seen* otherwise a hundred times.

The ground stiff with cold. The trees still bare of buds. The town center miles out. The cramps growing stronger, lasting longer as she hobbled.

The facts were enough to topple Maria, but she refused to despair. Not for this baby—Sam's child, their child. The happy result of the love they'd shared, no, *created* on the dunes all those nights ago. They'd be a family soon. It didn't matter how or where, so long as they were together.

Sam, she thought with a flare of anger, *where the hell are you?*

Another contraction walloped her, sending Maria to her knees. When it passed, she rose and fumbled forward, her lower back throbbing with pressure.

"Stay with me, Baby," Maria begged. "Please."

After what felt like hours of a slow, labored pace, Maria made out the shape of a small, dilapidated barn in the distance. Her throat tightened.

It would have to do.

Drenched with sweat, Maria gulped and steadied herself, hurtling herself in that direction, even if she had to crawl. She could go no farther; every instinct in her body screamed that it was time to start pushing.

Maria felt for the shears, heavy and cold in her pocket.

CHAPTER 28

Sam stared at the slick red stains on his shirt and shaking hands.

Blood. Viscous, dark, and pungent with iron. But not just any blood. Shipmate Caleb Dixon's blood.

Sam swallowed a gag and a sob, scrubbing his knuckles over a bucket of water, when he heard a knock on the captain's quarters.

Sam recovered himself, biting hard to suppress emotion. *Like Maria used to do*, thought Sam, *all those times she didn't feel she could be herself, all those times she had to hide.*

Oh Lord, how am I going to explain this to her?

"What did the surgeon say?" Sam asked, not daring to look up.

The footsteps neared, and Sam recognized the brass-buckled boots. His shoulders relaxed with relief. Paulsgrave Williams. His best friend and loyal quartermaster. Of all people, he could talk openly to Williams. He'd understand the loss. He'd known Sam as an unemployed sailor down on his luck at the Great Island Tavern in Cape Cod—before Sam had learned to perform this role of a tough but compassionate captain. Fearless.

Reckless.

It was the same distinction Maria used to question.

"Dr. Ferguson did his best. But old brother Dixon is gone," said Williams, hat removed, his mouth twisted into a frown Sam had never seen from the jovial character. "Three others are wounded, but Ferguson says they'll live."

Sam rose abruptly, bumping into the table and knocking over an hourglass. He winced, then deliberately slammed his forehead against the wall. "Williams, what have I done?" Sam ripped at his black hair and screamed through his teeth, his voice raspy from shouting orders all day. "How could I be so stupid? What made me think we could attack a man-of-war like that, built for battle?"

Was I too eager to prove myself as commodore? Too swept up in the chase? Impatient to secure an easy fortune?

Or is it all much simpler? Greed. Plain and simple.

Sam squeezed his eyes shut but still saw the day replay before his eyes: their eight small cannons against the man-of-war's forty, the sweat glistening as his crew wrestled to keep the *Marianne* positioned off the stern to avoid a broadside hit, the feel of Dixon's swaying weight in his arms after he'd been shot in the chest.

Dixon. At his side since the treasure-hunting beginnings. That faithful sailor with lines like a map across his forehead, that quiet man who would have made a better priest than a seafarer despite wearing his ridiculous oversize coat from Jennings's stash of pilfered clothes. Though he'd earned enough money for a passage back to England, enough to see his grown children and dying mother, he'd never lived to see his dream fulfilled.

Williams cleared his throat. "A terrible loss, though I hate to be the one to tell you that the flotilla sings a different tune. They are praising your name."

Sam balled his fists. "We sailed away."

"But *intact*. A feat. And not before standing your ground for more than an hour."

"We couldn't even board."

"Not this time, but maybe the next."

Another set of boots entered, and Sam stiffened his composure. In walked French Captain Olivier Levasseur, better known as "La Buse." La Buse had tag-teamed raids in his sloop, *Le Postillon*, until Hornigold's final days as a leader. When the Hornigold fleet had disbanded, Hornigold and Teach went one way, Bellamy and La Buse the other. Now he accompanied Sam's flotilla, looking for a bit of fun that could only be had by someone born of the bourgeois, someone granted an expensive education and every opportunity available. Someone who chose this life for sport.

"Commodore Bellamy, I must congratulate you on a most splendid display of courage," he said through a thick French accent. La Buse wore a patch over one eye to cover a slash wound from the Spanish Succession. He had smooth cheeks and a chiseled jaw.

Sam felt woozy. "Splendid?" he scoffed. His blood-soaked shirt chilled him to the bone. "We lost the prize, and a good man."

"We lost the battle, but not the bigger war," La Buse said, clicking his tongue. "They are calling you the bravest pirate of the Caribbean. News will spread of your deeds and name. In all my years as a privateer, then pirate, I've seen nothing like it. You fight like you mean it, and the men follow. I've witnessed the difference."

First Jennings, then Hornigold, now this rogue. If La Buse so readily dismissed spilled blood, no wonder they called him "La Buse"—the Buzzard. Everyone saw something in "Black Sam Bellamy," something Sam himself didn't much admire at the moment.

Sam removed his stained shirt, throwing it on the floor with a slap. He left without another word to prepare for Dixon's watery burial.

The humid night air clung to Sam's skin like a damp cloth, oppressive heat heightened by the fire of the stove. In hindsight, Sam felt gratitude for Williams's earlier warning. Though it was customary among the crew to celebrate a fallen brother's life by forgoing somber rituals, Sam struggled to pretend. His shipmates seemed to do better, energized by the earlier chase, or perhaps it was his cloudy mind; he knew people showed grief differently. But Sam saw good spirits, all smiles and clinking mugs of "kill-devil"—that nasty, strong concoction of rum and gunpowder—with loud gusts of laughter, a mood jarring a mere hours after wrapping Dixon in his hammock. They'd stitched up the shroud—with the final stitch through the nose, as is tradition—and secured two cannon-balls to his feet before sending him to the depths somewhere near Puerto Rico.

Sam kept silent. He snatched a bottle of brandy and paced the deck, taking in the general scene: snatches of brags about the fight, men lining up to sharpen cutlasses on the grindstone, a drunk man singing odes to Dixon backed up by a handful of even drunker musicians as the piper and fiddler played wildly off-key.

Near the tiller, Sam paused. Julian sat with a group of ship-mates with pewter cups raised in the glow of lantern light.

"I can toast to that," John Brown said. "There's nowhere safer for me than on a pirate ship like this, splitting responsibilities and an equal share of the booty and governing vote—more respect among races. Not perfect, we well know. Not with most crews relegating men like us to the worst jobs aboard. I tell you, even as a free man and honorable sailor, I used to get the shivers any time I stepped into merchant ports. Like one of the white men would snatch me, stow me away in one of those ships from hell. They don't care who I am or where I come from. They see any black or brown face and they see an opportunity, not a brother."

One of the listening black men spat. "Aye."

Then a man named Hendrick Quintor spoke, a rabble-rouser Sam recognized as a new recruit from a cocoa-carrying brigantine. "My mother was Dutch, my father, African—from the Ashanti people." He reached into his shirt and pulled out a necklace with an intricate bead shaped into a spiral shell.

"I never thought I'd hold Akan gold in my hands," Quintor said. "This is an *apupuo*, a symbol of steadfastness and defiance against injustice. Look at it. Have you ever seen anything so beautiful? Nothing those devils can understand. All they see is currency."

Sam did not know the name of the next speaker, but he rec-ognized him from Hornigold's original flotilla. "Half of Edward

Teach's men were black. He said a black man knew loyalty and how to fight for his freedom. Say, did you hear that there are two pirate fleets run by an entire crew of black men?"

Quintor exhaled with admiration. "I'd sail until the end of the world to join one of those ships."

"But the white, ruling world don't talk about those stories, do they?" said John Brown. "Not the millions stolen from their villages or sold by rival tribes to so-called Christians, nor we pirates demanding and creating a better world for folks like us. They call our lot pirates, not revolutionaries, and that's that. Written off. Worse than nobodies. To hang and be picked clean by vultures or to be clapped into chains."

Sam lost himself in their sobering words, caught in the moment of not wanting to intrude on the stories with his presence and also not wanting to invade their privacy. Heaven knows he could have used more privacy to process the loss of Dixon and his own inner griefs from the day.

That's when Julian stood and set down his cup, dismissing himself from the group and making way for the stern. Sam decided to follow.

"You all right?" Sam asked, elbows resting on the rail alongside Julian. He offered his bottle of brandy.

Julian shrugged, declining the drink. "Some days yes, some days no."

"I think I know what you mean."

Julian turned and glared at Sam. "No, you don't."

Sam blinked. "I—"

"You can't." Julian wrung his hands. "Sam Bellamy, I've sailed with you for half a year. I know you—your moods, your strengths, and your trepidations—yes, your trepidations. I see them in that faraway look on your face in the morning fog and at the end of the day during nights like this after a raid. And for the longest time, I shared your apprehension. It was me, on that beach in Florida, who warned us all of the dangers of going on the account."

"I remember," Sam said, swallowing a lump in his throat. He

recalled his speech to recruit the men, like Dixon, to abandon the futile effort of treasure hunting. How long ago that seemed. How much he had to answer for.

"But these past months have clarified something important for me," Julian said. "Brutal, but important." He cocked his head in the direction of the shipmates. "They're right. No matter how skilled I am as a pilot, or how many languages I learn to speak, no one on land respects me or my people—not in the way pirates respect the brotherhood aboard. Unlike you, I can't put on a fancy black coat and a new pair of shoes and erase who I am and the past I come from. On land, the white world sees me as below them. A savage. A brown Miskito boy from Nicaragua."

Sam listened without interruption.

"I've studied your ways," Julian continued, "and I've listened to the words of your speeches. I know you mean them—all of them, and ache for a better world, same as me. But I also know that your heart is set on leaving someday, returning to this Maria woman you profess to love. You're only waiting to secure enough riches to make it possible, then you'll put all this behind you like it never happened."

He wasn't wrong. A wind swept in from the open ocean and Sam gripped the rail. "I can't deny there is truth in what you say," Sam said. "And as a leader of a motley crew, with much to learn, I'm grateful for your honesty. I'm pained by humanity's unfairness and cruelty. I hope, no matter how long we sail together, we can create the changes at sea that we wish to see on land. I need you. You're irreplaceable as our pilot, and as a shipmate. As a friend."

Julian's lip tugged up at the corner. "Bellamy, I don't tell you this because I think you can fix it or make me feel better. I share this because it is an uncomfortable truth you should examine and wrestle with. The brotherhood aboard, while imperfect, is what has opened my eyes to the dimension of what freedom can mean for a person like me." Julian sighed, then made to return below deck for sleep.

"I'm sorry, Julian," Sam called out after him. How small it

sounded, for how much he meant it. "Thank you. For everything you've spoken."

Julian stretched his neck, massaging a tension at the base of his skull. He exhaled, as if Sam still didn't understand something. "I trust you, Bellamy, and always have—despite your foolish moments. But I'd urge you, as a white man, to remember that this has become a lot bigger than you. Bigger than your woman at home or your bouts of guilt. And for some of us in the crew, unlike you, there is no going back."

CHAPTER 29

"You there, can you hear me?" came a male voice overhead. "Speak if you can hear me."

Half-conscious, Maria's eyelids fluttered. With enormous effort, she opened one sticky eye to a crack. A horizon tilted onto its side: a dirt floor, oak beams, the stench of pigs, the scratch of hay against her cheek and chest.

A barn. I'm in a barn.

A whirl of agony. White-hot pain. A howl echoing somewhere deep within her.

Maria moaned, then tightened her grip around the cold bundle in her arms. She stirred but couldn't move her legs, frozen and numb. Wet and cold.

"This woman's alive," another voice said. "A runaway by the sight of her."

"She's lost a lot of blood," said the first.

"Your name, lady?"

A face, blurry and pink, came close enough for Maria to smell rancid breath. He swept the yellow hair from her face.

"My God, that's Goody Hallett."

"Sneaking off to give birth here alone . . . But why?"

"Go! Get Justice Doane. And find Hallett, if you can."

Hallett . . .

Hallett?

No. Not him! Anyone but him.

Maria pried both eyes open and pushed against the ground with panic. She fell back again, her whole body ablaze.

What happened here?

Sam, where am I?

After an unmeasurable amount of time, she awoke beside a pair of boots. Heavy. Pounding like thunder on the ground pressed against Maria's ear.

Someone lurched for the baby.

My baby.

"No!" Maria screamed, suddenly coming back to herself and covering her exposed breast. A pain ripped down her pelvis, but she covered the bundled child in her arms. She looked up with wild pupils at a man she recognized as Justice Joseph Doane, the same man from the docks the day she'd jumped, the day she met Sam. "Get away from us. Please. Let us be."

Doane ignored her and pushed Maria aside. She fought him, shrieking and biting, but the man tore the bundle away.

"Give me my baby," Maria demanded, summoning all her strength and courage to stand on wobbly knees.

Doane said nothing, unwrapping the swaddle and grimacing. "Dead."

No.

Maria lunged for him, scraping and hollering with animal frenzy. "He's mine! Give him back to me."

Doane threw her down into the hay. Maria's whole body convulsed with shock.

"Don't make a show of grief. You've always been such a willful young thing, taunting good men with your beauty," he scolded. "Look at you now. Trying to cover up your evil actions with a mockery of tears."

Maria's mind struggled to latch on to his accusations. Why was he acting so cruel? She glowered and balled her fists. "Give me back my son."

"Your son, you say, and whose else?" Doane kicked straw onto her bare chest from when she'd tried to nurse the baby back to life. He pushed the infant close enough for her to see, but too far away to snatch.

Her son was impossibly small. Tiny puckered lips. Velvet-soft skin. Coiled sweet ears. That snatch of ink-black hair. Maria's eyes blurred. She reached her arms out and Doane pushed her down again.

Another set of hurried steps returned. The farmers, along with Mr. Hallett.

No. Not him. Not here.

"What is this?" Mr. Hallett said, face flushed with shame at the sight of Maria's appearance. "What happened?"

"This woman hid in my barn to deliver a child."

Maria cried out, "I was trying to get to—"

"No witnesses?" Mr. Hallett said.

"No, sir. None to testify to the cause of death."

Without anyone noticing, Mr. Doane stepped on Maria's wrist, causing her to writhe with agony. Then he approached Hallett with the bundle.

"Married four months now, is that right?"

Hallett grunted.

Doane flipped open the swaddle. "Long enough for a child born of this size, with this much hair? One who conveniently happens to come up dead?"

Mr. Hallett's jaw hardened.

Doane covered up the baby. "We can have her arrested for infanticide."

When the stars cleared from Maria's sight, she rubbed her wrist and fixed her attention on her husband's face.

"John?" Maria whispered. Had she ever used his Christian name before? "John, please help. Please . . ." Her voice caught in her throat.

His beady eyes calculated the risks behind his spectacles. The shears. The blood and afterbirth. The stillborn infant. The mess of a scene—all that liability.

Maria's veins ran cold. Her look pleaded with him to say something. To show mercy.

"That is not my child," Mr. Hallett declared, turning on his heel. "And that whore is no longer my wife."

"Fornication. Deceit. The murder of an innocent child," Justice Doane said with a vague attitude of disinterest as he held up a finger for each crime. "Is there anything you wouldn't do?"

Maria sat on the wooden floor of the town jail, where she'd been kept since Doane had hauled her in—ignoring her weary, confused state. A terrible draft crept through the air where a single haze of light beamed in from a high window. She clutched her knees, tears flowing freely, soundlessly, and looked anywhere other than at Doane, who was now outside the bars of the cell cleaning his fingernails. She'd recognized his name among the wealthy Purchaser families in Hallett's notes.

"Speak, woman. Do you consort with Satan? Have you sold your soul to the Devil?"

What noise. Maria held her tongue, absorbing the unimaginable weight of her loss, unable to fathom what had happened, let alone what came next—like the immediate sting of a slap. She couldn't stand without pain, her vision drifting in and out of focus. She needed a doctor, not a prison, a chance to heal. Her skirts had soaked with blood. She'd delivered her baby as best she could, remembering what Mama had demonstrated all those years Maria had attended births. But Maria had no way of knowing. No way of saving . . .

Was there a way?

Did I somehow kill my own son?

Maria's abdomen seared with pain. She could barely move. She couldn't speak. She could barely even breathe. But she refused to let Doane's accusations worm through her head or poison the truth.

I did everything I could. I'm so sorry, Baby. I did what Mama would have done, if she'd been with me. If she'd been by my side.

As she should have been.

As Sam should have been, too.

Maria's whole body spasmed with fever and rage, and she hugged the dress stretched tight across her swollen breasts, from the milk that wouldn't come. She winced, then wept loudly.

"What have you to say for yourself?" Doane asked. "Answer me."

She stared from her dress to her inner wrist, skin purpled from where Doane had stepped on her, to keep her away from her son.

Oh Lord, my dear, darling son.

Where have they taken him?

Her lip quivered, but she found her voice. "Where is my baby?"

"This again," Doane scoffed. "You've much greater concerns now."

"Where is he? Where did you take my son?" Maria asked, tone sharpened to a pointed dagger.

Doane sighed, pacing outside the cell. "I imagine they'll find a place for him in the old cemetery. No family name, a pity. It isn't the departed's fault that he was a pirate's bastard."

Maria jerked her head, eyes ablaze. "Don't you dare—"

"I think you will find I will speak however I like, which you might find kinder than the treatment from others in the coming days toward a woman in your situation, with no witnesses of the death. A murderer."

Maria's mouth tasted of cotton. She attempted to stand, gripping the bars for support. Doane smiled, his white wig tight and fixed above wiry gray brows.

"I need to see my family."

"You have no family."

"You lie." Maria ground out. "Bring me my sister." *Bring me Sam. Papa. Mercy. Someone will come for me.*

Doane guffawed. "Goody Hallett, the famed beauty, the great prize, the woman with a spirit wild as the Nauset wind—now an example to us all. Oh, the fragility of the human condition, the weakness of pride . . . It seems you still don't appreciate your situation." He walked away, then returned with a whip gripped in his hand.

Her eyes widened with horror.

Mama.

"That's better. I see you're beginning to understand. Tomorrow, the town will gather to witness the beginning of your repentance. You might practice a night of humility. You'll need it."

CHAPTER 30

"Why's the black flag called a Jolly Roger?" nine-year-old John King asked Sam after the change of watch. The boy had a habit of trailing after him on deck or wandering into the captain's quarters, eager to please or pepper Sam with questions during long days at sea between attacks. John King, or "Little King" as the crew had affectionately begun calling him, had joined the flotilla a few weeks back when Sam's fleet, along with La Buse's *Postillion*, had given chase to an English merchant ship on its way from Jamaica to Antigua. One strategic cannon fire from the *Marianne* over the merchant ship's bow was enough for the wise captain to surrender immediately.

The Articles specified that no children were allowed on a pirate ship. And yet, here King was—knobby knees and bony elbows. Sallow-cheeked and weak, but hungry for a pirate's life with a determined excitement that rivaled any other recruit. After Sam's usual recruitment speech following the fruitful plundering, a small hand had shot into the air. Sam took one look at the boy, the green-blue bruises on his face, how he yanked free from the glowering woman gripping his wrist.

They'd cast a vote. The crew, reluctantly, let him join. That outcome had troubled Sam. He knew, better than most, what it meant.

"You're a pirate now," the crew had tried to tell the boy. "Not a child any longer."

Sam snorted with amusement at Little King's insatiable curiosity and his question about the Jolly Roger flag. "I suppose because we are such a jolly bunch. Wouldn't you agree?" It was easier than explaining Julian's theory of the corrupted French *joli rouge*, or "pretty red," of those flags promising murder.

Little King was at his heels, his forehead creased with dissatisfaction. "I don't jest. If that's true, why make it look so scary? Yours with that white skull and crossbones—and La Buse's flag's got a whole skeleton spearing a dripping heart."

Sam paused, then knelt down to the boy's level. He could see simple answers wouldn't suffice, a trait he admired in the lad.

"What do you see when you look at a flag like ours?"

"Death? Danger?"

"Yes," Sam said, balancing on one knee. "Most landlubbers do—and maybe they feel all of that and more when they spot our approach. But not pirates. In these symbols, we make a proud self-declaration." Sam explained the difference between the cloth colors: Black signaled mercy to anyone who surrendered, and red—one which they did not have—promised no mercy would be asked for, nor granted. "We learn to see resurrection in the crossed bones," Sam continued. "Rebirth. A new life. Ships fly their country's colors, right? But we belong to no nation. We are dead in the eyes of their shortsighted law. Instead, we are bound together in a cause. Flying this flag makes us a new nation, 'the Brethren of the Coast.' We are respecters of no king save for King Death. Our lives belong to nobody but ourselves."

Little King blinked with concentration.

"Remember the men the other day, the men we'd sprung out of that prison ship north of the Dominican Republic?" All had been desperate men: smugglers, debtors.

"Yes."

"Now that they're freed, how do you imagine they feel when they see our flag?"

"Probably pretty great," he said, lips transforming into a smile.

"I think you're right," Sam said, resisting the urge to fix one of King's baggy silk stockings that had fallen down into his leather boot. A paternal tenderness struck him in the chest, which he tried to brush away. "For many of us aboard, we've been debtors to an unjust system. Some of our brothers have paid unimaginable costs for freedom. We fly the only banner in the world to stand up to the corruption of power. Stealing from them, and hitting them in their deep pockets, seems to be one way to get their attention."

The seriousness in King's face said he understood. Satisfied that he held his captain's attention, and taking full advantage, he asked a flurry of additional questions: Do pirates make people walk the plank? (No). Would they ever resort to torture? (Not us, but some do, like keelhauling—throwing a man overboard, dragging him under the hull, then hauling him back up again on the other side). Why's the silver called pieces of eight? (Because eight of those make up a Spanish *real*, the most recognized form of currency across the world).

Then: "Am I the youngest pirate in the history of the world?"

"I imagine so," Sam said with a long-suffering sigh, more amused than annoyed by the indulgence. Little King knew Sam was taking a liking to him, despite Sam's vocal opposition to letting a child join. He ruffled the boy's snarled brown hair. "But don't let that go to your head. Shouldn't you have some washing to do? Some knots to practice? Be sure to have that dirk sharp and ready—there are no exceptions."

Little King nodded vigorously, then took off down the deck with the slap of those heavy boots. Sam couldn't help but grin at the sight.

"You're fond of the lad," Williams said, shouldering up beside him.

Sam shrugged. "Reminds me of myself. He's about the same age as I was when a ship nabbed me at the docks and made me a cabin boy."

"Mmm," said Williams. "Same except for the part where you

had no say in the matter, and Little King there threatened to throw himself over the edge of that merchant ship if we didn't adopt him into our crew."

Paulsgrave was right, Sam knew. "He's got spirit."

"Be careful of your attachment as commodore," Williams warned. "You're bound to get hurt. Children," he huffed. "They break your heart. Even the ones *not* risking their necks. I'd know. I've got two at home. Almost grown, but still merciless heartbreakers. The worst in the world."

"I guess I wouldn't understand," Sam said. Williams had rarely mentioned his children, and never like this. Most talk of Williams's home in Rhode Island included jokes and exaggerated tales about his fractured marriage. Hearing Williams now, his muscles clenched. A part of Sam judged his faithful quartermaster for spending so much time away. Sam's father had been ripped away by death. Williams's children still had a father.

Then a strange, wonderful pang swept through Sam's heart: *Maybe I'll be a father one day.* He hadn't talked about children with Maria yet. Would she want a big family? She'd make such a good mother: brave, sensitive, unafraid to speak her mind, adventurous. Would he make a good father, like his own? The thought of building a life with Maria, a life of their own design and making, filled Sam with a terrible sense of longing. He hoped with everything in his being that she'd received his letter by now, asking for additional months—enough to earn the funds to last them a lifetime over and to serve out his term as commodore with honor. Julian was right: Sam had to balance his pining for Maria with his other obligations as a leader, at least for a little while longer. He didn't think Maria would need proof of his love, but the gold necklace might ward off others and serve as evidence to her parents that he was a man of his word. They had no reason to know just how he came by such a gift. He'd retire well, putting all this pirate business in the past.

"Bellamy, what do you mean to do with Little King?" Williams asked with uncharacteristic seriousness.

Sam sighed and folded his arms. The mainsail flapped overhead. For a moment, he could sense the face of his former mentor, Lieutenant Evans, aglow in the candlelight beside the water-warped books. All those nights he'd taught Sam to read and behave as a gentleman, knowing Sam could likely never rise to be one. Where would Sam have been without Evans looking after him?

And how different would Sam's life look if he'd never been snapped up by the merchant ship to begin with? If he could have lessened the farming burden on his father?

So many ifs. But one thing was certain. A child that age didn't belong on a ship like this.

"I'll see Little King established somewhere safe," Sam said. "Once we amass enough to divide the booty—according to the Articles."

A few weeks later, on a cloudless day near an island called Saba in the Virgin Islands, Sam and La Buse captured a merchant ship based out of Bristol. Plundering English ships had improved their fortunes and crew loyalty, as Sam had suspected. This merchant vessel proved another easy victory without hand-to-hand combat: no need for swords or lobbing of sulfur-smelling grenades. The brace carrying Sam's four pistols had begun to feel decorative. Something about this felt too easy lately. Sam made his usual recruitment speech, resulting in thirteen new shipmates taking him up on the offer to go on the account. They'd need to add more sloops to their flotilla soon. The growth in numbers also meant splitting the profits with more men—profits that were already reduced to break even with Hornigold and his followers before departing, to say nothing of Sam's portion he'd welded into the necklace for Maria. Sam was aware with every new recruit, necessary as it was to the crew's success, that it added agonizing delays to his personal plans to quit and return with magnificent wealth. But this one time, he told himself, he had to trust his mind and the fruit of a well-planned future, not his blustery, moody heart.

But after Sam's recruitment speech, Williams appeared with a second appeal.

"Do you have a shipwright aboard—a competent carpenter?"

The grim faces glanced around. One sullen young man with startling blue eyes began to raise his hand before his companion slapped it down.

A pit lodged in Sam's stomach. With all the plundering of ships and cargo, they'd had to make physical adjustments to their sloops to accommodate the changes. They needed a skilled hand.

Williams approached the sailor. "Your name?"

The young man hesitated, but spoke with clarity through a Welsh accent. "Thomas Davis."

"Mr. Davis, so pleased to make your acquaintance," Williams said in his typical singsong voice. "You're coming with us as a special guest."

Davis looked up with horror. His pinched expression shifted from fear to vehement hate.

"I am no pirate."

Sam watched as Williams and La Buse ripped Davis away from his crew. He yelled like a demon out of hell until La Buse raised a pistol to his head. That silenced Davis, and his jump-ship crewmates tried to reason with him, seeing the many merits in what Sam's company could offer them if he signed the Articles.

But Sam recognized courage when he saw it, and standards—people like Maria, who couldn't be broken, no matter how much others tried. Davis wouldn't crack or be swayed. The realization unnerved him. His skin crawled with a feeling he couldn't shake during the return to the *Marianne*.

Back at their flagship, a cluster of Sam's crew had gathered around the commotion as the new recruits stepped aboard, followed by a snarling Thomas Davis. Hoof waved his hat like a victory banner. Julian whooped with delight. Isaiah Abell and Timothy Webb from the original crew joined in with claps, followed by John Brown, Hendrick Quintor, and all the others. That night, they'd throw a worthy celebration for all the new members in the flotilla. Shoot the cannons. Strike up the music. Silly themselves with drink. With any luck, get the arrivals fresh clothes—the rank sweat radiating from them was enough to singe nostril hairs.

Sam stepped forward, looking Davis in the ice-blue eyes.

"I regret we had to take you against your will," Sam said. "Though I hope to make your time worthwhile. We'll treat you well."

To this, Davis spat. A growl rumbled through the onlooking crowd.

Sam got close enough to whisper. "I will eventually set you free—I promise. Though my hands are tied by the votes."

Sam made out snarls and grumbles from the onlookers.

"He thinks he's better than us!"

"Devilish rascal."

"Such a sniveling, self-righteous puppy."

"Say what you will," Davis said, jaw hardened and eyes narrowed on Sam. "But I'll not be poisoned by your lies. God in heaven knows what's good and right. You can't twist truth. He'll see justice served. Mark my words."

Sam frowned. The hair rose along the back of his neck, but Sam dismissed his irritation. He'd long known God to be much bigger than the fickle-minded figure asserted by these supposed Christians. And who was Davis? One troublesome whelp, nothing more. Sam would be happy to see him gone. And soon.

Well, as soon as possible. They did need to make repairs. There was no denying that.

After his men ushered Davis away and situated the newcomers, Sam stood alone with Williams and La Buse.

"More news," Paulsgrave said.

"What now?" Sam groaned.

Williams cleared his throat and gestured to where La Buse stood.

"My crew in *Le Postillon* wish to head to warmer waters," La Buse said in his nasal English. "Fewer storms. Happy ports. Rest-

ful days with beautiful women and much-needed replenishing.
I'm afraid this is where we leave you."

Leaving?

To go on holiday?

Sam gaped, but caught himself from making a biting comment
about La Buse's spoiled upbringing. His flotilla could hold their
own without the Buzzard's help. But they'd feel the loss of him
and his ninety men. Sam's head spun with a flurry of thoughts
and feelings he couldn't calm down. He removed his hat, wishing
La Buse all his best, then escaped the conversation and his crew's
watchful eyes until he could be alone.

Sam bolted for the captain's quarters, somewhere away from
Davis's shouts of protest. Midstride, he bumped into Little King.

"Commodore Bellamy?" Little King asked, not apologizing for
being in the way. "I'm afraid I don't understand something."

Sam closed his eyes and exhaled, mouth pressed into a thin
line.

"I know freedom is important to pirates," Little King continued. "The *most* important thing that governs everything, along
with fairness and equality. But what does that mean for men
like—"

"Another time, King. As you can see, I'm busy."

CHAPTER 31

A hazy sun orbed overhead as Maria stumbled to the town square, her bruised wrists bound in chains. The whipping post, new and ominous, stood tall with an iron ring hitched to the top of the wood. A small crowd had gathered despite the cold March weather. The sneering faces she recognized from the community, mostly neighbors and stern church members she'd known all of her life. Most had attended her wedding. She saw no Abiah. No Mr. Hallett.

No Elizabeth.

No Papa.

No Mama.

But her mother had promised, after all, to abandon her if anyone ever discovered the baby's true parentage. Mama was a woman of her word. Where was she this morning? What memories seared through her mind as she lost herself in the day's work, brewing a stew or mending a sock? A knot of sorrow tightened in Maria's throat. She tried but couldn't recall the details she'd gathered over the years about Mama's public beating. Maria never thought she'd have to. She might have listened more closely.

There is so much I'd do differently now, Maria thought.

But there are other things I will not, cannot, regret, another voice answered back. *Not even now.*

"We bring before you Maria Hallett, known to most of us as Goody Hallett, the former Mehitable Brown," Justice Doane began, his voice reverberating. He thumbed the leather cords in his hand. "A duplicitous woman with more sins than names."

Maria straightened. Woozy from the physical aftermath of the birth, she'd spent the night in and out of consciousness on the jail cot. Each time she'd awoken in a state of delirious confusion—sweating and panting, her tender insides throbbing with pain—unsure where she was, only to remember. To remember everything all over again—the soul-splintering loss of her precious son. Her fever dreams brought the infant back into her arms, with Sam cooing to the baby and resting his head on her shoulder. *You are so brave*, he'd whispered. *You're the bravest person I've ever known.* Her eyelids had flung open, her pulse a steady thump. Chilling clarity hit her by morning, when the jailer found her standing in her cell. Waiting. Ready.

Under the watchful stares, Maria's eyes pooled with tears. There would be no helping that today. There would be time to grieve, time to rail against Sam's delayed return. But somehow, someway, she would not let these people win. She would not become their example. Maria wore the same battle-stained skirts from the day before, having done everything she could for the child she'd borne. Only she and God knew it, but what else mattered? She lifted her chin.

Best that no one I love is here to witness this.

But even as she said it, her heart cried out for Sam.

"Maria Hallett," Justice Doane continued. "You are charged with fornication and the murder of your bastard child. Do you deny it?"

"I do."

Doane signaled for his assistant. The man pressed forward, gripping Maria by the back of her elbow, twisting her around, and shoving her front-first against the pole. Her sensitive breasts ached. She clenched her jaw to mask the agony of the swollen tenderness between her legs from birth.

"Do you assist pirates and thieves?"

"No," Maria scoffed, forehead braced against the wood. Clearly. Sam wasn't here. And if she knew of any way to get to him, this is the last place she'd be.

A hand gripped the back of her dress and yanked it down with a tear. Maria collapsed, the irons on her wrists clanging, and the fist gripped her again and foisted her against the pole, tying her shackles to the metal hoop. A knife cut through the rest of the fabric with a loud rip, leaving her back bare to the onlookers. Her skin rippled into goose bumps.

"I repeat, will you repent of killing your bastard son?"

Where was Mama, to answer for her refusal to help? Or Mr. Hallett, for his neglect and insistence to keep her far away and secluded?

"I have done no such thing and thus have nothing to repent of."

She heard the whistle before the crack against her spine. Maria shrieked, the shock swift and clean. A thousand nerves screamed in protest, and white spots danced over her vision.

"Then have you sold your soul to the Devil?"

Maria's mouth hardened, aware of every inch of exposed skin tingling with warning. "I thought we'd all agreed to repent of that Salem nonsense."

Another crack, and Maria cried, biting down as hard as she could. She tasted blood.

"Have you forfeited your soul to Satan?"

Maria knew it would be easier to lie, to confess to sins she hadn't committed. She'd made mistakes, plenty. She'd put her sisters at risk. She'd hidden her secret and lied to Mr. Hallett at Mama's insistence. But she was not guilty of these other sins lobbed against her.

Don't believe them, Maria, a calming voice came to her.

Was it hers, or Sam's? Did it matter?

Don't let them confuse you.

Trust yourself.

Her lips tugged into a smile.

"You mock me?" Justice Doane accused, followed by a flurry of insults.

Maria closed her eyes, shutting them all out. The sun warmed her face. She brought herself back to the beach in late summer. Burning sand under her feet. Sam's impassioned speech. Her mind wrestling.

Hearts are meant to bend to God's design for us. To keep us safe, no?

What if God gave you a heart full of desires you could trust exactly as they are?

Damn her heart. That wild, unruly heart of hers along with all those pesky desires that made her such a misfit. But *her* heart it still was, and remained. She could confess without it, for the sake of appeasing these people, for the sake of easing the immediate pains and retreating into a supposed safety. But who would she be then? Her conscience was perhaps the last thing she stood to lose. The only thing they couldn't take from her.

"Answer me!" Doane shouted, impatience showing for the first time since his interrogations began.

"My soul is my own. Not the Devil's, and certainly not yours."

A lash bit into her flesh like a fire poker. Her vision blurred. With another thrash, then another, everything went black.

They left her alone in a cell, hoping isolation would make her confess. A week passed. No one spoke to her, and when she finally heard a voice, she mistook it for a dream.

Maria awoke to the noise in the stale dark.

"Maria," said a familiar voice.

Was this delirium? Maria stirred, eyelids twitching.

"Maria, where are you?"

Elizabeth?

The figure fumbled with a flint and steel, lighting a small lantern. Her sister's face glowed in the flame, her red hair hidden behind the hood of a black cloak.

"Elizabeth!" Maria said with a jolt, struggling to stand. The abrupt effort made her groan, forcing her to rise more slowly.

"Shh," Elizabeth hissed, attention darting both directions. Her gaze met Maria's, her eyes flooded with concern. "I'm here. It's all right. Everything will be all right."

Nothing was all right. It would never be all right again. But her sister had come. Someone had remembered her.

Coherent words finally spilled out: "They took him, they took—"

"I know," Elizabeth said. "I came for him. Papa and I gave the baby a burial in the forest. Before . . ." Her lip quivered. "Stay quiet, we'll get you out of here."

Her family had buried her child. Her son. Never mind that it wasn't in hallowed ground—for what could these cruel townspeople touch and still call it sacred? Her eyes misted as she became more and more conscious.

Elizabeth took out their mother's midwifery kit, reached inside, and pulled out a ring of keys.

"Where did you get that?"

"I worried I'd have to try and pick the lock or bribe the guard, but instead, I found him snoring," Elizabeth whispered.

"Elizabeth—"

"I'll put it back. Can you hold the light?" She nudged the lantern through the bars, and, with effort, Maria moved to help. "I've brought herbs. I've been worried sick. We all have, though Mama won't let us speak of it. She'll boil me alive if I get caught—but that's the least of our concerns."

Maria said nothing, relief and sorrow coursing through her like a riptide. "I'm so sorry, Elizabeth." She thought of her youthful recklessness, then her marriage to Hallett to try to fix her situation, to do right by her family. "I never meant to hurt you all. You shouldn't be here."

Her sister ignored her, tinkering with the iron key until the lock popped open.

"That's it," Elizabeth said, pulling the door open with caution to avoid a creak.

Once freed, Maria hobbled to her sister. Elizabeth rushed to embrace her, then froze. "Is it . . . bad?"

"Nothing like what they do to men," Maria said. "I think they stopped the lashes after drawing blood." She didn't mention that her back didn't need to be completely raw to feel aflame.

Elizabeth exhaled with audible relief. She looped her arm through Maria's for support, blew out the lantern with a quick puff, then they limped out of the jail—past the guard after replacing the keys—together.

Only once they took cover under a thicket of mountain ash a mile from town did they dare to speak or relight the lantern.

"We'll be safe here," Elizabeth said, tossing off her cloak and ripping open Mama's bag. "Take off your dress. I brought you a new one."

"I can't," Maria said, struggling for breath after the exertion. Though her body was recovering well from the birth over a week earlier, she could barely walk another step, let alone lift anything over her head. She wanted to suggest shears, but shivered from the memory of the last time she'd seen a pair.

Elizabeth helped remove the dress, sucking her teeth at the sight of Maria's back. The week's worth of bloodstains from the birth and afterbirth were also pungent. Maria washed herself with a waterskin as Elizabeth applied a clean cheesecloth to Maria's reddened back. The bandages stung, then cooled in the night air. Maria removed a pinch of medicines from the bottles in the bag, enough that Mama might not notice their absence: thyme for an antiseptic, St. John's wort for wounds, valerian for dreamless sleep, comfrey for her open sores. After a brief hesitation, she also pocketed some amaranth to reduce swelling. Some hinted that it also contained magical properties to repair broken hearts.

At least some things Mama taught her had stuck.

"Lydia's family has a furniture store with a large warehouse," Elizabeth said, preparing another bandage. "I've spoken with her. We'll hide you there, for now. Bring you food. Help you heal."

Maria shook her head. "It's too dangerous now, Elizabeth. I saw them, I heard them at the square. Eastham has turned on me. This isn't about Sam anymore, or even Mama's sensibilities. And shaming someone like Mr. Hallett? You need to stay away from me. For your own sake, at least for a long while. Scorn my name. Speak ill against me. Whatever it takes. You have your own reputation to protect."

Elizabeth hissed with frustration, "Your stubbornness will kill you, but this time, I won't allow it," she said, slapping on a layer of poultice with more force than necessary before securing it with cloth. Maria winced slightly, smelling the garlic and honey. Elizabeth reached for the new dress, helping Maria into it.

"I'm in earnest," Maria said with more force. "This is nothing like before. Elizabeth, I won't let them do this to you, too. I'm done risking the lives of people that I love. And you know as well as I do that we can't help who we love. We can only mind our actions."

It was the most direct Maria had ever been about her sister's relations with Lydia. But her days of caution were behind her. The words glowed like fireflies in the dark.

Elizabeth grimaced. "What if I found you money for travel, if I somehow found—"

"Whose money? Who'd take me in as I am, saggy belly and no child and no husband? Not even a name I'm safe to use? Besides, I know these lands. I can hide in the north, in Billingsgate. I'm not leaving the area without Sam, not without at least some word from him."

"Are you mad, or just daft?" Elizabeth huffed. She brushed dirt from her skirts and scrubbed tears from her cheeks. "Love," she scoffed. "You call what that pirate did to you love? How he left you here? All of this is because—"

Maria held up a palm. "I've been through enough without a lecture."

"What do you know of love?" Elizabeth spat with venom, her cheeks reddening. "Try loving your family. Or yourself. Behaving for just *once* in your foolish life in a sensible way that won't get you hurt. Or worse!"

Maria's jaw hardened. Was her son not family to Elizabeth?

Maria could let that pass, could see all that her brave sister had risked to protect her, to bury Maria's child. But it was too late for this conversation, too far past the point of return. She'd already faced "worse" and had emerged on the other side into a yonder, lonely world unknown to her sister.

And she couldn't let Elizabeth stop her. Or follow.

"Listen to reason," Elizabeth pleaded. "Have some measure of self-preservation."

The words rose like vinegar in Maria's throat, words she knew she'd regret, words she knew would rile Elizabeth's temper.

I'm sorry, sister.

"And is that how you live? Splitting your life in two? Hiding novels under your mattress, spending all your free time with Lydia because you think people won't suspect you, then nodding along at whatever Mama says as if you haven't a thought in your head?"

Elizabeth's eyes narrowed to slits. "Don't you dare—"

"Oh, I *do* dare," Maria shot back. "That's what makes us different. I dare to be myself, no longer content to parade around in fear as something I am not for the sake of those devils who pretend to be saints. That *is* self-preservation."

For a terrible minute, they said nothing. Even the stars seemed dim, as if looking the other way.

"What more can I do?" Elizabeth wailed with exasperation, picking up the midwifery bag and snapping it closed. "So long as you speak of that pirate, you are choosing him over me. I will not see or speak to you again until you rid yourself of this delusion. Otherwise, I only encourage it."

A promise. Desperate, but sincere.

Maria took her sister's trembling hand. She wanted to say if there was anyone she was choosing, it was herself. Her *true* self. Something Elizabeth might understand well. But the words were best unspoken.

Elizabeth did not jerk her hand away. This was not the goodbye Maria would have hoped for, but it was for the best. At least now, her sister wouldn't try to talk her out of her plan or come after her. At least now, her sister would be safe at last.

"After all this misery, you still imagine he'll come for you?"

"I don't think, I know."

I know.

But even as she said it, Maria's eyes watered. She wasn't the same person she used to be, even a week earlier. For the first time, maybe she *didn't* know. But Elizabeth would never hear it from her lips.

CHAPTER 32

As the *Marianne* and their other sloops approached Spanish Town, Sam inhaled the smells of fish nets and copper mines. They anchored in the aquamarine harbor, an area protected by perilous coral reefs. Beaches glistened like many others in the Virgin Islands, the color pale and soft as the center of a sand dollar. Had the beauty begun to lose some of its dazzle? Maybe, and the thought depressed him. His palms sweated and his pulse hammered, unable to focus on anything beyond searching for a letter from Maria and somehow sending her a second one in return.

In the loud town center, hagglers swapped goods with incoming seafarers under a bright sun. Meat roasted on spits. Sam didn't know quite how to handle himself in civilization again, even at a pirate outpost like this where they would restock needed supplies. His jittery fingers drummed against his leg. *How did she take my story of going on the account? What did she think of the necklace?*

He tried to conceal his eagerness from his brother sailors, as well as the other scrutinizing faces along the dusty road of the sellers hawking sawed-off muskets. He was suddenly conscious of how badly he, like all of his crew, needed a bath. A few of his men stood guard over the *Marianne* while Julian, Hoof, and Quintor accompanied Sam and Williams with hidden bags of coin beneath their shirts. The others explored the town, whooping and wild with elation to be in an actual port again, where they could gorge themselves on fresh salmagundi, visit a brothel, or gamble without the Articles' consequences for doing so aboard the ship. Sam wished they'd show a bit more reservation.

"Good news. John Hamann welcomes us," Williams said, interrupting Sam's thoughts.

"Does the old salt understand the opportunity?" Sam asked, eyes fixed on two women—Women! How long it had been?—who were arguing passionately over the price of a donkey. One held a shaking fist in the air as she shouted in a language Sam didn't recognize, while the other scoffed and gripped the donkey's halter tighter. Though La Buse had sworn that this man, Hamann, was an ally, a former pirate who'd pilfered for the Dutch on St. Thomas for many years and who now served as a makeshift governor of this town, Sam knew better than to trust just anyone, especially with bilge rats like Henry Jennings on the loose. Sam's stomach twisted, his pistols weighing heavy on his sash. He wanted to get the business part over with, then find where they kept the post on this island.

"I think so," Williams said, his own attention glued on the debacle as the donkey brayed. "Let's just hope we don't wind up the ass in the deal."

An old Spanish door cracked open when they knocked, and a hooded man stood at the gap. "Who goes there?"

"A friend of La Buse," Williams said, all politeness.

The man leaned forward, eyeing the group. His gaze snagged on Sam.

"Black Sam Bellamy?"

The name never sounded right. But Sam didn't deny it anymore either, embracing the pretense of authority. "Aye."

Then the hinge swung open, the lookout stepping aside to let the crew enter the musty room. Inside, a cloaked figure counted coins on a counter. The man sat alone, elbow resting on a well-marked ledger.

"You must be Hamann," Sam said.

The listener grinned without looking up. "No need to introduce yourself. Everyone here knows *you*."

The door behind them shut with a thunk.

"Is it true you took on a man-of-war with forty cannons?"

Sam reddened with the memory of Dixon's death, then straightened his velvet coat. "An attempt, yes. We've come as friends to discuss business." Sam nodded toward Hendrick Quintor, who placed a bag on the table with an audible clink.

Hamann lifted his chin, his sea-worn wrinkles sharp in the harsh lighting from an open window.

"What do you have to trade?" Williams rattled off a list of provisions they needed. With a crew growing after every successful raid, they needed to replenish. Fresh vegetables had been hard to come by, and Dr. Ferguson had been treating several on board for scurvy. They needed medical supplies. Hoof also wanted better maps.

"We can do that." Hamann tented his fingers, tapping them together. "The goods, yes . . ." He paused, furrowing his wiry gray brows. The orbs of his eyes appeared cloudy. "But how much would you pay for information?"

"What information?" Julian asked, always impatient with cagey conversation.

Hamann looked to Julian, then to Sam.

"How much might you offer me for a bit of news from home?"

Home.

Maria.

Sam blinked, a thrill billowing up from his toes to his throat.

"Agree to my price first," Hamann said, one spindly finger raised as he absorbed Sam's transparent expression. "You might not like what you hear."

His pulse thumped. Without hesitation, Sam reached into his coat and pulled out a fistful of silver. He threw it down, and his crew gawked.

"Give me the letter," Sam said, leaning forward and gripping the table.

"Captain?" the others called after Sam as he stormed out of the tavern.

Sam couldn't walk straight. He saw red on red and scratched at his hair, clenching his teeth hard enough to shatter bone. His stomach whirled, and he drifted off the road, throwing up behind a fern.

He fell to his knees and buried his head in his hands.

Maria.

Married?

"Captain?" Hoof's wary voice came from behind him.

Sam wiped vomit from his mouth, then stared at a startled Hoof in his oversize hat.

"Should I tell Williams and the others to load the ship? The provisions?"

Lines from the letter reappeared in his mind:

. . . whatever your eloquent excuses, all of Eastham knows . . .

Please understand. I could never accept you, or a gift, from a pirate . . .

Sam had a vague memory that he was supposed to put on a brave face for his crew, a dull sense that there had been some point to all of this.

. . . If you ever cared about me, you won't try to see or contact me again . . .

Sam dipped his chin in acknowledgment, and Hoof ran off, disappearing, leaving Sam alone. More alone than ever. He curled up again as if punched in the gut, suppressing a retch. He shut his eyelids tighter than a tomb, rolling onto his back into a scratchy frond. His gaze locked on the sky as the sun seared his pupils. He didn't believe it. It couldn't be true. She'd married so soon, after everything they'd shared? After all the hell Sam had been through to buy the support of her family? Hadn't it all been for her?

Yes, Sam reasoned. Yes, he'd asked her to come with him. He'd been clear from the start. *She'd* chosen to stay. Even if he'd re-turned on schedule at six months, according to her account, she would've already been Hallett's bride for three. She must have known she'd marry the old man all along. Had she lied to Sam out of pity? A terrible sense of eventuality?

How could the brave woman that he knew and loved accept this? To live out her days alongside that disgusting man?

. . . I'd hoped, despite your lowly circumstances, that you were dif-ferent . . .

Surely someone had tried to sabotage their love. Her family had successfully poisoned her against him. His whole chest shud-dered, imagining the hurts they must have inflicted on her. He should have never left. What a fool he'd been, believing he could elevate his social status by changing his circumstances.

Sam wanted to believe the letter was a trick. But he recog-nized that passion, and he'd felt the tenderness beneath the bitter words—a sincerity in the details she alone would know.

. . . my joy when you proposed under the apple blossoms . . .

Our night of love on the dunes . . .

Could Sam blame Maria? The whims of a "fickle girl," as Hamann had gleefully reported? Should he have hid the fact that he'd gone on the account until he could explain in person? No. They'd always told each other the fullest truth. And according to her, the town already knew. Explanation or not, Maria had already been married by the time she'd received his letter. She'd acted on one of her "whisperings."

Sam rocked onto his side, tears stinging. His lungs fought for breath. His mind tried but failed to reach out for his father, whose comforting memory seemed more and more distant with each passing day at sea, his contented smile and steady voice a long-ago feeling, fleeting as a snatch of spray off a cresting wave. His fa-ther's steadfast face, reassuring in a flicker of golden light between the swaying wheat shafts.

What have I done? Sam thought.

It wasn't until hearing Paulsgrave Williams's voice like a bursting grenade that he returned to the terrible present, his forehead sticky with sweat.

"Bellamy, wrap up your dramatic act and come quick. The prisoner, the carpenter—Davis. He's escaped."

Sam came to himself slowly, then all at once, vision tunneled, his whirling thoughts narrowing on a purpose, an outlet for the windstorm, a rudder in a directionless disaster. Bile lingered on his tongue. How dare Davis escape.

How dare she break our promise.

And just beneath that: *How dare I break mine?*

"Search the town," Sam yelled, springing up and balling his fists. "Find him." He bolted back for Hamann's tavern. The island was small. Too small for one person to hide. He'd threaten the devil out of Hamann if he had to. Davis wouldn't get away from him.

I'll burn the town down, Sam thought with blind fury that made his skull rattle. *I'll burn this whole place to ash if I have to.*

CHAPTER 33

"Don't lie to me," Justice Doane said, his lip curling as he glared down at Maria in the jail. His thick fingers wrapped around the iron bars. "You were seen. Who helped you? How did you escape?"

Here we go again.

Maria leaned against the stone wall, the fresh scabs shooting warnings in response to every word hurled at her. Despite the physical discomfort, Maria felt a strange calmness, a reassuring certainty similar to the night before the whipping. She would never give Elizabeth away. There was nothing they could do or say to change her mind. She merely had to endure.

"Shall I call in the witnesses?"

"Do what you like, but there is nothing to report. I got away. You got me back. You have me trapped here in this little cell, do you not, for a crime I didn't commit? What seems to be the problem here for you?"

"Wicked, disrespectful woman," Doane said, spittle flying. Maria hid a thin smile. Watching Doane had proved an interesting sport, perhaps a way to cope, seeking a distraction from her visceral fears of bodily pain. He'd begun to unravel like a botched weaving with each passing day. Baffled by Maria's lack of cooperation, he'd grown all the more insistent and appeared all the more ridiculous in his efforts to control. His flushed cheeks puffed out like a child's during a tantrum, and blotches formed around the edges of his mouth.

Maybe we can change the world, Maria said to the audience that used to be Sam, but sometimes their baby. She didn't know who she addressed now. Maybe God. Maybe herself. Maybe all of them at once. *In small ways. In risking everything, I have stumbled upon a startling power that I never knew I possessed.*

Fearlessness alongside fear. A refusal to participate in this narrow life they had on offer for her. An unwillingness to play the part they'd written for her to fill so they could congratulate themselves by comparison.

They'd found Maria the morning after she and Elizabeth had angrily parted ways. Limping down the brambly sand path, going northward to Billingsgate, she hadn't made it far without the cover of night. Fortunately her captors, more merciful than Doane, brought Maria to her cell without checking her pockets or confiscating her herbs. At least she'd have some meals, however meager, and shelter from the unwieldy spring weather as her body recovered from the birth and lashes.

Had Eastham ever elected to whip a woman more than once? Maria didn't know. But she took some small comfort in knowing they wouldn't kill her. Not after the united horror from the Massachusetts colonists following the events in Salem.

But what else they might do, Maria figured she'd soon learn.

"If you fail to provide a name, you will confirm our suspicions. This dark-hooded figure was Satan himself. You sold your soul in exchange for safety. Do you deny it?"

"Yes, I deny it. You speak nonsense, and you know it."

"Then who? *Who else?*"

Maria's eyes narrowed. "I have nothing new to say."

Doane kicked the bars, knocking over a bowl of murky water. He strutted out, leaving Maria alone at last.

*   *   *

On the day they finally led Maria, wrists bound, out of the prison, her vision strained against the May morning. Two solitary months without direct sun, two months without fresh air.

Though her body had healed, the muscles along her back clenched with fresh memory as her attention flicked to the post, then up at the too-bright sky—anywhere but at her accusers. She blinked. Globs of gray clouds streaked overhead in the cold air. She took a deep breath, then dropped her gaze. Another crowd had gathered. By the looks of it, the same hardened faces, their eyes rimmed with something new.

Fear.

She swallowed, bracing. But rather than tie her bonds to the whipping post, Doane unlocked the irons. Her hands dropped free, and she rubbed the green bruised skin.

Maria whirled, eyes scanning Doane, then the witnesses, for answers. A silence hung in the air like static before a storm.

"May I . . . go?" Maria asked, her voice hoarse from lack of use.

"This woman has been accused by spectral evidence." Doane clapped his hands over his ears, and Maria watched as another woman in the crowd did the same.

"Don't listen to her!" another person screeched.

"Enchantress."

"Satan worshiper."

"Witch."

Witch? Maria almost laughed. She didn't have time to react before a pebble glanced off her arm with a needle-like sting.

Startled, her head snapped in the direction of the throw: an elderly woman, Mrs. Walker, mouth twisted in revulsion. All at once, Maria understood.

Run.

Maria picked up her skirts and stumbled out of the commotion. Rocks began raining down, most missing, a few ricocheting.

"Witch!" came a wail as a stone struck her hard in the shoulder. Maria winced, but ran on with difficulty. Chest heaving, boots pounding, Maria pushed ahead as fast as her weakened body could carry her, the sounds trailing her like sharks after fresh blood.

"Witch."

"Witch!"

"Be gone!"

By dusk, Maria had reached the wilderness of Billingsgate in a state of total exhaustion. Sweat dampened the roots of her hair, and blisters ravaged her heels. She hadn't seen a soul since fleeing her accusers in Eastham, hoping she'd gone far enough. She needed to make camp.

Golds from the final breath of day bathed the meadow flowers, sending streaks like beams between the speckled alder branches onto carpets of budding mayflowers and white bayberries. How dare they appear so alive, audacious to grow, in spite of everything? Color itself seemed a strange sight after weeks of staring at a wall. How dare it be the height of spring, when her dear son should have been born? When Sam should have been home?

Heaving, with her hand clamped to the pulsing ache in her side, Maria stumbled across an abandoned fishing shack. A whaling cabin, from the looks of it, dilapidated beyond recognition save for the charred earth left from the try-pot fires for curing whale blubber and a stone chimney against the northern wall. The tucked-away shack sat among some pitch pines, close to a brook, neighboring the towering dune cliffs overlooking the Atlantic shore.

It would have to do.

She surveyed the empty room inside, then broke off a pine bough to sweep out the debris and insects. Sap stuck to her palms. If only she had Sam's hatchet. A swell rose up in her throat, which she pushed back down. With enormous effort, she dragged a few fallen pines to prop against the outside slats to cover some gaps in the beams. The cooking hearth and chimney seemed functional enough. She'd need to replace the roof. Make a door. Then a thousand other things if she had any chance of surviving in the forest on her own.

Just as well, Maria thought. When the initial adrenaline of urgency subsided, when the blinding thoughts of survival dwindled, then the harder thoughts and emotions would come crashing in again, the white-hot grief, the despairing isolation that pelted her during the harrowing nights in prison, and now, something more.

Witch.

There would be time. Far too much time. She'd need a fire, and a shelter, built by the strength of her own two hands.

Maria gathered a pile of sticks, propping one up against a rock. Using all her weight, she jumped and split the wood in two.

CHAPTER 34

"Thank you, Bellamy," one of the rescued pirates professed, bowing to kiss Sam's hand as they welcomed the new crew members aboard the *Marianne* two months after the incident in Spanish Town. The man's clothes hung like rags.

Sam held up a palm to stop the uncomfortable gesture. "You're welcome here, brother." Though in truth, Sam didn't know how grateful this survivor should be. By all accounts from these small-scale pirates they'd plucked off an island outside of St. Croix, they wouldn't have been attacked—and their friends' sloops sent to Davy Jones's locker—if it weren't for Sam's growing reputation. The British Navy had meant the ambush for Black Bellamy, not them. A tremor of guilt lodged in Sam's throat.

The navy was still searching. These few surviving pirates were lucky to have escaped with their skins.

Paulsgrave Williams took note of the influx of men by their names and skills, while Julian and Hoof aided with translation as needed. Webb and Abell divided the arrivals among the sloops in the fleet, with John Brown modeling his silver-buckled shoes and offering encouragement. Quintor and a few others distributed hammocks and immediate provisions. Even Little King helped, hauling buckets half his size filled with fresh water, which the rescued men gulped by the cupful.

The bustling noises seemed far away as Sam leaned against the rigging. The British Navy was after him. *Him*, Samuel Bellamy. He let the words knock around in his skull. The king's fighting arm at sea. Sam's former employer. His days and nights for the vast majority of his life.

And they felt threatened. By a cabin boy who hailed from a tenant farm in Devonshire.

His mouth went dry. Something about this felt different than evading Henry Jennings in those tiny periaguas eight months ago. Though a twinge of fear flooded his veins—for he knew what the vengeful British were capable of, and he could imagine that violent death well enough—another feeling met the nerves head on: something like satisfaction, or a tentative form of pride. Sam and his party had made a name for themselves. They'd collected prizes and amassed weapons and cannons to rival warships. They'd attracted the attention of the tyrants. They'd made a difference, a statement. Now, Sam had their attention, and he would keep it that way—brandishing the cause, inviting others to turn against oppression—all the while staying one knot out of reach.

Or get caught trying.

Maria, would you care?

Sam bit his chapped lip, careful to stop himself from that unbearable line of thinking.

Dr. Ferguson had joined the throng, tending to a few new arrivals suffering from dysentery. The doctor cursed, shaking his red curls at the state of the survivors. Sam could always count on Ferguson, a Scottish Jacobite fleeing retribution from the 1715 rising against England. Ferguson despised the King's Navy and foul treatment toward fellow rebels more than most. One patient of his had missing teeth and bleeding gums. Another's eyes glazed with fever, his frame trembling like an aspen leaf. The tender application of Ferguson's skillful hands to grind cinchona bark into medicinal quinine, as well as his gentle words to help ease the patients' anxiety about the syringe, reminded him of Maria's kindness and courage all over again. Or maybe it was Ferguson's flaming hair, akin to the fiery locks of Maria's sister.

There was no escaping it. Though it had been 52 days since he'd heard news of Maria's marriage (but who was counting?), he didn't think about her any less. Maybe the opposite.

He'd promised to raze Spanish Town to the ground in order to find the runaway carpenter, Thomas Davis. The memory scalded despite Sam's efforts to excuse his threat as something wholly outside of his usual character. And yet, he *had* threatened it, dragging Davis against his will back aboard the *Marianne*—Davis's ice-blue eyes shooting daggers. Though they'd set sail without lighting a single flame, Sam's whole body shook like he'd swallowed wildfire. He couldn't string together more than a few words for days. His men avoided him, making only necessary inquiries. Even Little King gave him space. Once the shock abated like a haze of smoke, then the blinding anger and self-hatred, Sam was left with gut-plummeting grief and unanswered questions that hovered around like phantoms. No matter how many times he paced the starlit decks after dusk, watched the waves rise and fall, tracked the majestic sun as it rose and fell along the horizon, or buried himself with his increasing number of duties as Commodore, the closure never came.

Did you mean it, Maria? That night on the dunes last August?

Did you really love me?

And each time, a swirl of infuriating tenderness in his chest that echoed an irrefutable *yes. Yes.*

Yes.

After the commotion had settled down and it was clear that Sam was only getting in the way of the intake process, he slipped into the quiet of the hold. He sat alone among the sacks of silver, gold, and ivory, and the barrels filled with sweet-smelling molasses, sugar, and spices he couldn't pronounce—alongside casks large enough to satisfy a palace. The *Marianne* never needed a guard; a happy crew serving under fair terms had no incentive to steal. He removed his tricorn, then unloosed his brace of pistols. The candle wick flickered as Sam summoned a moment of calm.

Her dancing eyes when they verbally sparred. The sweep of her collarbone during swimming lessons. Their vows, bound with their bodies on the sand beside the restless crash of ocean. Hadn't she too been willing to risk it all? Open-minded enough to understand his constraints and risks to give her a better life, and the potential to make a real difference, too?

Maybe he'd imagined it. Willed it to be true. Or maybe he thought too well of himself.

Her letter was clear. He'd crossed a line, become someone unworthy of her—intentions be damned. What must she think of him? A bloodthirsty pirate, no better than Jennings or any other brute raiding the seas. Maria may have broken her word to wait, felt she needed to marry Hallett despite her initial displeasure, but what about Sam's word? He'd been delayed, a point he regretted.

But he'd promised he'd return with a ship full of gold. He threatened to do nothing less when he stormed out of Mr. Brown's punitive presence. Recalling the memory, Sam's pride bristled like fur on the back of a wounded wolf still fighting.

Sam glanced around at the amassing loot in the musty hold. The wood creaked as the sloop rocked. He could hear the rocky ballast shift in the bilge beneath him and a rat scurry.

Not a ship-full yet—especially when split among his brothers. But with time, at this pace . . .

But it never would have been enough—no matter the amount—to be worthy. He seethed with regret. Did he owe it to her to return, to risk his neck to at least apologize in person? Did he owe it to himself?

Or, was that selfishness speaking? A chance to flaunt his success, to better explain, to prove his love, to beg for her forgiveness, to duel with Hallett, or to indulge his desperation to see her again, no matter the cost? Each motive pointed back to him, tasting like the bitter dregs from one of his impassioned speeches. She'd told him clearly not to try. Maria had her wits about her and the inner strength of a lion. She knew things about the world he didn't, including limitations placed on women that he'd never experienced. Dismissing her sensitivities and intuitions, her reasons—however unpalatable—seemed demeaning to everything he knew about her. He trusted her. He'd always trusted her.

Did he love her enough to give her peace, to not compromise her again, even if he knew in his heart he could not, would not, let her go?

Sam sighed, inhaling the scent of damp oak in the hold, noting the growing piles of treasure.

Had it all been for her?

Or is this about me?

"We need to clear these waters," Hoof hollered from the hatch above. "And quick."

Climbing up the ladder, Sam returned to the sun-blinding deck. He was greeted by the smell of unwashed bodies and the sound of shuffling boots. Sam blinked, and the mainsail flapped in the wind.

Julian caught up to Hoof and Sam, his lips pursed. "I'd rather *not* have a scuffle with the navy," he said.

Sam exhaled. "Aye." He glanced at Paulsgrave, who was finishing making post assignments for the arrivals. "Williams, how many men aboard the flotilla now?"

"One hundred and eighty," he shouted.

Sam's jaw dropped. They were running out of space to put them all—soon, they'd need another flagship. So many souls, from so many lands far and wide. Each man trusting him to lead them well. Sam still had a job to do, a world to see changed—with or without Maria by his side.

For now, they'd make for Hispaniola.

He placed a steadying hand on each friend's shoulder. "Navigate us toward the Windward Passage."

CHAPTER 35

The cold ocean felt sweet and electrifying, like a kiss against her bare skin. Maria dove under, her hair fanning as she wove her arms through the water. How *good* it felt to swim, a chance to stretch her sore muscles. She'd given up swimming during her marriage and through the long winter months. Here at the onset of summer, a mysterious oneness welcomed her without question, a balm for her constant nerves and aching loneliness, the surges of anger. Echoes warbled in her ear. Salt stung her opened eyes as she searched for bits of rope, a stray hook, anything to add to her collection of survival supplies.

This time while scavenging, her favorite chore, Maria's fingers curled around something shimmery buried in the sand along the ocean bottom. Heart leaping, she launched for the surface. She broke for air to examine her find.

It was a small hand mirror, corroded around the edges and coated with mud. Nothing she could use to feed herself, or hunt with, to her disappointment. Maria scrubbed away the sand, and the glass glinted with the summer sun. She caught her own reflection.

That's me?

She repressed the instilled impulse to look away quickly. Though the Browns kept no mirrors in the house—"traps of vanity," as Mama had taught—Maria had come across plenty at the docks and in Eastham's various shops. She knew her own likeness well enough in passing, but that wasn't who she saw peering back at her.

Maria forced herself to see again. To stare. There was no one here to tell her not to.

Her tanned cheeks had hollowed. Flecks of skin peeled away from her sunburned nose. But her eyes blazed with a quality that arrested Maria's attention while also making her want to break her gaze. She didn't.

That is *me*, she confirmed, satisfied that she looked as changed as she felt inside.

Would Sam recognize her, if he saw her now?

Would he ever see her again?

Of course he will, she countered, teeth gritted. And she'd be glad when he did. But first, she'd give that sorry sailor a speech to make his ears bleed.

She waded for shore with the mirror in hand. The waves knocked into her, pushing her off balance. The ocean on the Atlantic side of Cape Cod knew no mercy, no warmth, no rest. The swells rose and crashed every night and day, within earshot of Maria's shack.

Maria shimmied back into her sun-faded shift folded and waiting on the smooth beach. She hadn't brought her dress, the only possession she'd taken from the prison. Given the change in weather, Maria wore it only when necessary, preserving its uses. She'd extracted what she could from her skirts: the laces from the stays she used for fishing line (when all her attempts to spear fish with sharpened sticks had failed), and the whale bone from the bodice support she'd cut out and shaped with rocks to form two crude knives and a few shards she hoped to shape into needles.

"You are staying busy," came a voice to Maria's right.

Maria whirled with alarm. "Abiah?"

"They say you come here in the afternoons. Naked, I might add."

Maria blinked, eyes wild, unsure if this were a dream.

"What?" Maria stuttered. She hadn't seen or spoken to anyone in over a month, except to herself: cursing when schools of silverside slipped past her fingers, or singing as she scoured tidal pools for crabs and scallops.

Abiah's figure came into sharper view, her raven hair tied back into a thick braid rather than her usual English style. The same gray dress. Not a dream. A visage from her former life. Maria's pulse raced. "Where did you come from? How did you find me?" Her body shivered from more than her wet hair. Did she know how to converse with another human anymore? She didn't know if she should throw her arms around a familiar person, or bolt like a kicked dog.

Abiah smiled, then offered a wineskin. "There will be time for that. Show me where you live?"

Maria nodded in a daze, her mouth dry. She hesitated for a long moment, then lunged for the wineskin.

The fishing shack smelled of damp earth and hemlock bark layering the roof. The single room stayed dim except for the light streaming in from the entry. In one corner lay Maria's dress, nested into a ball for an insufficient bed. Along another wall stood small stacks of herbs and questionable foods—dried berries, mashed-up leaves, and shriveled roots from foraging. Across from that, an upright log a few feet in diameter acted as a table near the hearth.

Maria set the mirror facedown on the log alongside her fishing line and hook. "I'm still working on a door," she said, shuffling her feet.

Abiah sniffed, then glanced around the room without comment. Silence hung in the air. Abiah seemed comfortable with silence. Maria, after two months in isolation in prison, and another month here, could barely stomach the lack of sound.

"Creative," Abiah said at last. Her eyes returned to Maria, who stood in the entryway.

Maria flushed, defensive. "I'm still alive."

Abiah's gaze narrowed. "For now, during a gentle season of plenty. Though judging from the skinny sight of you, you'll fall prey to sickness at a moment's notice."

Maria stiffened. As if she hadn't thought of the coming frosts, months in advance, in her dawn-to-dusk struggle and preparations to survive.

"There *are* other ways people can live, if that is something you've ever had to think about before." Abiah rummaged through the piles of herbs. "You eat this?" she asked, wrinkling her nose and holding up a twig with razor-edge leaves and clusters of green buds.

"I've been through a lot," Maria snapped. *I don't need you mocking me like the rest of them.*

Even if Abiah was right.

Abiah blinked, pupils softening as she saw something in Maria's reaction. "You have toughened, I can see that. Good, you'll need it. But do not worry. I have no interest in pitying you, though you may be worthy of it, and I am grieved to hear you lost the baby." She sighed. "There is much I do not comprehend about your people and their petty, cruel ways. But banishment? That is a kind of death both of our people can understand."

Maria felt her lip quiver. Hadn't she been beyond tears by now? She strode out of the fishing shack, arms folded as she tried to recover herself.

Abiah followed, her skirt swishing against her ankles. "I respect you by telling you the truth."

Maria nodded, eyes squeezed shut.

"You should know that Mr. Hallett had your name revoked, erasing evidence of your marriage. He is engaged to a woman from Yarmouth."

Maria scoffed. Of course he was. Hallett had a reputation to repair, a triumphant career to uphold.

"You exist in birth alone in the town records. I'm sorry you and I have ever had to know such a vile man."

"Me too," Maria said, jaw clenched. "I'm not innocent, not by far. But I tried to do what they wanted, what everyone told me to do to improve my circumstances—for the child and myself." Hot tears slipped down her cheek as she thought of Mama and Mr. Hallett. "In the end, they were more than happy to wipe their hands of me, point all the blame, and save themselves."

Abiah offered the wineskin again, and Maria drank the sweet liquid greedily.

"You know, the first time your so-called Old Comers ever stepped foot from the *Mayflower*, they stole corn from the Pamet tribe's winter stores," Abiah said. "And robbed the sacred graves of our elders," she added with a shiver of disgust. "A violation we remember well and an omen we didn't heed well enough, even after one called Captain Thomas Hunt had already kidnapped and sold a group of the Wampanoag into slavery." She pursed her lips. "The Wampanoag Nation thought we might ally with these new invaders in Plymouth, strengthen our power against our rivals, the Narragansett to the west, after a white man's disease swept through our villages and sent two thirds of our people to the Creator. We signed a peace accord. Ousamequin taught your desperate people to farm, secure meat, and survive." She paused. "Now look at all that has passed, not even one hundred years later, our once-abundant resources growing scarce as we are pushed aside. And if we so much as outwardly refuse English dress and customs, we risk imprisonment—even death. Now it is we who must worry about survival."

She exhaled, then rounded on Maria, velvet dark eyes locked on her with intensity—willing her to make the connection.

"Please understand. I don't do charity for your kind, I do business," Abiah said. "And I have found our partnership to be useful. I miss your help, and so I come with a trade proposal. You know Hallett and the white man's mind-set—how to read English. I know how to live off these lands. You know how to weave and work with your hands like it's a calling from the Creator. I know people who would trade me for your work—all kinds of different work that I no longer have the time to do, including herb gathering for healing. I teach you to survive, and you assist me in raising the funds to fight the powers seeking to destroy and divide the common lands . . . and my people."

Maria nodded vigorously, a sense of hope and purpose wriggling into the cracks in her heart again, the same places that flexed whenever she and Sam had spoken of fairness, progress, justice.

"When do we start?"

"Now," Abiah said, holding up the bit of plant she'd examined in the shack, twisting the stem between her fingers. "This is woodbine. It's poisonous."

Chapter 36

"Commodore Bellamy?" came a tentative voice at the door of the captain's quarters.

It was Little King—the last person Sam wanted to face at a time like this, though even the boy had learned to ask fewer questions.

Sam lifted his gaze from the ship's log, his hand stained with ink that had dripped from the quill. He'd paused too long before putting the unretractable words to parchment.

One man killed in an accident aboard. A second man lost an arm. Another a broken leg. Others sustained minor injuries.

What followed next, the appropriate response to this strange incident, had yet to be determined. The Articles outlined the process for incidents in battle or blatant rule violations. But this?

Matter to be investigated.

As if the Windward Passage didn't pose enough risks, the fierce currents on one hand and the navy on the other making their way south for the winter like droves of geese. Sam's crew, on full alert during the day, had no time for this internal threat. Or, maybe too much time. They couldn't raid under these conditions.

What he should have written in the log instead: *Since double-crossing Jennings nine months earlier, I haven't faced such a dilemma.*

"We're ready for you," said Little King.

Sam straightened his black coat and followed King in silence, exchanging a nod with Williams, who was waiting outside. Sam's pistols jostled as he walked. Harsh lighting from the unobstructed sun illuminated everyone's faces. The entire crew had gathered near the mainmast: shoulders sagging; red-rimmed eyes, blood-shot and swollen. They still smelled of alcohol. Four suspects stared at the deck, wrists clapped in irons since the night before.

The night before. Was it the alcohol? The late hour? Pent-up restlessness from the tedious boredom? Residual nerves from be-ing constantly pursued, phantoms shimmering on the horizon: a warship flying the Union Jack, or the shape of Jennings's *Bersheba* coming for revenge?

An omen?

"We'll vote on the next course of action," Sam said, his fore-head throbbing. "But first, we need an honest accounting of what happened."

John Brown's eyes flicked up from his irons, his eyes as shiny as the silver buckles on his shoes.

Remorse. Unmistakable remorse.

"Might I begin? That is, since the skit was my idea. A fine ini-tial idea, don't get me wrong. Or at least it sounded like one—"

"Get on with it," Hendrick Quintor shouted. "Words won't bring a good man back from the abyss."

"Or our Alexander back his right arm," Julian added.

Sam looked around. He'd barely known the man who'd lost his life, a French-speaking sailor. An ache festered in Sam's chest: Had he known him better, he might have somewhere to attach his swirling emotions. The growing crew and responsibilities made life as a leader altogether different. Alexander was below deck, his bloody stump of a limb being tended to by Dr. Ferguson. According to the Articles, he'd receive six hundred pieces of eight for his lost limb. Sam flexed his fingers, just to feel the reassuring response of muscle.

"Fine," John Brown said with a huff. Then he began while Sam and the others listened to his and the rest of the testimonies.

They'd been too long at sea without a victory. The men, bored and sea-weary, sought entertainment. New entertainment. Brown, with a talent for minding the literal lines, as well as verbal ones, suggested they perform a skit: a one-act play about the hero, an everyman pirate character—witty, dandyish, and brave—being captured by none other than Alexander the Great. *The Royal Pirate*, Brown had called the drama. A large group agreed to the plan, recruiting a towering, blond-haired sailor named Alexander to take on the role of the namesake villain. They'd built a small stage and sacrificed sleep hours to make it happen. But at the height of the act, when the pirate hero was condemned to be hanged, someone lobbed a grenade. With a shriek, it exploded onstage, smoke choking out the dim room.

It was a gunner. The gunner had stumbled in after working the middle watch, horrified by what he saw. "I didn't know it was a performance," he said. He rushed the stage to save the fellow pirate, his good friend, from the evil Alexander as he yelled out the death sentence. The audience, shocked and provoked by the explosive attack, flew into frenzied action. Cutlasses clanked and cries erupted until Sam roared for the chaos to stop. The sulfuric haze cleared. A few whimpered or shrieked as they clutched their wounds. Blood smeared the floorboards, the iron tang in the air.

"A misunderstanding?" Sam said at the end of the accounts. "We are to believe a misunderstanding is what led to a dead brother, Alexander's lost arm, and our pirate hero's broken leg? I was there. Adequate actors you all may be, but you'll tell me the drama was *that* convincing to you?"

The gunner in chains lowered his chin. "It seemed too real to be an act."

Sam sighed. It was almost humorous. Should he trust this confession?

Of course. He had to. It was impossible to see a man's true intentions. But these were his friends, his faithful crew who shared his goal and vision. They were his country and countrymen of choice. He hadn't had to use the irons until now. He feared the worst was yet to come. A broken limb was one thing. But a lost life? A ruined arm? There must be consequences.

"Who severed Alexander's arm?"

"The dead Frenchman."

"Aye, it was," came a chorus of witnesses.

"I saw it, too."

That made things simpler. Slightly, especially if Alexander had acted in self-defense. Williams offered him an encouraging look. Sam exhaled. The irony of events was not lost on him: rulers of the sea they sometimes pretended to be, and often *knew* themselves to be—the dark ocean waving them on, the wind at their back, their reputation brewing fear in the minds of cruel captains and cowardly leaders. But the corrupt governments, the Alexander the Greats of the mind, lurked in every shadow. The pirate heroes? They remained nameless. How might the skit have ended, if allowed to play out? Sam wanted and also didn't want to know the true written ending of *The Royal Pirate*. The acting might not have seemed as "real" to Sam as it had to the gunner, but the feeling? That was real enough. The realest thing Sam knew, a deep undercurrent in his soul beyond language—that he'd never felt safe in this world. Not then, and certainly not now.

Life was only one act, one easily spent. Who'd ever promised safety? Better to focus on the immediate task: a rent sail, a tangled line, a day's ledger. Better to raise a blade against an enemy and a cup with brother sailors. To live the day, gold rings flashing in the sun, with only a vague sense for tomorrow. Nothing guaranteed a tomorrow. It never had and it never would again. Maria had taught him that much.

Had he known that ending, could he have savored their moments more? Done anything differently?

What nonsense, Sam thought, interrupting his fruitless musings. *It was just a play. You've got the loyalest crew in the West Indies. A hold growing full of treasure. A name that makes governors shake in their boots. The best is yet to come.*

"All in favor of releasing these men of charges?" Sam asked, voice hardened into confidence. "For a man acting in the service of a friend?"

Clusters of hands rose, followed by a few stragglers.

"That's a majority," Hoof said.

Sam exhaled. "Remove their irons. Everyone, return to work." Brown leaped to the task, and people shuffled back to resume the watch.

"Bellamy," Williams said, gesturing for him to look behind. "Davis still seems eager to befriend you."

In the background, Sam made out the hunched figure of Thomas Davis, their captive. He'd paused in his sawing, ice eyes narrowed on Sam with condemnation, maybe a promise. He shook his head, and Sam might as well have read his mind, the word enunciated with disgust:

Pirates.

CHAPTER 37

Maria tied her hair up and away from her neck. Sweat trickled down her scalp, which she wiped away while balancing a woven basket on her hip—a large reed basket she had woven herself.

"Not much longer," Abiah said, who gathered milkweed pods alongside Maria in the golden summer light. They worked in the forest, among the buzzing gnats, mostly in silence. Abiah used everything they collected for her healing practice or to sell at the docks to raise money for the cause. Though the pods could be eaten earlier in the summer as a vegetable, they could fetch a nice profit from colonists by selling the feathery interior of these seeds, which provided better insulation than goose feathers. Maria had already improved her sleeping quarters immensely by adding a silky-soft cushion against the ground. When Maria wasn't busy interpreting documents for Abiah or describing Mr. Hallett's habits and weaknesses, Abiah had also shown her how to use cattails and bulrush to create reed mats. Even for someone with Abiah's skills, it took two weeks to make a single cattail mat. Maria layered these on the outside of her shack to resist rain. Bulrush mats were even more effort. These required boiling, to remove the sap, which left them absorbent to fog, humidity, and dampness. Maria placed the bulrush mats inside her shack, like wallpaper, to provide insulation. Abiah also showed her how to use them to line food storage pits to keep out moisture. Maria marveled at the way each type of mat worked to keep the house warm or cool depending on the season.

"I can work until nightfall," Maria said, reaching for another pod. She'd never shunned hard work, and she welcomed it even more now. It gave her purpose. Digging a cellar with the metal hoe Abiah had brought her, making additions to the shack, or preserving food for the winter—it didn't matter what. Something to keep thoughts far away from the tragedies of her recent past and blinding losses. Something to distract her from the passing months with no sign or word from Sam, or anyone else. Through daily gathering—sometimes with Abiah, but mostly alone—they got one step closer to raising the funds for a loom. Any work Maria could do for Abiah meant more time for Abiah to devote to local politics, persuading voters to protect the common lands and to see this fight as beneficial and necessary to everyone in Eastham.

Abiah paused, examining the stems of a shrub covered in bright blue berries.

"Arrowwood," Abiah said. She snapped a few stems. "They make good shafts for hunting."

Maria snorted. "I'll be sticking with snares for a while."

"If you say so," Abiah teased. She pocketed the stems, then rolled her shoulders to let out the tension, breathing deeply. "Today I'll teach you how to make nocake by parching dried corn kernels. Nocake flour is delicious and filling on its own—our men used to carry it in pouches around their waists when they hunted or traveled. We also use it to thicken stew. But tonight, I'll show you how to turn the nocake into bread."

Maria salivated at the memory of fresh bread. She nodded, busy with her collecting.

"Do you know what this plant does?"

Maria stopped, craning her head to look.

The corner of Abiah's lip tugged up. "Your kind might not. This is meadow rue." She held up a white-prickled blossom that resembled a sea urchin. "It makes one burn for sex."

Maria flushed, despite herself. She didn't want to think, let alone talk, about Sam. But Abiah's silence on the subject of his return also made Maria anxious.

"Who taught you all this?" Maria asked, diverting the conversation. She'd lately thought of her own mother, who'd done small-scale gathering of herbs for her midwifery practice. But Abiah's knowledge of plants far surpassed that of any midwife or doctor Maria knew. Abiah had no children of her own. She served her people as a great healer—another calling, another demand on Abiah's limited time.

Did Mama regret what the town did to me? Does she know where I went, that I'm alive at all?

"My people have long understood the way Creator made the Earth to work," Abiah said. "But I'm called to it. We've thrived here for thousands of years, until now."

An emptiness filled Maria's chest, tightening with grief, the chasm of loss always a knife's flick below the surface. "I'm sorry." How small it sounded aloud, translated into language.

Abiah shook her away with a wave of the meadow rue. Though Abiah had been cautious in sharing personal details about her life, for reasons Maria thought she could appreciate under the circumstances—Maria was a liability to everyone these days—another question tumbled out. "Does your husband mind?" Maria asked. "You coming out here?"

Abiah laughed, re-tucking a strand of dark hair into her thick braid. "Though I am married, marriage means something different to your people and mine—something less restrictive. Take Weetumuw, for example. Her father was the Sachem, a chief among the Pocasset Wampanoag—a title she inherited after her father's death. She married five times. The first died abruptly. She spoke less about the second and third men, save for the child born to the second. The fourth husband she divorced when he took the white men's side during King Philip's War. And the fifth was a son of Ninigret Sachem from the Niantic Narragansett. They had a child together, too."

Maria's eyes widened with wonder. Women could serve as leaders of a civilization? She bit back the urge to wonder when she might tell Sam. "Does she live nearby?"

A shadow crossed over Abiah's face. "As Sachem, Weetumuw led three hundred men in the war against the invaders. But she drowned in the Taunton River, trying to escape the English after they defeated the Wampanoag forty years ago. We learned through the moccasin telegraph that white men displayed her head on a pole outside of Taunton."

Maria grimaced as Abiah went on. "My husband, since you asked, is a Punonakanit. I'm from the neighboring Nauset tribe. He's a Praying Indian, and a genuine convert to the Christian church. I go to the services, as many in the Wampanoag nation do, because it is how we can survive after the war. Reverend Treat learned the Algonquian language to deliver sermons. The more we speak and act like the invaders, the better chance we have of surviving. To do otherwise, to even wear the traditional dress of my people, invites dire consequences." She paused. "They fear what they do not understand."

Maria closed the lid to her basket. She'd not suffered the way Abiah and her people had; she understood how her community had viewed the Wampanoag. "Different" was an understatement; their words were crueler, condescending, inhuman. Eastham not only feared what it didn't understand, it attacked it—aimed to stamp it out.

Maria had always been different, a restless child and then an outspoken woman. Her "whisperings," her headstrong impulses to follow her heart instead of her head—at least the logic instilled in her from the community that had abandoned her—landed her here in the wilderness.

But to deem her a witch? She'd never recover from the absurdity, though she wished the shock would wear off by now. So much for Sam saying her intuition was a gift.

Abiah tucked the meadow rue into a pouch at her side, then straightened. "Let's return."

* * *

The sky had a greenish tinge with stars emerging out of the fading fog of daylight. The beauty seized Maria in the chest, a sight she'd come to anticipate with awe. They hiked to Maria's humble fishing shack to prepare the nocake. Abiah unpacked her supplies while Maria lit the fire, which sparked and crackled as it caught a taste of the pine kindling. Mosquitos fled from the heat. Whenever the walls grew warm, Maria swore she could smell the last fishy traces of whale blubber.

Abiah came for supper once or twice per month with documents in hand, but never for long. In the evenings, afternoons—and all hours, really—Abiah worked tirelessly to prevent any more loss of Wampanoag lands in addition to her services as a healer. Yet Maria always felt grateful when she did come for a meal, punctuating the dark, lonely nights with something to look forward to, a new skill to learn and hone, a political discussion where Maria might prove useful with her abilities and experience. Otherwise, Maria retired early, trying to minimize the amount of time spent awake, thinking, before dawn. She found that swimming and working long and hard during the day exhausted her by dusk, allowing her the mercy of a deeper sleep.

"I've pondered something you said earlier this summer," Abiah said, removing dried ears of flint corn from a basket. The basket still smelled of bearberry leaves and tobacco mixtures that Abiah once told Maria aided with inflammation, painful urination, and kidney stones. Maria watched step-by-step as Abiah cut the kernels away from the cob over a dry pan. Abiah continued: "You said that your efforts to keep you and your child safe backfired. You implied you may have been better off, or at least not banished, had you refused Hallett and somehow managed another way." She shook her head. "Today, I told you of Weetumuw."

"Yes," Maria said. How could she forget?

Abiah parched the kernels by stirring them over the budding fire. She gestured for Maria to follow her lead, and together they worked. After ten minutes, the corn swelled, browned, then split.

"Most people from the villages on the Cape chose not to join King Philip's War. White men continued to settle on our lands and bring disease, enforce Christianity, and pass laws that controlled every aspect of our lives. Resources became scarce. Our people declined in numbers while the number of white men increased. We lost our corn gardens, clam beds, and more. We tried to stop the invaders early on through petitions and laws to have the English fence in their animals. White men turned the soil to sand by letting cows, goats, and sheep roam wild, tearing life out by the roots."

Abiah poured the corn into the mortar, a hollowed-out log resting on the floor. A rich flavor hung in the air. "I am no longer sure the safest path is the safest path in the end. Not for me. Not for you. Not for anyone."

Maria examined Abiah's steady expression as she crushed the kernels into a flour. Then Abiah passed the pestle to Maria. "Do you have regrets?" Abiah asked. "Would you do anything differently, knowing what you know now?"

The question hit Maria like a thirty-foot wave crashing at her back. She remembered her parting words to Elizabeth, everything she wished she could have expressed instead of the words to inspire anger. For a moment, Maria lost her mental footing, her sense of up and down. Did she have regrets?

No.

No? Still? That couldn't be right.

It wasn't right.

I'd have ignored Sam's first invitation to meet him for a swim lesson. Never. Try again.

I'd have left with Sam when he invited me along.

I'd have run away when I first learned I was pregnant.

I'd have assumed Sam might not return.

I'd stop hoping for change.

I'd never be restless. I'd never be discontent: doing my chores with my head down, praying without questions, staying safe within the lines of propriety.

So what? I wouldn't be me at all?

Her eyes welled with tears, which she blinked away. A sudden tenderness swelled from her core. She used to cry without reason or warning. Elizabeth always teased her, and Mama always criticized her for it. Now, after everything, Maria rarely wept since that jail cell five months earlier, from the welts and throb of her heart. Maybe without someone shaming her she hadn't noticed so much. Mostly, though, she'd avoided staring down moments like this, questions like this, at all costs. Because somehow, underneath it all—despite the shattering loneliness—Maria couldn't imagine continuing her life as it had been. Hadn't the past months exposed the worst of the small-minded society in Eastham, alongside lessons about herself? The thought of an existence where she had not met Sam, or carried their child, made a deep voice in her revolt.

Here, there's no reason to hide my daily swims in the impossibly big ocean.

There's no one to tell me that I'm wrong.

No one here to put at risk over my differences.

Here, no one beats me or preaches about what is and isn't sin.

Or sighs with disappointment at what I say or don't say.

There's no one to tell me who I can and cannot love.

There are no rules outside of nature and my own conscience at all.

"I'd be wiser the second time around. There's no question about that," Maria said at last, a strength in her tone. She'd rather feel lonely here, gathering other emotions much as she gathered fragrant herbs from the meadow, than lonely in prison or in Mr. Hallett's dreadful home. "But . . . strange as it sounds to say, I'm better off in some ways. Almost none of the obvious ones." She gestured around the shack: the hooks on the wall, the nest of bedding, the room where she wished Sam or Elizabeth stood. "The fear is different. The fear doesn't live inside me like it used to." She placed a hand to her chest and shook her head. "I used to make choices by trying to walk two paths at once, wanting everything for myself while also trying to appease others—just enough.

I failed myself and everyone else for wanting different things. As a result, I've lost everything I feared I would, then somehow, I survived. I . . . didn't know I could. Now when the sun rises over the dune cliffs in the peaceful mornings, or when I see sprouts breaking ground in my vegetable garden, I don't long to return like I did when I first came to Billingsgate. Though there are many people I'll miss forever, and grief still weighs on me, I can't imagine myself fitting in there anymore."

Abiah paused to add water to the nocake mixture to form a bread dough. She kneaded in fresh raspberries and sunflower seeds.

"And you?" Maria asked. "Would you do anything differently?"

Abiah's eyes blazed. "Had I been born yet—knowing what I know, seeing the beach blow in gales against the barren land, watching our whole way of life slip away in a way that must make the ancestors lament, I might have thrown my trust in with Weetumuw. I'd do everything I could to ward off this slow death of our rightful place, our traditions, our homeland."

They completed the nocake by boiling the dough into small dumplings, then shared the meal in the glowing light of the fire. The nutty flavors filled Maria's belly, the nutritious bread sticking to her ribs. When they finished, Abiah shouldered one basket of the milkweed pods, then hefted Maria's. She'd sell the load at the docks tomorrow.

"I'll leave those with you," Abiah said, gesturing toward an impressive stack of letters and papers she'd left in the corner. "My elders want to better understand the internal frictions of the invaders, the arguments stated and those avoided in their slippery words. We hope to make use of the conflicts amongst themselves and their own private interests to convince more to oppose the land divisions."

Maria nodded. For a moment, she missed Elizabeth fiercely, imagining what her sister would think of her newfound stamina for reading. "I'll study them before your next visit."

As Abiah made to leave, another enormous question bubbled up.

"Do you believe real, meaningful change is possible?" Maria asked. "Still?"

Abiah considered the question, her eyes reflecting the fire embers. "Only the Creator knows, but my actions speak for my hopes. Sometimes nature shows the way."

CHAPTER 38

"Come see this, Bellamy," Julian shouted.

Sam flew down the deck, where clusters of men clambered near the rail and took turns looking through a spyglass. The boatswain whistled to remind everyone on active duty to keep minding the lines. Someone knocked off Hoof's enormous hat for obstructing the view. Everyone squinted at the speck of sails on the starboard side of the *Marianne*.

"It's a galley," Hendrick Quintor said, fingers tracing the gold bead on his necklace. "It's gotta be. Look at the long hull and square rigging of the three masts. That ship must weigh at least three hundred tons."

Williams leaned as far as he could for a glimpse, bushy eyebrows raised. His pupils grew with delight. "If it is a galley, as you say, and *if* we have any chance of outrunning the navy—to say nothing of our dear friend Jennings—that'll be our saving grace, aye?"

"If we could catch it," said John Brown. "Phew. A galley! A gorgeous, galloping galley . . ." He continued improvising the poem, sprinkling in as many g-words as possible.

"If we could *catch* it?" someone scoffed. "You mean if we win a raid with it! That there would be loaded with cannons."

"I counted sixteen."

"No, eighteen!"

Julian rubbed his thumb along his chin. "Something seems off. This 'galloping' galley doesn't seem to be doing much galloping. Shouldn't it track faster?"

Unless something is weighing it down.

All eyes locked on Sam. The entire crew fore-and-aft seemed to hold their breath. A salty breeze blew across his wind-chapped face. They didn't call this the Windward Passage for nothing.

Sam shivered to remember the failed fight with the man-of-war months earlier. Dixon's warm blood on his hands. The jarring reaction of the men. The rise in their confidence in him, all while more deeply questioning his own. They'd already collected a few sloops to add to their flotilla.

But imagine what they could do with a galley . . .

"Brothers," Sam said, fingers gripping the rail, a lock of dark hair falling into his face. His voice boomed above the standstill. His eyes narrowed to slits. "Make chase."

It was a galley all right, riding low in the water. With every hand on deck, breaking the fastest speeds their fleet could summon, Sam's flotilla closed in on the prey after a three-day pursuit. Inching closer to cannon range, Sam told Little King to replace their flag with the black Jolly Roger, then sent him below deck.

"But I want to fight!" Little King said, lip pouting as he unsheathed his knife.

"Captain's orders," Sam said, pointing to the steps. "You guard the stores." *Out of sight, protected.* He snapped his attention on the rest of his men: armed with raiding pikes, grenades, and glinting cutlasses. Just in case. Williams brandished his thin rapier with an audible zing, ready to lead the boarding party in his duty as quartermaster.

Five men apiece squatted around each gun carriage, preparing for battle: swabbing the cannon muzzle, packing the chamber with acrid gunpowder, rolling down the round shot, followed by the priming and lead apron cover in anticipation. One man crouched, fiddling with the quoin to adjust the angle.

Sam touched the four pistols in his stash for reassurance, then adjusted his old tricorn.

Maria.

A pang of longing. Why did he think of her? At a time like now?

At a time where he knew he risked death, as he did every time he claimed another ship?

He blinked away the intrusion.

"Gunners," Sam said as they reached the height of a downward wave, "fire a warning over the bow."

A roar cracked from their six-pounder gun, flying two hundred yards and crashing into the ocean on the other side of the galley with an enormous splash.

Sam's skin prickled in the haunting silence that followed. The sulfur made his nostrils flare. The galley did little more than fire two chase guns, wildly off target, in defense.

"Again," Sam ordered, his pulse spiking. A tendon throbbed along his neck. Anticipation flooding his veins.

Please don't fight back, Sam thought. *Not for the sake of king and country.* Any wise man aboard a ship in these waters knew avoiding a fight meant a merciful reception. The vast majority of Sam's victories, after all this time, had amounted to nothing more than an inconvenient transaction.

"Look there!" came a voice from Sam's right.

With enormous relief, the entire crew watched as the galley lowered its Union Jack colors, then the sails—a signal of total and complete surrender.

But the swift victory was no match for the terrible shock the seafarers discovered aboard the galley.

Sam put one boot down, then the other on the captured deck. His blood turned to ice.

Nets around the rail to prevent anyone from falling, or leaping, overboard. The emptied platform atop the pilot's cabin for additional space. A forecastle above the bow to sequester privileged crew. The defeated sailors—all white men, shrunken away into various corners—slimmed down to the essential rigging party, outnumbered against a band of pirates.

"A slave ship," Quintor said, spitting with disgust.

No one else dared to speak. Williams, rapier still in hand, waited for some kind of direction. "Search the hold for prisoners," Sam said with urgency, waiting for the captain to show himself. Julian and John Brown jumped into action.

A slave ship. The epitome of everything Sam's flotilla stood against. His soul shivered with revulsion. He'd never been aboard such a vessel, but he'd heard of the horrors: a death sentence for women, children, and men—bound by neck or hands yanked behind their back after being separated from their families, then stuffed into torturously cramped spaces as cargo; the stench of every body fluid imaginable as pressed, sick people wailed and screamed through the day and gruesome night while one in five perished at sea; innocents kidnapped, sold, and trafficked against their will after imprisonment in unthinkably small dungeons of colonial fortresses, the stone floors scarred with the clawing of shackles. Hell paled in comparison to those conditions. His men and others told Sam as much, especially the two dozen whom the rescued pirates had freed from a Guinea slaver just before Sam's company had intercepted them from the clutch of the British Navy. One freed man reported that he'd witnessed eighteen people, shackled together, choose suicide overboard rather than endure the unthinkable passage across the Atlantic.

Nothing good could come from being near such a cursed ship. Sam opened his mouth to speak, but no words came out. Then, the elderly galley captain emerged. He wore a brass-buttoned coat and a subdued scowl etched into a line across his weathered face. Anger, frustration, but not fear. This one knew the drill. A businessman, if such a man dealing in the business of slavery could be called one. What choices had he made, and not made, to get to where he stood? He had nothing to prove in fighting the band of pirates.

"Captain Prince," the leader said, introducing himself. The curls of his wig jostled. "We make for London. This *was* our maiden voyage . . ." he snarled. "In exchange for quick surrender, I request the best treatment your kind can manage. We will not resist."

Williams sheathed his rapier, and the other men lowered their weapons. Sam stared hard at Captain Prince. Though custom dictated the man and his sailors deserved mercy—a point of honor Sam would respect as he always had—Sam didn't believe Prince deserved that much. Not if his suspicions were true.

"No enslaved people above or below deck, Bellamy," Julian said, returning at a sprint. "But you should see what is . . ."

Captain Prince snorted.

"Anchor all ships," Sam said, thoughts churning with more violence than waves against a rocky shore.

Sam's crew stood in an enormous semicircle along the snatch of beach. His mind fluttered to that pivotal scene so long ago, on a beach not unlike this in Florida. Thirty men. That's how many he'd convinced to go on the account, so sure himself that he'd be able to extricate himself and be home to Maria in six months.

Now, a year later, how wrong he had been. About so many things he'd once thought so simple.

He pressed his eyes shut. Opened them again in the burning afternoon sun.

Now he faced a motley crew of almost two hundred men. Williams, Julian, Abell, and Webb from the original crew. Then Hoof, John Brown, Hendrick Quintor, Dr. Ferguson, and others. Little King sat there in the front row, using his finger to trace shapes in the sand.

And behind him loomed the galley, a vessel that Captain Prince called the *Whydah*. An enormous ship loaded down with the profits from the abominable slave trade. It had more treasure in its hold than Sam or anyone in his flotilla had ever beheld.

Sam caught Julian's eye, who lowered his chin with a subtle nod.

"Shipmates," Sam began. "We have an important decision to make, as a band of brother sailors."

He gestured at the ship.

"We've learned this galley, the *Whydah*, is named after the slave port Ouidah. This brand-new galley sailed from London to the Gold Coast to traffic four hundred people, enslaved and bound in chains. Eighty-eight died under the brutal conditions, and the remaining three hundred twelve, Prince says, were sold to sugar plantations in Jamaica." Sam swallowed, remembering Jennings's bragging about his plantation operations in Jamaica and Bermuda. He imagined the smoldering heat, the bite of a whip, the victims collapsed in the cane fields because of Jennings's food rations that bordered on starvation. "We intercepted the *Whydah* on her return to London, where the rich planned to pocket the profits, completing the cycle. It is a voyage we will never allow the *Whydah* to make again."

Embittered cheers rang out from the crowd, the loudest among the men who'd been sprung from the Guinea slaver.

"I'm tempted to send such a ship to the bottom of the ocean, for what amount of cleansing can erase such evil?" Sam said, pausing. "That is where we need your vote. Surely you've considered the benefits a three-hundred-ton galley might provide our flotilla. Another consideration to add: The *Whydah* contains more loot than we can possibly transfer to our current vessels. If it hadn't been weighed down, we might not have been able to catch the galley, which Captain Prince says can reach up to thirteen knots."

Jaws hung open at this staggering news, the men elbowing each other with renewed attention.

"Julian, will you share what you and John Brown saw below deck?"

Julian stepped forward, putting an abrupt end to the whispers.

"We haven't landed on an exact accounting of the money, but it's significant. In the hold of the *Whydah*, we estimate they carry thousands of British pounds. Hundreds of ivory tusks stacked like a pile of firewood. Valuable medical supplies like cinchona bark. Molasses and sugar and indigo and—"

"Akan gold," Quintor interjected.

"I saw a ruby the size of a chicken egg!" John Brown said.

The mounting excitement from the pirates drowned out Julian's and Brown's words. Williams raised a hand, pleading for silence. It took minutes to recover enough quiet to hear again.

"Profits from slavery," Sam said, clenching his teeth.

"Reclaimed for us! Sweet, divine justice for the oppressed."

"Aye, stolen from the tyrants. Back into freed slaves' pockets."

"Coin that could return some of us home when this is over," shouted one of the freed men. "Enough of this moral groveling. It disgusts me."

"An insult to God to send this gift to the deep. Our whole crew'll split the loot."

"We could weaponize the ship," said a man in a thick Irish accent. "Fight against the very practice that gave it foul birth."

They had a point, Sam thought, though he couldn't shake his unease. However, this was a shared decision to make.

"Hoof, will you give us a report of the ship itself?" Sam asked.

Hoof stepped forward to name the merits of a shallow-draft vessel with an ability to maneuver with sails and oars, no matter the weather. The *Whydah*, 102 feet in length, had an impressive caboose stove and space enough to expand the fleet. "She comes with the finest steering system available. With eighteen current cannons, we can make way for ten more," Hoof said. "Especially if we hack away the additions tacked on. We'll need the carpenter."

Thomas Davis. Sam tried to forget about him—and his promise to eventually free the poor bastard—though he knew the ice-eyed man stood somewhere in the crowd. Davis had been compliant and silent as the grave since his escape and recapture in Spanish Town. He deserved freedom, same as any of them.

After concluding the debate regarding the *Whydah*, they prepared to vote. Sam cleared his throat, speaking slow and loud enough for everyone to hear. "All in favor of taking what we can fit before setting flame to this vessel and seeing her charred and fed to the hunger of the sea?"

No hands rose, and Sam felt a sinking feeling in his gut. Was this a line he was willing to cross? Yet another point of no return? His own hand hung at his side.

A ship full of gold.

"Then all in favor of taking the plunder and purging the *Whydah* of its characteristics that marked its rotten history of slavery, reforging it to serve a new mission?"

The force of raised hands of every hue was enough to summon a storm.

No sooner had they boarded the *Whydah* than Sam gave orders to transform the galley: removing the platform above the pilot's cabin—where the enslaved souls must have been bound shoulder to shoulder under all manner of weather—tearing down the forecastle above the ship's bow for the sequestered leadership; ripping apart the quarterdeck and hacking off the lead sheathing of the hull to increase speed.

"Let me go," Davis said on deck, his Welsh voice as firm and clear as the bell announcing the change of watch. "Send me with Captain Prince in the dispensable ship you traded him. You swore you'd set me free."

Sam tensed, avoiding eye contact with Davis. He wanted to let the man go. Everyone knew it. Having a prisoner aboard against his will tugged at the mounting contradictions that swept through his mind when given a private moment, or when he imagined—as he still was foolishly prone to do—telling Maria all that had happened. A poisonous fantasy, both for the reminder of her and for the ways he struggled more and more to tell a coherent tale where he would come out a good man.

But it was also true that they needed an able shipwright to remake the *Whydah* their own: something beyond the typical mending of masts and yardarms. And Davis had proven more skilled in these matters than anyone else aboard.

"I'm sorry. I am. I'll make my wishes known again. But my word is bound to the will of the crew," Sam said simply, and they held another vote.

They called an immediate meeting. Sam made a case to release the carpenter. Davis, unfortunately, lashed out with the fire and brimstone of a pulpit-pounding preacher. The seafarers didn't take well to the judgments.

"No, *damn you*," someone spat.

"We'd rather whip ye to death at the mast before lettin' ye go."

They overturned Sam's futile position.

Davis would stay with the *Whydah*. Again.

Twilight settled on the horizon in a purple haze. Sam perched in a cherrywood chair in the captain's quarters, the door left ajar, with his spine stiff and rigid. He missed the familiarity of the *Marianne*—now in the possession of Paulsgrave Williams—and tried hard not to imagine what had transpired on the haunted decks of their new flagship under the command of the vile Captain Prince, who'd sat in this very chair. Shadows descended upon his mind. Sam studied the navigation coordinates while fiddling with a single piece of silver, a Royal Strike, that had been left on the table.

Did you know it has been a year, my darling? Over a year since I first dove in after you, that day at the docks? Over a year since our days of innocence?

Are you really, truly happy?

He exhaled. *Am I?*

"Voted commodore again," Julian said, taking the chair across from Sam. The chair legs scratched against the floor.

"Aye," Sam said, flinching slightly with surprise and glancing up at the incomer.

"Williams will make a fine captain of the *Marianne*."

Sam managed a smile. "Yes, he will." That vote had pleased him, though Sam would miss the constancy of Williams's buoyant presence as his quartermaster. Even if the *Marianne* never left the *Whydah*'s side.

Sam tried to spin the coin, which fell flat on the table. Julian picked it up.

"You know where these come from?" Julian asked, examining the cross-hatch markings. The scar along his eyebrow was clear and visible in the candlelight.

"Not really."

"Peru," Julian said with a faraway quality. "You can tell from the 'P' in the upper corner. Coins like this are made under some of the worst mining conditions you could imagine. They whispered of it at home in Nicaragua." He paused, turning over the silver in his palm. The reflection flittered in the lantern light. "The two columns here symbolize the pillars of the sea road flowing to the end of earth. And this here? The Latin *'plus ultra'* in the middle? In all, the message translates to something like: 'Across the Atlantic, past the Straits of Gibraltar, lies a New World which belongs to Spain.'"

Sam snorted.

"It's a brutal world, no matter where you go, Bellamy. We are all complicit in the cycle of it. No one is innocent. But at least we pirates own the ways we aren't."

Julian placed the Royal Strike down again, then stood with his palms against the table. He seemed to read Sam's ambivalence. But Sam caught the conviction in Julian's expression, his dark brows knitted together.

"We *are* building a new world, Bellamy," Julian said. "Not just an alternative to the oppressive system out there"—he waved— "but something in here." He jabbed a finger into Sam's chest. "It's something you've known since that day we voted to go on the account back in Florida. The men know it now, too." He paused. "We'll become the richest, most influential pirates that history has ever known—especially with a fast galley mounting twenty-eight cannons. We'll be a force to reckon with, a force they can't ignore."

CHAPTER 39

Maria paused in preparing her fresh-caught fish, iridescent scales sticking to her hands, as she caught the sound of heavy steps outside the shack. Her ears pricked.

The movement outside stopped. Maria wiped her palms on a rag, but didn't drop the fillet knife.

Abiah didn't sound like that, and she'd said she wouldn't visit again until the new moon.

It also wasn't the sound of the children, the ones who lived in the Billingsgate hamlet a few miles out. Since Maria had moved into her fishing shack six months ago, sometimes the children took to racing through the nearby forest shouting counter-prayers before crossing "Goody Hallett's Meadow" without harm. She admired their courage, recalling her own days of wicked innocence. Sometimes it took all of Maria's energy to not rush out and greet them, smothering them in hugs like she might for little Mercy. But what good would it do? For them and for her, to hear them cry "witch" and scatter as if she had the plague? But with the onset of harvest and the rise of autumn, even those voices had stopped weaving through the spindly tree branches.

If anyone else meant to hurt her, they'd have come well before now. Maria had stopped waiting in the dead of night for that.

A twig snapped, and Maria's heart raced.

Sam?

With a bolt of hope, she tiptoed to the door and peered through a large crack.

All she saw was brown fur.

Maria froze, listening to the heavy breathing of the enormous beast a few inches away. It stepped, and an antler scraped the upper wall.

A moose.

A moose!?

Maria had waited all her life to see one in the wild. If only she could tell Elizabeth. And now, finding one, she didn't know what to do.

Or did she?

Pulse galloping with a mix of awe and terror, Maria squinted through the slats. This time, she saw it was not a moose, but a stag, occupied with the piles of chokecherries she'd been drying in the sun to prepare more winter stores. It looked skinny and frail, maybe old, and the beast struggled to put weight on one leg.

A stag. Here at her doorstep.

Injured animals could be vicious, that much Maria knew. She wanted to stare with prickled fear, maybe flee. She wanted to witness and marvel at its beauty. Its huge chest close enough to touch.

Instead, she silently reached to her left for an arrowwood spear she'd modeled after Abiah's, the one with a sharpened-shale dagger affixed to the tip to practice hunting ducks and turkeys. Her fingers slowly wrapped around the shaft.

Aim for the heart?

No, too risky. Too small and protected. She was dead if she missed.

She angled for the lungs, her mouth suddenly dry.

One . . . two . . .

She plunged the spear with all her might through the slats. With a kick and horrible bellow from the stag, the wooden door shattered. The splinters smashed against her arms, shooting pain through her skin as the shaft tore through her grip. Rather than charging, the stag bolted, and Maria cowered behind the remains of the door until the sound of hooves and snorting grew distant.

After a few minutes passed, Maria stood to assess her injuries. Welts and cuts, but nothing broken. She grasped her fillet knife with trembling fingers and left to track her kill before something else did.

She found the old stag in a clearing with its knees buckled, spear lodged in its side, and crooked ankle on full display. How many days might this creature have lasted with a fetlock joint like that? Not many, Maria tried to console herself, though as a survivor she'd learned the bittersweet victory of a single day.

Her eyes misted, but she gripped her knife tighter.

This was never how it was supposed to be. Never how I imagined it.

Blood frothed from the stag's mouth as she approached with caution. It had collapsed onto its side, heaving with gale-force rasps.

Yet, here I am.

Here I am still.

A tear trailed down Maria's cheek, but still she crept forward, knife raised. She'd seen Papa's stable lad do it once. To a mare with a broken leg. Maria closed her eyes, then forced them open, slicing with the knife to end the stag's pain.

Maria didn't move for minutes. The silence circled, and the smell of blood filled the air. Then she stood, stumbling backward. Her spine rested against a tree, the stag carcass before her. She dropped the knife. She dropped to her knees, praying. Not the way Abiah did after a kill, nor the way Maria used to do at church. She prayed in the shape of the God she both knew and didn't have to know. For the stag, for herself—the cost of it all. For she would live to see another spring. The thought scared her almost as much as it offered reassurance.

When Abiah came again, Maria's stomach knotted with anticipation. Due to the weight of the stag, Maria had needed to skin the beast where it fell. But the pelt now stretched over a frame near the shack's outdoor fire. She would use the tanned hide for an insulated door and warm bedding. The antlers she'd set aside as a gift for Abiah, alongside seven baskets filled with her latest foraging finds: mostly mushrooms and medicinal herbs. Items to sell at the docks.

"You speared a stag?" Abiah asked, eyes wide as she surveyed the pelt. Little surprised Abiah, and Maria appreciated watching the shock cross her expression.

"I did," Maria said, savoring every moment of this exchange.

"You speared a stag before you were able to spear a small doe?" Abiah laughed, holding her sides for a full-body, melodic laugh. "You have gotten stronger."

The sound of her laugh warmed Maria straight through.

"I've got the bruises to prove it," Maria said with her chin raised, rolling up her sleeve to show a rainbow of scrapes and spots ranging from purple to green. Maria's chest swelled with pride as she recounted the story: the hunt as well as the long, laborious field dressing, which was nothing like preparing a goat or lamb. Maria had taken care to not puncture the intestines or the organs—as Abiah had modeled during the summer—to not spoil the meat. Her muscles ached from her many trips to bring the whole animal home. It was easier to tell everything as a story, as something that had already happened and not the fraught experience it had really been.

They shared their lunch outdoors in the mild afternoon sunshine, gulls calling as they rode the ocean breeze. Maria had prepared a venison stew, and Abiah brought some nocake flour she'd carried in her pack. After discussing how to use all parts of the stag and storing the meat away from coyotes, they moved on to other matters. Their thoughts turned to the latest political debates as they ate, the light mood dissipating.

"We've lost Great Island," Abiah said, jaw clenched. "Justice Doane, whom you will remember well from your time in prison, oversaw the division and sale of those common lands. Now, they'll

charge my people fees if they are caught anywhere on shore."
She glowered. "Private parcels were given to one hundred thirty-
five white men. I am organizing another petition to fight the plot
boundaries and restrictions, but the new inhabitants already felled
the pitch pines and oak to build boats and homes, plus the wood
fuel to heat them. The topsoil is gone, dry and dark as gunpowder.
Great Island has become a massive dune, the yellow sand blowing
into the bay. It could threaten the oyster beds." Abiah exhaled,
shaking her head. "How we got here is unthinkable. The Wampanoag do not believe in the selling of land. We told the First Comers
as much. They asked who owned Billingsgate. What a question.
The Nauset sachem said no one owned it. The English didn't understand. They then approached the Punonakanits sachem, who
struck a murky arrangement, agreeing the English could live on
the land south of the Sapokonisk stream. Now the supposed 'Pur-
chasers' not only try and dictate where we should live, but call us
'foreigners,' charging us fines if we walk on our own shores, among
the creatures, plants, and earth that have always sustained us."

Maria considered her savory stew, made with cuts of meat from
a creature she'd destroyed for her own benefit. Her shoulders
tensed. Sam had been right about the injustices of the world. He'd
also been right about her limited views. Maria *had* been sheltered.
Too sheltered. Shielded from the awful knowing that any of this
was happening all around her, that her own way of living had such
consequences. "Is there anything more I can do?"

"I'll ask for your thoughts before completing my next petition—
a response to Hallett's latest remarks in favor of the divisions."

Maria set aside her bowl. The name "Hallett" shot through her
mind. Land hadn't been the only thing men like him saw as property.

"Just continue the work you are doing," Abiah said, the unspoken between them clear: Beyond gathering goods, reading and
analyzing documents, or sharing scattered insights—as helpful as
those were to Abiah—there was little else Maria could do without
compromising the plans. Maria couldn't be associated with the pe-

titions. "Now, I turn my attention to Tuttomnest—our last main holdout. That area was never shared with the English, and not even they can argue otherwise. The whalers and fisherman who visit the harbor share our concerns also. No one benefits from the mass destruction of the land in the name of individual interests."

Abiah rose to her feet and smoothed out her dress. Maria hated to see her leave. She always hated this part.

"Any other gossip from the docks?" Maria asked.

Abiah's brow furrowed. "There is no news of Samuel Bellamy."

Maria looked away. It was the first she'd heard his name spoken aloud in months. To her own astonishment, the sting came, then went, as swift as it had come on—more a stab than a constant ache. In truth, she hadn't thought of him as often, not even in anger, and she didn't know what to make of that change. She brushed it aside. Besides, no news might be better than bad news. She wanted to believe this. She needed something to believe.

"It will be a long winter," Abiah said, gently changing the subject. "Already the days grow short. You'll need to finish readying your home." They'd already reviewed the changes Maria had been making, including the need for more bulrush mats to layer the floor and hold the heat of the cooking fire.

"There'll be little to find in the meadow when the frosts settle," Maria said. "I'll forage the beach, though I won't be able to withstand the water temperatures for long. What can you sell from me?"

"I have something else in mind," Abiah said. "Follow me."

Anchored near the shore was a rowboat. Inside lay pieces of a spinning wheel. Bags of wool and linen flax.

"Nails for the loom, too," Abiah said from behind. "We'll keep you busy through the cold months. And make a good shilling."

Maria whirled with joy, hands clamped to her mouth. "Abiah. I . . . Thank you. How can I begin to thank—"

"You will need to build another addition to your shelter," Abiah said evenly. "It will require daub and wattle."

This was the colonists' way of constructing buildings, Maria knew. "Could I not make an addition like a wetu, the homes of your people?"

Abiah laughed louder than Maria had ever heard her, even louder than when Maria had asked if anyone could weave a bulrush rug in a single week. "I assure you that making a wetu—a knowledge that remains with our people—is too complex for you to build, let alone during this season." Wetus, Abiah explained, were built around a frame of cedar sapling poles harvested during the spring when sap rises, making them easy to bend to form the dome shape. "This would be impossible so late in the year."

"I see," Maria said, tapping a finger against her chin. Though she could make daub using mud and some kind of straw, she didn't know what to do from there. She'd never been invited to learn construction skills as a wealthy girl growing up in Eastham. "Do you know what I might use to make the wattle?"

"Gather thin, flexible branches to weave a lattice around sturdier, horizontal pieces." They both agreed that repeated applications of the daub would secure a larger frame. "Just use material in the wattle that will bend and not break."

"Something like witch hazel?" Maria asked, arms folded across. She had been paying attention to Abiah's lessons about wood properties, and that tree grew aplenty in the meadow. "Something fit for a witch?"

"Try reeds," Abiah said, studying her. "It's not hard to be considered a witch, Maria. Surely you know that by now. All that is required is difference."

Maria snorted. "Then at least let me be pliable and useful." The skin of her neck prickled. Witch or not, she would need to summon strength beyond herself to endure the long, lonely season ahead. Harder, she knew, than any she'd faced yet, with long stretches of wet, bitter dark and soul-heavy questions, a season to sit in company with the griefs that refused to heal.

Let me bend and not break.

PART 4

1717

CHAPTER 40

"I don't like the look of that sky," Julian said with a grimace, fingers gripping the wheel. Bruise-purple clouds circled in the distance, blotting out the last glow of twilight.

A gust of bitter wind blew Hoof's hat off, which he snatched with quick reflex. He cursed in Swedish as his other hand clasped the tiller, waiting for instructions. The *Whydah* rose and fell with a rippling swell, causing Sam's stomach to roll.

Another gale attacked Hoof's hat, this time from the complete opposite side.

Curious.

Sam whirled to watch the mainsail, which snapped in multiple directions. The hair on the back of his neck rose. He peered over the starboard, where the *Marianne* sailed alongside the *Whydah*, to see if Paulsgrave had any message or signal. The crew aboard the *Marianne* seemed just as bewildered. Their gazes locked on the fast-approaching weather, while others stood by for orders. They had to act fast. But how, with these confused winds?

Only the boldest traveled the seas in winter, for good reason. So far, luck had favored them. They'd outrun the navy—who'd taken to shore or their Caribbean posts for the worst of the season—then sailed north for the seas near South Carolina, leaving behind the relative seclusion of the Windward Passage. They'd also evaded Jennings, who was rumored to be camped in New Providence. Sam's flotilla hungered after new prey, which they'd found. In the span of the last week alone they'd captured three ships without challenge or issue. Sam hadn't had a night free of nightmares since seizing the *Whydah*: images of Dixon's corpse blocking the doorway, children bound in chains, or Davis leering over him with a noose. But by all external measures, they were surmounting the odds, becoming self-made kings. It would have been enough—more than enough—to return to Maria, Sam knew with regret. But she had been clear in asking him to stay away. Without her, he would give what was left of his heart to the cause and to his men. They'd sung and whooped as they loaded more and more loot into the *Whydah*'s hold. Until now, no whiff of those famed, late-winter storms.

A clatter of thunder sounded in the distance, then an eruption of lightning. The dark blue inverted into blinding white, hot enough to singe the eye.

"The heavens are opening!"

"God's vengeance," someone shrieked.

"Oh hush," yelled another. To which a growl of thunder rumbled.

Little King quivered, eyes wide as he searched the faces of the adults. "What do we do?"

An excellent question.

"Bellamy?" came Williams's cry from the nearby *Marianne* as a wave plunged into the side of Sam's ship, ocean water sloshing onto the deck.

"To your posts!" Sam said to both crews as another swell slammed into the *Whydah*. "Stay together. Emergency protocols—man the pumps, reef the sails, mind the rigging. Prepare for the worst."

The boatswain whistled and shouted orders as Sam raced down the main deck, checking the mast hoops and scupper drains. A sheet of lightning flashed like a whip before a wave slammed again, throwing Sam hard onto his knees.

He cursed, then looked up at the whirling sky just as the rain began to fly like daggers.

Gales roared like ravenous demons through the night and into the morning, drowning out the groans of the tireless crew. Waves slammed against the hull, causing the oak to whine with strain as thunder boomed. The drenched men shivered but stood firm, tying themselves to the ship to prevent being washed overboard, dodging the snapped halyard lines thrashing on the deck like monstrous sea snakes. This tempest took on biblical proportions, though Sam winced at the desperate prayers and oaths uttered by his brother sailors in response—no matter what kind of wood-cracking groans he heard the ship make.

"Stay alert," Sam ordered with encouragement, to them and himself, to keep the poison of superstition in check. Thunder crackled.

Still the storm would not let up. Nor the mounting fear. For a day, then two. Battering mind and spirit. White caps slamming again, and again, into the *Whydah*. When Sam checked the roster, two new recruits were nowhere to be found, two new recruits he had sworn to lead and protect.

Gone. Swept out to sea, with no one who'd heard their final screams. Had no one taught them how to properly tie themselves to the ship? Sam couldn't even recall their faces. The guilt festered like a fever, like all the many ways Sam had failed. A chasm had grown between his outward successes and an elusive sense of contentment. The mounting fortune in the belly of the ship's hold did little to abate his gnawing grief, haunted by the faceless sailors who'd never hold a single piece of eight. Sam slammed his hand against a wall, gritting his teeth to contain a howl. Rain pelted his neck.

The men soldiered on, arms flexed and spines hunched against the onslaught. Sam lost track of how many times he'd vomited from the sickness. They'd eaten little more than hardtack from their pockets for days—unable to leave their posts without risk of boulder-size swells sweeping men overboard into the abyss. Their flasks alone sustained them. Remnants of torn sails flapped like villainous bats. The *Marianne* close by looked no better.

Night descended without mercy on day three.

Curse you, God, Sam thought deliriously, spiraling at last into superstition himself. How dare God snatch up those new recruits, who'd had no more than a few raids to besmirch their names? Bile soured on his tongue, and his heartbeat throbbed in his throat. No amount of pumping kept the frigid water at bay.

Heaven forbid anyone like us try to change this broken world, while you turn a blind eye to the suffering that drove us here.

He stood in an ankle-deep flood and could barely move his stiff toes. Mind murky and heart ablaze, God seemed no better than Mr. Brown or Hallett. A tyrant, same as Jennings.

I don't need you. I never needed you. I've always been alone. Better off alone.

Who was he talking to? Why now? He didn't know, or care, but he could think of no one else to blame for such a world. For the ways so many people seemed dispensable, invisible. For soul-crushing poverty under the heel of the rich. For the mother he'd never known, then his father's early death. His stolen childhood. His desperation that drove him, and so many, deeper into this dangerous life at sea, knowing life on land was even more dangerous.

In a weary flash, Sam recalled the last time they'd anchored in port, how he'd joined his crew at the local brothel to drown out the loneliness and sorrow. Sam slammed his eyes shut, remembering the young woman in front of him, her visible curves through a thin dress, her narrowed, feelingless gaze as she surveyed him, then gave a price. Sam gritted his teeth, seeing again her hand outstretched for his. Seeing her position, then his, the blatant transaction of it all, the imbalance of power. How heartbeats passed, loud enough to crack glass. Loud enough to drown out the whoops from his brothers, the clanking of brothel tankards, the drunken squeals and laughter.

How Sam had swallowed his bitterness, placed a large coin in the woman's palm, then walked alone back to the ship—unable, despite himself, to act otherwise. To forget as he should. To put behind him that night on the dunes.

Rain fell into his eyes. Better Sam had never tasted what he'd never have again. Better he'd never heard her name.

Why? Why, Maria?

Did you not know that I loved you . . . love you.

Do you know that I'm sorry?

A needling stabbed his numb fingers and he felt his dull pulse. Love. What foolishness. Love had been the common thread of his loss. The liability. The open door to endless pain.

And what of the pull of greed, of power, of vengeance that lurks in the corners of your own heart?

He could blame the void for that, too.

Woozy from lack of sustenance and sleep, Sam trudged toward a swivel cannon mounted on the stern. He kicked the side, then fumbled to light a slow match.

"Bellamy?" came a call that Sam ignored.

The spark extinguished in an instant. He tried another, then another, shaking to the bone. At the strike of a successful light, he aimed at the torrent of black sky. At the prison of fate. The damned pointlessness. The unfairness beyond his control.

To hell with it all.

He lowered the slow match to the cannon's touch hold. A bang rang out into the air, the round landing somewhere behind the ship, out of sight in the storm. His ears buzzed.

"Commodore!"

Sam loaded another cannonball, aiming the iron toward the clouds, toward the supposed Almighty behind all of it.

Kill me. Go ahead. You've killed the best parts of me.

Try the rest. Go on. Fight me.

The second ball ripped through the sky, kicking the cannon back hard enough to toss Sam to the flooded floor. He shivered as smoke filled his nostrils, and his head throbbed with fury.

I'm not afraid of you.

No more side blows. Fight me honorably, face-to-face.

Julian yanked him away, shaking him by the shoulders. "Bellamy, enough. The mainmast is going!"

Rain pelted Sam's face, his feverish eyes focusing on the blur of Julian.

Sam still had a crew. A responsibility. A mission—what was it again?

The mainmast.

The mainmast is going.

"Davis," Samuel shouted with the rasp that remained of his voice. He frantically searched the drowned decks for the captive carpenter. "Thomas Davis, get to the mainmast!"

"He's plugging another leak, Bellamy," came John Brown's voice warbling somewhere above the tempest.

That's when they heard it. The splinter of oak as the mainmast snapped, falling as if in slow motion.

"Clear out!" Sam yelled as the crew darted and dove out of the way. The center beam collided with the floor in a sickening blow.

A wooden deadeye that secured the shrouds was flung like a disc at Sam's feet. Salt stung his eyes as he kept them open, taking in the destruction and frenzied reactions of the men. He forced himself to see it all.

Then from behind: "Commodore Bellamy, the *Marianne*! Where's the *Marianne*?"

Sam brushed aside his drenched hair and shoved himself to the rail, gripping for all he had left. He held his breath, scanning through the choke of fog.

But Williams and the *Marianne* were nowhere to be seen.

CHAPTER 41

Maria held her elbows in the chill of the early morning. She could sense the first thaw of spring in that slice of golden dawn, though the blue-eyed grass and white mayflower blooms hadn't yet announced their arrival. What month was it? Maybe March. She stood atop a sand cliff near her fishing shack with a view plunging thirty feet below to reveal the Atlantic: that wild, cold horizon. Enormous. Unfathomable. Unceasing and restless.

It had been a year, more than a year, since she'd been Hallett's wife—the mistake she'd sensed in her bones despite Mama's pressures to marry. In a few months, it would mark a full year since the exile following her release from prison.

Swells slammed into the pristine shore, throwing seaweed in their wake. Maria's untied hair snapped in the briny wind and she pulled a red cloak—her own weaving work, the wool dyed using bloodroot—tighter around her. For months, she'd avoided this expansive view above it all. She'd purposely kept her gaze narrow, focusing on the next thing in front of her: scavenging clams along the white beach, skinning a single fish, gathering one kind of herb before the next, fixing the next broken thing on her shelter, preparing meals, throwing herself from sunup to dusk into the weaving she sent with Abiah to the docks where Maria could not safely visit. How strange, Maria thought, that the harbor had once been deemed too dangerous for her by others: the influence of the sailors, the worldly views, her own stolen attempts to swim. Now, *she* appeared too dangerous to them. And swimming? That terrible, improper thing? Though it had ruptured her life, it had also saved her in more ways than one.

A cluster of terns called overhead. Maria took a deep breath, then sat down in the smooth sand.

Last night, she'd heard a ghostly howling through the pitch pines. She woke up in a sweat, sure she had left her baby outside in the woods. He was so *real*. Just here, cradled in her arms and nursing a moment ago. Shuddering into consciousness, she tuned her ear to the wailing sounds of wind through bare branches and the crash of distant waves until she remembered it all over again.

Maria stared out at the ocean, looking hard. She inhaled the smell of salt.

The smell of him.

It didn't take a long winter as an exile to face the truth, or did it? *He isn't coming back.*

Maria felt her vision blur with the raw power of the simple statement. She clutched her fists into balls and bit her lip to contain the pain. She'd also avoided this view, she'd realized, because she'd known Sam would pass by this beach on his return. All boats passed this stretch on their way to moor. She would lose her mind if she watched every day, waiting in her gray homespun dress for the moment his ship graced the horizon. Though part of her had hoped to spend the winter working out a plan, a piece of her had resisted, not wanting to disrupt the surprising peace and contentment she'd come to enjoy here, weaving away each day. Focusing on the all-consuming tasks of survival had still felt more manageable than accepting this.

He isn't coming back.

Anger, for months, had protected her from this knowledge. She hadn't wanted to believe it, hadn't been able to believe it before now. Because though she had lost everything, she hadn't fully.

This was the last thing she had been unwilling, unable, to let go of.

Hot tears slipped to her chin, which she scrubbed away before they could freeze. With no one to tell her who to love and who to mourn, or how, she found she could do both simultaneously without fear or reservation. Samuel Bellamy, what they had, was over. He had not fulfilled his promise. He had not returned. He had not come for her, or their son, in time to build the life they'd envisioned. And yet, remembering him—what was—she couldn't hate him.

Because it was real.

It was *real*. And still hers.

She recalled her dream and shivered. Perhaps "real" wasn't best measured by facts alone. She'd spent many hours since Sam had left, talking with him in her mind, feeling the glow of his belief throughout her time in jail. Their imagined conversations had sustained her.

She'd loved him, and in doing so, she'd come to love herself. *Know* herself at last. Was it selfish, odd—that inextricable blur? To see another with unfeigned affection, then oneself a little better?

She had no way of understanding that expansiveness of a cracked-open soul. But she didn't have to understand to know its truth. She couldn't deny it because she'd lived it.

Maria ran a hand through the grains around her, letting them slip through her leathered fingers. Her chest physically ached as she tried to swallow down the hollowness. Without this final hope of his return, what kept her here?

She held her knees and rocked. She wouldn't remain here in vain. If she stayed, it would be on her own terms. To support Abiah. To save enough funds to travel and start anew. To somehow find Elizabeth and earn her forgiveness. Until she could . . . well . . . Maria didn't know yet. But it was time to live bigger, to imagine a different, full future. One without Sam.

She stood, brushing the stray beach from her skirts. Her cheeks stung with chill, which she patted dry with her sleeve. No sense lingering here: She had fish to catch, firewood to chop, water to collect before the day's spinning work. Maria walked to her fishing shack, her home, her back turned away from the view she would not allow herself to get lost in.

And on the next warm day, when her buckets of spring water did not rim with morning ice, she would start swimming again. She felt most herself, and did her best thinking, while swimming.

CHAPTER 42

"Thank the Almighty we live!"

"Don't be an auspicious fool."

"Thank the stars then."

"Upon my ass . . . Thank our own courage."

Sam overheard the debate as he checked the bolts on a gun carriage. The banter was a welcome distraction after the eerie silence immediately following the storm as they took in the ship's devastation, the chunks of shattered wood strewn across the deck. Since then, the men labored together to make repairs, each with a kind of reverence—directed toward many varied sources—for the air they breathed and the blue sky overhead. A solemnness over the loss of the two new recruits in addition to the *Marianne* shadowed every conversation. They took a week to pump out the water, with everyone taking shifts night and day. The stench of sweat and mildew clung to the damp quarters.

In place of the fallen mainmast, they'd rigged together jury masts. This provided a temporary solution until they could make more significant repairs to the *Whydah*. They retrieved a fallen stump from the mast, using the main boom as a yard, then cut a square from the damaged sail to form a square rigging with tripod stays. The new sheet fluttered as it caught the wind.

Davis, to everyone's acknowledgment, was largely to thank for keeping the galley sailable. He glowered at every spoken appreciation. He did not ask to go yet, but would—Sam knew—at first opportunity. Davis never showed interest in the company aboard and never flinched in his disdain for the Articles. He sawed and hammered with deep forehead creases, waiting. His judgment radiated hotter than the furnace at the heart of the ship, and his image seared Sam's conscience. He hoped the carpenter would hold his sharp tongue; given Davis's indispensable aid during a time of crisis, Sam could argue again for his release and persuade the crew to vote differently and release him.

The hold remained unscathed: the fortune from the *Whydah* and their other raids had stayed safe and intact.

"Will we find them?" Little King asked Sam as the crew worked to plug the remaining leaks. He didn't need to specify. Everyone felt the absence of their brothers like an amputated limb.

A few grunts resounded, but Sam placed a hand on his shoulder.

"Captain Williams and I made plans for times such as these. We have a meet-up spot. Hoof and Julian will lead us there. They'll be waiting and, with any luck, be in better shape than us."

"And if they aren't there?"

Sam stiffened. "They will be," he said firmly, as much to reassure himself as Little King.

No sound could rival that first shout of joy when, a few days later, the crew made out the familiar shape of the *Marianne*. Sam fought the instinct to cover his ears, instead letting the relief and shock and whoops ring through his skull. In the distance through a spyglass, he made out the figure of Williams, waving his arms frantically as someone on the *Marianne* let out a celebratory shot in the air. Sam, in response, pulled one of his pistols from his red sash and let it bang into the cloudless sky in response. An answer. His fingers tingled from the vibrations.

They'd survived. The flotilla had *survived*.

Sam spotted a snatch of an island sandbar. "Navigate to shore and make ready to anchor," Sam shouted above the crew's cries, to which Julian and Hoof nodded with enthusiasm as others fell into position.

"Tonight," he bellowed at the gathering of his brother sailors, "we'll dine and drink like kings."

"Then sleep ten years," John Brown said, clapping Sam on the back.

Around several bonfires, Williams's and Sam's crews lounged in the cool sand as they told and retold the story of the storm. The red glow danced across their skin and glinted off the pewter mugs. Fiddlers played into the starry night, a slight bite of chill in the March breeze. A briskness had set in the farther north they sailed.

"Thought I'd never see your sorry face again, Bellamy," Williams said, downing a gulp of brandy. "Hated the idea. Never seen anything like those waves, am I right? Three days of those swells, white-fanged devils charging us from the deep."

"Hope to never see their like again," Sam shuddered, swatting away a plume of smoke. "I'd hate to have to rescue you a second time."

This elicited a hearty roar from the listeners, though the fear of their escape still hung in the air, as did the reminder of the many ship repairs left to make. How could Sam have found the conviction to muster on without the good-natured Williams and all the crew on the *Marianne*? Sam gazed around the scene with appreciation. Some men snored as they dozed in the soft beach, their waistcoats unbuttoned to make room for their recent feast—they'd need to resupply again soon, Sam calculated. Clusters of others conversed in their individual tongues—some African languages, Irish, Welsh, Dutch, French, Spanish, Swedish, and Creole. A motley crew they'd all turned out to be.

"We should form a pirate kingdom," John Brown said. "Imagine it! No poor among us, every night like this. We'd build it at the mouth of a river, a center of trade, and become a beacon to the world, our conquests scaling well beyond those of any stinking royal empire. They'd send their princes and ambassadors to court our alliance."

"It's not impossible," Julian reasoned, studying his drink. "A place like the haven Hornigold founded in New Providence, but better. Bigger, too. A place worthy of admiration, a powerful sanctuary for outcasts and the common folk. Governed by votes, by consensus, just as on a ship. We know it works."

"I'd toast to that," someone slurred.

"Aye," another said, raising a glass.

"Pass a bowl of punch!"

Sam nodded with a faint smile, running a thumb along the side of his cup. A pirate kingdom. Would it work? A model to the supposed "civilized" world?

"If we build such a place," Sam said, "I nominate John Brown as our first prime minister."

"No, away with the old titles," Williams said. "We'll instead call him the 'quartermaster ashore.'"

"I accept," Brown said with a dramatic hand flourish.

At that moment, Little King cleared his throat from behind Sam, announcing his arrival. Sam glanced up into his earnest face.

"What does the boy king want?" Williams asked, hiccupping and wiping his mouth on his sleeve. "Come, join us by the fire."

"Sir," he said, addressing Sam. "Some men are calling us Robin Hood's men." His brows furrowed with concern. "You told me we have no ruler. Who's Robin Hood?"

"You're speaking to him, boy," Williams sniggered, toppling over into Quintor. The laughter spread through camp like the pox.

Sam shot an annoyed look at Williams. He'd balked when he first heard the title and told his men to quit the nonsense. He struggled to see himself, or anyone there, as a simple hero; it was far grittier and more complicated than that.

He gazed back at Little King. "We serve no ruler, not me or any man here," he angled at Williams. "But Robin Hood isn't a threat to us. Have you never heard the story?"

Little King shook his head.

Sam's chest swelled with a tenderness he hadn't felt toward anyone or anything in weeks. "Come. Sit. I'll tell it the way my father did for me back in England." And so he did, in all its familiar twists and turns, until even Little King had passed out, asleep.

"Did the boy break into the liquor?" Williams observed, chin raised with something like an accusation in Sam's direction.

Sam shrugged. Maybe? Definitely. He studied Little King's cheeks, flushed and filled in since that day the child had begged— no, demanded—to join the pirates. His light brown hair stuck to his pale forehead, slick with sweat. He looked so peaceful, so impossibly young. Young enough to believe in a commoner hero who stole from the rich to give to the poor and then managed to escape, uncorrupted and free to live with Maid Marian.

Sam believed in taking from the rich, from corrupted power and cruel empires. And yet, he was not so young. Nor innocent. And when was the last time he'd felt peace? "Robin Hood's men," his crew might sling with the courage of wielding a new rapier. But so far, they plundered for their own profit, shared only among themselves, and fought for individual dignity and power. The comparison fell short. How did their story end?

Could they build a pirate kingdom? Create an actual haven for the poor?

The *Whydah* loomed nearby. And somewhere, Sam knew, Thomas Davis slept on this same beach, with venom in his heart. Rightfully so. Reflexively, Sam placed a hand on a pistol for reassurance. The fire snapped as a log crumbled into an orange furnace of embers. Little King's small chest rose and fell. He couldn't fix the boy's past, nor his own. But he could give him a better world. A kingdom if he could.

"I haven't forgotten, Paulsgrave. I'll return the boy the minute we can find him a good, permanent situation."

Williams sighed, glancing around at the dimming fires, most of the crew of almost two hundred fast asleep. He yawned, wide enough to crack his jaw. "I have something to discuss with you, lad. On the topic of our next situation."

Sam's stomach clenched. They'd meant to circle the Carolina shores, avoiding the navy still gathered in the Caribbean. "Go on."

"Nothing like a skirmish with death to make one think things over. Oh, don't give me that look, Bellamy—I'm not abandoning ship. But I'd like to continue northward, spend a few weeks on Block Island. My mother lives there, you remember. Along with my sister and a niece."

"Rhode Island," Sam said, already doing the calculations. A mere day's sail from—

He shook his head, blinked. "Yes, I remember," Sam said, a wave of weariness washing over him. He knew no rest.

Do not entertain the notion, Sam thought. *Fight it. Show Maria at least that respect. She asked you to never come back. She asked you to never return.*

So he wouldn't. No matter what. Even if it broke him.

"You and the *Whydah* can prey on merchant ships in the meantime," Williams continued. "We can join forces again in the north. Maine has that wooded island Dixon used to talk about, with a deep harbor. A fine spot, no doubt, to rendezvous again. I won't need many men—just enough to make port and avoid notice."

Sam closed his eyes, inhaling the smell of sea and first whiffs of spring, the soft perfume of a magnolia tree. He preferred the open water, away from solid land and the memories, the feeling of being barricaded by that enormous, unfathomable blue.

"Very well, my old friend," Sam said, removing his tricorn to recline in the sand. "We'll see you and the *Marianne* to Block Island."

$\mathscr{C}$HAPTER 43

Farther, Maria's body said, arms threading through the bone-chilling Atlantic water.

Turn back, came the familiar pang of a whispering.

No, I can do it. I can go farther than I've ever gone before.

Her shoulder muscles strained as she pushed closer to an ever-moving horizon. Spring light glinted on the surface. She marveled at the sheer power of her body, so much stronger than that day at the docks. The day she jumped. The day—

Maria took a lungful of air, pausing to tread water. Her fingers and toes had numbed, the stabs of frigid spring ocean needling her bare limbs.

She craned her neck back toward shore, breakers pounding the beach where she'd set her hunting tools. She blinked away the sting of salt, squinting at the distance. She *had* gone far, better than her personal best. She relished the challenge. Each day, the cold felt less intense, her will strengthening and mastering the protests of her body.

A cramp pulsed in her right thigh.

Time to return. The snares wouldn't set themselves.

Maria kicked while her hands kneaded the water in front of her. The cramp returned, and she ignored the seizing. The aches always went away if she ignored them and pushed through the pain. Maria reasoned she was, if anything, good at pushing through pain.

Minutes later, Maria paused to rest, moving to flip onto her back to float the way Sa—no, *he*—had taught her.

Why is the shore still so far away?

No. Farther *away?*

Maria didn't need to ask, and her insides lurched with the knowledge. She'd been caught in a riptide.

All at once, her veins squeezed in protest, a shiver running down her neck.

Breathe, Maria said, rolling onto her side to angle parallel to the shore. *One stroke after another.*

The water sloshed over her stiffening joints.

I'm alone.

I'm completely alone.

She swallowed and coughed up water, the liquid burning her throat. She flailed a little, then righted herself.

Stay focused, Maria told herself. *You are strong.*

The cramp returned, her muscles spasming and forcing her to stop. Maria grimaced, maneuvering into a floating position and massaging her leg. She had to keep moving to stay warm. To keep fighting the current.

I'm too tired.

God, I'm so tired.

Something like tears sprung to her eyes as her teeth began chattering. She had to keep moving.

No one is coming to save me.

No one is coming.

She squeezed her eyes shut, then set her jaw. Behind the surging terror, a fire awoke in her chest. No one would come. No one would see this. But she would. *She* would save herself. Or die trying. She'd survived too much to perish here.

Maria seized but fought the cold, keeping her gaze on the shoreline.

Start counting, Maria said.

Count. Breathe. Anything. Just keep going.

You can't stop. Keep going.

So she did, her right leg kicking with shrieks of pain with every move, but she did move.

Keep . . .

. . . mov . . . i . . . n . . . g

A swell rose, carrying Maria with it, moving her closer to the beach like a snarl of seaweed. She couldn't feel her legs. Her heartbeat seemed to slow. But her arms rotated, caught in the waves, until she rolled, tumbled, and crashed in a torrent of water and light, landing against the hard beach, her mouth filled with sand as she coughed and convulsed, using her elbows to crawl one yard, then two, closer . . . closer . . .

She gasped, sucking for air, dragging herself to her feet. Her whole body shook, sand and seawater dripping down from her hair. She stared at her fingers, tinged blue with purple fingernails. Fatigue overtook her, begging her to slow, to drop to her knees, to rest.

Instead, she gritted her teeth and narrowed her eyes on her snares and red cloak. She tumbled toward them, forcing her eyes open, throwing the wool coat around her shivering frame. She shook harder than sea grass in a gale.

No one is coming.

She forced a labored breath.

I have only myself.

Capable as she'd proved herself to be, that echo stung. Maria pulled the cloak tighter, burying her face in its coarse folds.

When Abiah came to the shack a few weeks later, Maria had three coverlets and a length of homespun ready to sell at the docks.

"All this in a month?" Abiah asked, admiring the weaving work. "Fast, even for you."

Maria sat on a log bench near the extinguished outdoor fire. She used a stick to draw in the white ash. "Chores are quicker in the spring than they are in winter." She paused, a heaviness returning. "Though all I think of is how to prepare for the next winter. Then I wonder, why?" Maria looked up, circles under her eyes. Even sleep, that miracle drug, had eluded her lately.

Abiah studied her with soft dark eyes, not saying anything, and Maria returned to drawing shapes in the cinders.

"How fare the land negotiations?" Maria asked.

Abiah took a seat on the bench. "Great Island cannot be reclaimed. Now, we focus our efforts on protecting Tuttomnest."

Great Island. Lost forever.

Maria lifted her head at this sobering news, eyes boring into the wall ahead. "I hate staying out here, far away and removed from it all. We can't let Hallett and Doane win."

"Through their proposed way, no one will win," Abiah said, studying the small room. "No food will grow for anyone." She paused. "How is your appetite lately?" Her gaze lingered on the pile of bedclothes, then flicked to the unwashed bowls and crumbles of faded plants.

Maria shrugged.

"May I?" Abiah asked, raising a palm to feel Maria's head, as she'd done throughout Maria's pregnancy. The shock of a person touching her felt strange and soothing. How long it had been since she'd hugged Papa, tickled little Mercy, chided Elizabeth for her cold toes crowding into Maria's side of the bed.

The memory of Elizabeth, of knowing she could always turn to her sister for help or advice before all of this, made her heart squeeze. Now that she'd been branded a witch, Elizabeth would never be safe to speak to her again—regardless of how Maria felt about Sam anymore.

"No fever," Abiah said, rising for her basket and rummaging through her provisions. She hummed to herself. "Luckily, I have all my supplies with me. I was in Eastham just this afternoon, applying a poultice for another white woman with a strange lump on her chest." Abiah removed some dried herbs, then held them out for Maria. "I can't seem to help myself. Then wonder, maybe if I heal their bodies, maybe they can heal their hearts."

Maria extended her hand, fingers wrapping around the fragile stems. She recognized the mixture—a sleep aid. "Thank you." Maria felt her voice return.

Abiah said nothing, studying her. The silence filled the shack.

"Are you well?" Abiah asked.

Maria shrugged. "I have enough for my needs. It's better than I ever imagined when I first stumbled to Billingsgate."

"Survival alone is not living. The Creator made the world beautiful to remind us of that."

At this, Maria felt her heart rise in her throat. Damn those tears. Oceanic. Still, after all this time.

"I almost drowned the other week," Maria said, recounting the episode. Her throat tasted of salt at the bitter memory. "And ever since, I can't help but wonder what the point of any of this is."

When the sobs came, Abiah took Maria into her arms until the quaking stopped.

Abiah took her hand and squeezed. "I am sorry." She sighed. "It is difficult, the struggle of hope. I too know that war."

Hope. That was it. The shape of the wound, the hole.

Maria and Abiah looked hard at each other, an unspoken depth of understanding.

"I've been so focused on the past, then trying to forget the past—learning how to just get through a day on my own. But the future?" Maria's voice trailed off. "I need . . . I don't know. To believe I am making an actual difference to stop the land divisions, or something. I miss being part of something. Even Eastham." Maria scrubbed away a rogue tear on her sleeve, then scoffed. "After everything they did to me. Everything they do to your people. How can I still miss Eastham?"

How can I still miss him?

Abiah's lip tugged up at the corner, then she slowly exhaled. "I thought this day might come." She rose to rummage through her basket again, returning with a rabbit-fur pouch. Maria's eyes grew as Abiah revealed the contents.

"It isn't much coin, not enough to get you farther than Boston," Abiah said. "But it is your portion of the profits from the weaving. Knowing you had no need for money here, that it would only bring you risk, I saved it for you."

Maria's eyes brimmed with emotion.

"Forgive me for not telling you sooner. You are no child—you've proved that much. My people do not concern ourselves with money as much as yours. We rely on reciprocity and thanksgiving. Money is a white man's god, a corrupter of hearts. Also, I had wanted it to be more."

"Abiah, I couldn't. I can't—" When Maria didn't move, Abiah took her shaking hands and placed the pouch into her palms.

"It is yours," Abiah said with emphasis.

"But you don't do favors for the Europeans," said Maria. "Only business. And you've already saved my life."

Abiah laughed. "And what business we have done! Together, we have paid off the loom, raised funds to fight the land divisions, and gathered enough herbs to last a year for my medicine work in Eastham and among my own people. But the most valuable thing you have given me over the past year is your mind. Your knowledge of the invaders, of how they think and interpret their scriptures, how men like Hallett justify their greed. I am glad to have known you, Maria of no home and of no people. I am glad to have called you a friend. To know that people like us can learn to be friends."

Maria blinked away the tears. Time seemed to slow to a stop.

"But I can't go. I can't leave all of this. I can't leave you." Another loss. Loss upon loss upon loss. How much more could Maria sustain?

And yet, how could she stay? Alone. Stuck in a story that was no longer hers. Close but so far from her family. A stone's throw's length to those Atlantic-facing dunes.

Abiah closed Maria's fingers tight around the rabbit-fur bag, then whispered words in what Maria recognized as Wampanoag.

"You must, and you will," Abiah said. "The past is never lost. You already know this. You will not lose me, nor I you. My fight is here. Yours is elsewhere now, away from this people who despise you. And there is hope and life for you yet."

CHAPTER 44

"Sink it," called a man with an Irish accent.

"Aye, sink their miserable ship," echoed another man, his fist raised.

"That arrogant captain disparages us. Let him grovel for once."

Sam scanned the votes coming in. Hoof and Julian counted, then nodded in his direction. A clear majority.

He exhaled, then adjusted his tricorn. He left to tell the news to the waiting Captain Beer on his captured vessel. On the way, he passed giddy crew members plundering booty from the merchant ship to pack onto the loaded-down *Whydah*. Fresh supplies from nearby Boston: rum, sugar, molasses, and a dozen unopened chests—ready to be counted.

Captain Beer blinked, his puffy cheeks reddening by the second. Sam waited for him to say something, but he remained silent. From shame or fury, Sam couldn't say.

"I am sorry, Captain Beer. I scorn doing mischief to anyone when it isn't to my advantage. But we must sink your sloop," Sam said. "The crew has decided. They heard comments you and others on your ship made against them. And I stand by my crew."

Still Captain Beer said nothing. Was he shaking? For a moment,

Sam wondered if the bulbous British captain had stopped breathing, or if he might faint like some aristocratic woman. What an unpleasant business. He wished he could talk about it with Williams later—who always had a flourish for storytelling, stamping out some of the moral dilemmas of the events—but they had already said goodbye to the *Marianne*. Sam and his partial crew now focused on preying on the Atlantic coast for cargo vessels while they made for another island—Green Island in Maine—to wait for Williams and the rest to return.

"We'll set you and your men on a nearby island," Sam said, filling the silence. "Plenty of ships pass by there. You'll be saved by nightfall, no doubt."

Still, Captain Beer said nothing. Maybe there wasn't a point. Sam, eager to get on with the day and move off with his crew and the new loot, made to return to the *Whydah*.

The moment he turned, he heard the whistle of a blade.

Hand to his belt before he could think, Sam withdrew his cutlass and jerked around to meet the metal. Their swords erupted with a clang.

"You mean to kill a man with his back to you?" Sam asked, flicking his wrist and bending Beer's narrow blade to the side.

Beer advanced again, his white wig askew. "You filthy pirate."

Sam made out the sound of crew members from both ships gathering to watch. Beer held up a hand. "He's mine."

Sam exhaled. He preferred it when his victims gave up more easily. Beer must profit directly from his business, and well. How much value had he held aboard? Beer's weary crew proved no threat or beneficiary, and several had already defected and joined Sam's flotilla. But Sam's own loyal crew was another matter.

"At ease," Sam commanded his men. He saw this was an honor duel. Passing up his cutlass and brace of pistols, someone from the *Whydah* traded him for a rapier. He gripped the leather handle, remembering those hours and hours at sea as Williams and Hornigold taught him to use this gentleman's weapon.

He preferred a cutlass.

Beer struck again, and Sam parried.

"Have you no control over your mongrel men?" Beer growled. "Or do they control you?"

Sam felt the veins in his neck throb. An old anger billowed up like a storm as he gripped the hilt. Their blades clanged as they circled the deck. Diagonal rising cut. Retreat. Low, sweeping thrust. Jump. Evade, grapple, thrust.

Then again.

Focus, Bellamy, he could hear Hornigold say. *You're not half bad if you'd quit your daydreaming.*

Beer's edge grazed Sam's arm, tearing open his velvet coat. Sam gasped at a jolt of pain, then pushed the sensation away.

"Damn you," Sam bellowed through gritted teeth.

"And take company with souls like yours? With no shred of conscience left? I think not," Beer sneered, blocking a forward pass and making another thrust. Sam parried the blow, then ducked and rolled. He could make out the edges of what sounded like observers, but a drum hammered in his ears. His blood boiled.

How many men like you have I had to face?

Or worse, cower before?

"You sniveling puppy," Sam spat. "You and all those who submit to corrupt laws made to protect rich men's security." Sam angled a blow, which Beer evaded. Their blades met with a clatter at the cross section.

"They vilify us, scoundrels like you," Sam continued, words flooding his mind. "But there is only one difference: They rob the poor under the cover of law, and we plunder the rich under the protection of our own courage. Wouldn't it be better to join us rather than sneak after the asses of villains for employment?"

Beer guffawed. "And be bound to the will of a clan of savages?" he said, gesturing toward Sam's crew. He made a diagonal thrust and reformed his stance, which Sam swept away with a flick of his wrist.

Their blades slammed, the sound reverberating through the air and down to Sam's bones. An almost inhuman strength burned within him. The refusal to accept the world as it was. That despite everything, all the ways this dream had become complicated, he still believed men like Beer had no right to speak or act with such hateful views—that arrogant, unearned authority. No real conscience. No real morality.

No more.

Sam's blade rang as he relentlessly struck and thrust. Beer's eyes flashed with fear, but he blocked the attacks and stepped into the defensive. Their swords blurred in a circle of movement.

Finally, he trapped Beer against the wall, the shining tip of his rapier pointed an inch from the captain's throat. Sweat beaded across Beer's forehead, and he dropped his weapon. The hate never left his narrowed eyes. Everyone and everything had fallen silent, watchful.

You could kill him.

End him.

Be the man Maria fears, a man your father wouldn't recognize. The murderous pirate that self-righteous aristocrats like Beer mistake you to be.

He'd never killed a man outright before. The thought savored of bile.

"There is no arguing with men like you," Sam hissed, catching his breath. He stabbed the blade past the man's face, through the captain's jacket—pinning the silk fabric to the ship. Beer whimpered with relief.

"Keep your life," Sam said. "But think twice before you disparage me, or my brothers, in the name of what you call a 'conscience.'"

Sam wiped his mouth on his sleeve, then addressed Beer's gaping crew. "I am a free prince," Sam shouted. "My men and I have as much authority to make war on the whole of this broken world—with more right than anyone with a hundred sails of ships, or an army of one hundred thousand men—and this, *my* conscience tells me."

He sheathed the sword and returned to the *Whydah*. Clutching the bloody spot on his arm, he sent orders to deliver Beer and his men unharmed to shore, then to sink the merchant ship with due haste.

We counted a total of thirty thousand pounds below deck, sir.
Bags of precious gold and silver. Rare jewels and European goods, too. Drinks of every kind.
Enough money to last a lifetime.

Sam lowered his pewter cup, dazed despite the feast around him as the crew celebrated the news of their current fortune. A pair of fiddlers played as others stamped their feet in rhythm. Quintor swirled Little King around the deck, teaching him and a few others how to dance, an effort met with King's furrowed brow and guttural laughs from all observers. The boatswain whistled to remind the men on watch, once again, to mind the sails.

Without thinking, Sam fingered the clean bandage Ferguson had wrapped around his upper arm. A minor stab, and nothing more. It only burned if he remembered. He wondered if Beer and his men had been rescued by now. And where Davis now lurked on deck after supper.

Filthy pirate.

"What about you?" Sam heard John Brown trill to his right, snapping his attention back to the present.

"Lost in a fantasy," said Hoof, fanning Sam with his hat. "A ship full of gold!"

A ship full of gold.
That's what I'd sought. That was the goal.

"My apologies," Sam said. "What did you say?"

Brown and Hoof exchanged a look.

"How'll you spend your share?" Hoof asked. He elbowed Brown. "This brother here says he'll buy a herd of wild ponies to keep on his estate as quartermaster of our pirate kingdom. Not for riding, but for admiring. Free as all the people who live there."

Sam blinked. All the noise seemed to grow farther and farther away. For though he'd set out and done what he promised to do—though he and his men may very well be the richest men on the

Atlantic, enough to put any number of nobles and dukes and even some royals to shame—he still felt that insatiable gnaw to prove himself. Against what? To what end?

He'd won it all. Yet he'd never felt so adrift.

It's enough.

Sam, have you had enough?

Whether it was the voice of his father, Maria, his duel with Beer, or a cumulation of it all, something inside had snapped beyond repair. A sudden, inexplicable exhaustion swept over him.

Best if someone else took up the mantle. Julian, perhaps. He'd make a fine captain.

A quiet, retired life in a pirate kingdom doesn't sound so bad. A place to put ideals into action on land. Where votes count and all people matter. A place with no poor, a place like the haven Hornigold built in New Providence.

Maine, perhaps? Not too far to see—

He shook his head.

A chance to set Little King on a better path than mine.

"Bellamy," John Brown asked. "Are you ill?"

"I'm fine," Sam said, putting up a hand as he felt a tap from behind. He turned to see Isaiah Abell and Timothy Webb standing, their arms folded.

"Commodore, might we have a word?" asked Abell.

"Just a short trip ashore," the ever-sunburned Abell explained as Sam paced along the stern. "We'll raise the Union Jack in port and they'll never suspect us, all that traffic coming in and out with the shipments."

"Aye," said Webb, wringing his hat. "The three of us made out of Cape Cod together. With Dixon, of course—God rest his wise soul. It seems fair to use this chance to consider. To *re*consider . . ."

The memory of Caleb Dixon's crimson blood drenching Sam's shirt after they'd attacked the man-of-war made his chest tighten.

"Sir, in short, I am ready to return," said Abell, strands of straggly blond hair escaping his ribbon. "My parents may have lost the farm to the sand plague, but I can finally give them something else. A home in another part of the colonies. Where we might make a happier life for ourselves."

"I ache to see my children," Webb said, hiding his limp from the whaling accident. "I couldn't face them without shame, unable to secure a job again. But now I can. With a chance to give them a better situation than my own father could."

Sam placed a hand on both of their shoulders, then gazed north out at the dark sea.

"Your specific ask?" He needed to hear it clearly, to know it hadn't been born only from the shadows of his selfish mind.

"That we stop in Cape Cod Bay en route to Maine. In disguise. That Abell, and myself, might make our separate ways."

Sam closed his eyes. He'd done much since leaving Cape Cod a year and a half earlier—everything from treasure hunting, and raiding in the nude in those early periaguas, to storming a French merchant vessel with Jennings, then betraying him. Sam had then moved on to commanding a ship, then an entire flotilla, as they chased down prey and evaded the navy at every turn.

What loomed before him took more courage than all of it together.

Maria.

Forgive me, but I must return. Just this once, and not for long. To hear the truth from your lips. So you can hear the truth from mine.

"Lads, we've gotten enough," Sam said, swallowing hard. "It's time to go home."

CHAPTER 45

Maria paused the moment she stepped out of her fishing shack. A heron flew overhead as she set her heavy basket down. Closing her eyes, she inhaled the familiar smells of life bursting in the forest: damp pine needles, the sweet perfume of mayflower, the new growth of alder.

And salt. Always the salt from the unceasing Atlantic.

She smoothed out her gray homespun dress and patted down her freshly braided hair knotted at the base of her sun-tanned neck. She had no bonnet, alas, and nothing but the shard of mirror she'd retrieved from the shore all that time ago to judge her appearance. But this look would have to do. She couldn't appear like someone who'd spent a year hiding in the wilderness. Not if she wanted to secure lodging without too many questions. Not if she were to find weaving employment in Boston as a new arrival from England, as a widow perhaps.

She had a long walk to work out the story. To choose a new name. To sew a hem long enough to cover her deer-hide boots.

Maria forced herself to take one last look at the wooden shack she had made her home for almost a year: the cellar out back, the reed-lined walls, the almost imperceptible sprouts shooting up from the vegetable patch she'd planted last fall. She'd left almost everything. The loom, the snares, the milkweed filament bed. She could carry only so much. And Abiah might still find use for it.

She placed a hand over her heart.

Goodbye.

Her eyes misted and she forced back a pained smile. This year contained so much pain and struggle, but there was also joy. Peace and silence. The raw, sometimes cruel beauty of nature. And a kind of freedom she'd enjoyed and wondered if she might ever again. She took comfort knowing she could survive on her own if she needed to, or wanted to, in the future. Humans could be more untenable than the cycles of the earth.

She could always stay. Maria and Abiah had discussed all the alternatives. But without being able to appear in town, there was only so much Maria could do for the land division cause anymore. She was still a liability. With every conversation and potential plan, a springtide of hope rose in her chest. For she was not always this outcast, grieving woman. Irrevocably changed though she might be, somewhere inside she was still a young woman with dreams. A young woman who wanted to overhear all the conversations from travelers at the dock. A young woman who imagined she'd prefer spinsterhood to a marriage without love. A young woman who wanted, then succeeded, to learn to swim. A young woman with smiling eyes and a knack for trouble who wanted to see Boston . . .

"Goodbye to it all," she whispered to no one but the trees. "And thank you."

Strapping her basket to her back, a woven basket filled with meager provisions and her bag of coins, Maria made her way down the path for the cow-trail road that bypassed Eastham. Her mouth dried at the thought of passing so close to her old haunts, but she swallowed. She'd long forgiven Elizabeth and would find a way to send a coded letter, telling her sister what she needed to hear— that she was releasing Sam from her mind.

Maria would travel the path of the sun until the bay water's edge, then south until her destination. The shore would be her faithful guide.

Eyes on the dirt ahead, or gauging the cloudless sky, Maria walked on in the morning sun, resisting the powerful urge to look back.

CHAPTER 46

Sam gripped the *Whydah*'s rail as he peered out at the wall of fog. A briny April wind tore at his black coat, but he hardly felt it. Somewhere in the blurry distance was the Cape Cod shore, and between, a perilous coast. His insides churned with a thousand emotions, imagining the sight of her, bracing himself for the worst, pushing away the onslaught of memories: her lavender scent, her bold laugh, her hands finding his as they lay together on the dune under the stars.

It's not too late to change course.

"Bellamy," came Julian's voice from behind.

Sam gave an acknowledging grunt.

Julian stood beside him at the rail, his forehead creased with concentration as he peered down at his compass. The scar along his dark brow bulged. "I've rarely seen a midday fog like this."

"Nor I." It went without saying: a warm wind mixing with a bank of cold gray clouds rolling overhead. A storm brewed.

"To say nothing of the coastline," added Julian. "I have our best men in the crow's nest, but it's too hard to make out the dark and light spots to measure depth in these conditions. I asked Hoof if he knew these currents any better—something from his old maps. He does not."

Then Maria's voice returned, like an echo from the deep.

I know these waters better than your ilk.

Sam forced down a weary chuckle, recalling their conversation that first day. What "ilk" he'd turned out to be after all. What might she say now?

He'd find out soon enough.

"We'll remain dead in the water until the weather decides what to do," Sam said, answering the question Julian had really been asking. The pilot made to turn, to deliver orders to brace-box the rigging and make limp the sails, when Sam called after him.

"Julian, there's something I want to tell you."

Julian sighed. "That you are going to see your woman?"

Sam's eyes widened. "How—"

"Bellamy," Julian said with annoyance. "Have we not been brother sailors all this time? Have you learned nothing since your 'secret' little scheme with Jennings? I know you. We all know you. I knew this day would come the moment we sailed north."

A bittersweet reminder. Sam smiled, grateful that at least someone seemed to know him better than himself. That he was still recognizable in some way, somehow, to people he cared about. People who also cared about him.

"Truthfully, we're grateful. Maybe if she tells you off herself, you can stop moping about in private. You'll need a bribe or a means of quick escape, if she tries to turn you in. We can't afford to get caught."

Sam winced, the breath leached from his lungs. "I know." He'd plan for a terrible reception, to protect his crew most of all, but still he hoped the Maria he'd known would hesitate to see him captured and hanged.

"Besides," Julian said, "Abell and Webb made a fine case for the stop. Our original crew means to pay back that nasty Israel Cole and scrub their debts, then do a bit of black-market trading before we make our way to Maine." Julian paused. "We are *all* making our way to Maine, right?"

Sam folded his arms and ignored the brief jolt of pain from Captain Beer's stab. "Of course." And he meant it. No matter how wild his fantasies, he saw no other outcome after his conversation with Maria, given her marriage. At last he could put his hope to rest. "But once we get there, to this forested alcove on Green Island to build our pirate kingdom, I mean to retire in peace."

Julian's face fell at the news. This part, at least, the young pilot had not anticipated.

"I'll nominate you," Sam said, removing his tricorn and clapping it on Julian's head. "I'm sure the crew will vote you in, if you agree."

Julian whipped off the hat and immediately returned it to Bellamy. He blinked, then finally closed his jaw.

"I could never replace you, Bellamy," he finally said, back turned to the rail and taking in the *Whydah*. "But if given the honor, I'd try my level best to do right by our crew."

They were interrupted by a strong gust, then a riot of voices.

"A sloop! Commodore, a sloop off the port side."

Sam had no appetite for a last-minute raid. But this small vessel offered more than that.

The sloop drifted closer, perhaps curious and suspicious at the enormous galley flying the Union Jack in these waters on a day like today. When they drew close enough for Sam to make out the name, the *Fisher*, he called out for the captain. "Are you acquainted with these waters, sir?"

"Very well," came the croaky voice. "Who's asking?"

With a nod from Julian, Sam ordered the signal, sending four armed men with pikes to board the sloop to the shock of all aboard the *Fisher*.

The manifest ledger made the pirate crew cheer.

"What is it?" Sam asked with slight irritation, flinging open his cabin door at the chorus of excitement. Inside, he'd been coaxing the shaken Captain Robert Ingols and some of his shipmates—

including a stern-looking Scot named Montgomery—into collaborating with Julian and Hoof as they all navigated to safety.

"Madeira wine."

"More than seven thousand gallons of it."

Ingols's expression crumpled. Montgomery's mouth formed a grim line.

"I'll see you and your ship returned, along with the contents," Sam said with urgency. The ship crested on a break, then slammed down, knocking papers from the table and shattering a jar of ink on the floorboards.

The weather worsened. They all depended on finding deeper water, and soon.

Damn, but she was close. So very close.

"Please," Sam said, braced against the wall of the cabin as another swell rose. "We'll include a generous gift as a token of thanks. Will you help us?"

At the word "gift," Ingols's entire demeanor changed. He straightened his back and spoke with confidence. "I accept the conditions. I know this terrain better than anyone." To this, Montgomery glowered but remained silent as the team got to work to make sail again.

John Brown and a small pirate crew volunteered to go aboard the *Fisher*, ensuring the sloop would follow the *Whydah*. The pelt of rain began, and the crews on both ships manned the pumps.

"Make haste, brother," Sam shouted out to Brown. "Don't fall too far behind us." The Jamaican knew all the lines of the ship like the veins of his own body. If anyone could keep the distance close, it was him.

"Aye, Bellamy," Brown said, with a slight slur and giddiness that gave Sam pause.

"Brown, have you been drinking the wine?"

"No fear! I will carry the sail until she carries her masts away."

What on hell or earth was that supposed to mean?

"Captain," came Little King's voice. "Should I go with them?"

Sam closed his eyes and felt his head pulse. The thought of the lad on such a small vessel in the midst of a storm—even under one as capable as Brown, however many cups the man had downed—made Sam's throat tighten. But was he any better off on the *Whydah*?

He'll be safe in Maine soon.

"You'll stay here, King. Please. Take cover and stay away from the rails."

Barraged by a string of questions as the crew raced around the slick deck and readied the rigging, Sam knocked shoulders with Thomas Davis. They hit hard enough to shoot fire through Sam's fresh injury. They paused, staring at each other until Sam broke the silence.

"I mean what I said, and always did," Sam said, water drops drenching his hair. "I'm sorry for all of this. I want to see you free, and I mean to do it. I'll plead your case again with the men in Maine. You've saved our ship once. Your services—"

Davis bared his teeth and said nothing, picking up a saw and briskly turning away. Sam exhaled, unable to blame him.

The Atlantic swells rose, causing the *Whydah* to buck and dive. The wind torrented at vicious speeds, tearing away the fog. Before nightfall, Sam ordered extra lanterns to be hung in the stern and helm of each vessel. They'd need the light to stick together. They'd made this mistake before, and Sam refused to lose anyone in the flotilla again. Sam stared back at the murky outline of the *Fisher*.

That is when the waves started to rise like the hair on Sam's arms, the bolts of lightning flashing across the shrouded sky. A sickness crept into his gut.

"All hands on deck!" Sam said, running fore-and-aft to check the gun carriage mounts, drains, and any stray lines as waves began to pound like fists.

CHAPTER 47

There he is. Not her son toddling along the salt-marsh asters or cooing on her breast, but his father. More a clear image than a feeling. Knocked to his knees, he grips the rail of a tossing ship.

Is she the wind? The waves? The furious thunder, circling overhead?

Then she hears her name on his tongue. Sees faces—a hundred and more faces. Strangers praying, crying, sprinting in every direction. Diving into the abyss.

A coastline she recognizes.

Black-blue night. The whine of tearing wood. A crashing beam.

The jaw of the Atlantic cracked open, hungry to swallow them whole.

Maria sat up with a heaving gasp. "Sam?" she said aloud. Something wet pelted her cheek.

She squinted up at the thick darkness around her. Rain fell from the large rustling pine overhead, where she'd taken shelter for her first night of traveling. She'd learned the hard way not to seek sanctuary in anyone's barn or gristmill. To trust no one, especially on these outskirts of Eastham.

Throwing off her red cloak she'd wrapped herself in for a blanket, she stood up, her whole body tingling as consciousness returned.

I get these . . . whisperings, is what I used to call them. It's a burning feeling of sorts. What people are thinking, and . . . sometimes things before they happen.

Where I come from, we call that intuition, came Sam's honeyed voice. *Inspiration.*

How did she answer him again? On First Encounter Beach, all that time ago?

And where I come from, we call that "of the Devil."

People cry witch.

Maria took a step away from the pine thicket protection and placed her palm out to feel the downpour. Real and cold on her skin.

Her heartbeat didn't slow, but her focus sharpened. The clear choice before her: to believe. To not believe. Witch or not, she had little time to waste on the debate.

Suddenly, an image pressed against her mind: something of hers left on that same beach.

Maria paused before her father's shed, pushing away the memories and the wrongness that crept into her stomach. Wind whipped at her cloak, and she tightened the basket slung across her back. Taking a deep breath, she pressed her whole body against the door and slid it open. The horses inside whinnied at a bolt of lightning illuminating her silhouette.

"Whoa there," Maria soothed, smearing wet hair from her face and gesturing for Snip and Ruby to calm. "Shh. It's all right. Remember me?" She let them smell her. Snip snorted with recognition, and when he was ready, she stroked his velvet nose. *Stay quiet, please. I need you and your sure footing.* She fumbled in the dark for the wall with the leather straps: traces and reins and breeching. A difficult prospect on its own without the added challenge of knowing she still needed to hitch the one-horse cart. She needed it to—

When Maria threw the breast strap over Snip, Ruby squealed and kicked at the wall.

"It's me. It's just me," Maria begged.

"So it is," came a voice from behind.

Maria swung around, eyes wide, to see Elizabeth standing in the rain. Her heart leaped into her throat.

"Elizabeth!"

Before Maria could say anything else, her sister rushed at her, throwing her sopping arms around Maria.

"How did you know I was here?" Maria asked, her vision blurring with emotion.

Elizabeth laughed with joy, pulling away but leaving a firm grip on Maria's shoulders. "I'm always watching. I tried to sneak away and find you a few times on my own, but without luck. It took you long enough to return." She examined Maria's clothes. "They said you lived like a wild woman somewhere far in the north. Is it true?"

A cascade of memories hit Maria: their talks in the kitchen, sneaking away to swim, the thousands and thousands of minor, then serious risks.

The vow Elizabeth had made. That she would not speak to Maria so long as she still spoke of Sam. A vow that kept Elizabeth safe.

"You shouldn't be here," Maria said with conviction as Elizabeth closed the door and took a lantern out of her cloak. She ignored Maria and lit the flame before responding. The barn glowed.

"Well, I am, and so are you," Elizabeth said. "Now, care to tell me why you're stealing Papa's best horse in the middle of a storm?"

"It's a long story," Maria said, rushing back to harness Snip, an enormous draft horse. "One you don't want to, nor should, be a part of." It took everything in her to keep up her guard, to not dissolve into apologies. But Elizabeth couldn't be involved. Not in this. Not now.

Elizabeth guffawed. "I've been so bored and miserable and sorry without you."

Sorry. Maria had that, too. More than Elizabeth could know. But she had a duty to protect her sister.

"I have time," Elizabeth added. "For the long story."

"I don't," Maria said, her fingers shaking as she tightened the straps. For a bitter moment, she remembered the luxury of being bored. "I think something terrible is happening. And it's too complicated to explain."

Elizabeth stepped closer, looking her in the eye. "I've missed you so much." She exhaled. "How I've hated myself for letting you leave on your own, for getting jailed again, then everything else that happened. I even regret that stupid condition I put on you when we parted. I was acting like Mama."

Maria lunged for the bridle, then paused. Elizabeth was already on the other massive side of Snip, adjusting the saddle.

"Please," Elizabeth said. "Let me help you this time. Help me make it right."

She shouldn't. She wouldn't again. And yet: This might be the last time Maria would have to decide.

Heaven knows she'd missed her, too. Someone who truly loved her.

Maria sighed. "Only this once," she said with a weak smile, struggling to put her reckless plan into language. "Remember where I learned to swim? There was a raft there. A sturdy one Sam and I made."

Elizabeth pulled a face. The familiarity of that gesture overwhelmed Maria, and she embraced her sister once more—this time without any reservations—remembering all the times in the past year she'd longed for the company of her sister.

"Thank you. I'll explain on the way," Maria said with urgency. "But I'm warning you: You won't like it one bit."

CHAPTER 48

A wave washed over the deck as Sam reached the navigation team. They'd been battling the storm for the better part of the night. A swell forced the wheel to spin, and he sprang to stabilize it beside Hoof and Montgomery. They groaned loudly under the wheel's strong resistance. Sam's knuckles blazed white. Hoof cursed in Swedish.

Captain Robert Ingols, in contrast, lay curled up with panic beside them on the deck.

Sam wiped the frigid spray from his eyes and grabbed Ingols by the front of his coat.

"Where are we, man?" Sam shouted.

Ingols cried and tried to cover his face.

"Look at me!" Sam demanded, pulling him closer.

"I don't know," Ingols said, whimpering and tearing at his stringy hair. "By my life, I do not know!"

Ingols shriveled into a mutter of oaths and prayers as Sam whirled on the others.

"Where's Julian?" Sam roared, his voice raw from speaking over the incessant thunder.

Where was his capable pilot?

"Haven't seen him since the cannon on the lower deck got

loose, Commodore," Hoof said, straining to upright the wheel as another wave crested and the *Whydah* dove, causing Sam's stomach to lurch.

Julian.

Sam's chest seized. He rounded on the brooding Scot.

"And you. Do you know these waters better than your sniveling captain?"

"Yes." Montgomery's eyes narrowed. "I know them."

Again, the wheel spun and it took all three men to hold it steady. Somewhere in the distance, Sam heard a series of screams.

"Guide us to deeper waters," Sam said through gritted teeth. "I stand by my word to your captain. You'll be rewarded. If you fail, we all perish—you included."

A smash came from below, followed by the rip of a sail.

"I'll find more men to hold the wheel," Sam said, tearing away to look for Julian.

Every joint felt numb against the damp chill as Sam took in the nightmare through the flickering lantern haze—he'd never seen another scene like it. Lines lashed out like vipers as the crew scrambled to tie them back again. Some strained to pump out water, while others had abandoned post. Some climbed the ladders from the treasure hold, their pockets bulging and their eyes wild with terror. Many had scaled the rigging, clinging to escape the onslaught of water. Total darkness enveloped large portions of the deck, the men working blindly.

"Stay calm," Sam ordered. "Work together and mind your positions!"

He fumbled to stand, then stomped across the flooded planks. No sign of Julian.

A rumble of thunder clapped overhead.

So, Sam thought with a sinking awareness. *You find me again. This time, here at her doorstep.*

A swell knocked him to his knees. He bit through his bottom

lip as the ship angled to an impossible incline, then righted again. He spat out the metallic taste and pushed down the impulse to vomit.

This world knew so little forgiveness. It shouldn't still surprise him. Sam, whose crew had tried to justify benefitting from a cursed slave ship instead of sinking it. Who'd taken Davis against his will. Who'd stolen loot from a hundred ships.

"But are my methods so much worse than you?" he railed aloud with challenge. "You, an invisible force who stands aside as the ruling powers claim you for their own gain? I tried to change. I *am* changed. Not that it seems to make any difference to you."

I sound mad.

Maybe I am *mad.*

He pulled out a pistol and pointed at the indifferent rain. He might deserve this, but his brothers didn't.

"Have me, but not my crew."

I told you where to find me. Face-to-face. One-on-one.

The shot echoed for a moment before the thunder answered louder.

"COWARD!" he said, knocked off-balance again. He wouldn't— he couldn't—keep wasting his energy like this.

Not when he knew this was his own damn fault. Another wave swept over the deck, followed by the bloodcurdling shriek of someone washed overboard.

Then he heard it: the splintering of the mainmast again, still weak from the latest storm.

"Davis!" Sam yelled, scanning the ghostly faces of everyone within reach for a sign of the carpenter. "Where's Davis?"

"No sign of 'im, Bellamy," Webb said as a shudder from the ship slung him against the rail. He gasped with pain. "Not of him or the *Fisher.*"

Sam hurled himself at the rail, searching the void for any sign of the lantern from John Brown's sloop.

Instead, he saw land.

* * *

Sam shoved Montgomery away from the wheel, sending him sprawling onto his back.

"You've led us straight to shore," Sam spat.

Montgomery smiled. "I have."

Sam's mouth went dry. He balled his hands into fists, ignoring the confusion of Hoof and the others behind him.

"Never trust the word of a pirate," Montgomery said. "Your carpenter told me everything."

The *Whydah* rose on a swell and crashed down again as Sam steadied himself against a wall. A sheet of lightning blinded the sky. The wind wailed like a demon, and Sam saw everything cross his vision in a sickening instant. He clamped a hand to his chest and thought of his two hundred brothers. Julian and Abel. Little King and Quintor. All of them.

"Breakers!" someone shouted at the waves. "Breakers!"

They had no time to correct.

"Drop the anchors," Sam ordered, his voice ragged yet fierce. "Stop everything and drop anchor!"

The steadfast crew scrambled to follow the directive, a desperate tactic they'd recognize. They rang the galley's bell, and the *Whydah* pivoted into the gales.

The wheel spun like a frantic clock and Sam closed his eyes.

Work, he begged. He had no one and nothing to pray to anymore. For all his debates with Maria about the absurdity of predestination or a vengeful, justice-seeking God, he wasn't so confident anymore.

But if they could avoid the treacherous Cape Cod shallows a moment longer. If they could wait out—

An enormous jolt sent him flying across the deck, slamming him hard enough to crack the rail. His shoulder wound reopened. He gasped, but no sound emerged.

"Sandbar!" someone bellowed as the terrible scraping continued.

Cannons tore from their carriages, crushing through the lower decks. Barrels of nails careening across the flood. The world tilted.

Howls cut off in midair as a gigantic wall of water rushed the deck.

A shock of cold, a vortex of sound.

Then, Sam's body hurled into the deep.

CHAPTER 49

Rain and sea spray pummeled Elizabeth and Maria as they drove the cart onto the Atlantic-facing beach. Dune cliffs towered to the left. She set her jaw, bracing against the burning chill. Maria had tried to explain everything as they'd traveled, aware of her sister's silent and sometimes not-so-silent skepticism and doubts. Maybe Maria *had* been misguided, flushed with exertion and nervous about her new path into the unknown.

Still, her heartbeat rivaled the thunder. She'd refused to turn back despite the force of the storm.

"The waves," Elizabeth uttered with something like reverence. "I've never seen them this big."

The gusts and deep sand caused the cart to rock and drag. Maria whipped around and checked the knots, ensuring the raft they'd hauled from First Encounter Beach was still tied securely. They'd found it as Sam and Maria had left it: sturdy yet flexible. The clove hitch knots still strong, if a little crusted with dirt.

Snip tossed his head as a flash of lightning illuminated the torrential sky. Elizabeth made soothing noises and held the reins until the horse stopped.

"Did you see that?" Maria asked Elizabeth, her gaze fixed on something on the dark ocean. She covered the lantern with her dress to let her sight adjust, then pointed. "There—"

"Shh," Elizabeth said, eyes wide. "I hear something."

Maria's ears pricked, listening for sounds beyond the ferocious winds and the roar of the sea.

Is that a scream?

Snip snorted, redoubling his efforts to pull the cart through sand as his feathered hooves trudged forward. Gales sent the stinging grains flying into Maria's eyes.

"Someone's there," Elizabeth said, her voice suddenly less sure of itself.

Maria slipped from the seat, pulling her red cloak around her. A figure fumbled along the beach in their direction.

"You there," Maria shouted, waving her arms. She lurched for the lantern and raced toward the man.

It *was* a man.

A young one. A native boy, no older than herself. Teeth chattering and clothes torn, he limped quickly forward.

"Be careful, Maria," Elizabeth said, but Maria drew closer.

"Are you hurt?" she said.

He shook his head of wet hair vigorously, then looked left. A cry escaped his lips. "The ship."

"What ship?" Maria said, unable to breathe. Forgetting herself, she grabbed his trembling hand. "Tell me."

Tell me what I already know.

His bronze face reflected the lantern light, terror etched across his pupils. He had a scar along his brow. "The *Whydah*. My brothers." A full-body shiver overtook him, and Maria threw his arm around her shoulder, helping him stand.

"Does the name Samuel Bellamy mean anything to you?" she asked.

The man's lip quivered, and he shot her an evaluating look. "More than most," he said with despair, then stared with horror at the abyss.

The air sucked clean from Maria's lungs, and her ears buzzed. She snapped her focus back on the horizon. It gave her no pleasure to be right.

Elizabeth held Snip's reins. Her face had paled, all unspoken protests gone. Her brows arched with astonishment and recognition of the truth confirmed. "Maria?"

But Maria was already at the back of the cart, frantic to unhitch the raft. The shipwrecked man saw the task at hand and tried to assist her, but his blue-purple fingers struggled with the straps.

"You're Bellamy's Maria, aren't you?" He winced, then sighed with regret. "I'm damn sorry. He was eager to see you."

The raft fell with a thunk, but Maria couldn't bring herself to look at him.

Sam had mentioned her.

He'd remembered her all along.

He had returned.

Then they heard it: a terrible crack, the splintering of wood—violent and long, long, long as it shredded the distance.

"The hull," the man mourned, collapsing to his knees, burying his face in his hands.

"Get him to safety," Maria said to Elizabeth, dragging the raft toward the water with urgency. Was anywhere safe for a pirate? The young man surely understood his precarious situation. "He needs a hearth, and fast. Give him some food from my basket."

Elizabeth followed, locking the cart wheel and leaving Snip alone after uttering a prayer.

"Maria, it's too dangerous. Even by your standards. We have to go back. Find the right people who can help."

Maria bit her tongue, suddenly stiff with fear that had nothing to do with Elizabeth's usual rebukes.

A lifeless form lay on the beach, limbs and blond hair tangled like a wad of seaweed.

"Is that . . ." Elizabeth started.

Sickness welled up, and Maria gagged. The ocean tossed the

body farther up the beach like a straw doll. She couldn't unsee the cruel indifference.

"Tell me what the raft is really for," Elizabeth said with forced steadiness.

"To send to anyone thrown overboard," Maria said, swallowing traces of bile. "As I said."

Elizabeth balked. "You mean, risking *your* life by going out there."

A distant wailing echoed in the distance. A chorus. Maria saw by Elizabeth's widening eyes that they'd both heard it.

Maria needed to act. Now. Before Elizabeth could beg her not to go. Before her better senses overtook her. What had Sam and a group of pirates done to deserve her aid? After all this time and silence? When her new life—a good one built by her own hands— stretched out before her?

Why now, after so much pain?

But what of the good?

What of her heart? And that intangible, infuriating something beyond reasons "why"?

"Please, hold the light high and watch for survivors," Maria said as gently as she could. Thunder rumbled overhead. "Look for bodies." There would be more. "And guide the man somewhere warm."

But when they turned, the man was already gone, clambering up and over the steep dune cliffs toward town—beyond earshot.

"Oh, sister," Elizabeth cried, stumbling forward to wrap her into a hug. "I cannot lose you again."

Maria's throat burned, and she held Elizabeth tighter.

"Promise you'll return," Elizabeth sobbed. Though they both knew there was no way for Maria to return, to continue how everything used to be. If anyone saw them together, Elizabeth might still endure the consequences.

Maria's vision blurred. *Remember this*, she thought, holding her loyal sister, that familiar copper hair tickling her cheek. A wall of water crashed nearby, sending a chilling flood over their boots. But Maria did not move. Not just yet.

I almost drowned over much less.
Because of him, I am here.
But because of me, I've become a strong swimmer.

A warm conviction seized her chest. It was time. Now or never. She might still save a few. To turn back would mean a life of what-ifs. She'd lived long enough with those.

Maria removed her red cloak and flung it over Elizabeth's shoulders. She braced for the knife stab of cold awaiting her.

"There are still things I have to tell you," Elizabeth said with disbelief, shouting over the wind.

"I love you," Maria said, stepping away to tie a rope between the raft and her own waist. She chose her next words carefully. "Stay close. I'll be near."

CHAPTER 50

Red glowed behind Sam's eyelids, causing him to stir. Then he flinched with startling agony.

The churning black water.

Those howls and ghoulish shrieks.

Clambering for a piece of driftwood in the shock of cold.

A crackle of something familiar, something hot. His nostril twitched at the smell of smoke. Fire.

Was this hell at last?

Sam heard steps. Felt a cool cloth press against his forehead. He moaned but did not recognize the pathetic sound.

Had he been crying?

"You wake at last," came a voice. Rich and female. He tried to pry his swollen eyes open.

Sucked and thrown, like a pebble in a whirlpool.

Pounded like a nail. A mouthful of sand.

The stabs of pain with every bounce of . . . what was it?

A tangy smell.

A horse.

"Fever and scrapes, three cracked ribs, and an infected wound on your shoulder. I don't have to be the one to tell you how lucky you are to be alive."

Maria.

Sam jolted, attempting to sit as memory rushed back. He lay on a reed mat, a circular opening in the ceiling revealing a gray sky overhead. A fire pit burned at the center of the shelter constructed of domed tree poles. His lungs heaved for air as his blurry vision fixed on the speaker's face: a Wampanoag woman. Dark concerned eyes. Raven-black hair tied into a braid.

Not Maria.

"Look at me. Let me examine your eyes."

The woman propped him up and held up a candle, which made him wince. Sweat drenched his bare chest. He panted, peering down at his shaking, bruise-colored fingers. He tried to move, a throb searing through his shoulder. A fresh bandage had been applied.

His attendant pulled away the light and sighed. "You hit your head. Hard. Can you remember your name?"

A wall of water yanking him away from the ship.

The menacing thunder.

He could still hear their cries.

He nodded. "Samuel Bellamy." Orphan from Devonshire. Sailor in the King's Navy. Captain of the *Marianne.* Commodore of the *Whydah.*

A failure to everyone.

"I thought so," the woman said, scraping a mix of pungent herbs into a cup. "Drink this. What else do you remember?"

A silent sob emerged from his raw throat. He swallowed it hard, gritting his teeth to contain the pain and fury.

Montgomery's bloody trickery.

"I remember everything," Sam said. His fingers trembled as they grasped the cup. He couldn't bring himself to go on.

Were there other survivors?

But not survivors for long, he reminded himself. He could already feel the rope around his neck. See Maria's emerald eyes glaring up at him below the gallows.

The woman's gaze softened. "Drink," she demanded, and he

did. The tea was not as bitter as he'd expected, slipping smoothly down his throat.

"My name is Abiah. I found you far up the beach in Billingsgate. Before the whole town—those vile grave robbers—set upon the coast to search the bodies."

"Did you find others?" Sam asked, holding his breath.

Abiah shook her head. "Not alive. Only a few sets of footprints."

No.

It couldn't be.

Sam stared at the air between them.

I asked You to take your vengeance on me, not my crew.

This was worse. So much worse.

"But it is a wide coast, as you know," Abiah continued, yanking his attention back. "When I found your pulse, I brought you here to my home. You shouldn't be here. Yes, I know what you are." She twisted her mouth and sighed. "But I am a healer by nature, sometimes despite my better judgment. And besides, I have questions for you."

Sam put the tea aside and lay down again. Tears slipped out the corners of his eyes. If she'd meant to turn him in, she could have done it by now. "Thank you," he said with gravity, wishing he could trade places with anyone else in his crew. He recognized skilled hands when he saw them—skilled hands wasted on him instead of his brothers. "I am ready to answer honestly."

"What brings you back?"

He tried to breathe deeply, feeling his lungs rattle. He had nothing to hide, nothing to prove anymore.

"A woman I love."

The air seemed to still. A log on the fire popped and shifted.

"My men wanted to make the stop, too," he added. *Do not, do not, picture their faces.* He'd leave their names out of it, just in case they stood a chance. "Two intended to retire. The others wanted to make good on their debts with Israel Cole at the Great Island Tavern, or sell things on the black market." His eyes met Abiah's. "But for me, it was for her. It was always—all of it—for Maria."

Again he felt his throat tighten, spurring on a cough. He balled his fist, fingernails digging into his flesh.

"Did you know?" asked Abiah, offering him the cup again.

Sam whipped his attention back, trying to read her face.

"Did I know what?"

"That she was pregnant?"

Sam could barely see. Blood shot through his veins and his head pulsed, trying to take it all in. How could it be?

A son. His own child.

Dead.

His body shook with dizzying rage. He groped for his brace of pistols, long lost. Damn Hallett. Damn the whole of Eastham! Branding Maria as a witch. Fools! What hateful, ignorant non-sense. Blithering bastards! God-wielding devils! He'd tear down the town if he had to. One last flare of revenge. One last act of vengeance.

And what about him?

While she lived out a winter in exile, waiting, he was gallivanting to glory on a string of ships. Collecting gold and gold and more gold.

All of it, now settling at the bottom of the ocean. Along with the fate of his crew—their laughter, their rants over ale, their luminous dreams, their varied, valid reasons for going on the account.

Gone.

Another sob rose, morphing into a ringing bellow. He let it out, then tore at his salt-crusted hair.

"But the letter," Sam said, pushing himself up, his voice quick and urgent as he came to his senses. "She wrote me a letter to announce her marriage. She told me to never return. That she'd never have me again, knowing I'd turned pirate."

Abiah's brows knitted. "Lie down. You are fevered and confused."

"Where is she?" Sam asked, ignoring his body's screaming protests and forcing himself to stand. He stumbled, then stood again.

His ribs felt like they'd been shot clean through, but his legs were strong enough. He'd walk, however long it took.

Abiah studied him thoughtfully. A shadow crossed her face, and she didn't move or answer.

"Where is Maria?"

CHAPTER 51

Maria held her knees to her chest, hiding atop the dune cliffs. She'd wrapped the red cloak around her bruised shoulders to cover her torn dress. She rocked, then pressed her eyes shut. As if she could close it all out. As if she could ever be warm or happy again.

Three.

Three souls.

That was all she'd been able to pull to safety, who'd then made their way up and over the dunes.

Only three, among all those broken forms rolling in the waves, crashed onto the shore, as shattered and dispensable as flotsam.

And none of them were him.

A rustle to her right told her Elizabeth had returned. Maria did not look up but felt her sister settle beside her in the sand. The sky overhead was gray and flat as a dull blade, as if the night before had never happened.

"Maria?"

Elizabeth grabbed Maria's hand, holding it tight. The kind gesture made Maria's eyes water.

"Will you speak? If not to me, to Abiah?"

Maria felt her chest expand with air, then shrink again. She'd refused to risk her friend by entering the "praying town" sector relegated to the Wampanoag. Abiah had found Elizabeth among the wreckage by the sight of Maria's familiar red cloak, then borrowed Snip with a promise to find them again soon. Moments later, Elizabeth had dragged Maria from the water, the raft slipping from sight.

"It's done," Elizabeth kept saying, over and over, restraining Maria's weak attempts to fight and return to the water as a scarlet dawn cracked over the calming horizon.

No, Maria would not go to the praying town, however much she longed to see Abiah. The last thing Abiah needed was for the land cause to be associated in any way with a witch. Especially the day Maria's famed pirate crashed within sight of her fishing shack in Billingsgate. People needed far less to stoke the imagination. Far less reason to hate.

Elizabeth stirred the fire and put her arm around her sister. The touch shot pain through her muscles, but Maria didn't mind.

"The whole town is on the beach," Elizabeth said. "Searching."

Maria knew what that meant. Not searching for survivors, but for treasure. She'd seen snatches of it before fleeing. They left the bodies and groped for the loot. Pieces of eight from bulging pockets. Weapons and leather boots. She'd made out Mrs. Smith, who'd always sat in the front pew at church, cutting off a man's ear to snap up his gold earring.

Ruthless. All of them. Nothing new, but no less disturbing. Maria understood desperation. She knew the poor circumstances of many Eastham citizens. But she could never, *never* do what she'd witnessed that morning.

"I spoke with Lydia," Elizabeth said with feigned neutrality. "We can find a place for you to hide in her father's furniture warehouse. It might not be safe for you to be on the roads or in your fishing shack for a while."

This again? Maria rested her head on her sister's shoulder. How to make Elizabeth understand? She loved her too much. She would not risk anyone else she cared for again, and meant it. Destruction tracked her like a hunter. She seemed to make for easy prey.

"At least Mama didn't notice my disappearance," Elizabeth offered brightly to lighten the mood. "She and Papa think I made an early start, that I'm still hard at work gathering like the rest of Eastham before Captain Southack arrives from Boston. The governor himself summoned the captain to investigate the scene."

And to sweep up whatever treasure remained for the government, Maria suspected.

"You should return to them," Maria said, finding her voice again for the first time since the morning. It came out rough and scratchy. "Lydia will be worried."

But Elizabeth did not stiffen, as she used to do when Maria brought up the subject of her intimate friend. Instead, Maria felt her smile.

"She knows I am where I need to be. Besides," Elizabeth laughed with a playful nudge, "I'm better off than I was before. Thanks to you, I am in no danger of being married off to the next Mr. Hallett."

Maria tried to laugh, to savor these last moments with her sister. "How is it at home? Tell me about the family."

A snort and the sound of hooves behind them made the sisters startle. They turned to see Abiah, slipping down from Snip. The sisters rose and Abiah rushed forward, eyes intent on Maria.

"You're alive," Abiah said, with one of her rare, broad grins. She said something in Wampanoag and reached out her hands. Maria took them and squeezed.

"I have a habit of staying that way." It *was* good to see her again.

Then Abiah's gaze shifted, heavy with something unspoken. The intensity made Maria take a few steps backward, bracing herself.

"He lives, too," Abiah said. "Do you wish to see him?"

* * *

Under the cover of oncoming dusk, Maria paced while Elizabeth stood under a cluster of white pines. Crickets hummed. Her whole body vibrated with anticipation, like she might snap from the tension.

What if I don't want to see him?

Her stomach squirmed.

Or what if he doesn't want to see me?

If he blames me for the loss of his crew?

Losing focus, she'd tripped on her basket of provisions. To Elizabeth's credit, she did not chuckle as Maria muttered and righted herself.

Maybe he is unrecognizably hurt.

No, Abiah would have warned me.

Maria didn't know how to feel as she twisted the ends of her sun-dried hair, conscious for once of every yellowing bruise on her body, the way her torn gray dress hung off her bony shoulders beneath her cloak. The smokey smell of it, of her.

How none of that mattered.

"Do you want me to slap him when they emerge?" Elizabeth asked, arms folded as she watched Maria fret. "I'm sure I'd be good at it, with all the practicing I've done in my mind. Characters in my novels do it all the time."

Maria grunted with satisfying acknowledgment, clenching and unclenching her hands.

He didn't need to be hurt to be unrecognizable. How much she had changed. Maybe she didn't need to see him to forgive him. Or maybe she had already forgiven him. Maybe the idea of him, the memory of him, was enough. He'd lived. That could be enough.

A snap of twigs announced their arrival. Abiah led Snip by the reins, the cart rolling behind with a lantern swaying.

Maria gulped.

One heartbeat.

Two.

Abiah nodded at Elizabeth, who understood the cue and stepped away from the clearing, giving Maria space.

Heart hammering, Maria floated toward the cart. She held her breath, ready to see what was left of the man she'd known.

Then, a set of strong arms embraced her from behind, causing her to gasp.

Sam.

CHAPTER 52

Her lips finding his, his finding hers. Hard and bitter, yet sure. The thousands of words he had to say. *Needed* to say. All his talking and big ideas. The miles and months to cross.

And yet here. *Her.* A language beyond language. Theirs and theirs alone.

They still spoke it.

"Maria," he said, her name like the breaking of a spell, like the summonings from all those nights he'd stared into the stars from the rocking deck, willing her to feel him.

"You came," she whispered, sounding part furious, part disbelieving, part delirious with joy as she shook her head. "You came home."

Home. Yes, she'd always been home. His true and better north. Maria hugged him tight, and he gasped. "Ribs. Mind the ribs." Still he held her, ignoring the stabs of protest, feeling the heat of her close. He brushed a strand of her long hair from her shoulder, ran his thumb along her chin. How *strong* she appeared. Like a Viking goddess returned from war. A war she should never have had to fight.

Lord, she was beautiful.

Then with great effort he sank to his knees, holding her callused hands. They trembled, as did his.

The tears welled. "I am unspeakably sorry—no better than a sack of begging fleas." She stared down at him. He up at her. A hardened pain flashed across her face, and her jaw set.

"Abiah told me. What they did to you." He felt the lump in his throat return, forcing it down for a moment longer. "Our son," he broke.

"I know," Maria said, countenance softening as she knelt beside him in the dirt. He chewed his fists, biting back the sound. She took his hand, uncurled it, and pressed it to her heart. "I know."

"It's no excuse. I should have been here, I should have never left you."

"And I should have come with you when you asked," Maria said, reaching up to trace his ear, his neck, the V of his tattered coat. "Though piracy requires a serious explanation," she rebuked, raising a brow.

It did, he knew. And hoped, with time—though she may never agree with his methods—he might help her see the reasons why.

His throat tightened, imagining his men. Their sunken dreams.

"If I'd known—if you'd told me the truth, I would have come with due haste," Sam said, regaining his voice, combing his fingers through her tangled hair.

Her forehead creased with confusion.

"Why did you tell me to stay away? Why did you send me that awful letter?"

"She didn't."

Sam jerked his attention around.

"Elizabeth?" Maria said, staggering to her feet. Sam followed suit, pretending it didn't hurt like the devil. He placed an arm around her waist.

Her sister wouldn't.

She didn't—

Elizabeth frowned, looking between Sam and Maria, then back at Abiah. Her freckled cheeks seemed to redden to the shade of her tresses. "I had to tell you. Every night I waited at the bedroom window, hoping you'd come back," she said to Maria. "I tried to tell you at the beach last night. But I was too late. And I worried, after, that you'd go mad with grief."

Sam heard Maria's voice harden. "What letter?"

"His," Elizabeth said, nodding toward Sam. "I found it the Sunday before last. I was searching for a scripture. I came across it, tucked into Mama's Bible." Sam watched Maria blanch as Elizabeth summarized the contents. His temples pulsed. He had a foggy image of Maria's mother. Her rattling threat when she'd chased him from the house after he'd proposed.

Leave, she'd said. *Never come back.*

Mrs. Brown, the cause of so much anguish.

"Did you find a necklace?" Sam asked, his pulse rising with a swell of hope. Perhaps Hornigold had been able to deliver the gift, a prize that might deliver him and—if she willed it—Maria away from this place.

To marry her properly. With a ring. His chest squeezed at the undeserving thought.

"It'd be pure gold," Sam rushed on. "With small little beads, like pearls?"

Elizabeth shook her head and sighed. "No."

"So the pieces come together," Abiah said thoughtfully. "Interesting—they so rarely do." She nodded for Elizabeth to follow her. "Let us ready the cart for a journey."

But Sam reached out to stop them. What else did they know? "Have you heard news of other survivors?"

Elizabeth froze, then looked down. "Some knocked on doors. I do not know about the others, though they say a boat called the *Fisher* was captured. A few were found in a shed by Justice Doane."

Doane.

The same brute who'd taken his child from Maria.

The dog who'd dared to whip her.

He gritted his teeth. "Any man by name?"

Elizabeth hesitated, but straightened. "I only know the rumors. What folks said at the beach. They say a Mr. Thomas Davis survived. That he is prepared to bear testimony against the pirates."

He felt the blast like cannon fire.

"Sam?" Maria asked, gazing up at him. He hadn't let go of her hand, and his fingers tingled from how tightly he'd held on.

Suddenly, his dizziness returned. He leaned against Maria, who threw his arm around her shoulder. He winced, his vision blurring at the edges. The reality came crashing in, as visceral and pounding as the waves that should have swallowed him the night before.

"If there are survivors, I must stay," Sam said, his voice weary, longing to resume the fantasy. He cleared his throat, then strained to look at Maria. He found his balance again. "I am their captain. I must share their fate."

She ripped away, leaving him to wobble on what felt like sea legs. Losing the warmth of her filled his whole body with chills, the fever suddenly oppressive and near.

"Surely he doesn't mean it," Elizabeth said with alarm, whirling for answers. "Abiah, can we give him something to calm his nerves?"

"I mean it," Sam said with regret. Maybe Davis would do him in at last. Sam probably deserved it. Deserved all of it, and worse. He certainly didn't deserve Maria.

A terrible silence filled the twilight air. He longed to end it, to shatter the sorrow. To erase all that had happened. His culpability toward Maria, toward his friends.

"No," Maria said.

Nobody spoke, just turned and stared. Sam fixated on her back facing him, her arms folded.

"I said *no*," she repeated. Her face was etched with stony resolution. A kind of look he'd seen long before.

Not just courage. Conviction.

"You want to make things right? You want to talk about honor?" she said, rounding on him. "Do you think the hangman needs an extra pair of boots? That this would even the game? What good would you be to me, or anyone else who's escaped, if you're dead? You and I know exactly what will happen to the captured pirates, what will happen to you if you give yourself up."

Sam swallowed. He knew, all right. "I led them. They trusted me. They were—are—my brothers," he said, trailing off.

"And what am I?"

My heart. My whole, beating heart.

"Would you have a man without honor? Don't think I want—"

She yanked him by the coat, dueling with him eye to eye, soul to soul. Her blade sharper than ever. A thrill shot through him, from head to miserable, unworthy toe.

"Damn men's honor," she snapped. "I've heard enough about men and their honor. You promised me a shared life, Samuel Bellamy! You made promises to *me* first." Her anger fizzled into a sudden, fierce tenderness, and she pulled him close, pressing her cold nose to his. He touched her lips. He could feel her quick heartbeat against him, like a hummingbird's wings.

"I don't know if you were right," she whispered, the softness of her brushing his fingertips. "All those honey words and speeches. If people like you and me can try to heal any part of this broken world." She gazed up, intent. "But *I* have changed. And I imagine you have, too."

She had changed. Immeasurably. He could see that. A sense of groundedness. Surer of herself. Radiant in her knowing.

"As sure as the tide turns," he said, her breath hot against his mouth. He leaned in, closing the distance, every nerve responding. His insides ignited, his hands lunging again to find her body, to draw her into him. To burn the fever clean out of him.

"A pity, to be sure, that land-thief Mr. Brown will have lost a good horse in the storm," Abiah said by way of interruption, holding out the reins and circling the cart around. "The cover of night will aid you. The white men will stay busy with their plundering and grave robbing. You, at least, have coin to get you started." Then she addressed Sam. "Gained by the honest sweat of her brow."

Sam took a pace back, searched Maria's eyes.

"It's a long story." She tugged Sam's hand, a gesture that said, *Come.*

Please. Come with me.

Be free.

There could be time. Time to talk. Time to grieve. Time to unbury, then bury the past. To change, for the better. Together this time.

"Where will you go?" Elizabeth asked, her voice breaking as she flung her arms around her sister. "How will you live?"

Sam closed his eyes. Opened them.

An island green as spring grass.

More could come. If given the chance, anyone could follow. His men would know where to go.

He squeezed Maria's hand with a sweet rush of relief. What he couldn't do for the dead, he might still do for the living.

"I know a place," he said at last.

PILOGUE

Dear One,

If you receive this letter, give my thanks to L. for another safe delivery. I think of you often, as well as little M. Though you confess my "blatant rebellion" does not yet tempt you by way of choices, that you can enjoy life without so much pain and loss, I want you to know that there is talk of freedom here in this new place. I miss you terribly, though you may be pleased to hear I am happy. Happier than I ever thought a person could be. How can that be, after so much sorrow? I walk to the shore—the same salt smell of sea, the same yellow hue at low tide—to hear the gulls caw. The waves and the birds seem to remind me that the questions are more important than the answers, and perhaps the questions themselves are less important than just existing.

We read old papers for any news of the court proceedings in Boston. P.W. says the king is overwhelmed with the number of former sailors turned pirate and moves to make a general pardon. It couldn't come soon enough. How dreadful to have Cotton Mather involved in the case. S. can barely speak of it. I've never seen a man more eager to work: always chopping wood, or sweeping the floor, or building a shelter for a newcomer— whether for utter devotion to me, or to prove his worth again to

*himself, I do not know. Though he vows to never step aboard a
sailing ship again (despite training as a shipwright), I catch him
looking over his shoulder, casting his eye for another survivor. At
night, when he sleeps, sometimes he speaks with ghosts.*

*As for myself, I find I am not so afraid of ghosts anymore.
Maybe because of my darling son. Maybe because I think I used
to be a ghost. Or am one, a haunt that Eastham likes to feed and
keep alive for their own devices. I used to hate the stories you
described in your letters: how the Devil himself came to me in
the jail, how I sold my soul for the power to escape. The worst,
to have summoned that terrible storm four months ago, uttering
ridiculous curses on the dunes as I brought down the ship, then
scurried back into my fishing shack.*

*Perhaps we should encourage it. I find I like the idea of being
a ghost they can't get rid of. Spread stories like wildfire. Make me
into a legend. Talk of red shoes that make me fly, or where I keep
the buried treasure. Let them think I killed S., or that one of his
pirates slew me. Tell them the wailing wind they hear at night is
my vengeful scream. Let them fear me.*

What a relief, to no longer fear them.

*When you see A., please give her my regards, along with the
rare herbs I've included with this letter (she'll know what to do
with them). If you can reply, please give word about the fight
against the land divisions. A. would be keen for anything else you
might sneak from the office. They never suspect the women, though
mind you, be careful. Unless you want to end up like me, which I
wouldn't protest so much anymore. Not if it meant you'd join me
in this glorious place.*

With all my affection,
M.B.

Author's Note

The story of Maria and Samuel Bellamy swept me up while on a trip to Provincetown, Massachusetts, in the late summer of 2015. Walking along the hot wharf, I found myself lured into a museum advertising an authenticated, sunken pirate ship. Though I've had a lifelong fascination with the Golden Age of Pirates, what bowled me over was what I learned about this *particular* pirate, Samuel Bellamy: a poor navy sailor, unemployed once the War of the Spanish Succession ended—putting more than forty thousand other English sailors out of a job—who sailed to Cape Cod to see relatives and find work. Then, as many of the great tales go, he met someone who caught his eye.

After touring the exhibit, I had more questions. I asked a museum employee about Bellamy and his crew, confirming some of the information on signs that had described a democratic government aboard run by "articles" and votes, a system with equal pay, racial diversity, and an early form of workers' compensation. They called themselves "Robin Hood's men" and seemed to see themselves as part of a social movement against corrupt governments and oppression of the day. It felt remarkably modern.

Somewhat skeptical of this romanticized take on a grim period of history, and recognizing the dearth of primary documents by women and illiterate underclasses during this time, I asked the museum employee to tell me more. I expressed sorrow that so many answers sank with Bellamy and his ship, all within sight of where Maria was said to have lived in exile.

"I wouldn't go that far," the young employee said with excitement, contradicting what the museum itself seemed to indicate. Though Sam Bellamy had almost certainly died with most of his crew in an enormous nor'easter storm on the night of April 26, 1717, no one ever found his body. "They say people saw two sets of footprints leading away from Maria's cabin. After that night, she disappeared."

This was the first rumor of many others I unearthed over the years. But of all the varied, contradicting accounts accumulated over three centuries about what happened to Sam and Maria—some more popular than others, all impossible to confirm—it was this first image that arrested my attention. I swore to myself, right there in the museum, that I would learn more, then write a book about Maria and Sam. *This* book. A novel that grew from that single shred of hope, that looming "if." And when I finally sat down to write years later, the first thing that came out was the prologue—fully formed, ready, and haunting—exactly as you see it printed in this book.

This is a work of fiction. Period. A blend of purely made-up elements alongside legends, myth, folktales, and layers of history I interpreted and animated according to the characters I saw in my heart through a modern lens. This was a difficult time to be alive for most people, for women, lower classes, and especially people of color—a time of ruthless colonization, slavery, starvation, poverty, disease, witch trials, and more. Many pirates and privateers were bloodthirsty thugs, violent, complicit in slave trading, or blatantly racist (the notion of true racial equality aboard pirate ships is one worth interrogating, though there were large ratios of men of color among the motley crews, a few known all-Black crews, and Sam's flotilla had men of color—such as John Brown and John Julian—serving in important roles).

I claim no expertise on piracy as a whole. However, I have studied almost everything I could about this particular pirate's life, who seemed to be cut from a different cloth, or at least not recognizable in the kitschy, whitewashed pirates depicted in modern entertainment. This book does not give a history of pirates, but a story about one. Bellamy's flawed and idealistic crew, fascinating in their own right, ignited my passion to write with little need to embellish: young men, mostly in their twenties, who had a band aboard and put on skits for each other, with less sword fighting or walking of the plank (largely a Hollywood invention). Exaggerated swashbuckling did not interest me and seemed hardly necessary when compared with the excitement of reality.

But the more I leaned into the history, the more I wondered about the lore. Why do we know so much about Sam—how he eschewed wigs, wore a red sash with four pistols, and was fastidiously dressed in a black coat? Why do we know he had started as a treasure hunter with Paulsgrave Williams, son of Rhode Island's attorney general, with a small band in Florida, then went on the account with them in periaguas? Why do we know that he double-crossed Henry Jennings, was given the *Marianne* by Benjamin Hornigold—who saw so much potential and fire in Bellamy—then went on to replace Hornigold as commodore of the flotilla by an overwhelming voting margin? We know Sam had a way with words and have snippets attributed to him of epic speeches. We reasonably know the place of his birth, the names of his parents and siblings, that he was abducted to be a cabin boy before the age of ten, the places he traveled, the famous pirates—such as Edward Teach (later known as Blackbeard) and La Buse—that he worked alongside, the captains he confronted during raids, and the specific loot that he stole.

We know he advocated for Thomas Davis's release and cared about fairness—that when the crew didn't have enough hammocks for every person, he ordered that everyone would sleep on the deck in the meantime, himself included. We know that he railed against the sky during two epic storms that damaged and then destroyed the *Whydah*, shooting off cannons and yelling at the invisible force behind it all. We know he spoke with conviction, persuaded others to his cause, and, as he said to Captain Beer, that he "scorned to do mischief when it [was] not for my advantage." Samuel Bellamy, a twentysomething whose piracy career was short but illustrious, making him one of the richest pirates to have ever lived, has been given a fair bit of attention and research—if not as much as other notorious pirates. Still, he's gone down in the records and books.

But what about Maria?

What about the famed town beauty with a restless spirit like "the Nauset wind," to whom Bellamy was rumored to be returning when Montgomery led them into the perilous shallows? History cannot explain Bellamy's choice, though it shrugs and theorizes, pointing back to her—a character too specific, I believe, to be pure fantasy. (Sheryl Jaffe, coordinator of the Wellfleet Historical Society & Museum, agrees. "I'm sure she was real," Sheryl told me. "There are too many stories.") A similar thing happened with the *Whydah*. People took the ship for legend, another great Cape Cod folktale, until the *Whydah* and heaps of her sunken treasures were discovered in 1984 by explorer Clifford Barry and his team.

If Sam Bellamy and the *Whydah* were as real as it gets, inked in the authority of history, where is the third piece—the crucial motive for the story at all?

This is where I am grateful that I am a writer and not an historian. Truth can find many different forms. Like Kathleen Brunelle, author of *Bellamy's Bride*, I too am fixated on Maria, discontent with her remaining a footnote in this epic.

Brunelle undertook a search for the real Maria (whose nickname may have been pronounced as the less Spanish-sounding Mariah, though 'Maria' is how contemporary Cape Codders and legends know her). Brunelle outlines many possible theories about Maria's historical origins in her book. The one I found most compelling was that of Mehitable Brown, daughter of George Brown and Mehitable Knowles. Though there are records of her birth, "within a year of her nuptials to Hallett, Mehitable simply disappears." Less than a year later, John Hallett remarried. As Brunelle raises, why is there no record of her death, or her child's death? It is almost as if she has been deliberately scrubbed from the record. In another theory, our Maria was a girl named Mary Hallett, who never married but gave strange instructions in her will that she be buried in a string of gold pearls. I include the story of the lost necklace in this novel to nod to that hypothesis.

Countless folktales exist about "Goody Hallett," one of Cape Cod's favorite ghosts. The name "Goody" was short for "Goodwife." It was not Maria's legal name; it was a common, honorific title and identifier for women at the time, much like Miss, Mrs., or Ms. would be used today. The lore says that Maria was an outspoken, strong-willed girl with golden hair and an eye for mischief—the heartthrob of Eastham despite finding her local suitors dull. Others say she was a great weaver and healer, which is how she managed to get by later in life after her banishment. Still others remember her as an older version of her witch-self, who'd gone mad and terrorized the town or snatched up the souls of sailors. I couldn't possibly summarize all the variations: They are a genre unto themselves. Though intriguing in their own right, I wanted my Maria to have dimension and agency, particularly in her relationship with Sam. One popular legend says that Sam saw Maria standing in an apple orchard while he was staying at the Higgins Tavern. It was love at first sight, and implied that they had sex right then and there, before Sam sailed off with a promise to return for her with a ship full of gold and to marry her, despite her parents' disapproval. After giving birth alone in a barn, and losing the child, she was hauled into jail. Some say she escaped three times, that a cloaked family member sprang her out. Others say she gave her soul to the Devil. Eventually, she made her way to Billingsgate (modern-day Wellfleet) to live out her days, standing in a gray homespun dress and watching the horizon for Sam's return. Sometimes with longing, other times with an eye for vengeance. It depends on the tale.

The horrific Salem witch trials dominate most minds when we think of witches and Massachusetts. The events in this book start twenty-two years after that tragedy, a tragedy that seemed to have sparked a collective reckoning. The last hangings happened on September 22, 1692. On October 17, 1711, the Massachusetts Bay province finally declared general amnesty to (most) of the formerly condemned witches, reversing convictions, judgments, and attainers against them. Though killing witches was not as in vogue anymore, the idea of witches certainly did not go away overnight. Sometimes Cape Cod folktales about Maria/ Goody Hallett merge with other witches, such as the Witch of Truro or "the Screecham Sisters." Witch was a label hurled especially at Indigenous women, such as Delilah Sampson Gibbs (whom I discuss shortly).

Women like Maria, who found themselves pregnant outside of marriage, were not as uncommon as we might suppose as modern readers. Brunelle writes that "some records suggest that upward of twenty-five percent of children were conceived" before marriage. Brunelle continues to describe the Massachusetts Act of 1692 that added fines and whippings to make public examples of female fornicators, as well as the Bastard Neonaticide Act, which Brunelle indicates was a favorite of Cotton Mather's, and also endangered women in Maria's situation. If the infant died, the unwed mother had to have a witness. Otherwise, the guilt fell on the mother and she could be sentenced for infanticide. In 1733, Boston hanged a young woman, Rebekah Chamberlit, whose circumstances were eerily similar to Maria's. Women could also be punished for birth defects, similar to what we see with Mrs. Brown in this novel. As far as queer representation, two women—Sarah White Norman and Mary Vincent Hammond—were indeed charged with "lewd behavior with each other upon a bed" in 1648. I leave Elizabeth's choice to follow Maria at the end of the novel ambiguous as a tribute to the incredible LGBTQIA+ community that would later spring up in Provincetown, Massachusetts.

How could a young woman in the eighteenth century, whose survival depended on good standing in her community, withstand Maria's experience? How did she live? Why would she endure so much for love? The more questions I asked, the more she came alive to me. I knew I'd center her as the true hero of the story.

In addition to yanking Maria out of the shadow of mythology, reclaiming her power to wield the legend in the first place, I also learned about the political issues at the height of this period in Cape Cod over land divisions.

Though the stories of Maria and Sam I've read do not include a friend like Abiah Sampson, or many Indigenous characters apart from John Julian, I wanted to represent the land divisions that were the focus of Eastham's political attention during these years. Failing to do so would be an erasure of important events we should never forget. Things unfolded as best as I can tell the way Abiah describes in the novel. The colonists divided and regulated meadow lands, then common lands, creating a massive deforestation crisis while running both English and Wampanoag off land that was shared for wood, grazing, and gathering. Privatizing the land sparked opposition. According to historian Durand Echeverria in *A History of Billingsgate*, "On June 12, 1711, twenty-five English met and drew up a petition to Governor Joseph Dudley to prevent the division of common lands in Billingsgate." A group of twenty Wampanoag "signed a similar petition." The protests didn't work. Great Island fell next, divided into one hundred thirty-five pieces in 1715. Felling too many trees rapidly destroyed the soil. As Echeverria writes, "Soon the once verdant island was turned into a great dune." The sand plague not only ruined farming, but threatened to fill in the bay and destroy the oyster populations. Tuttomnest, the place the colonists called "James Neck" and later "Indian Neck," was the last holdout for the Wampanoag, who had existed sustainably on Cape Cod for an estimated ten thousand years—an existence and land that the colonists nearly destroyed within less than one hundred.

I loosely based Abiah's character on a historical figure named Delilah Sampson Gibbs, a woman sometimes purported to be "the last Nauset." As the Wellfleet Historical Society & Museum rightly points out, "The narrative of the 'last Indian' survives in many, many towns and area histories. It emanates from the concept of the 'vanishing Indian' that was established in the nineteenth century. These concepts erase Indigenous peoples from the history of their own homelands, allowing unfettered claim to those lands." The Wampanoag Nation still exists today as a vibrant community. (*We Still Live Here*, a powerful documentary by Anne Makepeace, tells the story of the revitalization of the Wampanoag language, the first time a language with no native speakers has been revived in the United States.)

We know precious little about Gibbs's life. What I did learn I gathered from the Mashpee Wampanoag Indian Museum, oral history documents, land deeds, and from Linda Coombs, an Aquinnah Wampanoag tribe member and historian, who helped put on an exhibit about Gibbs's life at the Wellfleet Historical Society & Museum. The Wellfleet exhibit describes Gibbs as a woman with a strong understanding of the landscape and the medicinal properties of plants. Around 1820, Gibbs used her vast knowledge of herbs to heal a case of breast cancer in a white woman who called Gibbs "Aunt D." Gibbs applied medicinal poultices to the tumor until one day, the tumor came off. Despite not receiving proper recognition during her lifetime, Gibbs "possessed the knowledge and skills she so willingly shared." She lived on land that is now part of the Cape Cod National Seashore and died sometime after 1838. At the exhibit, which acknowledged that "Indigenous people, even today, are the most invisible in American society," I saw a reconstructed portrait of Gibbs, a drawing made by Mashpee Wampanoag artist Emma Jo Mills Brennan. The image gives a face to this remarkable woman. I tried to imbue in Abiah what the caption described of Gibbs: "A very strong face, resolute expression, with very alive and piercing eyes." When creating the other visual descriptions of Abiah, I referred to museum sources, created or cocreated with the Wampanoag, and relied on my collaboration with expert Linda Coombs.

I am enormously indebted to Coombs. She was the one to name Abiah Sampson after reading my story and consulting documents from that period. During this time of imposed Christianity at the beginning of the eighteenth century, the Wampanoag peoples spoke English and had Biblical names. Colonial restrictions forced them away from outward manifestations of their culture, such as having tattoos, wearing traditional clothing, and using dugout mishoon canoes. Most people likely did not live in wetus anymore, though some kept wetus next to their European-style homes through the first half of the nineteenth century. The Wampanoag were forced to live in "praying towns" and on "Indian Lands," undesirable areas set aside as reservations by the colonists.

Linda Coombs's extensive knowledge informed Abiah's character and representation. Coombs's feedback and thorough notes were invaluable. Though Abiah works as a political leader, most Wampanoag—vastly outnumbered by the white population—relied on less obvious forms of subversion to avoid dire consequences, such as imprisonment or death. I chose to have Abiah keep her hair in an English-style updo when she is in Eastham, knowing that her appearance could interfere with her ability to influence colonists—and possibly even Wampanoag people who feared retaliation. But when she is away from watchful eyes, Abiah keeps her hair in a traditional braid. A person's attitude and way of speaking could show opposition. In Coombs's words, "like Abiah, people just kept doing many cultural practices." By continuing to hunt, fish, and use plants for medicine—to survive in the way they always had—they demonstrated their resistance, which Coombs argues "existed in myriad, more subtle manifestations."

It goes without saying that it is impossible, and not my goal, to represent an entire marginalized culture. Any mistakes in the rendering are my own.

What "really" happened in this novel, and what didn't? I wanted to represent a more accurate depiction of piracy in this book, at least from the lens of this crew. The conditions on typical vessels at the time were so poor that taking a ship often didn't require violence, with many uninspired seamen handing over the loot unceremoniously, uninterested in risking their lives. Many joined the pirates themselves. Other ships turned pirate by full-scale revolts against the cruelty aboard. I show these experiences rather than inventing battles that never happened, though I did add one sword duel between Sam and Captain Beer. Sam delivered a famous speech to Beer, one recorded in the somewhat-dubious historical source, *A General History of the Pyrates*, a book published three hundred years ago and often called the Bible of pirate history. Specifics about life aboard a pirate ship—the drinks they drank, the weapons they slung, the objects aboard (such as Quintor's gold shell necklace), and the detailed Articles of governance—are accurate.

The depictions of early Cape Codders' responses to shipwrecks, including their prayer regarding wrecks referenced in Chapter 12 or cutting off fingers and earrings from bodies as referenced in Chapter 51, are also documented. Many of the cultural details about wedding customs of the time come from historical accounts.

I also tried my best to stay true to the ordering of events, as well as depicting the actual places where Maria and Sam traveled. The cast of characters shows that I used known characters when I could, imbuing them with personalities inspired by records when I could find them. Sometimes I wove in direct or modern adaptations of their reported quotes.

Weighing historical accounts, alongside emphasizing certain perspectives, I also took some liberties for the sake of the story. In broad strokes, I compressed the timeline so that Sam's experience better paralleled Maria's narratively. There were no known letters exchanged between Sam and Maria, no swimming lessons, and no folktales that spoke of her dream of learning to swim (or her ability to do so). Stories describe Maria's eyes as blue or yellow, so I went with green, since I felt that was closer to yellow in certain lights. I once deliberately swapped events: the skit fiasco that appears in Chapter 36 actually happened aboard the *Whydah*, not before. In places, I simplified for the sake of the reader. For example, Edward Teach was not yet showing some of "Blackbeard's" erratic tendencies that he adopted years later. I also omitted some of Sam's other vessels—he had another flagship called the *Sultana* between the *Marianne* and the *Whydah*.

At the end of the novel, I simplified even more. The final flotilla had several vessels besides the *Marianne*, which was with Paulsgrave Williams on Block Island. The *Whydah* sailed with several others: the *Ann* (Montgomery's ship), the *Mary Ann* (the one filled with wine), and the *Fisher* (Robert Ingols's ship). Among the many variations of "Mary" and "Ann" alone, I felt it necessary to form composites. The *Ann* survived the storm, picked up the pirates in the sinking *Fisher*, then went on to Maine as planned. The *Mary Ann*, sailed by John Brown and the others (including Peter Cornelius Hoof), was captured the day after the storm. Montgomery was in the *Ann*, not the *Whydah*, so it is unlikely he had any conversations with Thomas Davis. I also do not give full justice to the storm conditions. The water was forty degrees, cold enough to kill, with waves as large as forty feet.

And yet, there *were* known survivors.

John Julian was one who made it to shore, climbing the steep sand dunes to get to town. The carpenter Thomas Davis also made it to shore, and his damning testimony was the one that condemned the survivors.

As writer Orson Welles has said, "If you want a happy ending, that depends, of course, on where you stop your story." The reunion of Sam and Maria in this work of fiction is not meant to overshadow the historic horrors of the one hundred and two men whose bodies washed ashore, or the terrible jail conditions that John Brown, Hendrick Quintor, Peter Cornelius Hoof, Thomas Baker, and John Shuan experienced before five of the six were hanged on November 15, 1717. At the gallows, Cotton Mather—who'd been visiting the prisoners regularly—declared: "Behold, the End of Piracy." Mather was right in a way, but the irony stings. On September 5, 1717, King George I, overwhelmed by how many of the former naval men had become pirates, issued clemency to any pirate who surrendered themselves within the year. The notice did not make it to Boston in time. However, many people (including Paulsgrave Williams and Benjamin Hornigold), accepted this pardon.

We don't know definitively what happened to John Julian after he endured the wreck. He disappears from the record. Though he might have escaped, some sources indicate that he may have been sold into slavery, but that he later killed his master and escaped (though met death himself when caught). If that person was the Julian in my mind's eye, he would accept no less than freedom. John King, the child and youngest pirate on record, did not survive the crash. His leg bone, along with his silk stocking and boot, are housed in the Whydah Pirate Museum.

I returned to Cape Cod as often as I could while writing this book. I'm not a superstitious person, but especially at night during the quiet offseason, I felt a strange aura I hadn't before on my carefree visits. Was it the pirates' decision to benefit from blood money that did them in? Could anyone else have survived, escaping to build that idealistic pirate kingdom they spoke of? Would they want their stories told? If yes, how might I do them justice? What did the Indigenous people see that the white historians did not? And if Maria's voice is the howl in the wind, as the folktales claimed, what is she trying to say?

My own hauntings, no doubt, a series of what-ifs. But still. I cannot walk along Marconi Beach at the site of the ruin without wondering if I'll see a silver coin in the sand, or stand along the dunes overlooking the Atlantic without thinking of them all on that night over three hundred years ago. Like Maria, I've let my intuition guide this story.

SOURCES

To write this novel, I synthesized material from many resources. Some of the books that informed my writing were:

- Brunelle, Kathleen. *Bellamy's Bride: The Search for Maria Hallett*
- Candlewick Press. *Pirateology: The Pirate Hunter's Companion*
- Clifford, Barry. *Expedition Whydah*
- Cordingly, David. *Under the Black Flag*
- Digges, Jeremiah. *Cape Cod Pilot*
- Dover. *Herbs and Herb Lore of Colonial America*
- Early, Eleanor. *And This Is Cape Cod*
- Echeverria, Durand. *A History of Billingsgate: Before Wellfleet Was Wellfleet*
- Johnson, Captain. *A General History of the Pyrates*
- Lynch, Patrick J. *A Field Guide to Cape Cod*
- Mather, Cotton. *On Witchcraft*
- Miller, John and Smith, Tim (editors). *Cape Cod Stories: Tales from Cape Cod, Nantucket, and Martha's Vineyard*
- Reynard, Elizabeth. *The Narrow Land*
- Sandler, Martin W. *The Whydah: A Pirate Ship Feared, Wrecked & Found*

- Schanzer, Rosalyn. *Witches: The Absolutely True Tale of Disaster in Salem*
- Simpson, Sharon, Kinkor, Kenneth J., and Clifford, Barry, *Real Pirates: The Untold Story of the Whydah from Slave Ship to Pirate Ship*
- Skinner, Charles M. *Myths and Legends of Our Own Land*
- Stetson, Judy. *Wellfleet: A Pictorial History*
- Wellfleet Historical Society. *A Special Exhibition: Wellfleet's Waterfront Revealed*
- Wigley, Nancy and Carr, Susan W. *Trailside Treasures: Plants of Cape Cod*
- Wright, D. B. *The Famous Beds of Wellfleet*

I am especially grateful for the invaluable information and support I received from the exhibits and teams at:
- Cape Cod Museum of Natural History
- Mashpee Wampanoag Museum
- National Park Service of Cape Cod National Seashore
- Provincetown Museum
- Salem Witch Museum
- USS Constitution Museum
- The Wellfleet Historical Society & Museum, including Sheryl Jaffe, Wellfleet museum coordinator, and Linda Coombs (Aquinnah Wampanoag), museum educator, author, and historian
- The Whydah Pirate Museum, with special gratitude for the work of the late historian Kenneth J. Kinkor

Acknowledgments

Once upon a time, there was a girl obsessed with pirates. As a kid, I tucked a plastic sword from Disneyland through the belt loop of my pants. In middle school, I sported a skull necklace under my shirt and drew boats on tests when I didn't know an answer. By high school, I was dressing up as a pirate every year to trick-or-treat until I was eighteen and went so far as to choose this costume for my senior graduation photoshoot.

To my wonderful, baffled family: Thank you for your patience. I'm grateful for the way this obsession fueled the curiosity that led to a more mature understanding of pirates, then a meaningful story that I can now articulate and share with you.

I wish I could name in full all of my loved ones, friends, and mentors, but they know who they are. They have set me free and shown me that yonder is a state of being. My relationships are my greatest treasure.

My enormous thanks to my early feedback-givers, as well as to my beta and sensitivity readers, who were instrumental to these pages: Aaron Newman, Alixa Brobbey, Kami Coppins, Angela Maxfield, Chaitra Earappa, Cynthia W. Connell, Elliott Eglash, Leslie Nielsen, Rachel Keränen, Rich Nielsen, and Stephanie Philp.

To Cami Carr: my steadfast friend since middle school who accompanied me to every midnight showing of every terrible pirate movie that ever came out, even when she fell asleep during most of them. She is now an incredible social worker, a warrior for those fighting systematic oppression.

To Victoria Hartmann: If I had a ship full of gold, it would go to her for being the first one to read—in full—every book I have drafted to date. Her support means the world.

To Mariya Manzhos: for all the writing comradery and her deep listening as I drafted and revised this book. *Slava Ukraini!*

To Carol Ann Litster Young: for teaching herself how to sail, then letting me tag along for countless inspiring adventures across the Charles River.

To my Paulsgrave Williams: for being an early reader and for the eternal love, loyalty, and joyful laughs.

To Toni: for helping me understand the "why" behind my pirate fascination, then helping me cope after I killed off characters and navigated the waters of writing fiction.

To Brenda Heaton: for having intuition as strong as Maria's.

To Ryan Davis: for a single conversation that changed my life forever in a recognizable scene in this book.

To Allison Hong Merrill: for being the best accountability partner I could ever ask for.

To Dayna Patterson: for her spellbinding poetry that showed me the potential and power of the word *if.*

To Rosalyn Eves: for her historical fiction highlighting real people that inspired the "cast of characters" list feature in this book.

To Pappy: for his unwavering support, always.

To Shevek: for showing me solidarity, equanimity, and a radiant example of social justice.

To Taylor Swift: for songs that got me through the hard days.

To Cape Cod: Thank you for capturing my heart and imagination, for the sacred solitude, and for bringing me back from the dead of depression. I'm grateful for the time I walked with ghosts along those white shores and rolling dune cliffs.

To the "Write or Die" writing group with Lisa Van Orman Hadley, Kim Ence, Barbara Jones Brown, and Katie Ludlow Rich: Thank you for lifting me and my writing game like the rising tide.

Warm gratitude to Sheryl Jaffe from the Wellfleet Historical Society & Museum for all her brilliance as a museum coordinator. I'm grateful for her interest in this manuscript and for believing, like me, that Maria was real.

One of the greatest experiences of this journey was the opportunity to work with Linda Coombs (Aquinnah Wampanoag), an author, historian, and museum educator with eleven years of service at the Boston Children's Museum, thirty years at Plimoth Plantation, and nine years at the Aquinnah Cultural Center. Representation was her primary focus at each of these institutions, and her expert notes were essential in creating Abiah Sampson's character. Coombs not only gave Abiah her name, but offered rigorous feedback throughout the manuscript. Her comments and insights were a gift beyond measure to this book—I hope you'll read her work in turn.

I owe a hearty shout-out to Michael Rueckert for his incredible book trailers. I'm also indebted to the full team at Kensington. Thank you to my delightful editor, Elizabeth Trout, as well as to Kimberly Witherspoon and Maria Whelan at Inkwell. Because of them, I can share Maria and Sam's story with you.

Finally, I want to thank the talented Crane Writers Group, including honorary and new members Amber Palmer and Megan Palmer. I've dedicated this book to Brittney Jenson, Megan Nordquist, Mikaela Benson, and Ryan Palmer. My forever gratitude, to these dear friends, for tossing me a line when I was drowning. For believing in me. They witnessed every stage of this book. *If the Tide Turns* would not exist without them.

If the Tide Turns

Rachel Rueckert

ABOUT THIS GUIDE

The suggested questions are included to enhance your group's reading of Rachel Rueckert's *If the Tide Turns*.

DISCUSSION QUESTIONS

1. *If the Tide Turns* opens with a prologue. How does this set the stage for the rest of the story?

2. The book alternates between Maria's and Sam's points of view. How did this impact your reading experience, and who do you think is the hero of the book?

3. The sea is core to the setting and characters. What do you think it represents?

4. Why do you think Maria chose exile? Have you ever found yourself in a similar position, forced to make a difficult decision between honoring yourself and belonging to a community?

5. *If the Tide Turns* moves away from Hollywood portraits of the Golden Age of Pirates in favor of historical accuracy. What surprised you in what you learned?

6. Elizabeth makes very different choices from the ones Maria makes. What do you think about this, and how can we make space for others to navigate their own life paths?

7. What do you think motivated the behavior of Mrs. Brown and Thomas Davis?

8. Why do you think the title begins with the word *If*?

9. Maria's powerful intuition gets her into trouble in her community. How do we consider and treat female intuition now, more than three hundred years later?

10. Though Maria and Sam's story has been passed on for generations, it rarely includes discussion about the Indigenous experience. What does including Eastham's politics and Abiah as a character add to this story?

11. Julian tells Sam, "It's a brutal world, no matter where you go, Bellamy. We are all complicit in the cycle of it. No one is innocent. But at least we pirates own the ways we aren't." Do you agree? Why or why not?

12. Many characters in *If the Tide Turns* ask themselves, in different ways, whether change is possible when confronted with class, race, power, and equality. In what way do these themes still apply today? Do you think change is possible?

13. Who would you cast in a film adaptation of *If the Tide Turns*?

14. What fascinated you most about the Author's Note and the true story behind this novel?

15. Before reading this book, what was your understanding of witches and pirates? Have your feelings changed after reading it?

Visit our website at
KensingtonBooks.com
to sign up for our newsletters, read
more from your favorite authors, see
books by series, view reading group
guides, and more!

BOOK CLUB
BETWEEN THE CHAPTERS

Become a Part of Our
Between the Chapters Book Club
Community and Join the Conversation

Betweenthechapters.net

Submit your book review for a chance to win exclusive
Between the Chapters swag you can't get anywhere else!
https://www.kensingtonbooks.com/pages/review/